VIA Folios 125

THE ARAB'S OX
Stories of Morocco

ORIGINALLY PUBLISHED AS *LARABI'S OX: STORIES OF MOROCCO*

Also by Tony Ardizzone

The Whale Chaser

In the Garden of Papa Santuzzu

Taking It Home: Stories from the Neighborhood

Heart of the Order

The Evening News: Stories

In the Name of the Father

Additional Praise for *The Arab's Ox: Stories of Morocco*
(Originally Published as *Larabi's Ox: Stories of Morocco*)

"An intriguing, beautifully crafted exploration of the human heart. . . .
Ardizzone writes like a poet, with a gift for capturing moments in perfect,
elegant images."
—William Rodarmor, *San Francisco Chronicle*

"Ardizzone is a first-rate storyteller who is not afraid to touch the 'big
subjects' of love, life, and death. He manages to avoid the sentimental
through powerful descriptions, intricate plotting, and subtle symbolism. . . .
This is the kind of book serious readers and writers are known to press upon
others with a command that's easily seconded by reviewers: 'Read this.'"
—Rita Ciresi, *The Hollins Critic*

"[*The Arab's Ox*] places Tony Ardizzone in our first rank of story writers.
His range is wide enough to embrace man and beast, infidel and Muslim,
the fallen and the saved; his empathy is such that he immediately makes
compelling any character that appears. These are wise stories, memorably
told, beautifully written."
—W. D. Wetherell, author of *A Century of November*

"In the Western World, few cultures have been so misunderstood as those of
the Middle East. All the more important, then, that there should appear a
beautiful and riveting collection such as [*The Arab's Ox*], with the power to
dispel ignorance while telling stories that are moving, compassionate, and
life-affirming. Without condescension or prejudice, Ardizzone brilliantly
explores the rich history, the deep rooted traditions, the magic, and the
cultural intricacies of Morocco, long considered the most 'enlightened' of
Middle Eastern countries."
— Carol LeMasters, *High Plains Literary Review*

"Ardizzone has gone into an alien land, taken it on its own terms, and
captured the essence of the place—the smells, the rhythms, the colors,
the philosophy. Some writers deal with the foreign by making it familiar;
Ardizzone has somehow kept it foreign, and so allows us to see what
connects and what doesn't. When he's done, the place is at it is—it is we who
are different."
—David Bradley, author of *The Cheneysville Incident*

"This year's winner of the Milkweed National Fiction Prize joins the growing ranks of novel/short story hybrids. Ardizzone weaves three distinct story lines in [*The Arab's Ox*], all involving Americans hoping to distract themselves from stateside problems in the disturbing beauty of the Moroccan landscape. . . . Beautifully designed and thoughtfully written, [*The Arab's Ox*] is a rarity: a book about Americans abroad that offers the hope of some rapprochement across cultures."

—Laura Pedrick, *Review of Contemporary Fiction*

"Who we aren't is as meaningful as who we are, and this is why I place a high value on stories like [*The Arab's Ox*], and storytellers like Tony Ardizzone, who writes with a poet's questioning eye, tracing the whorls of dangerous beauty in the fingerprints of a faraway world where, unexpectedly, we are offered the keys to our selves."

—Bob Shacochis, author of *Easy in the Islands*

"Tony Ardizzone has fashioned a stunning book around three lives, weaving a bright tapestry about their dramas and failures, crises and triumphs. His Morocco comes alive with sights, sounds, smells, and rhythms."

—Robert Philips, *Shenandoah*

"Vibrant, absorbing, and ingenious as a fine collage, [*The Arab's Ox*] is a collection of superb stories, and far more. Tony Ardizzone's stunning portrait of Morocco is a grave and intricate riddle whose answers reveal the soul of human striving. Look into these memorable characters and you will encounter your essential self."

—Susan Dodd, author of *O Careless Love*

"Imagery and spirituality layer the tales, swirling thick as Moroccan mid-day heat and the ever-present dust. . . . Spiced with Arabic, Islam, and vibrant geography, the stories astound."

—Sara Sanderson, *The Indianapolis News*

"Portraying three lives in crisis, the stories center on introspective moments, and often transform our clichés of tourism. With the collection set in a Moroccan landscape, it's difficult for readers to escape echoes of Paul Bowles, but the focus here is so clearly on an egotistical American perspective at odds with native culture that Ardizzone is able to offer fresh insights."

—*Publishers Weekly*

THE ARAB'S OX
Stories of Morocco

Tony Ardizzone

BORDIGHERA PRESS

Library of Congress Control Number: 2017951745

Cover Photo:
Fountain Outside the Mausoleum of Mohammed V
Rabat, Morocco

THE BORDIGHERA PRESS EDITION IS AN UPDATED VERSION
OF *LARABI'S OX: STORIES OF MOROCCO,*
FIRST PUBLISHED BY MILKWEED EDITIONS IN 1992

Printed in the United States.

Published by
BORDIGHERA PRESS
John D. Calandra Italian American Institute
25 West 43rd Street, 17th Floor
New York, NY 10036

VIA FOLIOS 125
ISBN 978-1-59954-120-4

for Anna

Contents

THE ARAB'S OX

In a ditch alongside the highway between Casablanca and Rabat lies the Arab's ox. Even in death the blue-black beast appears huge. Its open eye stares unfocused at the sky, streaked tangerine from the sun setting over the Atlantic. The ox's left foreleg, snowy white from hoof to knee, lies curled nearly to the swell of its stomach. The dying light lends its sallow horn a yellow cast. By the time Larabi—the Arab—finds his beast, the eye will be entirely milked over and covered with flies buzzing with greedy madness. Already the flies have settled on the blood clotted around the nostrils, lips, the black tongue bulging from the mouth. Other flies cling to the coarse hairs on the muzzle and the thinner lashes surrounding the eye, waiting their chance to bite something choice. Three egrets, white plumes unruffled in the still air, pick at a gash in the animal's side where its sweet blood has congealed, where a jagged spike of rib has torn through the skin. Beneath the skin the organs have bloated from the day's heat.

The ox has been struck by a shuttle bus from the Casablanca airport, then been prodded into the ditch by the bus's angry driver and by a dreamy boy pushing a red wheelbarrow loaded with two aluminum canisters of milk. It is mid-morning on the highway to Rabat. The driver stands on the hot stretch of road in front of his idling bus, a curse on his lips, his foot eager to kick the stupid snorting animal his bus has just struck. The driver is dark, built as thickly as the steamer trunks stowed in the bus's cargo drawers. Despite the bus's air-conditioning he has sweated through his shirt. Dark loops of sweat droop from his armpits. A rounded triangle of sweat stains the center of his chest. His pants cling to his thighs. He smokes so continuously that his first and second fingers are stained

gold from nicotine. He has never had a driving accident. He believes
in *maktub*, that what is written is certain to pass. Afraid to veer off the
road and risk a flat tire or, worse, a broken axle, he drives down the
road's center, with as much horn as wheel. The road belongs to the
strong, he believes. The ox failed to understand this.

The stupid beast. It gasps on the road before him, sitting on its
folded legs. Why, when other animals run from the bus, did this one
stroll into its path? The driver cares nothing for the animal's pain. His
sole concern is the worry that if the bus is damaged he may lose his
job. For a moment he turns from the ox and a wide-eyed country boy,
who hurries from behind a red wheelbarrow, and studies the front of
the bus.

At least the headlight is intact, he thinks. The bumper and front
panel are dented, spotted with blood. He glances back at the ox,
fearing if he is not careful it will rear up and charge him. His hands
try to jerk the bumper straight. Once he slit a sheep's throat for the
feast celebrating the birth of his first son, and when he turned for a
moment the animal stood and charged him. The dented bumper does
not budge. After the birth of his second son he held the sheep to the
ground. He jerks at the stubborn bumper. He straddled the animal
and held the neck fast while the thing's life spilled between his legs
onto the earth. He stares at the stupid ox, then steps into the bus
and returns with a rag with which he begins wiping away the blood
and the many dark hairs smearing the bumper and front panel and
headlight.

He'll lose his job. The thought is too terrible to consider. His job
is a big step up from what he used to do, which was drive a city bus.
No, he was not in the wrong. The right of way belongs to the strong.
He's no fellah from the countryside. He has opinions on many issues,
his time spent behind the wheel being ample. Also he has observed
much from the high seat of his bus. Force is what makes life work.
No matter the situation, the world belongs to the strong.

He remembers when he was young, after they buried his mother and burned her things so the disease would not spread, her brother came and took him to Casablanca. All he knew was life of the fellahin. The brother told him to stop acting like a donkey, to dry his tears, open his eyes, use his brain. The brother taught him how to lead tourists into shops owned by their friends, who would later share with him a percentage of whatever was bought. When he was older the brother taught him to steer and to shift the grinding gears of a friend's truck, and with luck and connections got him a job as a city bus driver. In the cool morning when the sun broke the darkness of the horizon, spreading over Casablanca's tan walls like a racing fire, and there were seats and room for everyone, the young driver saw that his countrymen could behave as decently as Europeans sipping tea. But in the thick heat of the afternoon when three buses wouldn't be enough—well, you risked your life sometimes trying to get aboard, to ride with the others, standing. Of course the weak ones were left behind at the curb, pushed aside, occasionally knocked down in the rush. With no room for them, he'd have no choice but to shut the door. Once, a woman with his mother's face was nearly trampled by a crowd thronging onto his bus. He watched her fall, remembers still her dark eyes.

He sees his image in the headlight as he folds the rag he used to clean the front of the bus. In the headlight he is fat and upside-down. The bumper and front panel look as they always look, he thinks. They must. A dent here, one there. And if someone were to point them out, why, the dents were always there, weren't they? No one needs to know the bus has struck anything.

Then he hears the boy with the wheelbarrow sighing. The boy is filthy, wide-eyed, so thin his hips hardly hold up his ragged pants. He wears a man's T-shirt torn at the neck. The driver takes out a cigarette, then spits with disgust. He was just like him before he was rescued by his mother's brother.

"Oh, oh, oh," the boy says, his dirty hands fluttering in front of his face. He leans over the fallen beast, which thrashes its legs on the ground. The driver would like to slap some sense into the boy, at least to shut him up. He steps toward the boy, raising his hand. At that moment the beast lets loose a great quantity of shit. The ox must have been saving it for just this occasion, the driver thinks. He lowers his hand. The shit lies repulsively in a mound, shimmering wetly. The stench is very high.

The driver considers for a moment the farmer who owned the animal. He might demand to be paid. Well, screw him. The stupid ox came out of nowhere, charged the bus. If blame is to be laid at someone's step, blame the fence the ox broke through or the sleepy boy who should have been watching it. The driver lights the cigarette, inhales deeply. There was no opportunity to stop without risking harm to the passengers. Of course, if accused, he can blame the passengers. He nods, looking back at the bus. The passengers are pushed against the windshield, gawking out like sheep at a fence. One, a fat American in a fedora and safari shirt, is taking photographs.

The driver waves for him to stop. "This damn American thinks it's amusing," he shouts into the bus's doorway. He speaks in Arabic to the group of Moroccans standing by the window.

"This is our life," one of the Moroccans answers, vigorously nodding, "the reality we live with each day, and he makes of it souvenirs."

The American smiles at the driver, then snaps his picture.

Screw him, the driver thinks as he walks back to the ox. Already he has decided his bus hasn't struck a thing. The dents were there when he drove the bus from its station. He grabs the animal's horns, lifts its head, trying to pull it from the road. The ox was already on the highway. The muscles in the dark neck twist against his grip. The black tongue lolls in the mouth. The country kid will have to help him.

The driver rolls what has happened around in his mind. He wants to put the events straight. He was driving along until he stopped the bus for a few moments to move an animal blocking the road. Obviously something hit it, then sped off. A car, a truck, a motorbike, perhaps another ox. Who can say how the beast was hurt? Who else but he knows what took place?

Not too bad a way to go, the American in the safari shirt reflects. He nods at his thought, then looks again at the beast through his camera. Quick, out of the blue, mouth full of tasty grass. Maybe dreaming about a cool drink of water, green pastures, a juicy heifer. You step out onto a road and then honk, honk, BAM! Welcome to the twentieth century. Probably shattered the poor thing's ribs, punctured a lung, a few of the vital organs.

The American lowers his camera and pouts. He looks somewhat like an egg and knows it, feels sometimes like a big Humpty Dumpty as he plods about. His face is very pink and since the chemotherapy fairly hairless, and he is quite fat, particularly now that he no longer cares what or how much he eats. Funny how they call them vital organs, he thinks, as if there's anything inside you that isn't. Well, there's the appendix. But who knows for sure? Life offers no reliability. You think your cells are inside your skin where they belong, minding their own business, behaving and carrying out their various God-given functions, and then you find out that a whole bunch have been traveling about your body acting like promiscuous sluts. Multiplying and dividing in places where there should be no arithmetic. He pushes his abdomen with the flat of his meaty hand and feels nothing but the hand's pressure. No pain. Funny how when it all goes haywire you don't even feel pain. As sure as his name is Henry Goodson he'd bet the animal on the road feels pain.

"He hit an immense black ox," he announces loudly, turning away from the windshield toward the Westerners, then the Moroccans, on the bus.

No one responds. Henry wishes someone would respond.
Because whenever he remembers how his body turned Benedict
Arnold on him, he aches to be touched, or at least acknowledged. He
fears his loneliness is so strong it can be smelled. His eyes scan the
others with visible urgency. Oh, see me and smile. No one does.

Pressed around him are several Moroccans, staring indifferently
out the window or gesturing and talking with one another. Others
relax in their seats. A pretty American traveling by herself smokes
a cigarette and fidgets, chewing her fingernails, pulling at the ends
of her red hair, which is shoulder length and, though unwashed,
breathtakingly lovely. What a shame beauty like hers is wasted on
boys in their twenties, he thinks. When he was a boy in his twenties
he had the sensitivity of a toad. He remembers what a bumbler he'd
been in bed. Like a bottle rocket. No sooner did he get all the way up
than he popped. He shakes his head, feeling pity for the girl and all
young women in general. Then he feels himself beginning to harden.

Oh Body, he thinks, how at times you amaze me. He covers the
front of his pants with one hand and blushes, not having felt desire
as strong as this in longer than he can remember. The young woman
peers out her window, puffing dribs of smoke out the side of her
mouth.

What a shame she smokes. What a shame she doesn't wash her
hair. Hair that beautiful should be shampooed, gently dried, brushed,
then held back from her face with fine combs. In a louder voice
aimed at her he repeats, "Our driver has killed an ox."

Instead of looking up, the young woman ignores him, eyes and
fingers busy with her cigarette and the ends of her hair.

Then he notices the older woman, reading in her seat. The
drabness of her turtleneck and men's hiking boots and trousers makes
him wonder if she's from England. Few American women dress that
way, he considers, at least the ones he's had the fortune to know.

Is she in her forties? Fifties? Her complexion is quite fair. Her nose, forehead, the backs of her hands, and her wrists are lightly brushed with freckles. Irish? Scotch? He imagines sitting next to her. What would he say? Surely she'll put her book down before they arrive in Rabat.

Then he sees the other American—or is he Spanish?—the one in the brown tie, gold-rimmed sunglasses. Corduroy jacket neatly folded next to him on the seat. Looking about like a cornered rat. No, he's from the States. You can tell by the button-down collar. Though the air inside the bus is still quite cool, the man is visibly sweating. Too tense a guy to go up to, sit down with, say howdy-do.

He turns and looks out the window as the Moroccans around him at first give him room, then press against him like a wave. They lean freely on him, touch his back, push against his legs, his arms, in their attempts to see out the windshield. Henry doesn't mind the contact, no, not in the slightest. It has been many years since he's been touched. He thinks perhaps that's why he has come to Morocco.

For a moment he closes his eyes and concentrates on the men around him. He feels their shoulders and hands rock against him, smells the sweet mix of their sweat and hair lotion and tobacco and some unidentifiable spice, listens to the lovely tumbling cadence of their speech. He turns, steals a glance at the young woman. She chews the ends of her hair, her tender face now buried in a guidebook. What a waste, he thinks. If only he could help her to be not wasted. He tips back his hat and gazes out the windshield.

The boy with the heavy wheelbarrow is glad he was not hit. Surely if he had been, his father would beat him. He is taking the two canisters of goat milk several kilometers down the road to his uncle. Then his uncle will sell the milk or take it where it will be made into cheese. The boy does not know what arrangements his father and uncle have made. All he knows is that he must not tip the wheelbarrow.

He has tipped many wheelbarrows in his short life. He has the welts to show for it. If he is as useless as his father and uncle tell him he is, he is sure to tip many more. Pushing a wheelbarrow is simple enough, difficult perhaps only over rocks or in deep mud. But pushing a wheelbarrow usually leads him to dreaming. As his uncle and father have told him, daydreaming distracts him and leads to mistakes. Dreamy boys tip wheelbarrows. He must not allow the wheelbarrow to tip.

Earlier, as the boy moved down the road, he daydreamed he was a horseman, like the ones he saw last summer in the magnificent fantasia held during the festival of Sidi Moussa el Doukkali, a saint buried in Salé, where his father's family lives. Traveling to the festival had been the most exciting event in the boy's life. Sidi Moussa had lived on wild onions and the salty air and could appear and disappear whenever and wherever he wished, leaping through any distance, no matter how great. He had given bread to the poor. Each year he had made a hajj to Mecca. He was the village's favorite saint.

The boy was imagining that he was a saint, a great horseman who lived on couscous and lamb and boulfaf—pieces of sheep liver rolled in luscious layers of fat—and who could fly through the air with his horse, and who rode in every fantasia in Morocco. In a fantasia the country's best horsemen, dressed in turbans and their finest robes, gathered at the far end of a field, forming a line, their steeds meticulously combed and decorated in red tassels and brilliant saddle blankets. At the field's other end waits the eager crowd. A hush falls. Then the horsemen charge, white capes flowing, raising and then twirling their long rifles above their heads. The horses break into a gallop loud as thunder. The men scream, "*Allahu Akbar! Allahu Akbar! Allahu Akbar!*" Allah is the most great! The earth trembles. The crowd falls back and screams. At the very last instant, when the crowd is certain it will be cut down by the horsemen like wheat beneath a sickle, the riders rein in and fire their rifles simultaneously into the

air, and then the great horses rear and the riders stand victorious in
their stirrups, again twirling their rifles above their heads. Then they
retreat.

The boy imagines the red wheelbarrow is an elegant tasseled bay
and he is starting the charge, crying, "*Allahu Akbar! Allahu Akbar!*"
He pushes the wheelbarrow down the road with what for him is
reckless speed. From his angle the bus appears to be charging a black
ox standing alongside a slight ditch. How exciting, the boy thinks. A
fantasia. Surely at the last moment the bus will brake. The ox takes a
step onto the roadway. The boy readies his mouth with the sound of
rifles. "Pa-tchoo! tchoo! tchoo!" the boy says. The bus speeds nearer,
and the beast—Larabi's ox, the boy realizes—continues on its way,
seeming to chew its tongue, the boy notices, gazing first vacantly at
him and then casually in the direction of the honking. For a moment
the boy has the giddy desire that the bus might actually hit the ox.
No. Yes, yes, it would be something to see. Then horribly, as all of
time collapses to a single moment, the bus does exactly as he wishes,
glancing into the ox's side, causing the great animal to skid drunkenly
up the road until its useless legs bend and then crumple and it
tumbles down, neck arched, its horned head raised to the sky as it
lows as if saying, "Oh, I am in such trouble and pain!" There is much
dust then and honking as the bus slides to a stop above the fallen
animal.

For several moments the beast twitches and snorts, sides heaving
like a punctured bellows. The driver rushes down from the bus, flares
his nostrils, spits. The boy hears the man's dark curse and lowers his
eyes. At that moment the animal begins emptying its bowels. The
feces is soft, dark as pitch, and smells of fear and metal. Or is the
metal just the taste on his tongue? The boy tries to taste his tongue,
but it has turned to sand. He tries to swallow but cannot. He fears
that by desiring the accident he has caused it.

The stench of the feces is so strong his eyes are tearing. He takes a deep breath and smells fear. Through the smell of fear he looks up, back at the ox. Blood bubbles like a spring from the wound where the bone protrudes. The bone is torn, tipped with pink. The boy steps over the mound of feces and puts out his hand to touch the bone. Perhaps he can push it back in place.

The driver tries to pull the beast to its feet. The ox seems to snore, as if asleep. The driver gives it a kick. The boy cannot comprehend why a man would kick an animal he is trying to save, though the boy knows that men often kick for no good reason the things around them. His two canisters of milk reflect the morning sun with a glare that is dizzying and blinding. In the same blinding light the dying ox's side flutters wetly.

"Wake up," the driver shouts. Again he kicks the ox, which lies now on its side. "Hey, donkey boy! Help me with this damn thing."

"As you like," the boy answers with a heavy heart. He knows if he had not imagined the tragedy nothing would have happened.

Together they try to encourage the ox into the ditch beside the road, with the driver grabbing the beast's horns, and the boy tugging the animal's right foreleg. The ox doesn't budge, shaking its head free of the driver's grasp and kicking the boy's hands, all the while lowing plaintively. Blood pools on the road beneath it. At the end of each of its labored breaths there is a gurgling, soft as a stream. The ox's hind legs scissor the air, and the driver and the boy stand back. The ox tries to right itself. It tucks in its forelegs, kicks its legs. Then, as if understanding the man's intent, it rolls and works itself to its knees. The driver holds its horns, trying to twist the head toward the ditch. The ox follows its head, crawling on its knees through its blood and feces toward the man, who steps backward as he pulls its horns. Then the beast collapses alongside the road.

The morning sun blazes brightly in the corner of the bus's windshield. The passengers stare down from behind the tinted glass.

The boy watches the driver pick up from the road a blood-stained rag and then fold it into smaller and smaller squares and then place the smallest square into his back pocket. Why does he want to keep the blood? the boy wonders. Tears fill his eyes. Oh, fantasia! Instead of a festival and celebration there is tragedy.

He returns slowly to the wheelbarrow. Without thinking, his hands fall to the wooden handles, which he lifts with a soft grunt. The boy knows he doesn't push his load so much as try to keep up with it. The weight of the load presses down on the wheel, which turns beneath the weight, covering the ground between where the barrow is and where it wants to go. His father told him it is the same with life. You run between the handles, trying your best to guide the wheel's direction and prevent the load from tipping. The bus roars now like a horrible monster. The boy is careful to push his load around the slash of feces. The bus's gears engage with a clank. Then the bus starts up the roadway, moving through the blood.

For a moment the three—boy, driver, ox—are in a line perpendicular to the road. The bus is in the center between the boy and the beast, which has stopped lowing and is nearly numb, feeling only a growing heaviness of breath and the familiar teasing sting of the flies. The driver gives the bus gas, thinking no one else knows what has happened. The chugging sound of the bus's engine soothes him. No matter what, he will not give up the comfort of this seat. The American in the safari shirt and fedora waves at the boy with the wheelbarrow as he passes below. The boy does not notice the wave. His eyes dumbly watch the road and the two canisters in front of him as he trudges in the opposite direction. But then he looks up and sees behind the window the lovely face of the woman with red hair. Her face is turned fully toward the window. Her beauty surprises him. The boy thinks her large, heavy-lidded eyes look sad. He stares at her openly, smitten by the ripe fullness of her lips, as the bus pulls even with him. The young woman looks beyond him and the rocky field

west of the road toward a blue sliver of the ocean, which she has just
noticed, and which pleases her, brings a smile to her lips. She knew
the road from the airport to Rabat ran parallel with the coast, though
she did not expect the ocean to be this close.

The boy's heart catches when he sees her smile. He imagines she
smiles at him because he is so handsome, so strong, so brave as to
drive an ox into a ditch. The idea is too delicious for him to endure.
His wheelbarrow strikes a sudden stone and all at once tips, one
canister shifting from the left side to the right with a bang, causing
the canister's top to pop off and some of the milk inside to splash out.
The milk splashes onto the side of the road, which drinks it greedily,
and into the belly of the wheelbarrow. The images of the woman's
smile, the dizzy tipping, and the splashing milk tumble in the boy's
mind as the roaring bus speeds past.

From a distance the boy's uncle watches the bus move past his
nephew and the wheelbarrow. The uncle stands sideways on the inside
slope of a slight ridge between the road and the pounding sea. In a
moment the boy will notice him, he thinks.

He has just peed, not without effort and pain, straining with all
his might to push out the last lazy drops that seem always to wish to
remain. He is pleased that this morning he's been successful. He is
sure the heavy drops contain grit from the food he has eaten in the
past day. That's why it's so difficult to cleanse the body of them. Like
the sediment you see settled on the bottom of a jug of water, so it
is with a man's tubes, he believes. If a person is not careful, the grit
builds up like silt at the bottom of a slowly moving stream. The grit
clings to itself, forming peculiarly shaped pebbles. He has seen several
such pebbles, picked up from the ground by men just his age after
they'd painfully urinated. He knew a few men whose tubes became so
choked with grit they died. There are far better ways to die than to die
of clogged tubes, he thinks.

He shakes a stubborn drop from the mouth of his penis, then

pushes his penis back inside the pantaloons he wears beneath his djellaba, which is wool, tan with sienna stripes. His dark eyes are set deeply in his skull. He has wrapped his shaved head in a white turban. Twice a month for a full day he fasts, and on the second day to break his fast he drinks bottled mineral water from Sidi Harazem, near Fez, to flush the grit from his bowels. During the thirty days of Ramadan, the ninth month, when Muslims forgo all food, drink, and sexual relations from sunrise to sunset, his body purifies itself further, becoming a flame of thirst and desire.

At first the flame flares brightly. The edge of desire is keen. The body cries out in need, like a pampered child. But then after several days the needs stop crying out. The flame of physical desire flickers, dies back to an ember, and the person becomes self-contained, like a plant, the uncle thinks, which takes in nothing, surviving on itself. Then appetite becomes more suggestion than demand. The body becomes servant to the soul. The mind is then content, and the soul is better able to submit to the will of Allah. Fasting is a pillar of Islam, which means submission or self-surrender, a voluntary act whereby a person places his or her destiny in the hands of God and submits to God's rule as revealed through the commands given to the Prophet.

In the pocket of his choukkara, his fingers touch his beads. The voice beneath his breath falls into prayer. "*La ilaha illa Allah, Muhammadur rasul Allah.*" There is no god but Allah, and Muhammad is His Prophet. He runs the beads through his fingers as the prayer spills from his lips. The prayers have not yet become part of his body, companion to each breath, heartbeat. His hand still needs to feel the beads. But sometimes once he has started to finger the beads he is able to pray through to their knot without a distracting thought.

He watches his nephew stop to balance the canisters in his wheelbarrow. Dawdler, inventor of excuses, dreamer and creator of unbelievable tales, the boy will need much discipline before he grows older, the uncle thinks. The man frowns, more from habit than displeasure. He deeply loves his nephew and would forgive him any sin. The boy is like the body, he thinks, full of need and desire. He is to the boy as the mind is to the body.

He notices far behind the boy an egret circle and then settle near a mound alongside the road. He does not know the dark shape is the Arab's dying ox. From where he stands it resembles a pile of freshly dug earth. He thinks no more of it, envying his brother, even though envy is a useless feeling and his brother is miserably poor. His poor brother lives in a shack made of scrap wood and tin with his wife, seven children, and scrawny goats.

The sea rages against the rocky coast. The man turns into his shadow, fingers his prayer beads, reflects. "*La ilaha illa Allah.*" The waves pound the rocky shore, shatter into droplets. "*Muhammadur rasul Allah.*" The water recedes, and the shore resists, though with repetition and time the sea will reduce even the hardest rock into sand. "*La ilaha illa Allah.*" With time and repetition the body learns complete submission. "*Muhammadur rasul Allah.*" The rock and the sea act in accord with Allah's will.

The uncle looks off into the distance, to the north edge of Casablanca, where there stands a refinery's flaming smokestack. This morning the sky over the refinery is especially gray, unclean. The man can remember when there was no flaming dirt in the sky. In time, he considers, even the refinery will be reduced. The candle will flicker, die. The towering cylinder of bricks will tumble. All of man's works will be reduced during the last hour, when the sun will be shrouded and the stars will no longer give light, when the mountains will vanish and the seas will boil over, and all people will be coupled with their deeds. Then the scrolls will be unfolded, and all will come to know what they have prepared for themselves. And the earth will be rocked in her last convulsion. The man returns his gaze to the furious whitecaps biting their way into the shore.

He knows his nephew nears, recognizes him, is thinking of a fantastic tale to explain why he is so late. Though the uncle is pleased to see his nephew, he clears his face.

Breathless, shouting with a high voice as he makes his approach, the boy tells him in a single tumbling sentence the story of the ox, the fantasia, the honking bus. As he begins to describe how the beautiful woman with hair the color of sunrise looked down upon him and smiled with admiration at his bravery, the uncle chides him for the wasted milk puddled in the belly of the wheelbarrow. The uncle believes the entire tale is a fantasy and is tempted to lecture the boy on the dangers of such idleness, but then he thinks better of it and holds his nephew close to his chest and in greeting kisses both his cheeks, and the boy tells him no more of his story.

The boy tells no more of the Arab, the simple fellah, who, untold, will set out on foot in search of his stray beast as the tangerine sun streaks the sky and dips into the pounding blue Atlantic. No one will watch the Arab walk into the dying light, shielding his eyes with one hand, his other hand grasping the staff he uses to drive his herds. He will walk into the sun, toward the sea. The birds in the air will lead him to it. At first the Arab's mind will deny what he sees, will tell him the animal is only resting, or asleep, or at worst has slipped, injured its snow-white left foreleg. Then when his eyes protest that the beast in the ditch is dead, he will think that it only resembles his lively animal. Surely this dead, bloated beast is another man's misfortune, the Arab will think.

Then he will fall to his knees in mourning and in recognition of God's will, and his fingers will scratch sad furrows into the darkened earth.

THE BEGGARS

He thought he'd lost every innocence.

The moment the air-conditioned bus that killed the ox on the road from Casablanca pulled alongside the curb in downtown Rabat, Corvino saw the crippled boy. The boy crawled out from beneath the shade of an ash-white building, scuttling on all fours, crablike, legs twisted behind his buttocks, which rode laughably higher than his head. His shoes struck the pavement at unnatural angles. He wore tightly belted blue jeans and a shirt that had once been white. Behind him hurried several thin-faced men—skin sepia, beards mottling their cheeks—who as soon as they could press against you would offer to carry your luggage, exchange money, recommend a hotel, serve as a guide, sell you a silver bracelet, kaftan or burnous or djellaba.

But it was the crippled boy that Peter Corvino noticed.

He rubbed his forehead, then pushed his sunglasses up on his brow and squeezed his eyes. His fingers were long, nails clean and neatly clipped. His mouth turned down naturally into a frown. A love song by the Egyptian singer Oum Kalthoum played loudly from the radio mounted beside the driver's seat. Now that the shuttle had stopped, the music seemed even more frenetic. He'd be all right as soon as he was in his hotel, he thought. He took a deep breath, at the same time blinking his eyes several times as if to clear them, then slipped his sunglasses down and felt the sweat broken out on his forehead. He wiped the sweat with the back of his hand. The others on the bus, a mixed group of Moroccans and Westerners, gathered their belongings, then stood in the aisle and lit cigarettes, pointing out the tinted windows at relatives and friends. Corvino exhaled slowly. His face, normally swarthy, appeared bloodless.

He'd tried without much success to sleep on the flight over, the flight that hurled him from busy morning in the States to this hot Moroccan afternoon the following day. But he was too tense to sleep, and the Frenchman in the seat beside him had wanted to talk. About New York, how it was safe to walk anywhere—the Village, Washington Square, 42nd Street, even Harlem in the dead of night— as long as you knew what to do. The whites of the Frenchman's eyes looked painfully bloodshot. His teeth were rimmed with black. Corvino found his powder-blue T-shirt too precious a shade and cut for a man to wear. His fingers waved a lit Gauloise.

"No, really, it is very safe. I just tell them I am French. They ask where do I live."

"Muggers talk to you," Corvino said, disbelieving.

"No, you are missing my point. There are no muggers. At least for me."

"You're very fortunate."

"It's more that you know what to do, to say, than fortune."

"Where do you live?" Corvino asked after a while.

"Many places." The man adjusted the conical nozzle regulating the flow of air above him. "At present, Casablanca."

"And you're not even hassled in Harlem? I don't believe it."

The Frenchman frowned. "I just say I am French. I give them a five." He raised his palm and slapped the air. "You know"—he smiled broadly—"some skin. It takes care of everything. It shows I am in solidarity."

"That's a high five," Corvino said.

"High five," the Frenchman said, slapping the air again. As he did, an arc of ash fell from his cigarette.

Later the Frenchman gave Corvino a card that listed his name—M. Alain Bornet—and a telephone number in Casablanca but no address. By this time the two had eaten and were sharing their third small bottle of Guerrouane, a Meknès wine.

"You say this will be your first time," Bornet said, eyes widening.

"I've been overseas before," Corvino said. "Years ago I hiked all over Europe. The summer before I married, when I was a student."

"You are married and you don't bring your wife?"

"Wife?" Corvino wagged his head. "Not anymore."

"Divorced? I am too. Every man today is, I think." For several moments they both were silent. "But you have never been to Morocco."

"No." Corvino smiled. "I've never been to Morocco."

"Never to North Africa?"

"Never to North Africa."

Bornet raised both eyebrows, then turned to the dark window beside him and coughed. When he faced Corvino again he rolled his eyes.

"It's not my business to ask."

"Ask what?" Corvino said.

"Why your university sends someone so—" He hesitated. "Someone who has never been before."

Corvino sipped his wine. "But that's part of the exchange."

"You don't send someone to the Arab world who has never been."

"But then how do you gain the experience?"

Bornet sniffed as he considered the question. "I think either you have it or you do not."

"Perhaps," Corvino said, "but the committee—"

"Ahh," Bornet said, patting Corvino's arm and winking his long eyelashes, "the committee! You didn't say a committee! That explains it."

Then Bornet began a story. "Once upon a time there was a frog and, and, how do you say"—he gestured with his hand—"a scorpion?"

"Yes," Corvino said, "a scorpion."

"Scorpion," Bornet said. He'd been trying to make one of his hand. He took a deep drag off his cigarette and nodded. "The two were standing on the shores of a river, and then the scorpion asked the frog if he would take him across. So the frog said, 'Why would I want to do a thing like that? I mean, you're a scorpion. I'm a frog. You'll sting me.' But the scorpion said, 'Me? Hey, listen, if I sting you I'll die too. Trust me. You're the only way I have to cross this river.'" Bornet smiled. "So the frog decided to trust the scorpion, and the scorpion climbed on the frog's back. Then the frog jumped into the river and swam. Halfway across, the scorpion stung him."

Corvino nodded. Bornet grinned as he lit another cigarette.

"So the frog began to die from the sting, and the scorpion started to drown. Then just before they both died the frog said, 'Hey, I just want to know one thing. Why?' Then the scorpion said, 'Welcome to Morocco!'"

Corvino laughed.

"It's good that you laugh," Bornet said. "If you laugh it means you have a chance to make it."

Then Bornet put on an eyeshade, turned off his overhead light, and went to sleep. Corvino tried to sleep. So sleep, he told himself. He prayed the Hail Mary over and over until he fell asleep. He was sleeping very lightly, dreaming of a river, as another part of his mind listened to the drone of the plane's engines as it crossed the dark Atlantic, when from the seat behind him came the loud and atonal song of a Muslim at prayer. Corvino opened his eyes. It took him several moments to realize where he was and that the deep, plaintive moaning behind him was language. Bornet started in the darkness, then without lifting his eyeshade turned his head and in French called the man an insect, then told him they were on board a public airplane in the civilized Christian world, and at least he could wait until they landed and he could crawl shoeless as a snake into his mosque before he bothered decent sleeping men with the crap dripping from his mouth.

The man paused for several moments, as if considering Bornet's speech, then sang even louder. Still muttering in French, Bornet seemed to settle again into sleep.

Later, after the sun appeared in the airplane's windows and the plane began making its approach to land, Bornet pulled a sweater on over his head. T-shirt covered, he looked older, more typically French. Bornet turned to Corvino and said, "I assume someone has told you about the beggars?"

Corvino shrugged. He wanted to rinse his mouth, brush his teeth. "No more than that I should expect to see them."

Bornet nodded, tapped a Gauloise against his thumbnail, glanced up at the lit no smoking sign, then frowned and slowly pushed the cigarette back into its pack. "Let me give you advice. Ignore them. Walk right past them. If ever you give to one, many others will be on you—how can I say?—like a mob, you understand? Like a big bunch of fish, you throw the smallest crumb of bread into their water and they all swarm up to the top." His fingers rose in the air like many fish in water. He smiled. "You give to one and the rest will be in front of you, blocking your way, next to you at your elbow, your arm, behind you, everywhere you turn. And once you give to a beggar, he will always remember you. Every time you pass his way he will see you and remember and want you to give him something more."

Corvino risked a smile. "Sounds like my ex-wife."

"This is no joke, my friend."

"No." Corvino was still laughing.

"Take it from me. Walk right past them. When they come up to you, just push the dirty fleas out of your way." Bornet swung his arm.

"Just like that," Corvino said.

"Of course."

Corvino stood in the narrow aisle.

"You're not convinced."

Corvino said nothing. He felt unclean. He wanted to brush his teeth.

"They don't need to beg," Bornet said. "There's no poverty in Morocco."

"No poverty?"

"Not like in America. In New York, Harlem, the Bowery, there's poverty. But in Morocco everyone has food. No one goes hungry. Bread is very cheap. Begging is a second job, something you moonlight, yes? An occupation."

Corvino had his toothbrush and toothpaste from his jacket in the overhead bin. In the seat behind him, a bearded Moroccan in an impressively beautiful white djellaba and what looked like a skullcap slept, open-mouthed. Corvino looked for several moments at the Moroccan, then back at Bornet.

The Frenchman smiled. Even with the morning light behind him, his teeth were edged visibly with stain. "Just wait and see, my friend."

Corvino saw as he stood in front of the ash-white Hotel Terminus. Immediately a man with dark eyes and a narrow mustache pressed up against him, offering to take his bags. Corvino said thank you, no. A second man tried to take his hand, smiling with broken teeth. Corvino waved the man away. He loosened the knot in the tie that hung from his neck, then checked the inside pocket of his crumpled jacket for his passport. He made a straight line of his mouth. His gold-rimmed sunglasses sparkled in the sun.

They'd told him at the university to act confidently, as if he had been there before and knew what he was doing. Then they laughed and Corvino laughed and the head of the committee said of course Corvino had their complete trust. No one on the committee trusted anyone else, of course. The distrust was typical of politics at his university. Distrust was why Corvino had been chosen. He was the compromise candidate, dependable and sturdy as his name, Peter, the rock upon which the committee finally agreed.

Corvino was grateful because he knew his election meant he had fewer enemies than the others, and because the assignment might eventually mean promotion.

His mission was simple, the committee instructed him after offering its congratulations. He'd teach, attend meetings, conduct interviews, arrange a tentative schedule of events. And return. Everyone laughed at the mention of the word *return*. The bus driver, a short stocky man who seemed incapable of hurrying, unlocked the luggage compartment of the bus. The committee suggested Corvino walk briskly, never carry a camera, stare straight ahead, not gawk at every new thing like a tourist. They'll eat you alive if you act like a tourist, they told him. Then all at once he felt a tug at the leg of his khaki pants.

It was the smallest of tugs, subtle enough to capture his complete attention. Corvino's mouth went dry from it. He stared straight ahead, at the luggage compartment of the bus. The other passengers pushed ahead of him. Corvino watched them to see if they gave the driver a tip. Then again he felt the pull on his pants leg as he heard a soft whisper, soft as leaves brushing the sidewalk below. Again he felt the smallest of tugs, and then he looked at the round face which was as brown as a nut, at the boy's wide eyes, the flat palm of his tiny hand next to his cheek, and in the whispering mouth something extremely white, twin rows of exceptionally white teeth.

A yellow button on the boy's dirty shirt was broken in half. His jeans were bunched at the waist, cinched by a black plastic belt, the long tongue of which dangled to the ground. Now that the boy had the man's gaze, he tilted his head from side to side—coyly, Corvino thought, mincingly—whispering more loudly, trying to plead with his large brown eyes, and then giving a half smile and trembling the palm of his hand that he still held open next to his cheek.

Then the fingers again tugged Corvino's trousers, and the head and eyes fell to the pavement, and the leaves rustled again and again, as if the child were telling some secret to Corvino's shoes. The open hand fluttered in the air above the bent head.

The driver bounced Corvino's suitcase and coat-bag from the bus to the sidewalk. Corvino stepped neatly over the boy, unsure of what to do. Give the boy a coin, tip the driver, accept the help of one of the bearded men whose hands were already reaching for the handles of his luggage.

"No," Corvino said, stretching his own hands toward his bags.

"*Merci, mais non merci*," Corvino told the others who pressed against him.

They'd told him how to find his hotel from the bus terminal, so he set off, acting as if he knew what he was doing. The terminal was across a side street from the train station, across a wide boulevard lined with government buildings, cafés, and shops. Streams of cars, motorbikes, and blue petit taxis roared around an oval grassy area fronting the station. Flying there were flags of several Arab nations and banners in Arabic, which Corvino could not read. Past a fountain to the west, the avenue was separated by a wide walkway planted magnificently with twin rows of palm trees. Lush ivy covered the trees' bark. To the south Corvino could see the minaret of the Assounna, Rabat's Grand Mosque. A woman in a dark djellaba hobbled past him, head bouncing up and down with each step, more on her right ankle than upon the foot itself. She wore babouches, slippers open in the back, on both feet. So here he was, he thought, in the center of the capital city. The walk across the boulevard seemed impossibly uphill.

A trio of shoeshine men clacked their brushes against their boxes as he strode past them. Then a heavy man in a brown burnous smiled and put out both hands and blocked Corvino's path. One of the man's eyes looked milky, gazing randomly, appearing to run with tears or pus. At first Corvino thought the man was trying to help him with his bags.

"No," Corvino said.

The man spoke in Spanish, then switched to French, English, then went back to Spanish. His good eye fixed squarely on Corvino. His hands brushed Corvino's shoulder, the sleeve of his jacket, Corvino's hand, then withdrew. For several steps the men walked together, Corvino saying nothing, the heavy Moroccan describing at first a hotel and then a friend's souq in the Rabat medina where they could go and purchase whatever the Spaniard liked—what did he like, silver jewelry? Corvino smiled when he realized the man thought he was a Spaniard. Then in the pit of his stomach Corvino felt a sudden chill. I am poor, the Moroccan told him. I am old but very able. Permit me, please, to be your guide. Corvino turned to the man and shook his head violently, then continued up the inclined street toward what appeared to be a bank. The hotel was just a few blocks farther. "No," Corvino said sharply when the man tried to follow. Corvino felt suddenly very happy when he saw in the window a chart for exchange rates and realized the building was in fact a bank.

On the next street, sitting on the broken sidewalk against the side of a parked car, was an old woman in a black haik, staring up at Corvino. Corvino had never seen eyes so big or dark or round. Were they so prominent because of her thin face? At his approach she dropped her eyes to his knees. The purple line of a tattoo ran from her lower lip down the middle of her chin. She had hennaed the palms of her hands. They looked strangely golden to Corvino. She raised one golden hand to him as he passed, further lowering her head, murmuring softly, as if to his suitcase or his shoes. Corvino walked past.

Once in his hotel room, he unpacked. Then he shaved and showered. For a few minutes the water was hot, and Corvino was happy, but then it gave out. By the time he rinsed himself of soap the water was cold and he was cursing.

*

His next two days passed slowly. At the university the people with
whom he was to meet greeted him with smiles, handshakes, and
a sweet glass of mint tea, but said there was no hurry for him to
conduct his business. Enjoy our country, they said. You found the
hotel? Good. Relax. This is your first visit? Take some time to get
over your jet lag. We suggest you go to Fez. You haven't seen the true
Morocco until you've been to Fez. Once seen, you'll never forget its
magnificent medina. But he should visit Marrakesh, another said.
Believe me, the South is another Morocco entirely. Marrakesh is the
gateway to the Sahara. When you are there be sure to go each evening
to the Jemaa el Fna. The Jemaa el Fna is too much *Arabian Nights* if
you ask me, said another. Well, who asked you? Really, it's a circus,
all snake charmers and fortune tellers, fire eaters, acrobats, monkey
trainers, men who swallow glass. If you want to see how lovely
Morocco can be, take a train down to Agadir. In Agadir are some of
the world's most beautiful beaches. But he should see Tangier. What
for? Tangier's a scandal. The only reasons to go to Tangier are boys
and drugs. I tell you he should visit Meknès. But not if he's going to
Fez too. You know between the two cities Fez is superior. Well, you
say that because that's where your family is from. But he hasn't so
much time to see both cities. He must see the South, Marrakesh and
Ouarzazate. What do you mean, not so much time? He has plenty of
time!

It lay heavy on his hands. After the hour of mint tea the
Moroccans smiled and left one by one by one, their English shifting
to French and then to Arabic. Corvino bade them goodbye and
remained in the tea room, watching a placid Berber busboy clear the
table. Outside the window, a bird-of-paradise flower stood indolently
in the sun.

Then he stood and recognized that he was alone. He could fall ill
at this moment, he thought, and he'd die utterly alone. He nodded

to the busboy and walked from the room. He thought he'd grown used to loneliness. After his divorce, he was sure he'd grown used to it. But now he saw that in the States he was never really alone. He was part of a university in a city in a country with a culture that he'd taken so for granted that its absence now surprised him in a palpable, embarrassing way.

He walked from the campus toward the center of town, trying to shake the lonely feeling. Rabat came from *ribat*, or fortified monastery. I'm walking toward the walls of a monastic fortress, he told himself. The town was once called Ribat el-Fath, Fort of Victory. The fortress was built in the tenth century, ruled by the Berber Almohads and later by the notorious corsair pirates who raided Spain, France, and England, and who challenged the Christian world for supremacy of the seas. The pirates took refuge in Salé, now a gentle town of cream-colored buildings just across the banks of the Bou Regreg. For two years Robinson Crusoe was enslaved in Salé. In 1912 Morocco became a European protectorate. In 1956, under King Mohammed V, the country regained its independence. The facts gave him no solace and seemed as dry as the dust mounded at the base of the crumbling walls.

Corvino looked up from the dust at the Bab Rouah, the salmon-pink Gate of the Winds, glowing in the light of the setting sun. The arabesque flourishes on its surface formed a series of concentric arches in relief. The arches rippled in the sunlight. For a moment he prayed he might find refuge within.

A stream of automobiles, petit taxis, sputtering motorbikes, and trucks and buses belching black smoke rushed beside him on the street. Sometimes he blamed his divorce. Or, rather, he blamed Ellen. She was the reason he was so unhappy, why he hadn't been able to advance. He held the idea in his mind for several minutes and felt comforted. Then he saw as he always did the real reason he hadn't advanced. Five years ago on an otherwise pleasant afternoon he had a glimpse of his research as if it were not his own.

His work said little that was new or significant, he saw that afternoon. It contributed nothing to what was already known. It was undistinguished, its irrelevance hiding behind the inflated dialect used by professionals inflicted with self-puffery, by second-rate academics hoping to advance.

Ellen had rushed from the kitchen, seven months pregnant, her apron taut against her belly, shouting what in God's name was burning? A mound of notes and papers blazed in the center of their backyard. Corvino set the gasoline can down on the lawn. From where he stood Ellen appeared to be running toward him through the flames. He wanted to explain but really didn't know how to, so he said, "It's just words, Ellen, just a pile of senseless words." He watched shock register on her face. "It's not like it was ever going to be published." Tears came to his eyes. The realization that he'd set fire to all of his work struck him with the intensity of a punch.

Later he realized that without the work his only route to promotion was by service. But arguments formed all too easily in his mouth. His tongue outraced his circumspection. Even when he genuinely tried to play the sycophant, he failed. Though bookless toadies were sometimes promoted, named committee head, department chair, even associate dean, he lacked the temperament and, when he pressed, appeared insincere.

The note on the dining room table the day Ellen left him said he was bitter and unbearable to live with. He was joyless. He was impossible to please. All her friends were really very worried about her. He never smiled! He hadn't even been pleased by Rachel's birth! He emanated disapproval and almost constant negativity, and did he think for one moment she wanted their daughter to grow up in an emotional environment like that? Women had a difficult enough time in the world without having neurotic fathers. She was sure he agreed. Their newborn daughter deserved only the best.

Corvino agreed. Ellen received custody of Rachel, the stocks, savings, most of the furniture, the newer car. He kept the house and his books. He placed a sagging lawn chair on the spot where he'd torched his academic future, in the middle of the scorched circle of grass, and sat there most evenings that first summer sipping one beer after another until mosquitoes drove him inside. Everyone agreed it was a model divorce. How ironic, Corvino remarked at department parties to whoever would listen to him complain, how ironic that his marriage could be so rocky, his separation so smooth. He went back to the Church, confessed his sins. He found the rosary his mother had given him the morning of his first Holy Communion. Taking it from its box up in the attic brought tears to his eyes. He was so penitent at first he thought he'd undergone a true conversion. Then instead of going to weekly Mass he began listening to a radio station that played the music that was popular when he was young. He drove around town, windows down, radio blaring, not caring to fasten his seat belt. His hair grew down past his collar. He felt young again, or at least every bit as young as a man in his mid-thirties could feel. Wives of colleagues began inviting him over to supper for eight or six or four, always seating him beside a smiling next-door neighbor in her early thirties, recently widowed, separated, divorced.

He stopped accepting dinner invitations.

Then he learned about the exchange with the university in Morocco. The word beckoned him like the call of a Siren. *Morocco.*

He was standing at the base of the Gate of the Winds. Two men in gray banker's suits hurried past him, mingling freely with others in djellabas and burnouses, their babouches softly slapping the ground. All crossed the street at great risk. You crossed the street not by waiting but by walking out into the traffic. The women not in traditional dress appeared to step out of the 1950s. High spiked heels, loose blouses buttoned to the collar, skirts just below the knee. They walked in pairs, heads bent to the other, frequently arm in arm, or holding hands. Sometimes men held each other's hand as they walked. Corvino wondered how painful it was for the women to walk along the cobblestones and uneven, broken sidewalks in high heels. His feet hurt, and he was wearing good walking shoes.

He was sweating. He tried to make himself relax. Above him on the gate were inscriptions in Arabic. The letters were sharp, angular. Kufic script. Corvino knew that Arabic omitted vowels and there was an essential difference between kufic and cursive—cursive was more modern, elegant—but he couldn't comprehend a word. What vowels had he omitted? he thought suddenly.

He stared up at the rippling flourishes on the horseshoe-shaped arch. "Bab Rouah," he said aloud, remembering that the gate historically greeted the people as they returned to the city each evening. He turned. The sun was setting brilliantly in the distance. He stepped through the adjoining gateway, pretending he was a Moroccan returning to the safety of the city, to the fortress. He kept pace with the others around him in suit and tie, burnous and turban, djellaba and clicking high heel.

On his way to the American Embassy the next morning to meet the cultural attaché, Corvino saw a woman walking up the street with a board on her head. Upon the board was a mound covered by a moist cloth. What was it? Laundry? A young girl in a Ghostbusters T-shirt skipped behind her. Rachel had a shirt just like it, he thought. Seeing the Moroccan girl made Corvino homesick for the home he didn't have. For a moment he bent and touched his sides.

He hurried to the embassy, then waited behind an iron gate as the armed guards approved his request to enter. Inside, as he sat waiting, a secretary brought him a copy of the previous day's *USA Today*, asked if he'd like some coffee, then returned a few moments later with a plastic foam cup of coffee so watery and bitter it was exactly like bad coffee brewed back in the States.

"I've been looking forward to meeting you," Corvino said as the secretary brought him in to see the cultural attaché.

The attaché stepped out from behind his big desk. The sleeves of his shirt were rolled up to his elbows. He extended a big hand. His smile was as wide as Kansas. "Judd Martin," he said. He had a clean, untroubled face. "Welcome. Have a seat. Take a load off."

Corvino shook the man's hand and smiled. "Did they deliberately teach someone to make it like this?" He raised his plastic cup.

Martin had a strong jaw and hair that looked as if he were growing out a crew cut. He gestured toward a pair of chairs in front of his desk. "You mean the coffee? That's our cafeteria coffee."

"That's what I meant," Corvino said as he sat.

"I don't know. I'm a de-caf man myself." He winked, then sat, slapping his stomach, which appeared fit, flat. "Corvino. Cor-vi-no. What's that mean? Something to do with wine?"

"No, actually it means 'corvine,' like a crow."

"Ahh, a crow." He nodded. "'Nevermore.' Edgar Allan Poe."

"That was a raven."

"I knew a Corvino, or was it Calvino, played guard for Oklahoma State. Any relation?"

"None that I know."

"He wasn't that big, but he had quickness. Excellent movement for a man his size. Anyway, Pete, we kind of expected you to drop by yesterday."

"The letter my university gave me said the thirteenth."

"Right. Yesterday was the thirteenth."

"No," Corvino said. "Today—"

"Today's the fourteenth, and believe me, I'm paid to know."

He leaned forward in his chair and reached across the desk for his calendar. "See?" He pointed to a 14 on the calendar. "That's today." He flipped a page. His finger pointed to a large 13. "That was yesterday." Martin kept tapping the 13 with his fingertip until Corvino nodded.

"No sweat." Martin flipped the calendar back to the 14. "So you're here in Rabat getting this exchange off the ground. Everyone cooperating?"

"Absolutely," Corvino said.

Martin spoke for a while about various people Corvino should meet while he was here, then gave Corvino a pencil and pad of paper and said maybe he should write down their names and numbers. Corvino wiped the sweat off his brow and did as he was told. Martin paced the length of the office, then slapped his hands together and said, "To tell you the God's truth, Pete, you look a little green around the gills."

"Yeah, lately I've been feeling a little funny."

"Off your feed?" Martin sat back behind his desk.

"I stopped earlier at a patisserie for a café au lait." He didn't add that there he saw a boy who looked exactly like the crippled boy outside the Hotel Terminus. The boy outside the patisserie stood straight, tall, begging silently until the French woman who operated the shop came to the door. Then the beggar ran off on two good legs. "I really don't have much of an appetite."

"Put that in a bottle and we'll make ourselves a million. What about sleep?"

"Some. I sleep for a few hours, then wake up. I try not to force it. So I read. Go back to sleep. This morning I was sound asleep until the morning call to prayer."

"The Fajr. Like a banshee wailing, huh? I'll never forget the first time I heard it. Made me jump out of my shoes." Martin laughed. "But after a while you won't hear it anymore."

"I woke up just as the muezzin began to sing. It gave me chills."

"Like I say, after a while you get used to it."

"I didn't have any idea where I was. I had to go to the window and look out."

"How are your digs? Any problems?"

"No. No problems."

Martin stared at his wristwatch. The pair stood, smiled, shook hands. As Martin led Corvino to the door he squeezed his shoulder, then patted his back. "Stop by again for a chat and more coffee," he said and laughed as he took the plastic cup of bad coffee from Corvino's hand.

"Sure," Corvino said, though he knew he wouldn't. As he walked beyond the guards and iron bars he knew he was having problems adjusting. Back out on the street he knew there was no one he could turn to.

"Olives and beer?" Bornet said with a laugh.

Corvino started. He hadn't expected his reverie to be interrupted. He was sitting in the lounge of his hotel, drinking his third bottle of Flag Speciale, making plans, plotting his escape. Alongside his glass was a plate of green olives—he'd eaten two or three—and olive pits. He would cut his trip short, telex the committee, take the following Saturday's flight from Casablanca back to JFK. He'd tell the committee that he'd completed the work early, that the Moroccans prefer he go sightsee, that he just couldn't hack it.

"This is a new thing," Bornet said, "olives and beer?"

"Hello," Corvino said with a sudden smile, standing and shaking Bornet's hand. "You don't understand. See, I tried to order peanuts."

Bornet was gesturing to the Moroccan waiter for a beer and a plate of olives for himself. He smiled at Corvino, fluttering his long lashes. "Peanuts?"

The men sat.

"I tried to get peanuts. He didn't understand, so I tried describing them with my hands."

"The Moroccan beer," Bornet said, pointing to Corvino's bottle. He lit a Gauloise. "How do you find it?"

"I think it's excellent."

Bornet frowned. The waiter brought him a bottle of beer, glass, plate of olives. Then Bornet spoke, too rapidly for Corvino to follow, then turned and shook his head.

"Sad, this beer is like all things Moroccan." He poured it gingerly down the side of his glass. "Many bottles are very good, and you decide it's a good beer. Then the next bottle you drink is sour."

"I'm glad to see you," said Corvino.

"The Moroccans lack, how do you say, 'quality control'?" He held his glass of beer up to the light.

"That's right. But it's still a developing country."

The waiter then brought a large plate of peanuts, which Bornet accepted with a nod. The plate was ridiculously large. "I don't care what excuses you make." Bornet shook his head and waved his hand at his beer to emphasize his point. "Sour beer is sour beer. It's the same with the wine. Some Moroccan wines are almost as good as the Italian. Then the next bottle you uncork is vinegar."

"I've been lucky so far," Corvino said. He ate a peanut. "What brings you to Rabat?"

"The train. My car is with the mechanics in Corniche, the dishonest sons of a bitch. So how are you?"

"Well, I'm happy to see you."

"Do you like this hotel? Is it agreeable?"

"It's good enough."

"You should be in a hotel where if you ask for peanuts you get peanuts."

They drank, Bornet eating several olives and then suggesting they go to a restaurant for a chicken-and-olive tajine. He wrapped a handful of the green olives in a napkin and said he knew just the place, past the Cathedral San Pierre. In front of the white stone cathedral, under two tall poinsettia trees in full flower, was a cripple hunched on the second step. Head lowered, he raised his flattened palm and called out as the two men passed. Bornet tossed an olive pit at him, then sucked another green olive into his mouth. In the restaurant Corvino ate his first real meal since arriving—salad with anchovies, a lamb tajine, and much bread. They drank a bottle of Ouled Thaleb Syrah and a liter of mineral water. The beer and food and wine made Corvino's head swim.

"It's a crime," Bornet said. "You are a visitor and no one takes you to eat. It's a disgrace. They are cold here, here in Rabat. Worse than Paris. It's typical, you understand. It wouldn't be the same in Casablanca."

"'Life is cheap in Casablanca, Rick,'" Corvino said and laughed. It was pleasant to be drinking, eating, with company.

Bornet's face sagged. "Life is cheap the world over. There's nothing special here."

"This vinegar is excellent." Corvino poured the last drops of the wine into his glass.

"We need another bottle." Bornet gestured in the air until the waiter noticed him. "If you think life is cheap here, my friend, you should see the rest of the Middle East. You're just standing at the edge, hardly in the doorway. You're on the top of the iceberg, do you know what I mean? The capital of the most gentle Arab country of them all."

Corvino nodded. He'd been trying to forget where he was, and now it was all coming back. The waiter brought Bornet the second bottle of wine.

"So drink. You need to keep up your strength." He filled Corvino's glass. "Get a tough skin, you understand? Don't be so American."

"What do you mean, 'so American'?"

Bornet's stare held Corvino's eyes. "I mean weak. I mean you asked a man in your hotel for peanuts, and he brought you olives. Then you left him a tip. The weasel's laughing at you right now, believe me. The story is going from one to another throughout the whole hotel. You'll be lucky to get clean sheets. You must learn how to handle these Arabs if you expect to stay here and work. It's not like they're people."

Corvino's eyebrows arched. "Not like they're people?"

"Of course they are flesh and blood like you and me. But they think whatever happens to them is the will of their God. Their destiny, their fate. They are stupid as animals, some of them. You see an Arab and his donkey, both filthy, covered with lice and fleas, loaded down with sacks of oranges. You can't tell which drives the other. You give them a fortune and they don't know what to do with it. You and me, we're men who know what to do with fortunes!"

Corvino shook his head.

"You took the bus from Casa, you've seen a little of the country. The *bidonvilles* along the road. Hovels made of scrap wood and cardboard, tin roofs covered with stones. Shacks you and I wouldn't even shit in. Some have a ditch that runs through, that they drink from, wash their clothes in, piss. Years ago the King tried to get some of them to move, so he built them apartments in the city. Beautiful places, better than what I lived in when I came here. So they moved to the apartments, stayed a month, two months, then sold them and went back to their shacks." He wagged his head. "Arabs stay poor because everything to them is *insha'Allah*. They think everything that happens is the will of Allah."

"But you can't just take people who've farmed all their lives and drop them in the city and expect—"

"See how American you are? You make an excuse for everything."

"The way out of poverty is education."

Bornet laughed. "That's right. How silly of me. I thought money had something to do with poverty." He poured himself more wine and lit another cigarette. "I forget you're a teacher, not a man in the real world."

"No. I live in the real world."

"You live in the land of Mickey Mouse and Goofy Duck. We have money because we know how to use it. We're not beggars, with our hands out, who know only how to beg."

"You're wrong."

"Not here," Bornet said. He tapped his middle finger against the table. A length of ash from his cigarette fell to the cloth. "In America maybe. But not here."

"You'd be wrong anywhere."

"This wine is sour," Bornet said, raising his glass. "Taste it. Don't you taste it?"

A startling thick depression fell over Corvino the following morning. What should he do? he thought. It seemed he hardly had the energy to do anything. In the shower he lathered his face, neck, arms. If he were going to change his plans and depart early he should notify the airline. The airline's main office was downtown, on Avenue Mohammed V, across from the train station. He could walk there, he thought. At least that was something. As the water in the shower grew cooler and cooler, he soaped his way down to his feet. He could stop for a coffee in the café at the Hotel Terminus. That was two things he could do. He could view the Grand Mosque. Explore the Chellah. Look at the grounds near the Royal Palace. That afternoon he could walk about the medina.

He felt exhausted. Even the bar of soap was heavy in his hand. He had slept like a dead man the night before, at least until the wine in his system wore off. Then he woke suddenly in the darkness, trembling. He sat up in bed. His rosary lay on the sheet alongside him. He gathered it in his hands, ran his fingertips over the beads, brought the crucifix to his lips. He felt on the verge of tears. This time he didn't have to go to the window to see where he was. He knew exactly where he was.

It was a chore to towel off and comb his hair. He felt he should exercise but was too tired. He threw himself anyway to the floor near the bed and did thirty push-ups, counting in French, then stood and touched his toes with his knuckles twenty times. Corvino twisted his torso until his spine popped. This is backward, he thought, exercising after showering. He ran his hand across his face. He'd forgotten to shave. He began walking back into the bathroom to shave, then stopped, thinking better of it.

The morning air held a crisp chill. Stepping from the hotel, Corvino shook his head at a man in a white coat wanting to sell him a bouquet of roses. Cars and motorbikes raced their way up the street. The high pitch of their horns was piercing. A boy approached him from a side street, one hand out, face gray with dirt. "*Un dirham,*" the boy said.

Corvino walked steadily, as if he had places to go. Yes, he thought, he'd tell the committee he'd finished his business early. What could they do? Call another meeting? He tried not to look at the old woman who sat on the broken sidewalk and begged with hennaed hands, but he looked anyway and noticed that she still spoke to his shoes.

They're out in force today, he thought. Before he was past the bank he saw another woman pleading from the doorway of a still-closed shop and a thin one-legged man, his leg hardly thicker than his crutch. Corvino walked on, past an old man with a straw basket full of oranges, past a boy offering matches and tobacco by the cigarette, past the shoeshine men who clacked their brushes on the sidewalk as he hurried past.

At a side street a man led a donkey pulling a cart full of scrap. A black Renault, honking, raced past them. There was the clatter of a jackhammer, men digging a trench in the next street. Corvino walked as if determined. Then a woman with a board beneath her arm stepped out from a doorway next to a bathhouse. Corvino smelled bread, and suddenly he understood. The mound of what he'd thought earlier might be laundry was actually dough covered with a damp cloth. Women must bring the dough they make each morning to the communal ovens next to the neighborhood bathhouses. Corvino stood outside the doorway leading to the hammam's ovens, smelling the rich odor of baking bread.

He was near the Grand Mosque. It was too beautiful not to evoke stares. He gazed at its white plaster walls, gold-trimmed windows, magnificent green tiled roof. He stared up at its minaret, from which the mosque's muezzin gave the calls to prayer. A thin woman in black sat along a wall in the shade on the other side of the street. Lying across her lap was a child, perhaps a year old. The child appeared to be sleeping. The woman held out both her hands to him, calling something out to him in a low voice he didn't understand.

He walked on, then stopped, unable to move past the gesture— her two outstretched hands, held to the sides, palms open and raised—that made him think of priests in Mass just before the priest consecrated the bread and wine into the body and blood of Jesus. His mind held both images as he stood still on the avenue. Mother and child, he thought. Oh mother and child. Quickly he turned and crossed the street, thrusting one hand into his pocket, finding two coins, two dirhams, one for the woman, the second for her child.

She'd turned away. She stared blankly at the sidewalk, nose and mouth darkly veiled. With the rush of his footsteps she looked back up at him. All Corvino saw were her two eyes. In a small voice she uttered something, some whispered phrase followed by a second, louder phrase.

He pressed the two coins into the palm of her hand, saying, "*Oui,
madame*, here, I am so sorry, may God bless you and your child."

The woman's dark eyes held him.

Corvino turned and took a dozen steps. Then a sob rose in his
chest. There was no controlling it, nothing rational about it. It rose
from just below his diaphragm, from the pit of what he was. His chest
heaved as he moaned, thinking of the Madonna and the Christ child,
of Ellen and Rachel when the girl was still at Ellen's breast. His chest
shook as he caught his breath. The images of Ellen and the Virgin
and the Moroccan swirled in his mind, and for a clear second he
held some small part of the weight of the reality of the world's poor
women and their children, and in that moment Corvino felt himself
in their place. It stirred something that had never been alive inside
him.

He looked back at the darkly veiled woman, knowing that now
he would be able to stay.

THE UNFINISHED MINARET

They were walking up the Rue el Mariniyne when Ahmed spotted the horses. The afternoon light was fading gently in the trees. "See," Ahmed Ousaid said, extending his arm. Too shy to point, the young Berber crooked his first finger until it formed an oval with his thumb. Then he turned and smiled with his eyes at the American. The American marched head down, twisting a dial on the camera that dangled from his neck. Ahmed's eyes were large and round and the most expressive thing about him. In his brown Berber face they were exactly the color of almonds. He couldn't see the American's eyes because of the man's low-slung hat.

The American huffed as he strode up the street. He wore a khaki shirt that was all pockets and brown pants that jangled with change, nearly like a tambourine. The shirt appeared new and sported buttoned epaulets. Ahmed knew enough about style to guess this one thought he was on safari. Ahmed dressed like the student he was, in a gray cotton jacket zipped halfway up over his checked shirt and a pair of cheap French-made blue jeans. His white sneakers were also from France. He raised his eyebrows to prompt a response, then shrugged and scratched his hair, which was dark and tightly curled, then ran a finger over his thin mustache. He put his hands in his jacket pockets. He was slight, thin. The American was more fat than a medina butcher's cat but nearly thirty times as big, towering over everyone and everything with his fedora and camera and kangaroo pockets.

They were on their way to the Mausoleum of Mohammed V and the nearby Tour Hassan, or Hassan Tower. Late afternoon was the best time to see them. By then the sun would slant brilliantly against the tower's north face, and the many rows of ruined columns beside the tower would cast their long shadows toward the new mosque and mausoleum, and a cool breeze from the ocean would carry down the river. Ahmed knew how to show off Rabat to strangers. The horses—one sorrel, the other chestnut roan—were now in plain view, pawing the ground, topped by guards in baggy red pleated pants, ornately buckled jackets, cream-colored capes.

The American's camera clicked and whirred.

"This was once to be a great mosque, greatest in the whole world," Ahmed said. For emphasis he made a grand sweep of his arm. "The whole area here by the river. Built in the twelfth century by Yaqub Al-Mansur, a mighty sultan. He desired to make a mosque big enough to shelter his entire army. He built too the Giralda minaret in Seville and the Koutoubia in Marrakesh. Maybe you have seen them?" The American gave no answer. "The tower he intended to be the mosque's minaret." Ahmed made an oval in the air.

"Yeah," the American said, "that's real nice."

The Hassan Tower rose thickly—nearly fifty-five meters—in the sky, its tawny south face fringed by arches and delicate stone lacework. The tower's internal ramps were so broad three horses could run abreast. The unfinished top ended in a blunt square rather than peaking in the narrow, slender tower typical of most minarets. Ahmed smiled up at the American, whose eyes were covered by his camera. Behind the American's head, Rabat's tiled roofs and whitewashed walls glittered in the late sun.

They walked past the guards and horses inside the pocked remains of the mosque's walls. The jagged walls were a rosier ocher than the tower. Ahmed and the American moved among the many stumps of columns that were intended to form arches and support the mosque's roof. The columns were round and set evenly in rows and made of thick slices of white stone. Some stood no higher than Ahmed. Some were taller than the American.

The American slapped several columns with his meaty hands. "Sort of reminds you of stacks of poker chips, don't they?"

Ahmed saw the American's smile. "Sure."

"Cut the cards and deal," the American said. He walked around several of the columns. "So why didn't this mighty sultan get the job done?"

Ahmed considered the question. He accepted the minaret's unfinished state so completely it was as if Al-Mansur had intended it to be that way. There was no other choice. The great mosque was in ruins and would always be in ruins, Ahmed supposed. It was the way it was. He knew the ruins still stood because of the will of Allah. He stroked his mustache and ventured, "Because at the end of his life he died."

The American pushed back his hat and laughed. "Better then than at the beginning."

Ahmed laughed too, though he didn't realize what he'd said was funny. He laughed because the American was laughing. He liked Americans. They laughed at unexpected times. He enjoyed being with them because they helped him with his English and because they gave him dirhams, of which he had only a few. He wanted to be like them, but not too much, perhaps someday even live with them, Allah willing. Even though America had many flaws, he thought it was the best country in the world. Some of his friends preferred Spain, some Italy, some France, but for him America was the ticket. Of course, everything hinged on jobs. In Morocco there were few jobs. The King did his best, but sometimes even a king's best is not enough. Besides, Ahmed thought, America was the land of James Dean. Ahmed admired James Dean. In James Dean's eyes there was such fire. A color picture of James Dean hung in the room where Ahmed slept, over the table he used as a desk. Alongside James Dean he'd taped a postcard of the Statue of Liberty and pictures of Stevie Wonder, Roy Rogers, and William "The Refrigerator" Perry. Ahmed was amazed that a man could eat so much he could grow as big as a refrigerator. But that was America. Many things were possible in America.

He and the American, whose mind held the images Ahmed craved to see, and whose tongue spoke so easily the idioms his books never fully explained, and whose pockets carried the dirhams Ahmed wanted a few of, stood laughing among the ruins of Al-Mansur's grand mosque. The cobblestone plateau upon which they stood overlooked the Bou Regreg River. Across the river's banks lay Rabat's sister city, Salé, her milk-colored houses glowing in the late afternoon light. Then a breeze stirred Ahmed's hair, and suddenly he smelled the ocean. He swung his gaze from Salé toward the ocean, which he couldn't see, which raged beyond the tower and Rabat's mellah and medina and kasbah.

"Now, that's a pretty thing," the American said. He turned his back to the tower and pointed at the Mausoleum of Mohammed V. Rectangular, its white marble walls opened in three arches supported by twin columns, mirroring the tower's design. Over the arches was the same delicate latticework that marked the unfinished minaret. A second set of polished marble walls enclosed the mausoleum itself. Golden lamps in the shape of pyramids hung over the arched inner doorways, which were flanked by guards with ceremonial rifles and the same imperial dress as those outside the walls on horseback. The mausoleum was crowned by a bright green tiled roof—like the lamps, in the shape of a pyramid—and topped by three progressively smaller golden spheres that shone in the sun.

"Looks like a birthday cake," the American said with a laugh.

Ahmed nodded but did not laugh. To him the mausoleum of the great king who led his country from colonialism to national independence and power in the Arab world did not look like a confection from a patisserie.

Then the American had Ahmed take a picture of him with the mausoleum in the background. The American took off his hat and raked his hair with his fingers. "How does my hair look?" he grinned.

The American's hair was thin and nearly colorless. It looked like dead grass. It was why the American wore the hat, Ahmed thought.

"Oh, your hair is very fine," said Ahmed.

He wasn't used to handling so complex a camera. Looking through it, all he could see was a bull's-eye. The American instructed him to turn a large dial this way and then that way. The bull's-eye was supposed to grow dark or disappear. Ahmed did his best to follow the instructions.

He was worried about the dying light. Nor so much for the photograph he was taking but because he had hoped to show the American the tower's north face as the setting sun shone down on it. There was one moment each day when the light made the tower the most beautiful and holy object in the world. Surely that was why Allah permitted it to stand for so many centuries. The tower was allowed to endure even the great earthquake of 1755, which leveled Lisbon and crumbled much of Rabat. It remained with the mosque's pitted walls and remnants of columns, unfinished but standing, symbol of the sultan's noble attempt.

The American propped his hat back on his head and took his camera, then seemed at once to pale. He leaned against one of the columns. Hands in his pockets, he fingered his change. Ahmed wondered why. There was nothing here he could buy. The American took several deep breaths, appearing to stare at the new mosque adjacent to the mausoleum. Then suddenly the man was charging ahead, toward the mosque's open doorway.

"No." Ahmed dared to grab the American's arm. "Please, it is not permitted."

"Rules were made to be bent." The big man puffed and winked.

"Not in Morocco."

"I'd like to go in there, kid."

"But it is not permitted."

"Why not? I'll take off my shoes."

"You are not of the faith."

"In Spain they let anybody into mosques. What's so special here?"

Ahmed frowned. "I am very sorry. It is not so much what is special here as what is not special everywhere else."

"Well, can't I even look in the door?"

Ahmed considered that at this hour there would be only a few Muslims inside praying. He nodded and told the American he could look inside as they walked past. But please, only for the slightest moment. They moved past, and the American paused at the center entranceway, raising his camera to his eye. A passing Moroccan with a dark beard, snow-white djellaba, and tight white skullcap called out to Ahmed, "Get that *Nasrani* away from the mosque before it is spoiled." Ahmed winced.

"Please, you must try not to give offense. A mosque is not something you sightsee."

"I can't sightsee too much from out here anyway."

"Then it is not something meant for your eyes."

"Listen, kid, you don't understand."

"Please."

Ahmed led him to the steps of the mausoleum. The American started up them angrily, clutching his camera, pockets jangling. Ahmed called out that in a few minutes he would meet him inside. It was a risk, Ahmed realized, because he could lose him entirely. An unescorted foreigner was fair game to anyone, beggar or tradesman, whore or guide.

Let him gawk around the inside of the birthday cake by himself, Ahmed thought as he called out to the Moroccan who had chastised him. Let the others have a chance at some of the dirhams in his pockets.

"Forgive me," Ahmed called to the man in Arabic. "I did not mean to offend."

"And yet you offended."

"Forgive me," Ahmed repeated.

"You should know a *Nasrani* can't enter a mosque." The Moroccan scowled at Ahmed, then raised a finger. "Allah is the one God, and Muhammed is His Prophet. The *mushrik Nasrani* believes in many gods, that Allah had a child. In the countryside an infidel like him caught defiling a mosque would be killed."

"Perhaps."

"The city is overrun by them."

"Ours is a crowded world."

"These imperialists should be controlled. They should be converted or kicked out of the country. They should not be allowed to wander about freely. They should be made to wear a mule's harness."

"And Allah will be praised, if we treat men like mules?"

"On this, Khomeini is right. May Khomeini kill them all."

Ahmed said nothing, then shrugged and waved his hand. The fundamentalist turned away. As Ahmed walked back to the mausoleum he hoped the American would be taken away from him. Then he'd have what was left of the day to himself. He'd hoped to study, and he'd wanted to have tea with his uncle, with whom he lived since he came to Rabat to attend the university. His uncle was growing sick. He enjoyed company with his mint tea. It was only a matter of time before he died. And later that night, perhaps in the medina, Ahmed wanted to eat a bowl of snails. He smacked his lips in anticipation. Yes, he thought, it had been much too long since he'd eaten snails in the medina.

One of the photographers working the steps of the mausoleum approached Ahmed, nodded in greeting, then touched Ahmed's arm as he lit a cigarette. He wore a dark suit with shiny stained lapels. A Polaroid camera hung from his neck. His mustache was dark and thin. He threw his paper match to the steps behind him, then asked Ahmed if he'd heard about the Moroccan athlete who'd been badly injured in a match the day before. Ahmed said he'd heard nothing. Oh, the photographer replied, he's been taken to the hospital for surgery, on special orders of the King.

"I see," Ahmed said, nodding, though he didn't care much for sports. "I wish that he is better soon."

"Bring your friend to me if he runs out of film," the photographer said.

He was hunched in his safari shirt over the mezzanine rail, puffed as a toad, looking down at the sarcophagus on ground level. Ahmed stood beside him at the railing without a word. Above them an immense brass chandelier, tiered and glittering, swayed from the mausoleum's domed ceiling, which was ornately layered in thick gold leaf and pierced by stained-glass windows. The opulent heaviness of the ceiling and chandelier always made Ahmed bend his head and avert his eyes. The tomb rested on a floor of black marble so shiny it looked wet. The walls around them were richly tiled. In each corner stood a guard in the same red-and-cream uniform.

"That guy down there in the corner on the rug," the American whispered, "he's a priest from the mosque next door, right?"

Ahmed shook his head. "No, not a priest. He is a fqih. He reads from the Quran."

"Think he'll mind if I take a picture?"

Ahmed's eyes grew large. "Flash?"

"Not a big one."

"Perhaps it would be better if you did not."

"I really envy him," the American said after a while. "This is what I call having it made."

"Who has it made?" Ahmed said. "The fqih?"

"You couldn't ask for a better setup, having a priest praying by your side, greasing your way up to Heaven." He hesitated, then pulled at his lips. "Arabs go to Heaven, don't they?"

"A few." Ahmed smiled. "Just the good ones."

The American's face seemed to fall. His eyes darted about, then stared at the coffin. When he spoke again it was in a coarse whisper. "What about me, huh? When I die. You know, I think about it a lot. All I come up with are blanks."

Ahmed didn't know what to say. He gazed at one of the guards, whose face was nearly black. "You will find out soon enough, I think."

"I appreciate the cheery prognosis."

Ahmed nodded, confused. He didn't know the meaning of *prognosis*.

They descended the mausoleum steps. "You know," the American said, "I think about it an awful lot. 'Don't dwell,' everybody tells me." He waved his white hands as he spoke. "I go to a party and stop smiling for one lousy minute and they start yelling at me, 'You're dwelling again. Stop it.' You know what I mean? People, they're always telling me to put on a smiling face." The American pushed his hat back on his head. "Sometimes I wonder if it'll just be darkness. Or if I won't even know—" Suddenly from the steps below came a flash.

"Ten dirhams." It was the photographer who'd spoken earlier to Ahmed.

The American blinked his eyes several times, then put his hand in his pocket and clanked his change. Ahmed stepped forward, eyes narrowed. "We did not ask you to snap a picture."

"He's willing to pay," the photographer said in Arabic, "so why don't you shut up?"

"He has plenty of his own film," Ahmed replied, also in Arabic.

"He's rich enough. What do you think, you own him!"

"The thing you do has no honor."

The American stood a few meters from them, studying the snapshot. He cupped it in his big hand. The photographer and Ahmed huddled around him and watched as the picture developed. For a few moments it remained slick and white and then some of the

white darkened into gray that became black and then Ahmed forgot
he was looking at a developing picture. The mausoleum's central
doorway exactly framed the American, whose left leg was bent slightly
as his right leg took the step below. The American's featureless face
was in crisp focus, his mouth forming the letter O. Though Ahmed's
mouth was closed, he seemed about to speak. He was a step behind
the American and so appeared to be nearly as tall but considerably
younger and more slight.

The American nodded several times at the picture, slipped it into
one of his pockets, then began picking coins from the flat of his hand.

"No," Ahmed said. "Put down your money." He pushed the
American's hand and turned to the photographer. Ahmed gave him a
few dirhams and warned him not to pull the stunt on him again. The
photographer stared at the coins in his hand, then looked at Ahmed.

"I said ten," the photographer said in Arabic.

"For him, ten," Ahmed said. "For me, be thankful for what I gave
you."

"That was nice," the American said after the photographer walked
away. "I really appreciate it."

"He should have asked you first."

They walked again among the columns, then through the gates
on the river side of the stone escarpment. The horses on this side
of the ruins were dun. The dying light was just reaching the point
that Ahmed so dearly loved. Only if they ran, and ran hard, Ahmed
thought, could they reach the spot in the garden from which they
could watch the last golden rays slant off the tower's silver northern
wall. Ahmed imagined what they might see, then pictured them
seeing it. Then he surrendered both images because he realized the
American was not something he could make run.

Below them traffic jammed the bridge to Salé. Mixed with the
autos, trucks, buses, and motorbikes were many carts pulled by
animals, and men on foot driving their donkeys with sticks. Ahmed

pointed to the bridge, again making an oval with his thumb and first finger, then invited the American to look west up the river at the cluster of small rowboats ferrying the poorer people across. "The modern exists side by side with the traditional," Ahmed said in the tone he used to answer his professors at the university. He was unsure if he should continue to explain, then thought no more of it because the words that might begin the explanation failed to come to him. So instead of speaking he turned back and gestured at the tower and ruins and the mosque and mausoleum. What he meant was there for anyone with eyes to see. Then he saw that the American's eyes had filled with tears.

"I think I'd better sit," the American said.

Ahmed led him slowly to a patch of grass. The American squatted, folded his legs, reached behind him with one hand for the ground. "Whew," he said. Ahmed knelt and stared at the American. Now their eyes were on the same level.

"See this?" the American said after a while. He pointed to his stomach. "I bet you can't guess what I got hiding in here."

Ahmed laughed. "Do not ask me to do it. I can not."

"Come on, take a guess."

"OK. Your stomach and some fat."

"You lose. Try again."

"I have no idea, no thoughts."

"I had no idea either, to tell you the truth." The man leaned closer. "It's a crab."

"A crab?"

"You heard me." The American guffawed. "A goddamn crab, with its claws and legs and pincers all twisted up inside of me." He made his hands into claws and pincers. "You understand? I got cancer up and down my guts."

Ahmed moved back on the ground.

"Don't be a goose, you can't catch it."

"You are dying?" Ahmed said. He was very impressed.

"You better believe it," said the dying man.

"How does it feel, this crab in your stomach? Is there great stabbing?" The thought that the man was dying made Ahmed bold.

"Nope. Not a damn thing. Isn't that amazing? You'd think I'd be able to feel it." He pushed on his abdomen, then sat back. "Ahh, I guess it's not so bad. Besides, they said it's in remission. You know"—the man waved a thick hand—"it's sleeping."

Ahmed put a finger to his lips. "You must not swear, or you will rile it. Is that the word, *rile*? You must not wake it up."

The dying man smiled. Ahmed could see his eyes clearly now. They were pale blue, the color of the morning sky.

"And you must eat only mild foods."

"That's why I came here to Morocco," he said with a laugh.

"My father in Ouarzazate had many stomach pains."

"Did he die of cancer?"

"Perhaps. One evening after he ate a very spicy tajine he died. Maybe it was only worms."

The dying man laughed again. "Hey, worms I can live without."

The light on the tower's north face had passed, and now the sky was graying. It was the time between times, Ahmed thought, the time when you did not know if it was day or night. For a moment Ahmed wanted to explain this to the man with the sleeping crab of cancer in his stomach. Since he'd been a child, Ahmed had felt an unexplained sadness at this hour. Once he had tried to explain it to his mother, who told him it was hunger, nothing more. She said sadness was the beginning of hunger.

Or are we hungry because we are sad? he had thought.

The dying man was on his feet, arms folded across his chest, looking down at the river. Ahmed stood. "Are you hungry?"

The sad man shook his head.

"See," Ahmed said, straightening his arm and pointing with his ovaled fingers, not knowing what else to do. "If you like, we can follow the river to the ocean. See, there beyond? Take a deep breath and you will smell it. And there by the trees are the walls of the Kasbah des Oudaias. We can walk outside. Would you like for me to take you?"

"It's too dark for pictures."

"But not too dark for our eyes."

In the wan light they began the walk down to the river. Then they heard the sudden call of the muezzin, amplified from the minaret behind them.

"Allah is the most great," sang the muezzin in Arabic. "There is no god but Allah, and Muhammad is His Prophet. Come to prayer. Come to completion and fulfillment. There is no god but Allah, the one and indivisible God."

The prayer held them where they stood. The dying man turned back to face the tower. "Everybody asked why I wanted to come here, to Morocco. What, you're knocking on death's door and you want to go off to the Sahara for a camel ride? You want to see Arabs? A trip to Venice, Rome, the Vatican, you know, something like that they could understand. It's not like I'm going there for a cure, I told them. I want a cure, I should get myself a bottle of Lourdes water. I should go to the Mayo Clinic. Stay on chemo till all my hair falls out." He wagged his head. "My father had stomach pains too. You should've seen what his cancer did to him. Sunken face, cheeks. Down to seventy, maybe sixty-five pounds. The only hair left on him was fuzz. And this was a man who worked every day of his life on a loading dock. I mean, in his prime he was a tree. Arms hard as rock, big barrel of a chest. I went into his hospital room, I nearly turned right around. Who put the corpse in Pa's bed? I asked. Henry, they said, that's your father. At the end I held him in my arms. He was a bird, I swear."

"In the end," Ahmed said, "I held my father too."

They turned again toward the river and walked in silence.

"The priest back there on the rug," Henry said, "he prays there all the time? I mean twenty-four hours a day?"

It seemed important so Ahmed said yes, even though he wasn't sure.

"Then what happens to people like us?"

Ahmed said he did not understand.

"Sure you do," Henry said. "What happens to people who aren't kings or sultans, who don't build mosques or end up in mausoleums?"

Ahmed thought as hard as he could. He wanted to tell Henry that death was merely a passage, not something to fear. It was like the boats on the river ferrying the poor people to Salé. Death brought you back to where you began. Death returned the droplet of rain to the clouds. But the words would not come. "They walk along the river to the kasbah," Ahmed heard himself say, "and then afterwards they go together to the medina." He looked at Henry to see if the answer pleased him. Henry held his gaze and nodded.

"Are you hungry?" Ahmed asked. Henry said yes. "Have you been to the medina?" Henry said no. "Then we will go there to eat. You will like it, I think. And tomorrow, if you like, I will show you more."

They reached the spot from which Ahmed liked to view the tower's north face, and he and Henry stopped and looked at it in the dusky darkness. Then they followed the sandy rubble of the river's south bank to the Oudaias Kasbah, which, Ahmed explained, had been built just before the Tour Hassan and was the site of the original fortress from which Rabat took its name. Because of the hour the kasbah's imposing gateway was closed, but Ahmed pointed out the shell-shaped palmettes radiating from its circular doorway and then showed Henry the citadel's turrets and musket slits and cannons, and Henry nodded and smiled and seemed to forget about the crab in his stomach as he ran his hands along the kasbah's rough umber walls.

Then they entered the crowded medina, walking past the doorways of rug sellers, tinsmiths, herbalists, barbers, past stalls offering djellabas and kaftans of all colors and sizes. They walked past men hawking bunches of mint, baskets of oranges, paper funnels of roasted chickpeas, women displaying stacks of flat, pocked baghrir, butchers with cages of squawking chickens, rows of blackened sheep heads, trays of fresh tripe buzzing with flies. An old woman sat on a stool behind a mound of dark henna powder. Beggars called out to all who passed. Sometimes a motorbike or automobile tried to force its way through, pushing everyone to the sides of the narrow streets.

Later, after Henry paused before one of the stalls and bought a large brass plate, when it was dark and a thick crescent of moon shone in the black sky, Ahmed stopped by the medina's Andalusian wall and purchased a steaming bowl of snails. Immediately he gobbled one then two of the snails with a straightened safety pin stuck in a lemon impaled on the side of the vendor's pot.

Then he blew on the hot broth and offered the bowl to Henry. As Henry bent to take a sip, Ahmed saw the reflection of the moon fill the bowl. Henry's hands covered Ahmed's. For a moment the Moroccan moon gently skated on the liquid's dark surface. Then Henry seemed to swallow the moon as he tipped the bowl to his lips.

IN THE GARDEN OF THE DJINN

Sarah didn't pause to watch the water seller scurry from his spot in the shade to the path leading to the ruins and gardens. The shallow copper bowls ringed to the belts crisscrossing his bright red shirt jangled softly and flashed in the sunlight. The water seller made a show of splashing the ground in front of the young American woman and then arcing a steam of water into a bowl held in his outstretched hand. His dark eyes stared at her between the twin rows of tassels dangling from the broad brim of his hat. Sarah couldn't help but stare at the man's outrageous red hat. She assumed no one was expected to actually drink the water—it was sour, no doubt squirting from the hairy goatskin waterbag beneath his armpit. Tourists were expected to gawk at the man's quaint costume, smile, give him a coin for his efforts.

The water seller said something Sarah didn't understand. He grinned at her expectantly, holding a hand up to his eye and cocking his first finger, then nodding with a smile that revealed many missing teeth. When he pressed the air again and made a clicking sound Sarah realized he wanted her to take his picture. She saw that a mole on his cheek was really a fly clinging to his skin. The fly flew in a tiny circle after the man flicked at it with his fingertips. Then the fly landed on the same spot. The tassels on his hat swung in the hot air. He grinned again as the red-haired woman hurried past him. Then he dumped the water from his bowl to the hard dry ground and returned to the cool shade beneath his tree.

Sarah knew about water sellers from Zach, who'd found a picture of one in a book Sarah brought home from the library. Zach had a friend who'd recently traveled through Morocco. That was how it started for Zach. One winter night the friend came to dinner at their apartment, and while Sarah rinsed lettuce for the salad and Zach rolled a joint to go with the wine, the friend bragged about all the great sights he'd seen and all the fantastic hashish he'd smoked, hiking up in the Rif mountains.

"See this?" the friend said, making a fist. "Let me tell you, I must've smoked a hunk of hash this big every week I was there." The friend's mouth melted into a smile. His head bounced up and down. "Hashish so dark you thought it was fudge. Blond hashish crumbly like halvah. Some hard as a brick. Every morning I drank it in my tea. Ate it every day for lunch and supper, man."

When Zach asked if he'd brought any back, the friend's eyes grew big as saucers. "No way, José, I didn't even try. They've got prisons over there you would not believe." Zach said he could believe it. Zach was rail-thin and had curly brown hair he let grow long in imitation of an afro. He twisted the joint's ends, then nodded to Sarah. "Yo, Red, can you believe it?"

Sarah stood by the sink in jeans and an old sweater, the sleeves of which she'd pushed to her elbows. She was long-boned, with big hazel eyes and full lips. She lifted the cutting board and with the edge of her knife scraped a mound of chopped scallions into the salad bowl. "Oh sure, Zach." Then she washed her hands, and the three smoked the not very good marijuana. After dinner, while Sarah did the dishes, she could hear Zach and his friend trying to remember the words to the Crosby, Stills & Nash song about Marrakesh. For the next week whenever Sarah came upon Zach he was humming the tune or singing some mangled version of the words.

Fascination with Morocco started for Sarah years before, when she first read Anaïs Nin's diaries and essays, particularly the piece on Fez, which Nin portrayed as a splendid labyrinth that took you back to the Middle Ages. Morocco was a magical place that smelled of cedar and the rarest oils, a land of azure skies, earth-colored kasbahs, carpets from Persian fairy tales. Veiled women, tiled fountains, handsome guides in canary-yellow slippers that slapped the ground softly and with the utmost dignity. It was the enchanting land of genies—Sarah delighted in the Arabic form, *djinn*—the playful and sometimes evil spirits who could take on any form, human or animal, and whom Allah made from smokeless fire. They lived in the world just beyond the world of people, beneath the earth's seventh layer. So one night when Zach suggested going there for a month, six weeks, maybe the whole summer if he could get the bucks together, Sarah eagerly agreed, her face flushing with excitement.

"Sure," Zach said. He pulled his T-shirt over his head, then reached for a cigarette. Sarah lay on the mattress on the floor of their bedroom, across from a window frosted over with a mosaic of ice. She'd pulled the sheet and blankets to her chin against the draft that ran across the floor from the baseboards. "Maybe we can split for Casablanca in June."

"Casablanca," she said, then laughed at how easily one could say the name of a place and truly consider going there.

"That's where we fly into. I called the airline." Grinning, he took a drag off his cigarette. "Then it's off to the Rif mountains."

"And Rabat and Tangier," Sarah said. "Meknès and Fez and Marrakesh."

He laughed. "Sure. Once we're there we can go anywhere you want."

Sarah's dark red hair fell to her shoulders as she sat up. Zach crouched beside his side of the bed, stubbing out his cigarette into an ashtray. Sarah touched his arm, then held him, the blankets dropping from her shoulders and breasts as Zach murmured her name, as if she'd surprised him. He stroked her back, then kissed her shoulders and neck. A tendril of smoke drifted from the ashtray to the ceiling. Then with his hands he kneaded where he'd kissed.

"Not so hard," Sarah whispered. She drew her elbows in over her breasts, rounding her back. Though his touch felt good she was cold.

"Know why I love you?" he said as his hands dropped to her waist. He lifted the blankets from her thighs.

"Why?"

He ran his hands so gently down her back she shivered. Then he pushed her onto her back, and as she pulled the sheet over herself he began to stroke her thighs, then her calves, then her ankles and feet. She closed her eyes and thought of the Morocco she'd never seen. "This is why," he whispered, as he began kissing the inside of her legs, which were now relaxed, open, bent at the knee. She heard the click of the switch as he turned the lamp off. In the darkness she tried to imagine the winding narrow streets and many souqs of the Fez medina as the hands softly massaged first one thigh, then the other, as the mouth kissed and licked the back of each knee. She imagined a stall full of scarves of all colors. "This is why," the voice whispered. She tried to hold the image but it slipped away. For a moment Sarah saw only blackness. Then she saw the rolling dunes of a desert, something dark moving slowly across the sculpted sands. Was it a woman? The mouth moved slowly across the inside of her thighs. Yes, the figure in the desert was a woman, dressed in a black djellaba, dark as winter's night. She walked so softly she left no footprints on the sand. The mouth was higher, settling in on a spot that made the dunes ripple with heat. The sands shimmered in warmth that spread outward in white circles. Then the woman in the djellaba melted into the white circles, which turned into the sun, which spun blazing over the desert. Sarah held the sheet between her clenched teeth. The Moroccan sun spun faster and faster, turning into twirling multicolored scarves. Her hips arched. Then the heat broke upon her in ripples, and she tried to push the whirling scarves away, push away the spinning sun that throbbed and pulsed through her and made her cry out into the bedroom's blank winter night.

By spring Zach hadn't saved any money for the trip. When she asked him about it he blamed entropy. Dollars simply refused to mass in orderly fashion under his care, he told her with a grin. Besides, it was the nature of money to resent being imprisoned in cobweb-filled bank accounts. Money had a sense of its own, a yen to get out at night, see the sights. He began spending time with the new woman in their apartment building. At first Zach claimed he was only helping her move in, get cinder blocks for a bookcase, paint her kitchen. The three shared a few meals. Sarah was even willing to lend Zach some money for the trip until one spring night when she came home.

She sensed something was wrong the moment she put her key into the lock. She didn't hear the stereo. The lamp by the living room sofa wasn't on. A triangle of light from the hallway lay like a block of stone on the carpet. The apartment was strangely quiet. Then she heard sounds coming from their bedroom. *Mmmm*'s and drawn-out *O*'s. For a moment she thought it was Zach by himself trying to trick her. She'd open the bedroom door and there he'd be, pretending to be making it with her pillow, a big smile on his face. She stole down the hallway, pushed open the bedroom door.

On their mattress. On the sheets she just took to the Laundromat. With the pillow her mother gave her eight years ago when she left home for college propped beneath the new woman's fat ass.

Sarah booted Zach's bare ass with the toe of her sneaker. The new woman scrambled from under him and tried to cover herself with a sheet. Sarah ripped the sheet away, shouting, "Out! Both of you! I want you out!"

"Not to worry," Zach said. "Be cool," Zach said.

The new woman was already at the doorway, one arm holding up her droopy breasts. Sarah stepped across the mattress and kicked Zach's thigh. He knelt on the mattress, cupping his groin. "I'll give you cool," Sarah shouted. She slapped his face with the back of her hand. She didn't consider the thought he might strike back. "Here's cool," she yelled as she gave him another kick, until he and the woman fled.

Later, the day he carried away his clothes and albums and took down all his posters and left thumbtack holes in all the walls, Zach said please cut me a little slack, Red, it was just sex, mindless and harmless, if there is still a last piece of harmlessly irresponsible sex left in the cold world. And in case she cared to know but was too busy assaulting him to notice, he had been wearing a raincoat for protection against disease and progeny. They drank a bottle of expensive red wine neither could remember buying. It wasn't as if he'd meant to hurt anyone, he said. She wasn't supposed to come home when she did. And she didn't have to drive them naked from the apartment, like a wife, finger pointing to the door, like some kind of disapproving mother, all lightning and thunder, just like a redhead.

"Give me a break with the melodrama," Sarah said. She sat across from him at the lovely walnut table they found the year before in a junk store, then refinished, and smoked a cigarette and waited for him to start to beg.

He sipped his wine, scratched his curly hair, then let his eyes grow soft as velvet. He deserved anything she wanted to lay on him, he had never been more wrong in his life, of course she was right, he was a jerk, he'd change, he'd be a new man, she was so strong, he'd never seen her that way before, such righteous anger, it turned him on so, couldn't she maybe let him come back? Could she, you know, try the new Zach out for a month or two, then make up her mind?

Sarah sat back and laughed. "And after then if I'm not pleased I get to throw you out again with the rest of the trash?"

That began the argument that ended it, that allowed them to hurl their favorite weapons at each other for the last time. They started slowly, as if they each knew this would be the last time, with the chronicle of the other's faults. Zach brought up one of Sarah's weaknesses, and then Sarah topped it with one of Zach's. Sarah sipped the very good dry red wine, secure that she could list Zach's faults far longer than he could list hers. When he began doubling back on accusations, Sarah smiled and said he was slow-witted and repetitive, and then Zach called her an uptight bitch.

Sarah called him a childish asshole. In the middle of the shouting, as Zach searched the cupboard beside the sink for another bottle of wine, Sarah realized she was enjoying the fight as much as anything she'd ever shared with him. She sensed her face was flushed and that she looked beautiful. She and Zach argued with more commitment and conviction than they did anything else. All at once she saw that the best thing they did together was compete. She was suddenly relieved he was leaving. They were both catching their breath as he uncorked a bottle of something pink and most likely sweet, something Sarah knew would give her a headache if she drank it, when he said, "And without me you can't go to Morocco."

She hadn't considered that. "Like hell I can't."

"Hey, Missy Miss, we're not talking about a stroll through J. C. Penney. We're talking foreign country. You have trouble on the interstate."

"I've already made my airplane reservation," she lied.

He shook his head. "Take my word, they'll eat you alive."

Sarah smiled. "Something you'll never have the pleasure of doing again, let me assure you."

"Aren't you a bitch."

"I don't need you, Zach, if that's what you're trying to prove. I feel nothing for you. I can travel overseas perfectly well by myself."

"You're a Barbie doll, Sarah. You were born a Barbie doll and you'll always be a Barbie doll."

"That's right, tear me down to build yourself up."

"You won't last a week. You'll break a fingernail and get a run in your panty hose and come running home in tears."

"You're like a little boy on stilts. Trying *so* hard."

"You want something hard, Sarah?" He slammed the bottle on the table. "Want me to give you something hard?"

She stood and walked past him from the room. She wasn't enjoying the fight anymore. She had a headache even though she hadn't drunk any of the pink wine. Maybe just looking at the pink wine gave her the headache. Then she realized he was trailing her down the hall.

"Come on, Sarah," he said. His eyes were glassy slits. "Just once. For old time's sake."

"Forget it, Zach."

"Hey, come on. One last time. I promise you I'll be quick."

She turned, took a deep breath, and told him to think about what he was doing.

"Oh, I'm thinking about it, all right. So what do you say?"

"I've already told you. No."

She walked into the bathroom. Before she could close and lock the door he grabbed her arm. "I need an aspirin," she said, reaching for the medicine cabinet. He pushed her against the wall, held her arm, nuzzled her neck. His other hand pulled at the clasp and zipper on her jeans. As she pushed open the cabinet's mirrored door she looked at their reflection. How sad to have come to this, she thought. She felt as if she'd swallowed cold grease. She said, "Don't you think it's sad?"

Her free hand hovered over the toothpaste, stick deodorant, cough syrup, razor blades. There was a loose razor beneath the tin. "What?" he said. He let go of her arm, crooked his elbows around her. The razor was stuck to the bottom of the cabinet. She rested her right hand on his shoulder, slipped it down to his chest. "What?" he said again, after she didn't answer him.

"This," Sarah said, as she brought her knee up between his legs as hard as she was able, at the same time pushing against his chest with her hand. He fell back against the toilet bowl, legs sprawled. In a moment she was out of the apartment, down on the sidewalk in front of their building. Zach's new woman was rounding the corner, a bag of groceries in her arms. Sarah shouted hello and ran up to her and clutched the bag from her. "Zach's up in my place getting his things together," Sarah said in a rush, "so it'd be just great if you let me stay with you for an hour or two." The woman looked confused, then nodded. Sarah then told her all about Morocco and its labyrinthine medinas and history and beliefs and how in Arab folktales the travelers had to ask everyone if they were human or djinn, because when you were traveling you could never tell and you'd think someone was good and nice and then suddenly he'd turn into a monster—

Sarah smoked one cigarette after the next in the neighbor's kitchen that Zach had painted, talking more rapidly than she'd ever talked in her life, until she heard him walk down the stairs, slam the trunk of his car, then drive off into her past.

The crumbling brown walls and twin turrets flanking the arched gateway of the necropolis of Chellah loomed ahead of Sarah on the stone path. She could hear the water seller's tinkling bowls as he walked away. She braced herself for what lay ahead. This was her third day in Morocco, the first on which she attempted to travel freely.

At the suggestion of the guidebooks, after her flight from JFK landed in Casablanca she left for Rabat, about an hour to the north, to recover from her jet lag. She knew enough about Casablanca to conclude it was an urban sprawl too complex for her to navigate before she'd rested. She felt she had made the right decision once the shuttle to Rabat pulled away from the airport, and though the bus struck a large black ox wandering on the road, she forgot once she had a glimpse of the sea. The sky-blue ocean pounded the rocky coast with hypnotic freshness. Staring at the ocean through the window of the bus took the edge off her long flight and calmed her nearly as much as the bath she took once she'd secured a room in a downtown Rabat hotel.

She'd made the reservation under her last name, Rosen, and first initial. The Moroccan at the desk asked to see her passport, checked the reservations list, looked again at her passport, then in French said, "I am sorry, but we were not expecting a double room."

"No," Sarah said, "the reservation is for a single."

"But where is Monsieur Rosen? The reservation is for Monsieur Rosen."

A hot ripple of fear ran through her insides. Sarah stood at the desk not knowing what to say. The man said, "Perhaps the monsieur is not traveling with you?"

Yes, she said, Monsieur Rosen was not traveling with her. He has not yet arrived in Rabat. Monsieur Rosen has important business in Casablanca.

"And may I have his address there?" the hotel keeper said.

Quickly Sarah said, "I'll give it to you when he arrives."

"And when will he arrive?"

"Why, when he has finished with his business in New York, of course. Now, please give me a room. I've just come from far away. I am very tired." She enjoyed saying the phrase. "*Je suis très fatiguée,*" she repeated, bringing her hand up to her brow.

She double-locked the door of her room and then unpacked and took a long bath and tried to rest and ended up smoking so many cigarettes she had to open the glass patio door. The next morning she ate breakfast in the hotel dining room, then slept until noon and spent the remainder of the day at the doorway, gazing down at an outdoor café that fronted the hotel and the wide boulevard separated by a walkway lined with twin rows of palm trees. She watched the palm tree fronds sway in the wind, then gazed for a while at an imperial-looking building across the boulevard. Nearly everyone who came to the café smoked. She smoked at the patio doorway, feeling very European. Then Sarah saw that the only people who sat alone in the café were men.

The few women who came to the café were accompanied by men. She made a game of it, waiting for a woman to come by herself to the café. She smoked another cigarette. She watched for an hour, then two, three, until dusk, when the muezzin from a nearby mosque gave the call to evening prayer, and then muezzins from all across the city cried out the call to prayer. Tears ran down her cheeks and dripped on the tile floor. No women sat in the cafés! Sarah had always imagined Anaïs Nin sitting by herself in a Moroccan café, a French cigarette burning in the clear glass ashtray in front of her, a cup of coffee made light by warm cream at her side, the clean crisp blank pages of her journal open before her, everything open to the marvelous life parading before her senses.

Three dark-haired boys in dirty T-shirts ran toward her from the doorway of the Chellah. "Mademoiselle, I be your guide." "*Un dirham, madame.*" "Hey, you want me, I know every place." They pushed one another aside, their eager brown eyes staring up into her face. The one wanting a dirham touched her arm and then tugged her skirt, immediately stepping back with hands raised to his lips. Sarah was wearing an ankle-length skirt, white blouse, cotton jacket. She wore no makeup. Her purse was tucked tightly beneath her arm. Her dark red hair was brushed simply, away from her face. The tallest boy said, "I pay for you now, you pay me later, OK?" "I know better, I show you better," the other boy said. The boy wanting a dirham asked again for a dirham, the word popping in nearly a single syllable off the tip of his tongue.

Inside the shadow of the doorway several older boys sold trinkets, film, cigarettes. As Sarah approached they knocked their wooden boxes against the ground. A boy with a mustache fanned postcards in his hands and spoke rapidly to her in French. A man with a cashbox sat at a table. The boy who said he knew every place was already

telling her that djinn lived within the Chellah's walls, guarding the
tomb of the Black Sultan, King of the Djinn. "I pay for you, OK?"
the tall boy said again. The boy who knew every place touched her
hand. "Come, I show you his grave." There was a tug on her jacket.
"*Un dirham.*"

Sarah whirled and tried to push them away. All three were
touching her, pulling her clothes or hands. She felt besieged, as if she
were bread tossed to a school of fish. "No," she said as she pushed
their hands away. "No! I don't need any of this, do you understand?
Leave me alone! Go away!" She spoke first in English, then French.
The boys took a step back, eyes large, then ran from her as first one of
them and then all three pointed to a tour bus coming up the winding
road from the city.

She silenced the knocking wooden boxes by ignoring them, then
paid the man with the cashbox a few dirhams and stepped through
the dark cool shadow thrown on the ground by the high gate. She
knew from her guidebook the place had once been an ancient Roman
town, and after it was abandoned it was used as a cemetery, and
later, sometime during the fourteenth century, a mosque was erected
alongside the necropolis and nearby gardens and the entire area was
enclosed by the large wall.

It was so peaceful walking through the first garden that Sarah
could believe djinn protected the place. She could no longer hear
the pulsing clatter and screech of the city outside the gates. The high
walls of the Chellah made her feel enclosed, secure. The air was warm
and still and smelled sweet. Finches flew from a pair of olive trees.
Willows swayed on a nearby hill. A fence on the hill was draped with
pink bougainvillea, and before it was a stand of fig, holly, jacaranda
so blue the flowers seemed painted by the sky. Rhododendrons spread
their waxy leaves to the sunlight amidst oleander and tamarisk. A
dozen sparrows chattered on a stone walkway to her left. She paused

before a poinsettia tree in full flower. The tree was twice as tall as she, the blooms big as both her hands.

She thought she saw a blur of white in the sky, so she looked up. Then she saw a pair of storks at the top of a minaret. They were building a nest. The larger stork held a twig in its beak. Only a few crumbling walls remained of the mosque. The tops of the walls were overgrown with vines, and Sarah had the impression that if the vines could they'd swallow the stone walls and pull down the slender minaret, and she realized that of course the vines and trees and even the swaying grasses and flowers were attempting to do just that, to reduce rock to stone, stone to pebble, pebble to dust, and for a moment she felt she too would be pulled into the ground and reduced to dust.

She turned, hearing the scrape of foot against stone and the sudden gabble of the group from the tour bus. In the afternoon light her hair resembled flame. Sarah hurried down a pathway deeper into the gardens, her skirt catching on a spike of camelthorn. Not wanting to tear the skirt, she squatted alongside the low spiny plant and carefully worked the fabric free of the thorns, though when she was nearly through she hurried and pricked her finger.

A bright drop of blood swelled on the tip of her finger. She licked the droplet of blood, then squeezed her finger so it would bleed more easily and wash away any poisons or dirt that might have been on the spike. Her blood dripped freely onto the camelthorn and made splashy circles the size of dirhams on the sloping pathway as she fled through the garden toward a section of what had once been the mosque.

At once the air grew cooler. The uneven ground leveled off. Sarah walked slowly, sucking her bleeding finger. She stood in what had been the mosque's sanctuary, then stepped from the enclosure and entered the large prayer hall. In the corner of her eye she saw something move but by the time she turned she was unable to see anything.

Perhaps it was a snake, she thought. It would not be unusual for there to be a snake sunning itself on one of the flat sun-baked slabs of stone here in the ruins. She gazed at a mound of stones, certain she would see a snake. Then she saw something move again, more quickly than her eye could follow.

It looked like a boy, small and brown, though she wasn't sure. She had only a glimpse of its back as the figure scooted behind the stone wall of the mihrab—the chamber facing Mecca—toward which those in the mosque prayed. She squinted at the mihrab, hearing the high, winding pitch of insects, then the softer sound of wind rustling the leaves of trees.

Her finger had stopped bleeding. Sarah looked at it and then saw a cat step from where the boy had disappeared. The cat was brownish orange, the color of the earth. Sarah crouched, extending her hand, saying, "Here, puss, puss." The cat cocked its head, then pushed out its front paws and raised its tail and arched its back and gave Sarah a yawn.

She followed the cat past the mihrab to a shaded place outside the mosque where there were many graves. The earth was hard, pounded gray, and pebbled with many flat brown stones. Sarah stooped and picked up a stone that made an almost perfect circle. Then she saw a dozen or so cats sitting before a white domed sepulcher. She wasn't sure *sepulcher* was the right word.

"Qubba," she heard a voice say. Then the voice added in French, "The tomb of the Black Sultan, King of the Djinn."

The boy walked beside her silently, then held her hand and pointed. For a moment Sarah wondered if she was supposed to give the boy the stone. The boldness with which he took her hand surprised her and at the same time seemed natural, not unwanted. She gave his small hand a gentle squeeze. He made a sharp sound with his tongue, and the cats ran off into the trees behind the grave.

Like in the stories, she thought. So she, traveler far from home, asked, "Are they djinn?"

The boy looked up at her with round dark eyes and said nothing.

He led her wordlessly to the tomb. She stood before it, not knowing what she was supposed to do. She bowed her head and held her hands together at her waist, standing reverently, as she did whenever she stood before a grave. After a few moments she looked up. A long-legged spider crawled across the surface of the qubba. She brushed it off. The wall was smooth, dazzling white, surprisingly cool. She laid both her hands against the flat surface, then moved her hands in cool half-circles.

Then she saw that the boy stood some distance away. She followed him, descending a steep slope to where an old man sat on his folded legs beneath a tree and beside a pool of dark water. The boy greeted the old man in Arabic, then kissed his hand. Between the man and the pool there was a plate of what looked like eggs. One of the cats that had been by the tomb pawed the eggs. Several other cats crawled about the man or lay still at his side or tussled near the tree behind him.

The hood of the man's djellaba was dark and partially shaded his face. His beard was mottled black and gray. His face was olive, etched with deep lines. He lolled his head at Sarah, eyelashes blinking in mild spasms over his clouded eyes, which stared up at the sky. The blind eyes jerked from side to side between the twitching lashes. White flecks of spittle creased the corners of his lips. Sarah looked around for the boy but he was no longer there.

The old man scratched the back of a tawny cat. "You have come for the eels?" He spoke in French.

"I don't understand," Sarah said.

"The eels," the man said. He raised his hand from the cat and made a vague wriggling motion. "They've been waiting. They're very hungry."

"Eels?" Sarah said.

"In the pit." The man gestured toward the dark pool of water.

Sarah took a step closer. The walls of the pit were squared, made of stone, and thickly covered with black slime. Repulsed, she held her breath.

"If you feed the sultan's eels, they'll grant your wish."

Around her all was absolutely still. Even the cats were motionless. She tried to read his face. "What are you?"

The eyes fluttered, then seemed to gaze inside the man's skull. "A grain of sand. And you?" He emphasized the formal *vous*.

Sarah stared down at the ground. "I don't know."

"The eels will tell you, if you ask."

He turned and reached for the plate of eggs. His hand found the plate's edge, then an egg, which he cracked with a sharp rap. At once the cats ran toward him, mewing as they ran. Several more dropped softly from the tree. The cats filled the lap of the old man's djellaba, crawled up his back, over his arms. He gently pushed the cats away, then began peeling pieces of shell from the egg. The cats fought for the pieces of eggshell until the man barked in Arabic and made them pause, and then he said something else and the cats retreated to an arm's length of him, and then suddenly Sarah saw squatting among the cats the small brown boy.

"The cats are all djinn, yes?" Sarah smiled with a mix of amusement and fear.

He held the peeled egg before his sightless eyes. "But of course."

She could hear her pounding heart. "And you. Are you a djinni too?"

The mouth gave a dry laugh. "If I were, would I tell you?"

She paused. "If you were a good djinni, you would."

"And if I were evil?"

She thought about her answer. "If you were evil, you'd lie. You'd do evil."

"Of course. Here's the egg."

She knew she had to be careful or he'd trick her. "If you were evil, you'd tell me you were good. You couldn't do otherwise because of your nature."

"Take the egg." He turned it round in one hand, and then his other hand brought out from behind his back a small brass plate upon which lay several dirhams. The man bowed his head and uttered in Arabic. Several of the coins were dark red, as if they had somehow rusted.

She reached into her jacket pocket for a coin and placed it and the stone she'd picked up by the sultan's qubba on the djinni's plate, then accepted the egg and knelt by the dark water. The pool's bottom was coated with dark slime. The sides were clotted with clumps and strands of black algae that began to swirl and sway as the eels rose suddenly from the dark depths toward the surface, toward the reflection of her face. Shocked, she dropped the egg into her reflection.

Her face shattered. The egg slipped beneath the water, hesitated, then broke surface, bobbing. The eels coiled darkly around it, baring their teeth. Sarah cried out as they bit. For several moments the eels twirled her between them, their blunt mouths biting her in turn. The dark lengths of their bodies thrashed the silver surface, breaking the light above into smaller and smaller pieces, like mercury, until there was only the darkness of the bottom of the pool. The beasts nosed her into the depths, and she saw only the darkness.

Without thinking she reached into the churning pool, fighting the frenzied things. Her hand brushed one of the eels as it made a pass at the egg. Finally she pulled what was left of the egg from the water. Blood beaded brightly on her fingers and wrist. She let out a long breath and turned, imagining Zach standing behind her, laughing.

In the shade of the tree the blind djinni sat as if dead. The cats mewed at her expectantly. A pair of young females rolling in the dust at the djinni's feet stood, ears back, and stared at her. Sarah looked at the torn egg in her bleeding palm. She shouldn't have thrown it to the eels, she thought. She should have given it to the cats.

She crouched, stretching out her hand. They bounded toward her in a rush.

EXCHANGE

"Well," Mohammed Abbassi said, "what do you think of it?"

Peter Corvino looked out from the third-story window in Abbassi's apartment. It was afternoon in the bustling Habous Quarter of Casablanca. Gorgeous Rabati rugs and hand-woven Berber carpets spilled onto the sidewalk from a shop on Rue Abdelessam el Khattabi below. A coppersmith stood proudly in his doorway, surrounded by his shining wares. Farther down the road the owner of the Islamic bookstore laughed with two men. Cars and motorbikes rattled by in the street. It seemed all the young men sitting idly in the café near the patisserie on the corner wore short sleeves and chain-smoked cigarettes, though now and then an older man in a brown burnous or djellaba hobbled past, eyes fixed on the ground, like a monk or someone out of the Middle Ages. Women hurried by in high spiked heels, crossing the street in front of barefoot peddlers driving carts pulled by donkeys. Everything Peter saw in Morocco was still fascinating and new. The bright sun made rectangles on the varnished hardwood floor where he stood.

"You mean your neighbors?" Peter said, unsure.

Mohammed laughed. "So your gaze was through the window. Forgive me." He pointed at the picture on the wall beside it. "I thought you were looking at that."

The picture was a reproduction of something, that much Peter could make out. But to his raw Western eyes the image appeared surreal, like a Rorschach or something from the Museum of Modern Art. The picture was mainly brown and gray, dappled with pink soft-edged shapes that bumped randomly against one another, with no apparent purpose or design. A few of the shapes seemed more sharply defined, crisscrossed by long meandering lines and squiggles spotted with Arabic's dizzy dot and swirl.

"Sorry," Peter said, turning back to his host, "but I don't have the slightest idea what this is."

"But as an historian you must," Mohammed said. His teeth glistened as he laughed. He was thin and slightly taller than Peter, with dark, closely knotted hair and a complexion the color of sandalwood.

"Very well then," Peter said. He was dark too, though not nearly as brown as Mohammed. The corduroy suit Peter had chosen to wear to the lunch meeting felt warm and, with a tie and button-down shirt, too formal. He adjusted his eyeglasses, then reached inside his jacket to the left inner pocket to check whether his passport was still there. His interview with Abbassi wouldn't take too long, he thought. With his fingertips he tapped his passport's hard upper edge.

Mohammed wore tan pants and a soft cotton shirt open at the neck. "May I offer you something to drink?"

Peter knuckled his glasses to the bridge of his nose. He shook his head. "I tell you, I don't know," he said, referring to the image.

"I have water, soft drinks, brandy. Whatever you prefer."

"No. Thank you. Nothing for now."

"As you like," Mohammed said. The white of his teeth flashed as he smiled. "Would you care to hear some music before we eat? I can offer you some excellent Arabic folk music." He folded his hands, as if waiting for Peter's assent. "Or, if you prefer, we have classical music or jazz."

Peter glanced again at the picture on the wall. All he could conclude was it was some sort of ancient chart. "You have classical music?"

"A few recordings. Aisha's." Mohammed crouched over a wooden box of albums. "Mozart, Shostakovich, Beethoven's symphonies, Vivaldi—"

"Oh, the Vivaldi. Please."

Mohammed lowered the record onto the turntable, then read from the album jacket. "*Il Giardino Armonico*. Concerto in F major, 'La Tempesta di mare.'" He placed the album jacket back into the box. "You'll forgive me, my Italian is very poor."

"No, your pronunciation is far better than mine."

The opening notes of the concerto leapt from the stereo's speakers. Peter closed his eyes. For a moment he had the pleasure of recognizing a familiar sound. The music brought to Peter's mind the image of the cold January night Ellen announced that she'd become pregnant. They were sitting in the dark drafty den of their old house, listening to the same recording, sharing a bowl of unsalted popcorn. Peter had been trying to read. He'd wanted salt but Ellen didn't for fear it would make her bloat. Putting down his book and getting salt and his own bowl seemed like too much trouble. Then Ellen told him the news, with more whisper than voice. Outside their windows high drifts of snow sat motionless, sculpted by the wind. The moon hung full and heavy in the trees. Black branches coated with ice stirred and clacked. The wind whistled through the cracks of the old house. After the announcement Ellen said she wanted to be by herself. Peter remained standing by the windows and watched her walk from the house away through the snow. She had to step high with arms out for balance to work her way through it. She didn't look pregnant at all. At the time Peter honestly believed she was content. He had mistaken her quiet for contentment. Standing now with his eyes closed in the sunlit apartment in Casablanca, he could nearly see the bright stars in the wavy glass of the den's bay windows, could almost feel the bracing cold of the night air. Mohammed adjusted the stereo's volume. Then Peter felt the heat of the Moroccan sun and he remembered where and what he was.

Mohammed stood beside the record player, an unopened album in his hands. He ran his fingers up and down the album's sealed plastic seam. There was Arabic writing on the album cover. Peter saw at once he'd made a mistake requesting the Vivaldi.

"Have you given any more thought to what it is?"

"I'm sorry," Peter said, looking about. Mohammed raised a palm and smiled. "I'll take a wild stab," Peter said. "It's some sort of chart." He pointed. "Here's writing—"

"But you can't read it."

"No, I can't." He returned to the window, glanced out at the street. "I should have studied Arabic before I came here. I feel like a child. I can't read or speak."

"God willing, in time you will learn to do both."

Mohammed crossed the slanting rectangles of sunlight on the floor and dropped his hand to Peter's arm, then led him with a slight touch of his fingertips back to the picture, which, he explained, was a reproduction of an ancient map made by Al-Idrisi, a twelfth-century Arab geographer. In Al-Idrisi's eyes there were only two land masses, Africa and Eurasia. North Africa was the most prominent and detailed section on the map. Peter made out the Atlantic coastline and the land bordering the Mediterranean. He traced his finger along Italy, which thrust itself up into a sea beneath a Sicily nearly as big as the peninsula itself. Mohammed explained that in Al-Idrisi's world view north and south were inverted. The shores of Africa sloped upward, dominating the map's upper half and the nearly formless expanse of Eurasia to the south. He explained to Peter what was known and not known about the world in Al-Idrisi's time. Then the men stepped back.

"You must understand the bulk of contributions made by the Arab world," Mohammed said. "It was Arabs who gave the West the medieval basis for modern science. Their knowledge of the earth was wider than Ptolemy's. Arab mathematicians were the first to come up with the concept of zero. Algebra is an Arab invention. Arabs discovered irrigation and gave Europe the orange, cotton, cane sugar, rice. Arabs understood the working of the solar system five hundred years before Galileo. Augustine, Christian saint and philosopher and bishop of Hippo, was a Berber." Mohammed smiled. "We are not all camel drivers or rug merchants, in the same way the people of your country are not all Texas cowboys or Manhattan millionaires. In fact, Arabs may have been the first to discover North America, as Thor Heyerdahl has suggested in his writings." He raised his eyebrows. "Should I spend the rest of the afternoon citing further examples?"

Peter shook his head. "Let's not forget to mention the wonderful tales of Scheherazade. I enjoyed *The Thousand and One Nights* very much when I was a child."

"You should read them again, as an adult."

"Don't you know it is only power that determines north from south?" A woman's voice. Peter turned.

"Let me introduce my wife, Aisha. Evidently she has never heard of the magnetized needles used by the sailors of Genoa."

Peter and Aisha said hello.

Aisha wore a soft yellow kaftan embroidered in shades of gold and brown. Her dark hair was pulled away from her face and gathered together at the back of her head in a bun. Her eyes were large, the same color as her hair, and thickly lined with kohl. When Peter looked at her face, her eyes were all he saw.

"The needles were stuck in a piece of straw," Mohammed was saying, "then floated in a bowl of water. A brilliant idea, wouldn't you agree? In the thirteenth century they became what we know as the compass."

"What would be the difference," Aisha asked, "if the top were the bottom and the bottom were the top?"

"Listen to her," Mohammed said, one man to the next. "She wants to flip-flop the earth."

"I don't want to flip-flop anything. I'm merely pointing out that those in power reserve the higher position for themselves."

Mohammed smiled. Peter felt in the middle of things. He knew Mohammed was trying to be polite, impress him so he'd report favorably on him when he returned to the States. But now he didn't know what to say.

"But if I did want to turn the earth upside-down," Aisha said, "I'd have to invert the entire universe. It isn't possible just to reach in and change one detail. You have to change the entire context." She reached toward the map, twisting her hand in the air. She looked at both men as she spoke. "It would take a great deal of doing."

"Indeed," Mohammed said with a laugh. "Certainly much more than we are capable of." He turned to Peter, eyes twinkling. "We haven't even had a drink and already we're discussing politics. Please, you must allow me to bring you something."

"I didn't say we weren't capable," Aisha said. "We're capable. The earth doesn't care what we call north or south. And certainly the universe has no opinions on the matter."

"Of course not," Mohammed said in a professorial tone. "But the magnetic pole—"

Aisha raised a hand. "I'm not talking about magnets."

A breeze shook the shade on the window. From the street below, a car gave a shrill honk. Peter didn't know what to make of the tension, though he suspected they'd been arguing before he arrived. It explained Mohammed's overly conciliatory tone. Peter felt strangely relieved to see that Moroccan couples had their troubles too. If the world had no happy marriages, he thought, maybe he'd feel better about his not having worked out.

Mohammed was nodding, eyes down, as if he understood.

"The intelligent mind welcomes the new into its house," Aisha continued, "no matter how strange it first appears."

"One would need to remake all the maps," Mohammed said.

"You're right, but so what?" Aisha looked at them both and laughed, as if they'd just said something ridiculous. "Maps are mere paper, made by mere men. Remaking them would be difficult but not impossible."

To Peter the pair appeared suddenly wistful. Mohammed ran his hand over his mouth, then tugged his lower lip. Aisha crossed her hands at the waist and stared at her husband. Her long lashes blinked several times, and then her eyes fell on Peter.

"Welcome to our home. Has Mohammed offered you a beverage?"

"He said he—" Mohammed began.

"Yes," Peter said. "No thank you." He looked about. Near the window a philodendron snaked around a stick. Beside it stood potted dracaena and sansevieria. The walls of the apartment had been painted white. On the far wall hung an elegant Berber carpet above several pillows. "You have a very lovely home."

"We're most fortunate." She shifted slightly, one arm gesturing casually around the room. "We're privileged, if truth be known, to be able to rent this place. It costs us nearly everything. So Mohammed said you're here as part of the exchange."

"Yes." Peter smiled, to show her he liked her. "Both here and in Rabat."

"And how long will you be visiting?"

"Six weeks. Two months or even longer, indefinitely, if I like."

"You will like," Mohammed said with a nod and a wide grin.

The recording of Vivaldi's concertos came to an end. The turntable shut itself off with a click. From another room could be heard the sound of plates being laid on a table. Aisha walked to the doorway, then turned and said something to Mohammed that Peter couldn't understand.

Mohammed answered in Arabic. Peter made out the word "Vivaldi."

Aisha's eyes fixed him with a glance. From the tone of their voices they were arguing again. He wondered if it was over the unplayed album, then turned his attention back to the lopsided world. The expanse of Africa stretched east—or would it be west?—toward a yet undiscovered America. His eyes followed Africa extending off the map toward America.

"One doesn't need to eat the whole loaf to know what it's lacking," he heard Aisha say in French.

"We'll discuss it, please, after we have the details."

So they were arguing about the exchange, Peter thought. Aisha gestured for him to follow her into the next room, which was small and lined on three sides with a low sofa. Before the sofa was a round table set for three. Peter slipped off his jacket and loosened his tie and, at Mohammed's suggestion, rolled up his sleeves.

They sat. A barefoot girl entered the room carrying a kettle of water and an aluminum bowl which contained a sieve and a bar of soap. Over her arm hung a towel. Peter was the first to wash. He described the exchange over salad made of chopped tomatoes, cucumber, mint, onion, lemon juice, oil. On the table were several round loaves of bread, scored in fourths, and liter bottles of Sidi Ali mineral water as well as an orange drink. Mohammed seemed excited about the chance to return to the States. He asked about the course load, the size of classes. Aisha ate a few forkfuls of salad and said nothing. The girl from the kitchen cleared the plates and returned with a raisin-and-onion chicken tajine, a great platter of *frites*, more bread.

Immediately Mohammed ate a raisin and then broke off a piece of bread and dipped it into the sauce surrounding the two chickens in the tajine. Then he deftly tore off a leg and a choice piece of breast meat and placed them before Peter at the lip of the tajine, and then he placed several pieces before Aisha, who was already helping herself. The girl returned with a bowl of radishes and another of a spicy vegetable mixture and plates for the fries.

"Don't be bashful," Mohammed told Peter.

They ate with their hands. Peter could not recall chicken ever tasting so delicious.

"You know," Mohammed began, "the Moroccan sense of privacy and ownership is quite different from the European perspective. It wasn't until I attended the university, for example, that I had my own bowl. A bowl in my house in Ifrane was simply a bowl, belonging equally to everyone and to no one. Western children are given their own bowls, their own forks and spoons. The family's food is partitioned, separated." He made cutting gestures with his hands. "American children sleep in their own beds. In my family the children had one bed."

"You're romanticizing," Aisha said as she raised a piece of bread soaked with sauce to her mouth.

Mohammed shrugged. "Perhaps. But I enjoy eating like this. From one bowl, with my hand." His white teeth flashed. "I find eating with my hand more sensual and enjoyable than eating with a piece of metal. With my hand I can feel the food's warmth and texture, and thus I enjoy it with my fingertips as well as my mouth. In contrast, Western meals can be quite cold, I think, particularly when one is forced to forget the food and focus on selecting the proper utensil."

Peter was pulling some meat from the chicken closer to him. The meat felt smooth and warm and fell easily from the bone. As he took a bite of the meat, some of its juice ran into the cup of his hand. He ate the meat, then licked his palm and reached for more bread.

At once Mohammed turned to Peter and smiled. "Even the height of the table makes a difference, doesn't it? Here we sit close to the earth, close enough to fold our legs beneath us, but not so far away as to forget the earth is there."

Aisha shook her head. "Tell him how sensual it is to sleep on a bed with your six brothers, who have not washed, who are too young or too lazy to get up and make water in the chamber pot. Tell him how enjoyable eating from one dish is when that dish serves first the men, and then after they're finished, the remains"—she tossed a bone onto the plate meant for her fries—"are brought to the women and children."

"At one time the French were the same," Mohammed said. "Even the mighty English were so uneducated as to require women to eat with children and dogs. My comments are about the contemporary Morocco."

"As are mine," Aisha said. She sat up and stared at the men.

"Perhaps," Mohammed admitted after a while. To Peter he said, "Both realities exist, side by side."

Aisha rolled her eyes. "That's what everyone says about Morocco. Pick up any book. It's the land of contrasts where the ancient—that is, the quaint, backward, oppressive—exists side by side with the modern, or shall we say European, particularly French. Neither image is complimentary, you understand. What they miss is the real Morocco that lies between."

Mohammed's hands fell loudly to the table. He looked squarely at his wife and then turned to Peter. "You can see that in this house there is a healthy reverence for freedom of speech."

"As there should be in all houses," Aisha said.

For several moments the three ate in silence. The barefoot girl entered and cleared the table along with its plastic cloth, then returned with the kettle and washbowl. After they rinsed their hands, the girl brought out mandarin oranges and grapes. Most of the oranges had a stem and a leaf or two still attached. Mohammed gestured to Peter to help himself. Aisha raised her eyes and asked Peter if in his house he and his wife experienced similar exchanges of opinion.

"I'm afraid my home is very quiet," Peter said.

"And why is that?" Mohammed asked.

Peter took a breath. He didn't enjoy talking about himself. The barefoot girl brought Aisha a tray upon which were four glasses, a bunch of fresh mint, a box of sugar cubes, a small dish of green tea, a silver teapot. Aisha poured the green gunpowder tea into the pot, packed it with mint and sugar cubes, then filled the pot with hot, steaming water brought a few moments later by the girl.

"I no longer live with my wife," Peter began. "I'm divorced." He looked to see if there was any reaction. Mohammed was peeling a white thread from a section of mandarin. He nodded and brought the fruit to his lips. Aisha sat with hands folded.

"We're very sorry to hear that," Mohammed said as he swallowed.

"Of course," Aisha said.

"Do you have children?" Mohammed asked.

Peter nodded. "One."

There was a pause, as if Peter were expected to explain. He didn't have to say anything more, he thought. But being in a foreign place gave him a new, peculiar sense of freedom. "She got fed up. With me, with my personality, my attitude. She said I was too dark, overly negative, always disapproving." He picked up a grape from the bowl before him. "I've never been much of an optimist. I think optimism is naïve. I was raised Catholic but I'm not sure I believe in God. I guess I believe in things"—he held up the grape between his thumb and first finger—"and in randomness. Chance. You know what I mean? The world exists, and we happen to exist too, cursed with the awareness of our inconsequential existence. It's a cruel joke."

"Your wife," Aisha said, looking back and forth between Peter and Mohammed, "she couldn't live with you because of your beliefs?"

Peter chewed the grape. "She said nothing pleased me." He swallowed. "And she was right. Forgive me, you two have been so polite. Don't think I'm anyone special, here interviewing you for this exchange. I'm only a mediocre historian reciting the past to students who often regard a knowledge of history as about as useful as a tail. I'm what's called an academic burnout. I can't remember the last time I had an original idea. I'm tired of writing obscure articles in pretentious prose for journals read only by experts. I no longer publish, or even try." He lifted his eyebrows, then smiled. "My current goal is to become an administrator in my department, at which point I'll have fewer courses to teach, and after which I'll be able to retire with a decent pension." He laughed. "If there was one thing Ellen liked about me it was that at times I could be brutally honest. Particularly when chronicling her faults."

There was silence. He decided to continue. "She had a baby, thinking it would turn me into a happy man. I'd hold the baby in my arms, forget all my problems, be filled with optimism. When I wasn't thrilled enough she packed her bags and our child and left."

"Just like that?" Mohammed said.

"Well, she had the good manners to first leave a note."

Sunlight stretched across the far wall. Aisha placed a few mint leaves in three of the glasses, then filled the fourth glass with tea, opened the teapot's lid, and returned the tea back into the teapot. Then she poured the tea out, beginning just above the lip of each glass and gradually raising the teapot as high as her head. The steaming yellow tea splashed up the side of each glass, making a bubbling foam.

"Why do you—" Peter began. He raised his arm.

"Here," Aisha said, handing him a glass.

"One pours from a height so the liquid breathes," Mohammed said. He nodded as he accepted his glass from Aisha. "And one returns the first glass to the pot to distribute the sugar."

"It's quite delicious," Peter said. "Everything"—he waved a hand over the table—"the entire meal, has been quite delicious."

He felt for a moment that his shirt was unbuttoned. He looked down at his chest to check. There was a crumb of bread on his pants leg. He picked up the crumb, raised it to his lips. All his buttons were buttoned.

"Sometimes women need room," Aisha began. She held her glass of yellow tea at her lips, then set it down. "No, women always are in need of room. Their lives are so closed, so—how do you say?—so claustrophobic. They need room, place."

With his thumbnail Mohammed pierced the skin of another mandarin.

Aisha leaned toward him. "Shall I tell him about last winter?"

"I agree," Mohammed said at once. "Men need to give women space."

Aisha sat up straight. "No, you are wrong, my husband. Women need space, yes, but space is hers to take, not the man's to give." She clutched Mohammed's hand, then squeezed it. "There's a vital difference, yes? In the first case, it is a right. If it is the man's to give, it is a privilege."

Mohammed's face had no expression.

"If only more men were more wise," Aisha continued. "Last winter I felt very closed, shut in, claustrophobic."

"She needed some moments of time to herself," Mohammed said.

"All my life, from the minute I was born, it seemed as if everything I was belonged to a man. And my father was a good man who didn't give his daughters beatings. But still, every decision was his."

Mohammed's expression was defiant, as if daring Peter to object. His eyes blinked rapidly. "For a month we slept separately."

"In the next room," Aisha said, "on a pallet. Is that the word? Or is it *cot*? Leaving me to our bed, where I had a place."

"It was not inconvenient," Mohammed said, picking up his peeled mandarin.

"I needed to be able to decide. Whether that night I wanted to be alone, or to share a bed with my husband."

"It was a temporary situation." Mohammed ate a sliver of fruit.

Peter was surprised at how easily the man was able to speak about such intimate concerns.

"You must realize that not many Moroccan women can make this choice. Their husbands would throw them out—"

"They would beat them," Mohammed said.

"—beat them without mercy, call them whores. Then they'd divorce them, leave them nothing, and of course the qadi would decide in the man's favor."

"Don't judge us too hastily," Mohammed said, "or by Western standards. The Quran granted women economic rights a dozen centuries before European women were given the same."

"Before European women began to seize what is theirs," Aisha said, "while we slept. Though the Arab world is beginning to awake."

"All things change in time."

"Though there are many who resist. '*Les chiens aboient, et la caravane passe.*'" She smiled. "The dogs bark, and the caravan passes."

"A wise saying, yes?" Mohammed said. "It makes those who do not change into barking dogs." He laughed, long and loudly, as if from great relief.

Peter laughed too, picturing a caravan of camels, explorers on the edge of the frontier. He was glad he'd told Mohammed and Aisha about himself, though their apparent ability to work through their problems made him envious. He wondered if he'd missed some moment with Ellen that might have saved them.

The girl brought more boiling water and after a while Aisha refilled their glasses. "The decision on this exchange—how shall I say it? It must also involve me. I don't want the decision to be only Mohammed's since I'll be asked to pick up, undo my life here, all for him."

Peter's glass felt smooth, warm in his hand. "I understand."

"She's against it," Mohammed said. "But it is something we can discuss."

"Yes," Aisha said, "we'll talk about it."

Then the three rose, holding their glasses of tea, and went up to the rooftop. From there they looked out at the tan houses and buildings of Casablanca. Nearby rooftops sprouted a jumbled geometry of antennas, a forest of metal spines spread open to the sky. Clothes hung in rows from washlines and swung in the breeze. From one open window a woman stared idly at the next house as she brushed her long hair. The air smelled of spice and cooking meat. All around them the horizon was pierced by the spikes of minarets. In the distance the slate-gray Atlantic stretched beneath an orange sun.

On Rue Abdelessam el Khattabi, cars and motorbikes raced past a hunched man in a dark djellaba driving a gray donkey laden with twin, bulging sacks. Peter wondered what the sacks contained. From the height he couldn't tell. A teen on a ten-speed bicycle zipped past. In the rubble between two apartment buildings, a gang of boys kicked a soccer ball. The ball was black and white and angled high in the air. The boy spiking it with his head toward the goal gave out a yell. Then a light came on in the tower of a nearby minaret, and the call of a muezzin could be heard. Then a light shone from a second tower and a second call to evening prayer began, then a third in another minaret, then another. The effect was at once beautiful and eerie. The air tumbled with song. Peter shuddered and touched the stone wall edging the roof.

"There," Mohammed was saying, pointing out something to Aisha in the streets below. Aisha held an arm at her waist.

One by one the calls of the muezzins faded, and one by one the lights in the minarets twinkled off. The sky grew dark. Peter raised his arm and pointed to the horizon, where the sun had set, unnoticed.

"America," he said.

Aisha and Mohammed turned and looked at him strangely.

"My home," Peter said, though suddenly he wasn't so sure where his home was. He shouldn't have let Ellen go so carelessly, he thought.

He should have followed her into the snow. He envied Mohammed
and Aisha, and all at once felt old, alone. With a quick toss he drank
what was left of his tea.

"There in the west," he called, "or should I say there in the east?"

They seemed not to understand his joke.

In the streets below, a dog began barking. Mohammed put his
arm around Aisha, who shivered, then accepted the arm and drew
close to him. Peter nodded as again from the streets below came the
sound of barking dogs.

THE WHORE OF FEZ EL BALI

"*Balak!*" a voice barked. "Watch out!"

And she was pushed aside suddenly by a foul-smelling donkey loaded down with unwashed sheepskins. "*Balak! Balak!*" the donkey's owner cried, his hand snapping a stick across the wide curve of the animal's back. She watched the miserable donkey lift its tiny hooves, the load on its back shift and sway.

Her guide led her up to Bab Boujeloud, the blue gate that opened into the narrow cobbled streets of the ancient city. Around her were several men selling various kinds of fruit, a score of idling tour buses reeking of diesel fuel and spewing black exhaust, a line of petit taxis, the soft stutter of motorbikes, the squeal of brakes, and now the tin sound of a horn. Women in dark djellabas, hems powdered with dust, trudged steadily past with eyes fixed on the ground, their unveiled faces clear and impassive. An old man in white hawked bouquets of flowers. Behind him the empty hands of beggars rose hopefully to the sky, and as she approached she could hear their cries, repetitions doleful as a Kaddish, growing sharper and sharper with insistence and need. "Allah! Allah! Alms for the love of Allah!" No sooner could she make out their stumps and twisted limbs, their rheumy eyes, the hideous shadow beneath the veined bulge of one beggar's elephantiasic head, than the guide she'd chosen, mainly because she thought his height and long hair would make him easy to follow in a crowd, grasped her arm and pulled her wordlessly forward into the throng, bumping her into a woman who held a round loaf of bread beneath her arm, past a man thrusting tomatoes the color of blood into the air. Next to him a peddler waved a thick bunch of green mint. A sudden group of boys threaded their way past her, somehow keeping between them a black-and-white soccer ball. "*Khizzu! Khizzu!*"

shouted a toothless man, raised fingers twirling green-topped carrots round and round like a baton. There was too much to see, to take in. She lowered her eyes and pressed her temples with her fingertips, trying to surrender to the extravagance of detail before her.

Then from her right a man clutched her arm and said, "Allah! Allah! Allah!" over and over so many times she thought he'd never pause, not even to breathe, his blunt parrot tongue not hesitating for even a beat. As she stared into the collapsed sockets of his eyes she realized he was blind. It made her wonder if Allah—or Yahweh or God—had intentionally caused the man to stumble into her, of all the people who passed the gate. She reached into the pocket of her skirt for one of the coins she kept there specifically for beggars. He was up to his fiftieth Allah, his bird tongue putting even stress on both syllables. She stared at the crust of spittle caking his lips as she tried to push a dirham into the hand that squeezed her arm. "Here," she said, "in the name of Allah." The coin unlocked his grip. Then her guide tugged her other arm and pushed the blind beggar away before she could hear the blessing he gave her.

She very much believed in blessings, particularly in those offered by beggars. She imagined it purest when it came from the blind, who couldn't tell she was a foreign woman in their midst. Stripped of one sense, the blind were somehow closer to God. She believed beggars could give away some of their baraka, their holiness or grace, or whatever the source of things called it. She thought of it as spiritual energy, a light unseen. Beneath the colors of its spectrum all but saints and animals were blind. The few moments with the sightless beggar made her feel holy, as if giving away a silver coin and smelling an unwashed man's suffocating stench and breath were a spiritual act. She had not traveled to this edge of the African continent unprepared. Giving alms was called *zakat*, the Arab word for purification, and was one of the five pillars of Islam. Giving alms was a ritual cleansing, as purifying as taking a bath.

Ever since she'd been a schoolgirl she had great admiration for Helen Keller. She envied her Catholic friends for having so many saints. They even had women saints. She used to ask her friends how many of their saints were blind or deaf or mute, and she was sorely disappointed to learn that most had all their senses. Her friends then took her to their church, which smelled of dreamy-sweet smoky perfume, and she gazed open-mouthed at all of the statues and at the gold box up beyond the altar where the priest kept the Holy Bread. On the feast day of Saint Blaise they brought her to church again, and as they knelt at the communion rail the priest blessed their throats with a scissors of crossed flaming candles, and for a whole year the children were protected against all sickness, choking, and the swallowing of bones.

As a Jew she felt she had only the Old Testament's dark, unbending fathers. Bearded and stern, they raised a sharp knife over their children's throats. They were ready to slit your jugular as easily as killing a goat until the innocent boy Isaac was rescued by an angel. Thank God for angels! she learned. Beware if your father comes after you with a knife. Through her early years she lived with the fear that God might tell her father to sacrifice her on an altar of stone—just because she was Jewish—and then the public school boys began chasing her home with shouts that her grandmother was a bar of soap. She had to ask her mother what they meant. At first she refused to believe, stomping her foot on the kitchen floor and shouting, "No! no! no!" until her heel was sore, her voice raw as grated beet. "Yes," her mother said, stroking her hair. She wept so bitterly her mother kept her home from school the rest of the week. From that time on the girl couldn't wash her hands or face without remembering.

Her tall guide was staring at her with eyes the color of ground coffee. He wore a pink cotton shirt and plain, unbelted black pants. "Don't give to all who ask," he said slowly, with the elongated vowels and soft consonants of English dipped in French. "Or else we will be, how you say, surrounded, and then I will not be able to show you anything."

Already other beggars were making their way toward her. "I don't mind," she said. "A dirham or two is nothing to me, compared to their poverty." She walked slowly, trying to take everything in. So this is the ancient city of Fez, she thought, Fez el Bali, the medieval labyrinth, the Fez of Anaïs Nin, the reason she'd traveled to Morocco.

She was very conscious of how she appeared. She wore no makeup save a bit of liner around her eyes, and she concealed her long red hair beneath a plain gray scarf she had paid too much for in a French shop in downtown Rabat. She'd quickly learned to hide her hair and to dress conservatively, in modest skirts that came down to her ankles and loose long-sleeved blouses. She knew she was expected to button her blouse to the neck, but she kept the top button unbuttoned. At times in the solitude of her hotel room or even now, about to enter an ancient city she'd dreamed of visiting since she was in college and first read Nin, she felt like a spy, a voyeur, an alien on some distant planet. Here she was, finally, Sarah Rosen, an American woman traveling by herself in a world of foreign men, a Jew among Arabs and Berbers.

"If what you give is nothing, then you give nothing," the guide said with raised eyebrows. His name was Ibrahim.

"But for them," she said, "a dirham can buy a loaf of bread."

"Two loaves, if they know where to buy."

"Two loaves. I didn't realize."

The first to reach her was an old woman with a lined, almond-colored face. She stood as high as Sarah's elbow, speaking rapidly and raising one hand, then pulling the hand to her breastbone with a bow of her head. "Here, in the name of God," Sarah said, pressing a coin into the woman's palm. The woman raised her eyes and gave thanks. Behind her one of the blue petit taxis was trying to make its way through the crowd. A woman with a lighter face and the purple line of a tattoo dripping from her lower lip to her chin thrust out a hand that was yellow with henna. Strapped to her back was a sleeping child wrapped in a swath of cloth. One of the baby's arms stuck out, its dappled, half-opened fist dangling like an apple on a branch. Sarah looked at the graceful curve of the child's fingers, and the mother raised her golden palm nearly to Sarah's face just as a man with half a melted face—fire, Sarah thought suddenly—mumbled a few words and raised his hand beside the mother's. Sarah gave a dirham to the woman, then quickly got another and gave it to the burned man, whose face she could hardly bear. Several other hands pulled at the sleeve of her blouse and at her waist. Women. Cripples. Children demanding *un dirham*. Sarah took from her skirt pocket all the coins she had and filled the open hands as quickly as she was able, and then she had no more coins, and yet the hands around her had multiplied. They pressed at her from all sides. Where there had been half a dozen hands now there were fifteen, twenty. Her eyes sought the long-haired head of her guide, pleading with him to help her escape.

"Now you are, how you say, a marked woman," Ibrahim said after pushing the cripples and children away. "You can never pass this way again unbothered. They have long memories, beggars. You have made many friends."

"What did they say?" Sarah asked. "After I gave them a coin."

He frowned. "A few words. A prayer of thanks."

"And did they give me their blessing?"

He squinted, as if he were measuring her. "Why of course."

From the narrowing cobblestone street inside the gate and adjacent walls, she could see the top half of Bou Inania medersa's grand minaret. The guide walked a step in front and told her that from this point on no cars or trucks were permitted, that everything coming in and going out of the ancient city had to be carried on a man's or woman's or donkey's back. The streets sloped downward because the Fez medina was shaped like a bowl, dipping down to the river, Oued Fez. The guide made a bowl of his hands. At the bottom they would find the tanners, who washed their hides in the river fed by streams and the snow covering the mountains surrounding the valley in which the ancient city lay.

"The walk in is very easy," Ibrahim said, "the walk out, very hard."

She saw he was looking at her shoes. They were flat-soled, comfortable. "Don't worry about me. I want you to show me everything."

"Not everything," he said.

"Yes, everything."

"No, that will not be possible, unless you choose to live here like one of us for your whole life. The medina is complex, a maze, unlike the Ville Nouvelle, unlike Fez el Jedid, unlike anywhere in the world you can see."

He wants me to hire him tomorrow, Sarah thought and smiled. She liked the way he had treated the beggars. He was firm but not cruel or rough. As he pushed her past them he seemed almost apologetic, as if asking them for their understanding or forgiveness.

"What did you say to the beggars so we could pass?"

Ibrahim shrugged. "Not much. That you were not the Bank of the Maghreb."

They passed the doorways of a few shops and then walked past several closed doors that, Sarah imagined, likely opened onto splendid courtyards and gardens. Each time they approached one of the elaborately designed doors she hoped it would be open so she could look in and have a different view of Fez, but each door was tightly closed. She knew the traditional Moroccan house opened into itself, that it was built around its courtyard and garden. All the rooms fronted the garden and its light. The tiled roof sloped inward, to drain the rainwater into the garden where it could be used. Usually the garden had a fountain that was the house's sole source of water.

What the outside world saw were walls of bare, unembellished stone or plaster, sometimes broken by a high narrow window inserted more for ventilation than for light, and a square boarded window near the kitchen, so waste water could be thrown down onto the street. The architecture protected the house from attack, held in night's cool summer air, and prevented the women inside from being seen. Unlike Western houses that were open to any passerby who cared to look, these houses hid their faces, just as the women hid theirs. For the rich Fassis these houses must be like castles, Sarah thought. The poor had to pool their money to rent a room in a house like these, so where a single rich family once lived there now lived a dozen or more families. But none of that life could be seen or even heard as long as the door to the street remained closed. She ached to see and hear that inner life. She paused before the next door and pressed her cheek and the palm of her hand against it.

"You are already tired?" Ibrahim asked.

"No," Sarah said, "curious."

"You know what is said about the curious. It cuts off your nose."

"It also kills the cat."

He shook his head. "I don't understand."

They continued walking. The high blank walls of the houses squeezed the street more and more, funneling the pair down a cobbled walkway barely wider than their shoulders if they tried to walk abreast. Then the path took several sharp turns and wound its way into the darkness beneath overhanging floors. As Sarah entered that blackness she had the sense of being walled in.

No, she thought as she and Ibrahim walked back into the light and passed an arched doorway and a black door. No, in walking these streets one was walled *out*. How curious that the details of ordinary life were so concealed here, so hidden from outsiders, whereas the city's commerce was so open, so nakedly displayed in the souqs of the medina, where everything for sale could be touched, smelled, seen.

She felt proud of the connection she'd made. For a moment she was tempted to tell Ibrahim.

"Where are we now?" She realized she had no idea where she was. She reached out toward his pink shirt. "I thought we were going to walk past the Bou Inania medersa."

He corrected her pronunciation, then said, "But at the hotel you told me to show you the true Fez that is, not the touristic sights."

"But there's nothing to see here." Then she winced, regretting her words, their implication.

If he was insulted it did not show on his face. A fly lighted on his forehead. With a wave of his hand he brushed it away. "If you want to change your mind, change your mind. It is your mind to change. Follow me, I can take you there straightaway as you like."

"No, that's not what I'd like."

"If you want to walk with the other tourists we can walk with the other tourists."

"Forget I said anything." She took several steps, then stopped. "I just didn't know where you were leading me, that's all."

He nodded and began walking ahead of her. "On the first visit many find the Fez medina, how you say, distorting?"

"Disorienting," she said. "Confusing. It's like a medieval maze. It makes me think of Anaïs Nin." She laughed, looking at his blank face. "You wouldn't need to read about Fez, I guess. Forget I said anything, all right?"

She felt she'd given him offense. "I have read Graham Greene," he said. "Paul Bowles. And some stories of a man named Joyce."

"Show me whatever you'd like."

"Whatever you like," he said with a shrug.

They turned left down a narrow pathway Sarah was sure led only to a dead end, then turned right and walked perhaps thirty yards. The next right opened onto a busy, crowded street. Sarah walked

behind, ever downward, stepping to the side and pressing herself thin
as possible against the rough walls whenever the cry *"Balak! Balak!"*
bellowed behind her. Voices and footsteps echoed between the high
walls. The wooden shutters of a window above her banged open, and
a woman spilled a pan of water to the street. For a moment Sarah
could see the woman's dark hair and round face, the graceful curve
of the upper arm that held the pan. The water splashed, then ran
in jagged lines between the stones at Sarah's feet. The woman had
appeared and vanished as quickly as a lizard's tongue. Sarah wished
their eyes had met, if only for an instant. What would the woman
think, Sarah wondered, if their lives were to touch? How would they
judge each other?

She walked on, looking up from the trickle of water for Ibrahim,
for that tall head of long hair and pink shirt in the crowd, but she saw
only the dark heads of strange men, men wearing white turbans, men
in gray skullcaps, men with the hoods of their djellabas bunched at
the neck. Shorter veiled heads of women bobbed darkly, wordlessly
among them. Another donkey passed, pressing Sarah again to the
wall. Her heart pounded in her ears.

"Mademoiselle," said a voice just as suddenly beside her, "that
man you are with, that guide, he is not reliable."

She turned. Before her stood a boy in a djellaba the color of
polished ivory. He'd pulled its hood up over his head, though it didn't
conceal the startling blue of his eyes. Sarah was sure his olive cheeks,
which were slightly flushed, had never known a razor. He was twelve,
thirteen at best, and beautiful, she thought, every bit as lovely as a
young girl.

"Believe me, mademoiselle, I know him. He is a clever thief who
pretends to be your friend, but once you give him your trust and turn
your back he will steal from you all the things you have."

Sarah brought her hand to her mouth and laughed.

"All you need do if you don't take my word is ask the keepers of the shops here, because that man is known, you know? He is famous over Fez. Perhaps he is even wanted by the police for these thievings. Come with me and I take you to the shops. You can ask the men yourself. No charge, I mean only to help, don't insult me and say no."

"Where did you learn English?" Sarah said. "You speak very well."

"Please, I beg you, we must hurry to the shops before he comes back." He took her hand in both of his and pulled gently. "Or if you do not desire the shops you must come with me."

She stood her ground. It was not unpleasant holding the boy's hands. His touch was cool and soft. The lashes around his eyes were long and dark. His lips were red, full. She smiled and walked several steps with him. "What is your name?"

"Whajid. The one who finds."

She laughed again. "So the one who finds has found me?"

"Yes, Lalla." He smiled and stroked her hand. "I was on my way to the house of my father when I saw the clever thief lead you into the darkness, to a place where no one would hear your screams. So I followed, to rescue you when he made his attack."

His fingertips had worked their way past her wrist and were massaging the inside of her arm. Sarah found his words amusing and smiled again, then pulled her arm free. "But I don't need to be rescued."

"Then pardon me a hundred times." He dropped to one knee, clutching her hand and brushing his lips against her fingers. She didn't recognize what he was doing until he sucked one fingertip into his mouth, then released it and whispered, "Pretty Lalla, rich Lalla, do you want a fuck, do you not, I know what you want, Lalla, let me give you a fuck." He whispered so softly at first Sarah thought she was only imagining the words, but his smile was so sly only an idiot could miss its intent. The boy's proposition became more apparent as he rubbed his head up the length of her leg and said, "Give me dirhams and we can fuck."

In the moment before she acted—before she didn't just walk away and put a simple end to it but instead chose to raise the hand that in turn raised the other hands, setting into motion a sequence she'd realize later no one wanted or deserved—her temper flared like a lit match as she flashed on how she'd been treated in recent days, on all that had been said and unsaid to her. She recalled how difficult it was to secure a room in a hotel, how in Meknès she couldn't even get one after she admitted to the manager she was alone, how in both Rabat and Fez she'd had to lie and say her husband was on business in another part of Morocco and would join her later, and then after he didn't appear she had to lie again and say he'd changed his plans. She remembered the looks the waiters gave her each morning at breakfast, the comments and solicitations she heard while walking the streets. The first time she'd tried to rest in the cool shade of a sidewalk café in Rabat the embarrassed owner refused her service, explaining in halting French that the prostitutes frequented some other place, and besides they did not normally show their faces until dark, until after the evening prayer. When she informed him, indignant, that she was not a prostitute, he laughed.

Of course she was a prostitute, the café owner said. He looked around, as if to check who might be seeing him speaking to her. There was no other explanation. Why else would a woman be out on the street by herself? If she was married, how could her husband allow it? And if she was not yet married, how could her father and brothers permit her to travel to a foreign land? She must have been disowned by them. She must have done something to disgrace them. They must have caught her whoring. Surely if they loved her, if she were deserving of their love, they would not allow her to travel out of their sight, where her reputation could be ruined.

Besides, he said, he'd been to the cinema. He knew about
America. In the movies American women were either daughters
or wives or— He raised his eyebrows and laughed, then put his
thick middle finger through a circle he made of his other hand. She
understood, he said. He was a man of business, he added quickly,
more open-minded than most she would meet. He liked America.
He thought America was a good place because you could make a lot
of money there and then return to Morocco and live the rest of your
days in a country that knew and feared God.

Believe me, he said, I like you, but if I let you sit here my
business will be ruined. Come around the back when it is dark,
he said with a wink. I'll show you something. I pity you, because
prostitutes are to be pitied, because it is their fate to be unloved. Now,
because others have seen us, I must pretend to be angry and yell.
Then he yelled, waving an arm, shifting from French to Arabic.

As Sarah walked away, her body trembled. Only after she'd locked
the door of her room and taken off her shoes and sat on the edge of
her bed and rubbed her feet did she begin to feel the impact of his
words. She could not believe she'd been so passive. Did I sit there
and listen unprotesting, she wondered, because he spoke clumsily
in French and his words were difficult to follow? Or was I simply
shocked? She felt numb. She wanted to be strong. Travel tests what
one is made of, she told herself. She tried to laugh it off, thinking it
would make an amusing story to tell when she was back home. Then
she walked calmly to the bathroom where she crouched on the cold
tile floor beside the toilet and waited for her nausea to pass.

So she slapped the boy's face, as hard as she had hit anything
in her life. The slap jerked his head to one side, knocking him back
onto the cobblestones where for a moment he lay, unmoving, as the
red impression of her hand flowered on his cheek. The hood of his
white djellaba spilled from his head. On his head and neck were welts
the size and color of plums. At once a crowd of men gathered, as the

slap echoed down the medina's narrow walls and the boy began to whimper and then writhe like a serpent at their feet.

She couldn't understand a word of what the boy said to the men once someone helped him to stand. All she could do was try to read his eyes and gestures. His eyes were slits of blue ice, burning with hate. He pointed toward her, making incomprehensible gestures. All at once she knew she'd crossed a line beyond which there was no going back.

She brushed a lock of hair that had fallen to her forehead, then ran her hand over her gray scarf. There was nothing to fear, she told herself as she listened to the men speak. They spoke to one another in Arabic, a tongue not usually unpleasant to hear, though the sounds now were harsh as stone grating against stone. Coming from the back of the men's throats, it was nearly as if they were spitting. Their eyes pinned her to the wall. The boy pointed at her, nodding, then knelt before one of the men and kissed the hem of the man's djellaba.

"He says he has been rescued," said a man in excellent French. In his hands was a folded newspaper, *Le Matin du Sahara*. After Sarah turned toward him he looked away, at the boy, as he spoke. "He says you purchased him from his mother, who accepted the money because she was poor. He says you beat him and sell your body to any man who asks."

Sarah took a deep breath, trying to make herself calm. "No." She shook her head back and forth. "What he's saying is absurd."

"Of course," the man with the newspaper said, "but they believe him."

The boy was pulling up his djellaba, which was dirty now that he'd rolled on the ground. A pair of donkeys loaded with thick beams of wood neared. The donkeys swayed beneath the weight of their load as they walked in front of two men supporting another beam on their shoulders. The crowd around Sarah had to push against the wall to give them room. Then a beam slipped from one of the donkey's side bags, and the men lifted it from the street and made the least of them carry it by himself. Although the beam was obviously heavy, the man seemed to accept it without complaint. Sarah watched him drag the length of wood down the cobbled street after the other men and the donkeys.

The boy was holding up the hem of his garment. He pointed to the purple bruises on his legs, then pulled the dress higher. On his thighs were round marks that looked like burns.

"He says you inflicted these wounds on him," the man with the newspaper said.

"That's ridiculous," Sarah said in as calm a voice as possible. Her mouth was so dry she thought her tongue would crack. "He's lying. All of it, it's a lie." She wanted to add *disgusting* but she didn't know the word in French. "I was separated from my guide, a man in a pink shirt, named Ibrahim. Then he"—she pointed to Whajid— "approached me and—" She didn't know the word for *propositioned*. "He said very dirty things." She spread her hands. "I've done nothing." Her hands tightened into fists. "What do you think I am? It's him. It's him!"

The man with the newspaper translated. The weight of the others' eyes made Sarah feel like a little girl, cornered, caught on the public school playground. She breathed deeply and bent her knees so they wouldn't buckle.

"They say they wish to believe you but point out that several saw you strike him."

"It was because of what he said, because he insulted me."

He translated. "They want to know how you were insulted."

She stared at the boy as he cringed beside the man whose dark djellaba he'd kissed. "I told you. He suggested filthy things."

Again he translated. The men in the crowd all spoke at once.

"What are they saying?" Sarah asked.

The man with the newspaper raised his eyebrows, then answered in English. "They are trying to decide who is the whore."

Sarah felt unable to breathe. She closed her eyes for a moment, trying to calm herself. Who were these men anyway, she thought, that they could judge? Who was anyone to judge? She realized her mouth was slightly open, that she was panting. One of the men was examining the bruises on Whajid's legs. Then a second man seized the boy's waist and flipped him head down, and two other men took the boy's legs and held them still, and another bunched the boy's djellaba down onto his back at the same time pulling up the boy's underwear. The boy raised a fierce, angry scream. The men held him facedown as they split his legs. They spoke loudly, nodding their heads. Those at the fringes of the crowd pointed. The boy screamed and kicked. The man with the newspaper was nodding.

"See?" they said, bringing the boy's raised buttocks closer to her. They held his legs apart like an open scissors. The boy wailed, as if he were about to meet his death. "See?" they said again. The boy's buttocks were bruised. The anus appeared caked with blood.

"They have found their whore," the man with the newspaper said triumphantly. "Now they know he is the liar and you are innocent."

"Innocent?" Sarah said. Tears filled her eyes. They put the screaming boy back on his feet, and the man in the dark djellaba hit him. The others shouted. Some men laughed. A shove knocked the boy against the wall. A kick to the side brought him down. The boy tucked himself into a ball at the wall's base. If there were loose stones on the ground, Sarah thought, by now the first would be picked up and thrown.

"No one is innocent," she said, pushing the men away from the fallen boy. The man with the newspaper stood beside her. "Here," she said, removing her scarf, "wet this cloth with water in one of the fountains." The man nodded and merged into the crowd.

Sarah knelt. "I'm sorry," she said. The boy lay without moving, his back to the wall. Tears puddled along the ridge of his nose. She wiped away some mud near one of the bruises on his head, and then the man with the newspaper returned with her wet scarf and she began washing the boy's wounds.

She made what she hoped were soothing sounds, drawing out the sound of *m* and the *ue* in *blue*. The boy made no response, not even to wince, as Sarah wiped the dirt from the wounds on his head. It was as if he were made of wood, she thought. She washed the boy's arm, which he held out stiff as a branch, as if it did not belong to him, as if the flesh weren't his. Now she could see a pink shirt—Ibrahim— standing behind the man with the newspaper. "There," she said, gently lowering the boy's arm to the side of his djellaba. "There," she said, stroking the flesh of his arm with her fingertips.

The side of the boy's face still bore the faint red imprint of her hand. Sarah refolded her scarf and was wiping his forehead and cheeks when she heard the scrape of boots on the stones behind her. She turned and stared at two men behind her. They looked past her as they lifted the boy from the street, then dragged him between them until he began to walk.

"Where are they taking him?" Sarah shouted.

"Where do you think?" said the man with the newspaper. "To a place where he can be questioned."

"But why?" Sarah said. "Because they think he's a whore?"

For a moment his eyes met hers. "I think because he is the cause of a disturbance. And because you a foreigner, a guest."

"What will they do to him?" She feared the answer.

The man shrugged.

"I've searched the entire medina for you," said Ibrahim. "One moment you were behind me. The next, you had disappeared."

She sighed and turned back to the wall, picking her gray scarf up from the ground. Her hands unbunched it, snapped it open. She feared the reaction her long, uncovered red hair might cause so she folded the scarf into a triangle and tied it over her head.

"Forgive me," Ibrahim said. "I am very sorry you were lost." There were shiny crystals at the edge of his mouth, as if he'd eaten something sweet.

"It can be a terrible experience for a *Nasrani* to be lost here," said the man with the newspaper. He opened and refolded it, then tucked it carefully beneath his arm.

Sarah laughed. She knew *Nasrani* meant Christian, one from Nazareth.

"Please," Ibrahim said, "forgive me." His tongue licked the sugar from his lips.

She nodded. "And what do we do now? Pretend nothing happened?"

"Life goes on," said the man with the newspaper, "*insha'Allah.*"

"*Insha'Allah,*" said Ibrahim.

If God wills it, *insha'Allah*, Sarah thought with a sudden bad taste in her mouth.

Ibrahim then led her deeper into the medieval labyrinth, down the busy, twisted streets to the spice merchants' souq, where the air was laced with a soft rainbow of smells. There, it was easier to forget what happened. Odors dangled and hung in the air, like vines. One caught and returned her to the sweet smoky church of her childhood, and Sarah remembered how once she'd imitated her friends and dipped her fingers into the bowl of blessed water, splashing a few drops on her forehead in the hope that it would always keep her safe.

The sky grew as gray as her damp scarf, and it was time to depart. Ibrahim cupped his hands and nodded. "Remember that the walk in is very easy," he said. "The walk out, very hard."

EXPATRIATES

"So I said to the driver, 'What do you think I am? A tourist?' I mean, really. Do I look like a tourist?"

"I've never thought so."

"I should say not." Leonard gave the air a petulant sniff. "My Arabic was just as good as his, the stupid donkey."

They sat in Rosemary's courtyard, drinking gin beside a cracked plaster wall covered with bougainvillea. Fat, furry bumblebees bumped the blossoms nearest Leonard's head. In the courtyard's center, an untended mess of poppy and auricula fought with the weeds beside a large Barbary cactus and several small banana trees. Tiny black ants scurried up the legs of the wooden table beside Rosemary. On the other side of the wall, on Rue de l'Atlas, the traffic skirted a rut in the road's center, rattling by a toothless man who sat by the curbstone next to a brazier on which he roasted ears of corn.

"You look like that character out of Evelyn Waugh."

Leonard shook his head. "Please, no literary allusions. Not today."

"I'm sorry. I was only trying to compliment you." Rosemary's laugh had the wet, throaty catch of a lifelong smoker. In the afternoon light her face was much less wrinkled than in the morning, when the sun did her few favors. Her graying hair puffed out on both sides of her head. "Oh, you know the one I mean. We saw him on that series Margaret taped off the BBC."

"I didn't watch the series. I read the book."

"Oh, what was his name?"

"I know who you mean," Leonard said, sipping his drink. "The handsome soldier." He smiled and waved away a black fly that lit on his forehead.

"His name's on the tip of my tongue. You know, the rich one who died in the end from too much drink—"

"The faggot." Leonard feigned insult. "How flattering."

" —or was it pneumonia? I remember him lying feverishly in bed."

"Please. No illness or death today either, if you don't mind."

"That's a healthy attitude." Rosemary believed wholeheartedly in healthy attitudes. Healthy attitudes and good intentions gave her form, a start to each day. She sipped her drink. The gin bit into her tongue, warmed her throat. A cloudy ice cube floated in the center of her glass, emanating rippling lines into the liquor. She knocked the cube idly with her fingernail, then licked a drop from her fingertip and stared at the wavy lines in her glass.

"After the bad news I received." He brushed his long hair from his eyes.

She saw she shouldn't have tried to compliment him. "Endurance," she said. "Fortitude." She made a fist. "Remember, it was the tortoise who beat the hare."

"Tourists ruin it for the rest of us," Leonard said. "Really, how can you stand them? Clogging things up, overpaying everywhere they go. They make begging in this town a thriving industry."

"Fez has always had its unfortunates."

"If I could just get a sign, hang it around my neck. You know, something that said I wasn't one of them, here for two days and nights on tour."

"In time you'll grow used to them."

"I will not. I'm serious. And the traffic, well, it's as bad as the States. Did I tell you yesterday I was power-walking out on Avenue des Français and I came this far"—he raised his first finger and thumb—"from being run over by one of those huge tourist buses?"

"What?" She looked up from her glass. "Power-walking?"

"It's obscene the way they travel about. Sitting behind their tinted windows, removed from everything, breathing their cool air-conditioning, fresh from a morning shower. They come here to see this place, they should be made to smell the street, the soot, the sweat."

"You could have a bath each morning if you wanted. We've wood for the water heater. I told you, it's not much trouble."

"You'd think they're in a theater watching a play the way they look down on you from their windows, oohing and ahhing, pointing. Then the big bus slides to a stop, the door hisses open, and they all tramp out, cameras at the ready, expecting everyone to do something colorful or scenic."

"Well, that's why some people come here. They're camera buffs."

"The other day in the medina there was a group of tourists gawking near the entranceway of the tomb of—you know who I mean—that old dead king."

"Ahh, yes," Rosemary said, laughing, "that old dead king."

"Don't make fun of me. You know the spot, where boys sell candles to the Muslims. Anyway, I was passing by, trying to work my way past this tangle of tourists clicking and whirring away with their cameras, when this rather tall Frenchman waved the group away from the boys so he could take their picture. The boys smiled, smoothed their dirty little shirts, held up the candles they were selling like little angels. Then when the tourist was finished the smallest boy asked for a coin. The boy was very polite, asking the usual, a dirham for each, less than some and certainly less than the water sellers. The man shook his head, smiled, told the boys no. The boy asked again and the man said don't bother me. Then all the boys whose pictures he'd taken asked at once, still quite polite, and the stupid man shook his head and actually elbowed one away."

"How horrid."

"So imagine, there I was, having watched all this, and meanwhile dozens of Muslims have streamed past, entering the archway, slipping off their shoes, and dozens in turn have come out, doing the reverse, and this guy has taken free photos of it all. So I pushed my way up to him and told him it was customary to give people who pose for a picture a coin, or more if one's taken several."

Rosemary smiled and raised her glass. "My valiant nephew."

"Oh wait, you haven't heard the best part. He looked down at me as if I were speaking Portuguese. Then he repeated what I'd just said, *correcting* my French pronunciation. I tell you, the man had absolutely no concept that he was being humiliated. By now the boys had gathered behind me, insisting he give them money. The man wouldn't acknowledge what I was saying so I snatched someone's camera as politely as one can snatch a camera from around someone's neck without taking the person's head off in the process and began snapping his picture, all the while shouting in my inferior French, 'How do you like it? Does it feel good? How do you like it?' until he turned and ran away."

"Marvelous."

"I should write it down, make a story of it, don't you think?"

"You should." She drew a cigarette out from her pack.

"Do you really? I exaggerated the ending."

"I think it would make an excellent story." She wanted to be encouraging. She knew since he'd arrived he'd done little work.

"Do you think the boys are colorful enough?"

She drew on her cigarette and nodded. "They're absolutely fine. Just describe them. Get in the sounds and smells. You know, the local color, the shape of the candles, all that. Let the story tell itself."

"That's easy enough to say."

"Oh," she said, "sorry." She remembered his bad news.

He drained his glass and grinned. "I was beginning to think Moroccan mailmen didn't exist. You know, that they were a myth, something on the order of ifrits and flying carpets." He made a flying carpet of his hand. "That postal delivery was a sham, a pretense designed to sell stamps to tourists from Boston."

"It's true what they say about no news."

"No." He shook his head pensively. "I'd rather know."

They were silent for several moments. Rosemary stared into her glass. Maybe now he'd go back. She wasn't sure if she wanted him to go back. She'd lived here alone for so long—since her husband Bill's death, at the start of Reagan's first term—she'd gotten used to it. They had come here when Nixon was in office, back before all his mess. After Bill died, staying on just seemed easier. She swirled the ice cube in her glass, then took a long swallow.

Leonard seemed on the verge of tears. "To all the good books that go unpublished," he said with a grand wave of his empty glass.

Now she didn't care who was in office. She feared she couldn't live back in the States even if she tried. She stubbed out her cigarette. She could feel the warm liquor emanate from her abdomen out through her limbs. Her hands and fingers were peacefully still. The gin floated like a melting ice cube inside her, emanating ripples that made her numb.

"You do it with your arms, like this." Leonard stood, imitating a toy drummer, power-walking in place. "I was expecting the news, I suppose. So I guess if I can't be any good at writing at least I can try to look good." He slapped his flat stomach. "You know, it's what's on the outside, the surface, that counts."

"Nonsense."

"I'm serious." He pumped his arms. "My eyes are open. The package is more important than its contents."

She didn't know if she had the strength to humor him. "So what really happened in the medina?"

He sat down. "You mean with the Frenchman? What one would expect, I guess. He refused the boys. I watched, did nothing."

"You did what you were supposed to do. You imagined a fine ending. I hope you write it."

"A sign of the times. We watch and do nothing."

She suddenly remembered the young woman. "A few days ago I met a young woman, very pretty really, wandering about the medina by herself, just as lost as anyone could be. Had some sort of trouble with her guide. Literally going around in circles, trying out one street after the next, until I walked up."

"See, that's the difference between us. You initiate things."

Rosemary smiled. "I invited her to dinner this Thursday."

"You mean tonight. Today's Thursday."

"No it's not. It can't be. Tomorrow's Thursday."

"Tonight. Should I show you on a calendar?"

Fear spilled warmly down Rosemary's neck, across her shoulders. She gulped her drink. She didn't like being caught losing track of the days.

"Is she very pretty? Do you think she'll fall for me?"

"Not if you let her sit for this long with an empty glass." Rosemary extended her empty glass. "Tell Halima to make more ice."

"I fear our bottle's passed on to its next incarnation."

"There's another beside the table."

She watched him pirouette past the cactus and banana trees and walk into the house, which seemed to shimmer. She pressed the flat of her palms against her eyes. Inside her was a tug-of-war. She didn't know who pulled against what. All she knew was that she was in the middle, being pulled.

In the mornings, after she awoke, the forces would be at their quietest, and she'd sip mineral water mixed with the juice of half a lemon so as not to wake them. She'd feel fine until afternoon, until the sun slipped in the sky beyond the edge of the Ville Nouvelle, over the snow-tipped mountains that embraced the three cities of Fez within their arms. Shadows would spill down the avenues named for dead kings and long-past dynasties. An uneasy feeling would fall over her, as palpable as an itch. She'd sit in the courtyard with a magazine or book and pour her first drink. It was the hour when Bill returned from the consulate, when night would begin to descend. She'd read until the pages grew gray and hid the letters. Then she'd go inside. The garden would seethe with unseen things—lizards, snakes, cockroaches big as her fingers, centipedes long as her hands—things that ran over her ankles and cracked beneath her bare feet whenever she stepped beyond the circle of yellow light pooled by the metal doorway. Sometimes from high up in the mountains, even as she stood in the light, she could hear the wild call of wolves.

Now as she sat, eyes closed, waiting for a fresh drink in the afternoon sun, she tried to listen to her beating heart, but all she could hear was the rumble of the traffic beyond the wall on Rue de l'Atlas and the slowly rising whine of insects in the poppies and the weeds.

"Of course you've never heard of them." They were standing in the sala. Leonard had put on a pale blue shirt, loose white pants, and sandals, all of which made him look very French. He'd cornered the American, who stared about the room as if she were trying to take everything in.

"Relax, please," Rosemary said, feeling very Moroccan. She took a sip of her drink. "My home is your home." She had changed into a cinnamon kaftan and was barefooted. Two tortoise-shell combs held back her hair.

"No one's heard of them," Leonard said, sitting on the low seddari that lined three walls of the room. He leaned against one of the sofa's cushions, propped a second behind his back. "That's just my point. No sooner were they out than they were thrown off the side of a cliff."

The American nodded. She had brushed out her red hair, which she'd hid in a scarf the day Rosemary found her in the medina. Rosemary was sure she would have remembered such striking red hair. Now the woman's hair hung freely to her shoulders. She sat demurely. Flowered skirt, tan blouse, sensible shoes. No ring, Rosemary noticed. Sarah something, that was her name. She'd said her last name at least twice, but Rosemary was never any good at last names. Sarah nodded at something Leonard said, then immediately looked away and picked a string of lint from her skirt.

Rosemary listened for a moment for Halima, who was in the kitchen frying briouats. Now that Sarah was here and it seemed they'd have a party, Rosemary wondered if perhaps she should have invited more guests. There were the Peace Corps people, of course, and always someone here on a Fulbright, and that nice man who owned the American bookstore. He knew all the Americans in Fez. She'd throw a big dinner party next time, she thought. Tonight they'd just get to know one another.

"That's how it's done," Leonard was saying. "They toss these helpless newborns off a mountainside, hoping that on the way down some will miraculously grow wings. A few do, you know. It happens once, maybe twice a season. Instead of disappearing they fly right out of the abyss, and everyone gazes up at them and applauds, thinking it's great, how it proves the system works. They don't notice what happens to the nine hundred and ninety-nine that spin and fall and vanish, splattering like ripe tomatoes, smashing their little heads against the rocks below."

"Please," Rosemary said, "don't be quite so graphic." They were having tomatoes later, after the briouats. Then the mechoui Halima had picked up from downtown. Then tea. Rosemary thought if she were really Moroccan she'd serve couscous after the mechoui but she didn't appreciate couscous after something as heavy as lamb. Besides, she thought, she wasn't Moroccan. She wouldn't have to serve a feast to show her guest she was welcome.

"Old woman, take the blinders off your eyes. Writers are supposed to be graphic." He gave the ceiling an empty laugh.

Rosemary bristled at the phrase. Old woman! Mumbling the words, she shook her head several times, then reached for the tongs and dropped an ice cube into her glass, filled it with gin, then lit a cigarette.

"That's a terribly brutal way of separating the good from the bad," Leonard was saying, "but that's the way it's done."

"You can't mean they do that deliberately," Sarah said.

"Can I get you anything, dear?" Rosemary said.

"You mean the editors?" Leonard said.

Sarah shook her head, then turned to Leonard and nodded.

"American publishing is an industry," Leonard said, "no different and no better, certainly no more noble, than any other. They take the result of your labors, pay as little as they can, try to market it, which in most cases means slap on a cover peppered with clichés, then toss it to the wind. And you're *grateful* to them." He rolled his eyes. "Ever so grateful."

"More to drink?" said Rosemary cheerily. Then she noticed Sarah's untouched glass.

Leonard stood. "It's their pretense that's so galling." He nodded vigorously, as if to convince himself. "These poseurs, who themselves more often than not have never written a book, have such authority over those who have. It's a brutal and humiliating process, publishing a book. The horror stories I could tell."

"His novel has become an orphan," Rosemary said, wanting to join the conversation. She'd remained near the liquor table, settling into the sofa beside it. "*Orphan* is the right term, isn't it?"

"I never realized the situation was so complex," Sarah said. She accepted a briouat from Halima, who'd bowed before her with a brass tray.

"Be careful, darling," Rosemary said. "Don't burn your mouth."

Leonard nodded glumly.

"His editor was fired after his publishing house was sold to a conglomerate that makes cat food." Rosemary looked up at her nephew, who was now pacing the room. "Do I have it straight?"

"The cat-food conglomerate owned the house in the first place," he said, "then sold out to another conglomerate."

"Oh," Sarah said suddenly, "your publisher is the one with those cute little kittens reading the book on the spine."

"Sweetie, listen to what I'm trying to tell you. The rabid dogs of corporate America have taken over. There was a *merger*. Those charming little pussy cats have been sent straight to the pound."

"Think positively," Rosemary said. "The letter didn't—"

"You know what the new spine design will be? Pit bulls tattooed with dollar signs, ripping the last non-commercial American novel to shreds."

"Positive, positive."

"This new house, what a reputation! They haven't touched poetry in twenty years. Out-of-town writers who make the pilgrimage to New York to meet with their editors get stuck with the bar tab. One senior editor has the habit of taking promising first novels under his wing, then tying them up for years, all the while promising they'll be published just as soon as the lawyers can draw up a contract. None of his books ever see the light of day."

Sarah turned. "These are delicious."

Rosemary nodded. "That's what Leonard thinks will happen to his book." She didn't like to give voice to negative thoughts because then they existed, at least in sound and mind, but she suddenly understood Leonard's fear. He stood between the two women, basking in their attention.

"Wait, it gets worse. Let me tell you the World's Greatest Horrible Publishing Story. There was a writer who rewrote her novel extensively in galleys, made thousands of changes, edits, cuts, and because of the due dates didn't have time to keep notes or make copies of anything she'd done. She rushed it all back to the house, which rushed it to the printers, where it was printed and then shipped, plates and all, by accident to the shredder, where the entire run—I mean every single book—was turned to confetti. Computer error, they said later. The writer never saw one copy."

"You mean they didn't print any more copies?"

"They couldn't, then decided that to start the process over would be too expensive. Then they had the gall to ask the writer to give back her advance."

"Eat, dear," Rosemary said.

"New York is the most self contained, provincial city in the world. If Manhattan dropped into the sea tomorrow I wouldn't shed a tear."

Sometimes what you fear takes place because you fear it. Rosemary nodded at her thought, then took a gulp of her drink and touched the combs holding up her hair. Particularly if your fear is strong and you dwell on it, give it details, dimension, substance.

"I know you're tired of listening to this but I'll say one more thing and then shut up." He crossed the room, then whirled toward the two women as he spoke. "I wish the world's careless editors would come back in their next lives as writers, and after their years of sweat and labor they'd be handled by someone exactly like themselves. Now that would be sweet revenge."

Sarah smiled, then gave a soft laugh. She was beautiful, Rosemary thought. Then her face fell as she gazed at her own reflection in the silver tray beneath the bottle of gin.

"Right now I'm just traveling," the red-haired woman was saying in response to something Leonard said. "I've always been fascinated by Morocco."

Rosemary pulled the combs from her hair and set them carefully next to the gin bottle, then teased her hair with her fingertips, trying to make it look lovely, like Sarah's. Her hair was gray and thin and, since she hadn't washed it in nearly a week, rather greasy. It hung in two clumps on the sides of her head, like ears on an old cocker spaniel.

"You're traveling by yourself," Leonard said.

Sarah nodded. "Sometimes I have to tell lies to the hotels, say my husband will be arriving in a few days, then that he's changed his plans. But it's not really much of a hassle. I'm getting used to how I'm treated on the streets."

Halima entered, carrying a brass tray upon which were plates of salad and a basket of round Moroccan bread.

"And how are you treated on the streets?" Leonard said, taking a wedge of tomato from one of the plates. He held the tomato in his fingers and waved it as he spoke. "Aren't you hassled all the time? Don't guys pull on your arm, want to walk with you?"

"Please bring forks," Rosemary managed to say, even though Halima was no longer in the sala. Then Rosemary noticed her purse, reached for it and drew out a lipstick, which she twisted and held in her fingers like Leonard was holding the tomato. Halima appeared suddenly with forks. The lipstick was as deep red as the tomato. For a moment Rosemary wondered if she was expected to eat it. She smeared it on her mouth instead, coating the left side of her upper lip well beyond the lip line, barely touching the right side. "Mmmm," she said loudly as she blotted her lips.

"Get you something?" Leonard said from across the dizzy sea of the room.

She stared at her image in the tray. Her complexion was pale, like uncolored wax. She looked like an old clown.

"Balls," she said. When embarrassed in a social situation, one should try to make a joke of it. "To juggle with, since I look . . ." She pointed to the silver tray, then hesitated. She took a breath, then sat as straight as she could.

"Aunt Ro's been putting quite a dent in Morocco's gin reserves," Leonard said, laughing. "You know, she nearly forgot—"

"Just because you got bad news," Rosemary managed to say, "no reason to be cruel."

"Cruel? I get the most devastating news of my life and you accuse me—"

"Devastating, devastating. You don't know devastating."

"No," Leonard said, "but if you hum a few bars."

She could feel them staring. Well, she'd stare right back. "You're in grief over nothing. Words on paper." The rest of the thought hung in the air beyond her reach.

"She actually told me this afternoon that the tortoise could beat the hare." He waved his arms at the young woman, who'd stopped eating.

It wasn't what rewards the words brought you, Rosemary wanted to say, but your putting them down, the steady doing of it.

"Tortoises!" Leonard sneered. "It's wolves who win races."

Her fingertips stroked her shoulder. "Excuses."

"Look at her, all dressed up in her kaftan, like something out of the ancient Moorish court. Can you believe the day before I arrived she'd hennaed her hands? At first I thought it was some kind of disease."

"You won't exist," Rosemary said, "if I refuse to listen."

"I won't exist if you keep drinking like that."

"And you didn't drink your share?"

"I wanted to keep you company. There's nothing quite so sad as an old woman getting soused by herself."

"You should be an old woman! Die and come back an old woman. Worse, a poor one. I curse you!"

"Didn't I tell you? She's gone completely native."

Halima came in at that moment with the mechoui. Rosemary covered her face with her hands until she heard Halima's soft voice tell her not to cry, then ask if there was anything else she could do. Halima was bending over her, stroking her hair. Tell me if you're going to be sick, Halima whispered in Arabic. I can bring you the bowl. Leonard and Sarah murmured in the background and for a moment the light was very bright, and then a cold cloth was wiping Rosemary's forehead and a cool hand was pressing her neck, lifting her head from against the wall where it had fallen.

"Forgive me, please, so embarrassed," she tried to say but wasn't sure anyone understood her.

Someone lifted her from beneath her arms. Halima. Rosemary could smell her, the gentle mix of some oily perfume and the soft black soap—beldi soap—the Fassi woman used to wash her hair. Rosemary pictured a mound of the dark soap, the scoop used by the men in the mellah who sold it. Halima's voice said walk, so Rosemary moved her legs and walked. The red Rabati rug on the sala floor spun like a child's pinwheel. Then she felt her bare feet on the hallway's cool tiles and let her head fall to the crook of Halima's neck. Her arms held Halima and she was happy. Her tongue licked the neck, and then her lips reached for the skin—soft, salty—and kissed it, and Halima's voice said something soothing as a hand pressed against the back of her head and she opened her mouth to say how very sorry, but instead of words— She felt her stomach buck as if it had been punched. Halima held her head over the bowl.

Poison! The body, which knows better than the mind, repels the poison, saying I will be well! And Jesus said to those who dared defile the temple Out, I say to thee! And in the Quran it was written that drink is a loathsome evil of Satan's doing. Shun it so that you might obtain a happy state! Alcohol is a Soul-Snatcher, a woman beckoning from the shadows, a man creeping into your room at night. When you open your mouth in longing, the Snatcher sucks out your marrow, turns you hollow. You're left breathless and walk as if empty.

The voices fell into the bowl along with her vomit, which was nearly clear and which glistened in the light. Tears blurred Rosemary's sight. She held Halima and knew no words could repay the care the woman gave her. She who cooked her meals, washed her clothing, cleaned her filth when she was drunk. Was this the bottom? Rosemary thought. She burned with shame. She fell to her knees on the cracked kitchen tiles, head bowed, arms wrapped around Halima's legs. Give me your forgiveness, Rosemary's mouth tried to say, though what her ears heard was more the growl of some drugged beast. She slipped to the floor, kissed Halima's feet.

"Forgive me," she said as clearly as she was able.

A cockroach waved its long antennae from the room's corner. Then some part of Rosemary's mind answered yes, I forgive you, just don't drink again.

The American lay sleeping on the seddari. Halima must have brought her the blanket, Rosemary thought. She stood in the darkness in an old, unflattering dress that made her look nearly as aged as she felt. Thank God for aspirin. It softened the pounding so. She sipped a cup of lukewarm water mixed with lemon juice.

So Leonard hadn't been up to taking her back to her hotel, Rosemary realized, looking at the lovely young woman asleep. Oh, to be young and beautiful again! She silenced the envy with a gulp of lemon water. Apparently Leonard also hadn't bedded her, or else why would the girl sleep here alone? If she were a young man who resembled Lord Sebastian Flyte—the name of the character from *Brideshead Revisited* surfaced suddenly in her mind—she certainly would have tried to instead of boring the poor dear with stories about his failures. She wondered if her nephew preferred men. Perhaps he preferred no one, nothing. Then he'll be content, she thought, if his middle years are as lonely as mine.

She must have made a noise then because the girl stirred, then sat up.

"Hello. Is it morning?"

"Not quite."

"How long have you been standing there?"

"Only a few moments. Go back to sleep."

"No. I'm awake now."

Rosemary sipped her lemon water, for courage. "I want to apologize to you for last night."

"You don't need to apologize." She stood and began folding the blanket. "You just got sick, that's all."

Rosemary smiled. She liked this girl. "Why don't you go back to sleep?"

"I'm not tired, really."

"It's sweet that you make excuses for me. Sarah, isn't it? For a moment I'd forgotten your name."

Sarah nodded. "The dinner was delicious. I want to thank you."

"You enjoyed the mechoui. I'm glad."

In the room's fuzzy darkness Sarah rubbed her eyes, then reached down, trying to smooth some of the wrinkles in her skirt.

"Can I get you anything? Something to eat? Coffee?"

"No," Sarah said. "It's too early. I can't eat when it's this early. I'd like to go back to my hotel, if it isn't too much trouble."

"No trouble."

Sarah nodded. Rosemary looked for her car key after Sarah excused herself to use the bathroom. The key wasn't hanging in its usual place, on the hook by the door. It was difficult searching for it in the darkness. Rosemary's hands kept finding things she didn't want or had thought she'd lost. A scapular from when she was a girl, a pot holder her mother once made, an unopened letter from her daughter.

Sarah came out from the bathroom, even prettier now that she'd washed her face and brushed out her lovely hair.

She showed Rosemary where Leonard had put the key after he'd tried to drive her back to her hotel. They walked out into the courtyard to the gravel driveway. The air was heavy, wet. A squatting rat ran from their path. In the distance two birds called to each other repetitiously. Sarah explained that after they ate, Leonard insisted he drive her, not help her look for a petit taxi. She had no idea where in Fez she was, she said. Rosemary unlatched the metal doors at the end of the drive, swung them open, then propped them open with rocks. But the car stalled, Sarah said.

"That's because he can't drive a standard transmission," Rosemary said once they were in the car. "He had it in fourth. See?" She put the gear in neutral. "No wonder he kept stalling."

On the streets there was little traffic. The Renault's yellow headlights sliced a wedge ahead of them.

"Leonard received some bad news yesterday," Rosemary said as they drove. "I hope you'll forgive him for what he said."

"I know," Sarah said. "He told me."

"He's not usually that bitter."

"Well, everyone has a right to say how they feel."

"He's really quite a good writer."

"I'm sure."

They passed an old man brushing the curbstone with a sheaf of palm leaves. "You must think us strange"—she waved a hand—"for living here."

"Not particularly," Sarah said. "I could live here. In a way I envy the life. Fez is an enchanting place."

"To visit, certainly, but to live? You think you could live here?"

She didn't answer. Light from the street played on her face.

"You'd be giving up a lot," Rosemary said after a moment. "I think I'm here because I can't live anywhere else, if that makes any sense."

"You mean the States."

"I mean more than that. I mean the place and its pressures and who I was when I was there. Did Leonard talk to you last night?"

"He told me for the past two years he hasn't been able to write. He said that when he sits down at his desk he writes sentences which he later erases. He said he has nothing really to say, only the ability to say it."

"Is he planning on staying here?"

"He thinks America failed him. Or that he failed America. Something like that. He goes back and forth on it. He isn't sure."

Rosemary smiled. "Sounds like you two got along."

"We talked, that's all. Considering the circumstances, what other choice did we have?"

"You're angry with me, aren't you?"

"No, not at all."

"You're a darling, but a very transparent liar. You're a lot like my daughter before she got wise. She'd let me say anything, then make excuses for me." Rosemary reached for the envelope on the dash. "Here. Read this. Is there enough light?"

"What is it?"

"A letter from my daughter, in Minnesota." Rosemary stared at the envelope. Not even the house number. Just R. Fisher, Rue de l'Atlas, Fez. "It says she and her husband and children are fine, and they miss hearing from me and hope someday soon I'll return. But if I return they pray I'll stop being a drunk because they don't love their old grandma when she's drunk."

They were on the main boulevard now. Sarah's hotel was just ahead.

"And if it was Christmas when she wrote, it says the snow is really beautiful, and last week Ted took little Mark and Christy and Luke sledding while she stayed home and made sugar cookies, and afterwards everyone drank hot chocolate with marshmallows. And if it was spring—"

"You haven't read it?"

"I don't have to read it. I know what it says."

She saw the lit white sign—the hotel's name above three squat stars—and pulled the car alongside the curb next to the grassy walkway that separated the boulevard. "If it's locked you may have to ring the bell to get in. I'll wait here until you're safe inside."

Sarah nodded. She handed Rosemary the unopened letter.

"She's about your age, you know. Husband, kids. She doesn't have to go into lonely hotel rooms in foreign countries at five in the morning."

"You don't have to be mean."

"Don't become one of us. You don't belong here. Go back to wherever you ran away from. I'm only trying to warn you, so you don't turn out like me."

"I can't remember when I had a less pleasant time."

Rosemary smiled. "You said you liked the mechoui."

"By the time we ate, it was cold." She put a hand on the door latch. "You should have heard yourself last night. Your daughter's name is Louise, isn't it? You kept calling the Moroccan woman Louise."

"Was I"—Rosemary swallowed—"less than cordial to her?"

"Less than cordial?" Sarah laughed. "You were vicious. That poor woman must need her job desperately because I can't see how anyone could put up with so much abuse." She opened the car door. "I don't want to be ungrateful to you for inviting me to dinner, but I don't welcome your comments about me or my life. Believe me, being here hasn't been very easy. Your invitation was like a port in a storm."

"I apologize."

"It should be obvious I really don't know what I'm doing. I was supposed to come here with a friend. But things didn't work out. I didn't want some man telling me what I couldn't do, so I came anyway."

"I'm very sorry," Rosemary said. Tears welled in her eyes.

"I'm not your daughter. And I certainly have no intention of becoming like you."

Rosemary breathed heavily, eyes closed. "Could we have a drink together later, try again?" When she heard no response she said, "Please?"

Sarah had closed the car door and now leaned in through the open window. She sighed, shook her head. "All right. This afternoon at two. Just tea or coffee."

"Of course. That's what I meant. Just tea or coffee."

She idled for a while at the curb, then dried her eyes, blew her nose, stared her reflection in the rear-view mirror. The instruments on the dashboard flickered and grew faint, so she pumped the accelerator, then put the car in gear and drove up the long avenue, away from the French city, to Fez el Jedid on the road that ringed the mountainside and looped Fez el Bali, the medina of ancient Fez. The air from the open window was cool and felt good on her face. She gave the car gas. On her right was a cliff that separated the road from a grove of olive trees. Light from her yellow headlights played on the tops of the trees.

Just for fun she swerved into the trees. At the last moment, as the wheels bit the gravel edging the steep cliff, she fought the car back onto the road.

She dropped into second gear, her heart racing. Now she could never drive up this road again without thinking of steering her car into the treetops, without imagining the car crashing in a tumbling ball of flame. The car lugged its way up the mountain. No matter what Louise was doing, at that moment she'd feel a chill, pause, cry out Mother! Ted, something's happened to my mother!

"Your mother is dead," Rosemary said to the darkness, pretending to be Ted. She imagined him standing by a telephone. "No," she said, not wanting to give in to it, and at the same time speaking Louise's line. "No, it can't be." She laughed out loud. "Mother would never kill herself. She likes to drink too much."

Ted would smile at the joke. "You're right. At this moment she's driving up Route 501 thinking of the bottle hidden beneath the passenger seat."

Louise: "Even the Moroccan police who'd searched the car when she was stopped for speeding couldn't find it."

Ted: "She's a master drinker. She holds her liquor better than anyone. They never even suspected she was drunk."

Louise: "Mother, drunk? That's absurd. She only drinks a little."

Ted: "You're right. It doesn't even affect her anymore."

She brushed away her tears with the back of her hand. She once had such pretty hands, she thought. In the dim glow of light from the dashboard they looked young again. The road leveled out, then began again to climb.

When she neared the Kasbah Cherarda and the hospital, near the road that led to the famous blue gate, Bab Boujeloud, she pulled over to the left on the mountainside and set the hand brake. It was still dark. The rim of the hill skirted Fez el Bali. Carefully she took the gin bottle out from the springs under the passenger seat, then began climbing the rise jutting from the road. Before her, a black-faced lamb chewed a thistle in the shadows. A shepherd in a tattered cloak was driving his herd alongside the road. As she climbed the rise she stared at the ground so she wouldn't trip. Lights twinkled in the Fez medina below, like stars in some undiscovered constellation.

She sat and breathed deeply, relaxing. Her concentration merged with the medina's lights. After several minutes she felt something hovering behind her, some idea or presence, or perhaps it was the black-faced lamb. It knew about her bottle of gin. Spill it on the ground, it told her. Start again. Renew. Become like an empty bottle.

She took the bottle in her hand, hefted it weight. She cracked the seal, tossed the cap into the darkness. Here it goes, she thought. She poured the gin out on the ground before her. The liquor glugged as it slipped from the bottle. Rosemary's mind held an image of the earth, balanced in a dark sky, turning so ponderously that eventually she'd feel the morning sun, though from where she sat it seemed as if there was no movement and it would be forever until morning.

SONS OF ADAM

They were sitting in the back room of the Café Restaurant de la Saada spooning runny mashed potatoes next to the grilled lamb on their plates when Ahmed said, "Henry, I have just thought, tomorrow we must go to Moulay Yacoub." Ahmed's cheeks bulged with meat as he spoke. He held up a fresh piece of charcoaled lamb. Before Henry could ask how far away Moulay Yacoub was, a boy crying, "'Garro, 'garro, 'garro," like a softly firing machine gun rushed up to their table offering them an assortment of cigarettes. The boy had everything from Marquis to Gitane, Best to Casa Sport Blue, precisely arranged and tiered in an open Marlboro carton. Then another boy waltzed in from behind the counter in the first room and pushed a tray covered with brown paper against Henry's arm. On the tray were roasted peanuts and salted sunflower seeds. Henry gave the boys a smile and a shake of his nearly bald head, then reached for the platter of salad—green pepper, tomato, garlic, parsley in vinegar and oil. He was pretty hungry but didn't want to eat birdseed. The boy with the tray drummed his thumb seductively. "'Garro, 'garro," beckoned the boy with the cigarettes. Henry spooned some of the salad beside his mashed potatoes and said, "Cut me some slack here, amigos. Thanks but no thanks."

"Eat," Ahmed said. He held his fork the British way, with his first finger pressed against the back of the tines. "You will feel better."

"I don't feel bad," Henry said.

"Good. I am very glad to know."

"To tell you the truth," Henry said, patting the swell of his stomach, "tonight I think I just might do a little damage." He stabbed a wedge of tomato and with a grin stuffed it into his mouth.

"Sure. It is why you are here."

Not quite, Henry wanted to say. He hadn't traveled all the way to Morocco for a plate of lamb. He'd come here, plain and simple, to die. Something like how elephants were said to march for miles to some special clearing before lying down a final time in the weeds. You do it by yourself, he thought, with some dignity, style, a little privacy. Once you've heard the jury deliver the verdict you pick your spot. Sitting in a travel agency back in Chicago he'd thumbed through a stack of brochures, the insipid agent behind the desk saying, "Many of our clients are opting for Barbados this time of year, but then again maybe what you might enjoy is a cruise to the Caribbean." Henry shook his head, then on south Wabash came upon a store whose broad front windows displayed several maps. He bought a globe embossed in relief. That night in the darkness of his North Side apartment Henry let his fingers run across the world, trying to read the globe like a blind person learning Braille. He wept over the sentence the oncologists had pronounced on him. His tears fell on the oceans, wet the bumpy surfaces of the continents. He hugged the colorful ball to his chest. Then he wiped his eyes, sucked in a breath, let fly a fist. It wasn't fair! He pounded the hard ball until his knuckles ached. In the morning light he saw he'd cracked the globe's paint and dented Australia. It was then that he noticed the tan, flat stretch of the Sahara. His fingertips traced the tips of the Atlas mountains, and then he knew where he'd begin.

He pushed the images from his mind and tried to concentrate on where he was at the moment. He was in Fez, sitting with his friend Ahmed in the back room of a crowded café restaurant. They were in Fez because Ahmed's uncle suggested that Henry take the healing waters of nearby Sidi Harazem and Moulay Yacoub. Henry closed his eyes so he could feel the throbbing pulse of the place. Like an unprepared student taking a difficult test, Henry felt time slipping by too fast. He'd never have enough minutes to answer all the questions.

He tried to center himself so he could stop time from spinning by so quickly, but the passing moments seemed elusive as smoke.

"Something is wrong?" he heard Ahmed say.

Eyes still shut, Henry waved his words away.

"You are very sick now?"

He tried to calm himself. His heart thudded dully in his ears. "Don't be a dunce."

He grew suddenly aware of the smell of cigarette smoke. It wasn't entirely unpleasant. Nor was the room's noise, which grew louder now that he concentrated on it. He opened his eyes, looked about. No women were in the place, he realized. He raised a bowl of what appeared to be lentils to his nose and sniffed—the vegetable smelled faintly of garlic and freshly dug dirt—then put a spoonful beside his mashed potatoes.

It was the first Saturday night after Ramadan, the month of fasting from dawn to dusk. The other tables in the room were filled with noisy young men drinking beer. Seeing them when he entered, Henry's initial reaction was surprise. He hadn't imagined that Moroccan men drank. He'd thought that the only people who drank alcohol in Morocco were foreigners. Then he realized the only bars he'd been to were ones that catered to foreigners. Now he'd see some of the real Morocco. He tasted the garlic and lentils.

He was pleased to have stepped off the path normally taken by tourists. These Moroccans were like any boys out for a drink, he observed. They were loud, rowdy, alternately tender to one another and crude. He watched a pair argue animatedly and seem nearly to come to blows, then drape an arm around the other's neck and bring the other's head so close Henry thought the two were about to kiss. One table of drinkers broke suddenly into song, and now others from the next table joined them, and after a minute everyone but he and Ahmed was singing. It was a sweet song, Henry thought, about courage and love. The boys pounded time with the flat of their hands on the tables. Great courage and love that endures. A somber man with a dark mustache and white apron moved among them, bringing them beers. The bottles were green as summer's fields. The young men kept their empties in front of themselves to display how much they'd drunk. They sipped their beer from squat, clear glasses and sang loud enough to rattle the table tops. Now Henry knew by their laughter the song was bawdy. Then the words of the song stumbled, and a few of the young men clapped their hands, and everyone laughed.

"The food," Ahmed said, "it does not please you."

"No," Henry said, "it's fine." As if to prove it, he scooped a mound of potatoes and lentils into his mouth. "I was just taking a minute to smell the roses."

Ahmed looked about, then frowned. "But there are no flowers here."

"Sure, there are," Henry said. "They're everywhere. Just take a look." He cut a piece of the mechoui with the side of his fork. The tender meat melted on his tongue.

"I want to know, to be taught. The other day you said the world was something else." Ahmed had to shout to be heard. "Was it a clam or an oyster?"

"An oyster," Henry said, remembering.

"Your oyster." Ahmed dropped the hand he was eating with and frowned.

"You know," Henry said, swallowing the meat, "there for the taking. Could be you find a pearl." He picked up a slice of green pepper with his fingers and tasted it. "Hey, I once heard that the bravest person who ever lived was the first one to eat a raw oyster. Imagine, breaking open the shell, wondering what the slimy thing inside would taste like."

"When you are hungry you eat many things." Ahmed nodded knowingly. "The stomach does not have eyes."

"I'd like to think the first one was eaten out of curiosity." Henry ate more of the lamb. "Someone just wanting to put one in his mouth."

"Perhaps."

"What was the strangest thing you've ever eaten?"

"I do not know. I do not eat things that are strange."

"You sure do."

"I do not. Look at me. Look at my arms, my wrists." The young Berber was skinny as a blade of grass. Looking at him, he was all eyes and brown curly hair. "See? I am thin. Not fat like you."

Henry had to smile. "What about that plate of grasshoppers?"

"Locusts," Ahmed said. "You said they pleased you."

A week after they'd met, Ahmed took Henry to his uncle's house in El Youssoufia, south of the Chellah. Late evening, they sat in a narrow room, a seddari lining three walls. Ahmed's aunt entered wordlessly, bringing them tea and plates of almonds and dried locusts, and just as Ahmed began to pour the tea his uncle came in. At the carpet's edge he slipped off his shoes. He said a few words to Ahmed, then shook Henry's hand and pressed the flat of his hand to his chest. Henry smiled and slowly, deliberately, imitated the gesture. It meant he took the friendship to his heart.

"I did," Henry said. "But I normally don't eat grasshoppers."

"I do not too. I told you, my cousins sent them from the South. They are—what is the word?—a delicacy."

The locusts were brittle and crunchy, with the consistency of dried paper and a subtle nutty taste. After Henry had eaten several the uncle told him to break off the heads and not eat the wings. Ahmed translated. On the table before the uncle was a neat row of brown insect heads and a small pile of wings. Henry snapped off the heads and wings. The insects had a darker taste and were considerably less crunchy.

"Yeah, I wish we had a great big plateful of them right now."

"You do not mean it," said Ahmed, laughing. He was chewing a
big mouthful of lamb. The waiter paused at their table, bringing them
a platter of potatoes.

"Just what we need," Henry said, "more *frites*."

Ahmed helped himself to the fries at once. "They are very good.
Eat. Do not be shy. You need to keep up your strength."

Henry patted his stomach. "Oh yeah."

The group of boys nearest them was singing again. Henry caught
the eyes of one, an attractive, clean-faced young man with a wide
spread of green bottles on the table in front of him. Henry counted
eleven, twelve, thirteen. He smiled at the boy's reddened eyes. Ahh,
to be able to drink thirteen bottles of beer! Henry tried to imagine it.
He raised his glass of mineral water in a gesture of friendship toward
the boy's table. To be a young man again, out on a Saturday night,
surrounded by friends, drinking!

It didn't matter where they were, he thought. People were the
same everywhere. A raw energy Henry found romantically attractive
sprang from the place, an unimposing café on a Fez side street. The
energy was what made Henry stop as they passed. He wished he could
drink some of it in. Oh, to be young and have the world on a string!
The boy at the other table stared back drunkenly, then dropped his
head and spoke to his friends.

"You like the water," Ahmed said, "to raise it in the air."

"I was toasting the drinkers."

"Sure." Ahmed again filled both cheeks and chewed.

From behind the rows of locust heads the uncle said he had a
brother-in-law who lived in Fez. If they traveled there after Ramadan,
they'd have a place to stay. Henry and Ahmed drove north to Kenitra
and then east to Meknès and then up to the Middle Atlas mountains,
passing fields of wheat and sunflowers and barley, groves of oranges,
palm, olives beginning to ripen on twisted trees. As the sun set they
drove along the dusty edge of the Ville Nouvelle, where a knot of

boys kicked a ball in a clearing beside a pile of broken stone and
many orange peels, where every other minute a rooster crowed. The
boys gathered around the car, a rented Peugeot, hanging on the open
windows, trailing their fingertips along the grime on its doors and
hood. They pointed Ahmed and Henry toward a squat building. A
light bulb dangled dimly inside a wooden door. The first room was
bare, save for a stack of cardboard boxes on top of a bench in the
shadows and, at eye level, a drooping clothesline. A water faucet a
foot off the floor protruded from the wall. In the other room were
two small sofas and a table upon which rested a small television
whose black-and-white picture rolled continuously. It took Henry
a while to realize the place was windowless. Taped to one wall were
pictures of oiled weight lifters scissored from magazines and a torn
poster of the singer Madonna leaning forward to display her cleavage,
her red lips protruding in an exaggerated kiss. On the opposite wall
hung a cardboard print, most likely French-made, of an unsmiling
mother holding a baby. The brother-in-law made a pot of tea, boiling
the water on a hot plate beneath the bench, and insisted they stay
with him. He crushed a water bug beneath his sandal after picking it
out from inside his box of sugar cubes. "All I have is yours," he told
Henry. "The honor's mine," Henry said, pressing his hand against his
chest.

"You must stay for a long time, long as you like," the brother-
in-law said. Then he and Ahmed talked about their families, shifting
from English to Berber. On the small TV, its rabbit-ear antennas
covered with crinkled tinfoil, Henry watched the rolling image of an
Egyptian soap opera.

The next afternoon they drove to Sidi Harazem. The radioactive
waters there were so potent they were said to break up kidney stones,
cure liver problems, disorders of the bladder, stomach, intestine,
spleen. Further, Ahmed claimed, it was well known that drinking
a cup fresh from the warm springs made you urinate within ten

minutes. No matter how blocked your tubes, you had no choice.
How do you know all this? Henry asked, as Ahmed pointed to a
rutted field filled with parked cars and tour buses. Henry pulled the
car off the road. Ahmed said he and the brother-in-law had a long
talk after Henry had fallen asleep. The brother-in-law had left by the
time Henry awoke, on some kind of business in Sefrou.

The land around the spa at Sidi Harazem was as desolate as the
moon. A nondescript hotel for tourists stood baking in the sun.
Concrete slabs led to a large rectangular fount and swimming pool.
Water from the natural springs flowed freely from the many taps
on the fount's sides. They stood on the edge of the crowd. "Perhaps
here," Ahmed shouted, before the force of the crowds separated them,
"you will find a cure for the crab in your stomach."

Already several children gathered around them, reaching for
Henry's hands. "Think so?" Henry yelled. "You can't be serious."

The children thrust earthenware cups at Henry, trying to lead
him to the fountain. Ahmed cast his eyes down as if he'd been
insulted. "Yes, but of course. Or else I would not have said it."

There was a palpable excitement in the air. The children bounced
around Henry like rubber balls. "Hocus-pocus," Henry said. "Lead
on."

Like a giant among elves he let the children take his hands—he
followed where they pulled—and have him. The water was so warm
Henry nearly spat it out. Then he held it in his mouth and swallowed.
It had a clean, full taste. He drank from each cup the children offered
him. Water spilled down his chin, wet his neck and chest, darkened
his shirt. The children remained around him, requesting dirhams.
Henry gave them what he had.

"All I have is yours," he told them, and then he understood
that the brother-in-law's story about business in Sefrou was a lie
that would enable Henry and Ahmed to have the tiny place for
themselves. Henry marveled at the stranger's generosity. Then he

belched with such rich wetness it made the children laugh. The
boys laughed openly, heads back. The girls giggled behind their
hands. Henry loosened another belch. It rattled the air. His stomach
had never felt so full of water. He laughed at himself because of it.
Moments later, after he and Ahmed hurried to the men's toilet, as
they stood together over an open trough, Henry let loose a stream
that was so copious he felt lightheaded when he was through.

He looked across the table at Ahmed to share the memory, but
Ahmed seemed displeased.

"Eat," Ahmed said. "We should soon leave."

"What's the rush?" Henry broke off a piece of bread. "The food's
not going anywhere. We've got all night."

"There is no rush," said Ahmed. Carefully he poured some
bottled water into his glass. "It is just—" He stared at Henry, then
raised his eyebrows and appeared to drain all feeling from his face.

"Come on," Henry said. "Spit it out." Then he saw that the
young men at the next table were watching them, laughing. When
Henry's gaze caught the eyes of the drunken boy, the boy laughed and
sneered, then put his lips together and made a kissing sound.

The insult was clear enough in any language.

Henry's mouth went dry from it. As an adult he led a life that
avoided unpleasantness. As a child he'd been victim of the usual
scrapes, the fat boy taunted by the bullies on the playground,
tripped whenever he drew near. He learned to avoid playgrounds.
He learned to avoid gangs of boys. One winter when he was in high
school a group of his classmates mocked him for wearing a woolen
cap with earflaps. The cap smelled faintly of mothballs and always
made Henry picture the closet where his mother stored it along with
extra scarves and gloves in neatly labeled boxes—GOODSON, WINTER
HATS—beneath the smooth folds of plastic dry-cleaning bags. As
young Henry tried to make his escape, the boys—cool, hatless, the
type of boys girls liked—snatched his cap from his head and tossed it

back and forth, playing keep-away. Henry ran between them, trying
desperately to get it back. He imagined the disappointment on his
mother's face if he were to come home without it. Then the strongest
and handsomest of the boys spat into Henry's cap before throwing
it to the next boy, who snickered and did the same, until all of the
boys had spat in the cap. By the time it was given back to him Henry
was in tears. He held it in his hands like a bowl as the boys circled
him, laughing. Henry tipped the cap to spill the spit on the ground.
Only a little of the spit trickled out. The rest had soaked into his cap.
Oh! Henry thought, breathless. There was nothing to do but put it
on his head, twist the visor, walk away. It was a moment of pride or
foolishness that formed what he was to become. Another boy would
have cried for help and run. Another would have thrown the ruined
cap away. Another would have lunged at the bullies and despite their
numbers fought them.

Ahmed turned and said something in Arabic to the boys at the
next table. Henry leaned forward in his chair. One of the boys with
whom Ahmed was talking stood and shoved Ahmed's shoulder.

Henry stood and shouted, "Hey, you don't need to do that."

"*Tante*," called one of the drunken boys.

"I said get your hands off him!" Henry shouted.

"No," Ahmed was saying, "sit down."

"This is my fight," Henry said, raising his hands to chest level,
balling them into fists. The young men behind the beer bottles
hooted and jeered. The boy who'd made the kissing sound stood
and pointed a finger at Henry, then unleashed a string of curses that
silenced the room. Henry pointed at the young man and said, "You
don't think I can fight, do you, you dumb drunk, I can fight, you
jerk, come on, come on, let's mix it up," trying to match the power
and strength of the boy's words. He felt a delicious excitement.

The boy swept his hand drunkenly, knocking down several of
the empty bottles in front of him. The bottles tumbled like tenpins,

crashed to the floor. Henry swept his hand down too. He knocked over his water glass and upset the platter of salad and then managed to cover the back of his hand with mashed potatoes, which he then flung at the shouting boy. The potatoes spotted the boy's shirt. The boy threw a beer bottle. It whizzed by Henry's ear. Then the waiter ran in between them, and the boy's friends pulled him back and surrounded him like a great wave, and then the wave receded and there was a great deal of shouting and finger-pointing. The boy and the waiter were arguing, nearly bumping chests, faces a whisker's length away. Henry wanted to yell some more but there was no one else to yell at. He wiped the mashed potatoes from his fingers with a napkin. It was then he heard his pulse pounding happily like a hammer in his ears.

"There were at least thirty of them, weren't there?" Henry said the next morning as they drove from the city.

"More," said Ahmed. "I think perhaps thirty-five."

"Maybe forty." His eyes gazed at the clear road ahead. "Five tables, easy, with maybe eight, nine guys sitting at each one."

"Many were there," Ahmed said conclusively.

"It was a gang," said Henry. "A gang. And I stood up to them."

"I was afraid you would fight them all," Ahmed said with a laugh.

A wide grin creased Henry's face. "So was I." He gripped the steering wheel hard for a moment, then laughed and slapped the dash. "And I would have, by God, if I had to."

"Sure."

"Believe you me, I would have bloodied a lot of noses."

"Oh, sure."

"The entire gang."

"Every one."

"Like Muhammed Ali."

"Of course."

"Joe Louis. Rocky Graziano."

"The champ."

"Henry Goodson, heavyweight champion." He laughed, slapped his abdomen. "Even though it's full of cancer, it's good to know I've got guts."

They drove for a while in silence, winding their way up the soft gray checkerboard of mountain. The concrete road was barely wide enough to hold two compact cars. Henry had to pull the Peugeot over and drive on the shoulder whenever another car—rear wheels spitting rocks—passed them. In the fields beyond the dusty windshield, shepherds tended their flocks of goats and sheep. Henry drove slowly so he could take it all in. The graceful curve of the land, the expertly terraced gardens, the simple stone houses behind which tethered donkeys grazed, flicking away flies with their tails. In one field, women were making stacks of freshly cut wheat. They carried the sheaths on their heads, threw them down on mounded stacks. Henry and Ahmed drove past a shepherd squatting indecorously beside a patch of cactus, holding up his djellaba's hem. The man stared abjectly at the ground, as if he were carved of wood, while around him his flock roamed the mountainside. In the wind the bells around the animals' necks rang softly.

"That young man from last night," Ahmed said, "he makes me think of an old joke."

"I'm all ears," said Henry.

"There are two guys," Ahmed began, "talking about what happened to them in the jungle. There they are attacked by a fierce lion. The lion says to all those he attacks, 'Hey, I will give you a choice. Either I screw you in the ass or I kill you.' So the first guy asks his friend, 'When you met the lion in the jungle, what did he do to you?' The second guy answers, 'Well, he killed me.'"

Henry laughed. "I'll have to remember that one."

"I was thinking of last night," Ahmed said.

They drove for a while in silence.

"I'm an awfully easy target," Henry said finally. "Don't worry yourself about it. People have been making fun of me for years."

"That is sad. I am very sorry." Ahmed paused. "I think it is difficult for some to endure Ramadan. I have heard there is a thirst. Myself, I do not drink but for someone with a thirst, to go for a whole month—"

"I never knew Muslims drank."

"Oh, sure. Muslims are people, like everyone."

"They could have been kids in a bar in my hometown."

"Sure. We are all Adam's sons, sons of the first prophet."

"You really believe that?"

Ahmed seemed shocked. "Yes. You do not?"

"I know if you go back far enough we're all related. But I think it's just as possible we're all sons of the same monkey."

"You do not believe in Adam? Do you believe in Salih? Houd? Shoaib? Noah? Moses?"

"Those last two, sure. Them I believe in."

Ahmed looked amazed. "But you think Adam was a monkey?"

"The first man? He was a caveman. You know, some half-naked lowbrow fighting saber-toothed tigers with a spear."

"I do not think you can pick and choose. Either we are from God or we are not."

"Could be." Henry drove down the center of the road until a truck wanting to pass blinked its yellow headlights and forced him off onto the shoulder.

The sulfur and sodium baths of Moulay Yacoub were at the bottom of a hill terraced by stalls offering trinkets and food. Men waved away flies with strands of palm. A girl blew notes from a water whistle shaped like a bird. Beggars and cripples squatted alongside the concrete steps, mumbling to all who passed. They held their hands out or rolled their eyes up at Henry, who sprinkled them with dirhams and fifty- and twenty-centime pieces until his pockets were empty of change.

He and Ahmed walked down a few steps past a cage where they paid to enter. Next to the cage hung a sign in both Arabic and French listing the diseases the waters were known to cure. At Henry's request Ahmed began translating. Nearly every ailment known to modern science was listed. Below the sign was official assurance that no disease brought to the baths could be transmitted to another due to the water's high temperature and mineral content.

Henry changed in a stall barely bigger than a phone booth and put his belongings along with Ahmed's in a plastic bucket, which a man behind a counter stored. He tried not to look at Ahmed's bare chest and legs. Ahmed wore brown bikini briefs. From behind he was as hairless and slender as a girl. Henry understood how the boy in the restaurant could have thought he was an old French poof out with his young Moroccan whore. Henry wore large yellow boxer shorts pulled up to the widest part of his gut, which protruded roundly. In a mirror slanting against the far wall he looked like Oliver Hardy.

The air smelled of boiled eggs, which grew increasingly more rotten as they neared the pool. Already Henry could feel the water's heat. The thick air left a metallic taste on his tongue. They rounded a corner. Light streaked from the glassed-in ceiling, between dark wooden beams. From the far wall gushed water fresh from the hot springs.

A veil of mist hung in the room. Clinging to the pool's sides were several old men with shaved heads. So that's what they look like without their turbans and skullcaps, Henry thought. A few stood as he approached. Their chests and arms were covered with dark scabs or red sores, and now Henry noticed several cripples—twisted legs floating just beneath the water's surface—and one man so skeletal

Henry marveled at the fact he was alive. Skin stretched tight as a drum over bones, little more. The man's eyelids drooped over his jaundiced eyes. Gray water swirled viciously around them all.

He thought about turning back. Then the skeletal man's eyes rolled up and met his, and the skull face broke into a smile. For a moment Henry saw himself as the others in the pool saw him—a pale white fat man wearing preposterous yellow boxer shorts. Could they see the death growing like a mound of dough within him, or did they see only what the young men in the café restaurant had seen? What did the beggars on the steps outside see as he passed them? And Ahmed, what did he see? Did Ahmed know that young Henry had let the lion take him? Though now, in his physical condition, he felt beyond anything much more than concealed admiration, abstract desire. He smiled back at the skeleton, who strangely connected him to these men in this desperate pool. He recognized in them all a patient sorrow.

Henry slipped into the water cautiously. The others moved back to give him room. The water was surprisingly hot but not so hot he couldn't take it. The odor of bad eggs had filled his lungs, and he breathed out deeply, then in, out, then again in, as he spread his arms, bent his knees and let the hot water rise to his neck, then his chin, and then for a moment he slid beneath the surface and let all that was there surround him.

As he broke surface one of the bald men took his hand and led him to the far wall and the gushing mouth of the hot springs. At first Henry held back—the water was too hot—but then he gave in and allowed the man to lead him to the pool's hottest point. "*Nasrani,*" one man said, "you follow, OK?" Henry said OK. The other men spoke to him in Arabic. They splashed hot water on their arms and chests, washing themselves, then looked up at him and nodded. He did as they did. The men smiled, encouraging him. Henry smiled back, then splashed more of the very hot water on his chest and arms.

Then a deep voice began to sing, sound slicing the air like a knife. The others in the pool sang the word *Allah*, and then the lead sang a line that twisted in the silence like rising smoke. Around Henry the others repeatedly sang the word *Allah*. Even the sickest of the men sang, smiles wrinkling their toothless faces. The bass voice hurried ahead, driving his dark sound up into the moist hollow of the room. The other men followed with their string of Allahs. From across the pool Henry could see Ahmed singing. Henry tried his best to sing along too. Then the man who had Henry follow him waded beside him, put an ear to Henry's mouth, and corrected his pronunciation.

"*Allah ya Moulana!*" Henry sang, "*Allah Allah, ya'Allah Moulana!*" He drew in a breath and asked what the words meant.

The man smiled. "Allah O our Master! Allah Allah, O Allah our Master!"

The nasheed bounced off the walls, the glass ceiling, the dark wooden beams, the water. The little room could barely contain the joyous sound.

The singers led Henry to the pool's opposite side, where on a ledge several men were giving other men rub-downs. A dark burly man with a thick mustache pulled Henry up from the water like a mighty fish, then had him sit up beside the pool and began massaging his back and neck. The man had Henry lie flat on his back as he kneaded Henry's arms and legs, then turned Henry over on his stomach and worked him over, twisting his limbs, bending Henry's flesh, twisting Henry's back, cracking Henry's neck, cupping his own hands and popping them up and down Henry's spine. As the man finished with each limb he made a kissing sound, then popped Henry's skin with a hard, hollow-handed slap.

All the while the men in the pool were singing. They took Henry's hands again as the dark man slipped him back into the hot pool.

A few hours later in the Marhaba, a café restaurant upstairs, Henry and Ahmed sat at a table sipping mint tea. Henry's skin tingled and glowed. He felt aware of muscles he'd long forgotten about. A smile he couldn't erase hung on his face.

"That washed the States right out of me," Henry said.

"Good," Ahmed said. There was a sparkle in his eyes, a pink blush on his cheeks. "Or is that a bad thing?"

Henry considered the death waiting inside him, lying coiled like a sleeping snake. Then he looked about and sighed. He had the sensation he'd just entered the nearly empty room and was seeing it for the first time—the stark afternoon light slanting through a wall of open windows, hotly falling on the wooden tables and faded carpets, the flies circling the air that quivered with the beggars' soft staccato from the steps below, a sudden breeze from the windows, on his tongue the sweet bite of mint tea.

"No," Henry said, "it's a good thing."

THE SURRENDER

He learned to pace his day by the color of the sky. Beyond the tall palm trees lining the walkway that separated the wide boulevard, the cloudless blue of a perfect afternoon was fading to silver. Soon the muezzin from the Grand Mosque would begin the call to evening prayer. Then the muezzins from the many other mosques would begin their calls, and for a full minute or more the air would throb with song and black would streak the sky and it would be night. Peter looked forward to night, particularly this night, Sunday, because on Sundays everyone in Rabat promenaded up and down the boulevard. He enjoyed the sight of them, walking with them. Walking with the crowds made him feel less alone.

No matter that he'd come to Morocco as a committee's compromise. The assignment might shore his bid for promotion, nudge his salary, earn him fewer classes, classes which Peter taught not nearly as well or enthusiastically as when he was young. When he was young he'd been full of fire. Now, after a decade of teaching, he'd come to expect the kiss on the cheek, the knife to the back. Peter fervently believed that in the order of things deans ranked slightly below devils and vampires. Twice he'd been refused promotion because of recommendations made by deans. So he joined the cynics who gathered each morning in the history department mailroom to sip bitter coffee and trade complaints and mordant jokes. They analyzed everything from what their department chair was overheard whispering in the hallway to the size of the potholes in the faculty parking lot.

Buried by student papers and exams, he'd let his research slide. After the divorce, Ellen became more trim and lovely than she'd been on the day they'd married but markedly guarded in an off-handed, upbeat way that clearly told Peter he was on the outside, an enemy. Rachel was five, in kindergarten, very much her mother's daughter and, since he'd arrived in Morocco, very much on her lonely father's mind.

"Dear Rachel," the postcard he'd sent that morning began, "What fruit do ghosts most like to eat? Boo-berries! Love, Dad." On the other side was a picture of a handsome young Arab on camelback. Before Peter mailed the card he drew a bubble next to the camel's mouth and inside it wrote, "Come away with me to my kasbah!" He hoped Rachel would smile since he'd made the animal, rather than the man, talk.

He stepped toward the fountain across from the railroad station, hand in the side pockets of his pants. Soon it would be night. He was wearing a gray corduroy jacket that was slightly darker than the sky. He expected the evening to be cool. His shirt was open at the neck. His mouth turned down naturally into a frown. That morning he had decided not to shave, thinking a slight beard would make him look more like a Moroccan. In another day or two he'd resemble Yasser Arafat, he thought, though certainly he was more handsome, his nose not nearly as long, face not as pinched. Peter was dark, swarthy, sometimes mistaken for a Spaniard by the boys who approached him, wanting to lead him to some shop.

When the boys spoke to him in Spanish, he smiled and responded in Spanish. When in French, his tongue tried answering in French though like legs unused to shoes he'd trip after the first few sentences. The street boys leapt from language to language like playful goats on a craggy hillside. They knew Moroccan Arabic, several Berber dialects, French, English, Spanish, Italian, German, even some Russian. He'd lumber his way through conversations with them, butchering nuance, murdering syntax, with a slight smile on his face. I wasn't much different from you when I was a boy, he'd try to tell them in as many languages as he could. Now I'm just trying to get by from one day to the next. He lifted his wire-rimmed glasses from his face and dipped them into the water at the edge of the fountain as a pair of women in stylish djellabas and light-blue head scarves walked past without a glance. He dried the lenses of his glasses on the front of his shirt as he walked on.

On either side of him a row of towering palms, barks covered with ivy, swayed their fronds in the early evening breeze. The walkway itself was wide and edged with grass and three-pronged streetlights that were not yet lit. Beyond the trees on both sides streamed the city's traffic. People were careful not to step on the grass, Peter observed, and then no sooner had he made the generalization than he saw a man bound onto a patch of the grass and run behind one of the palms. The man was chasing a child, who ran laughing from one tree to the next. The father held out his arms like a pretend monster, howling, calling to the child as he chased. The child giggled with glee. Then the man scooped the child up into his arms, and the child resisted, still absorbed in the game, then looped both arms around the father's neck, nuzzling his shirt.

"You have a beautiful child," Peter said in French and smiled.

The child's dark eyes looked up suddenly at the father and then back at this stranger who'd dared to speak to them on the street. Peter smiled and gave the man a nod. The man's face showed no expression.

Then just as quickly as their eyes had met the pair was behind him. Peter cleared his face. As he continued on his way he wondered what his reaction would be if he were with Rachel in a park back in the States and a foreigner smiled, told him she was beautiful. For a moment he ached with longing for his daughter. What had he done to have lost her? What hadn't he done? He pulled in a sudden breath, gazed across the traffic at a man in a dark blue business suit and red fez walking past the first row of tables outside the Hotel Balima.

"I must not have been ready," he said softly, hardly moving his lips, the words more exhalation than voice. He slowed his pace and pushed his hands into his pants pockets, recalling the day he'd gathered his notes and the drafts of the book that was supposed to make him a full professor and with melodramatic flair set it all on fire. A veiled figure with downcast eyes hobbled past, right leg shorter than the left. Then the first cry of the muezzin pierced the air that now was as dark as his jacket. He shivered as the call ran down his spine to his unpolished shoes, and then a second muezzin from another mosque took up the call, and then another, and another. The sounds spun round his head like whirling whips, then turned into song, harmony in praise of an indivisible God. How could anyone not answer the call, feel the urge to submit, fall to his knees, press forehead to the earth?

It was why Muslim hats had no brims. He smiled gently. He'd always been good at facts. Expressing feelings was where he stuttered. He had a historian's mind that retained facts in their proper folders, filed the folders in the proper drawers. Rabat was the capital of Morocco, a constitutional monarchy that regained its full freedom in 1956 under Sultan Sidi Mohammed V, who returned triumphantly from exile in Madagascar—

Ellen had said, "What in God's name are you burning?"

"Just words," he had answered, just a pile of senseless words. He crossed against the traffic, fingering the dirhams and fifty-centime pieces he kept in his pockets for beggars. One crouched there in a doorway with her child. Since Peter walked up and down the boulevard nearly every night at this time, he knew all the beggars and they all knew him, and he had a coin for every one. The woman murmured to him, and the child in her lap opened its brown eyes. Peter dropped a coin into her outstretched palm, saying, "Just a pile of senseless words, mademoiselle," then turned and walked several steps and entered a patisserie thinking how he should have told Ellen that perhaps the right words might have eased the load he carried at work by giving him a sense of true worth and dignity, which in turn might have made him less objectionable to be around, might have returned him to the hopeful man she married, not the bitter cinder she disbelievingly stared at in their backyard.

He told the young Moroccan behind the counter he wanted a café au lait and then pointed to the sugared puffs and pastries, which she removed from the trays beneath the glass counter with silver tongs and placed on a paper doily on a white dish. He was suddenly hungry. The young woman's hair was covered by a three-cornered scarf that matched her blouse, buttoned modestly to her neck. He accepted the plate and cup and saucer, then asked the girl for an extra paper napkin, on which he placed the two sugared puffs. He raised a finger and told the girl wait, he'd be right back.

He'd read that the Moroccan per capita consumption of sugar ranked among the highest in the world. Drinking their mint tea and eating bastilla and sampling some of their honeyed pastries made him believe it, he thought, as he carried the sugared puffs to the beggar woman and her child.

"I suspect you'd enjoy these as much as I would," he said, leaning down to hand the woman the sweets. Then he returned to the patisserie and chose a table near the windows where he'd be able to look out onto the street.

Even after five years grass still wouldn't grow in the circle where he'd made the fire. It was because of the gasoline, how it had soaked into the earth. He bit a sweet square filled with cocoa-flavored cream, sipped his coffee. Ellen's therapist said the bonfire symbolized the ritual murder of their marriage and future. Peter told Ellen where her therapist could shove that theory. He glanced at a man in suit and tie sitting by himself several tables away. The Moroccan in the suit lifted to his open mouth a pastry shaped like a horn.

Peter pulled several postcards from the inside pocket of his jacket and sorted through them, looking for one Rachel would like. For a few moments he stared at a snake charmer from Marrakesh seated in front of three fierce-looking cobras, then chose a Berber shepherd standing guard over his flock. The patisserie door swung open, then banged closed.

"Dear Rachel," he wrote, "Where do sheep get their hair cut? At the baa baa shop! Miss you. Dad." Then he took the other card and flipped it over and scribbled, "Dear Ellen, Can you guess why this picture reminds me of you, your lawyer, and your therapist?"

He addressed and stamped both cards, then thought better of it. He couldn't send the cobra card to Ellen. They were a modern couple. Their divorce was amicable. Appearances were everything, particularly where Rachel was involved. Both the lawyer and the therapist tried to get Ellen into bed after the papers were signed, the property distributed, everything else settled. She seemed flattered when she told him, as if the offers somehow asserted her new independence, as if the men's interest in her meant now she and Peter were really divorced. She was drinking white wine from a long-stemmed glass and became angry at him after word of the solicitations made him upset.

Something was tugging at the sleeve of his jacket so slightly that at first Peter tried to brush it away. It was a boy with a strangely familiar face, wearing a smudged shirt, standing just behind him, so close Peter could smell the sweetness of his sweat. The boy tilted his head to one side and gave Peter a coy smile as he raised a tiny hand to the middle of his chest, then slowly pushed the hand outward in the street beggar's familiar gesture. His teeth were square and very white and made Peter think again of Rachel. Then the man in the suit scraped his chair back along the wooden floor and gave a shout.

Though the shout was in Arabic Peter understood it was directed at the young beggar, disapproval for his bold entry into the patisserie.

Peter wondered what he could do to restore the easy, dreamy quiet of the place as night grew ever darker outside the windows and he awaited the evening promenade. The boy crouched beside Peter's chair, and the Moroccan shouted at him and pointed, and the girl in the three-cornered scarf hurried out from behind the counter, a straw broom in her hands.

"It's OK," Peter said, raising his hands. "He's OK. The boy's OK." Though he wasn't, Peter realized. He'd seen him around the city before. The boy was a fraud, a charlatan. The angry man continued to shout at the young woman with the broom, no doubt encouraging her to sweep the little beggar into the gutter. Peter stood and scowled at him and then pulled out the chair beside his, pushing the boy into it.

"*Non*," the young woman with the broom began, and then explained in French that under no circumstances would the boy be allowed to remain. He belonged out on the street, she explained. This wasn't a café, she told Peter, her voice thick with scorn. If the boy didn't leave immediately she'd have to call the authorities. The man in the suit stood behind his chair and wiped his mouth angrily with his napkin, then shouted at Peter and flung the napkin to his table with disgust. The boy sat still, head down, hands at his sides. The angle of the boy's head and exposed neck made Peter think suddenly of a guillotine. He stared for a moment at his postcards and uneaten pastry, his coffee now skimmed over by a film of milk. He looked past the girl with the broom. Above the counter was a framed portrait of King Hassan II in a sky-blue jacket, staring pensively.

"I think even if the King himself were here," Peter said in English, "he'd respect my right to invite a guest to sit at my table." He studied the girl's eyes to see if she understood. If she did, her eyes showed nothing. "You're much too young to be a slave to rules," he told her in French. To the man who was outraged he said, "And you're a donkey's ass." He gathered his postcards and uneaten sweets, then pushed the boy ahead of him out the doorway.

He'd always been pompous when he felt he was right, he thought, striding down the boulevard. The night was surprisingly cool and dark. How many times in arguments did Ellen toss that accusation at him? He always denied it. It made him argue all the more. But it *was* pompous to make such a show over nothing. He realized the beggar boy was trailing him, so he turned and handed the little faker the pastries and, unthinkingly, the two postcards beneath the paper doily.

The boy bent slightly at the waist and stuffed the sweets into his mouth, a soft rain of powdered sugar spilling from his hands. The sugar glistened in the glare of the streetlights. No mistake, Peter thought, studying the boy's face. This was the crippled beggar who'd crawled toward him on the sidewalk the afternoon he'd arrived in Rabat. He hadn't given the boy anything—he'd been told to ignore the beggars, though after a few days in the country his heart thawed—but the image of the crippled boy had stayed with him. Now the cripple stood behind him on two sound legs, licking sugar from his dirty fingers.

"Why aren't you crawling around on the ground?" Peter said.

The boy's eyes opened wide and the pupils darkened, like a cornered animal.

"I know you're a liar, a cheat. I've seen you begging outside the Hotel Terminus. Don't pretend you don't understand."

The boy sucked crumbs and sugar from the doily.

Clearly angry, Peter shook his head. He'd had a hard go of it trying to adjust. He didn't appreciate being deceived. Only two days ago, teaching at the university, trying to engage the sixty or so students scattered in his classroom—some listening raptly, a handful doodling or taking notes, others gazing out the window or rocking in their chairs as they read from another book—there was a sharp knock on his door. Peter was just reaching the point in his lecture where abstractions turned concrete, when meaning and significance might congeal in their minds. He opened the door quickly, prepared to wave the interruption away. A young man asked if he could deliver a note. In his hands was a folded piece of paper. Peter glanced back at the class and told the young man to wait, then closed the door to resume his lecture. The intruder rapped again on the door, pushed it open, said, "Please, there is so little time." Then instead of taking only a moment to hand the note to one of the students, the young man walked to the center of the room and addressed the class in Arabic.

Some students clapped, stomped their feet, whistled shrilly. Others hushed the ones making noise. The man read his message without pause, his voice rising to a shout. More students were clapping now or pounding their notebooks against their tables. Peter retreated to a corner of the classroom, watching his lesson unwind. The young speechmaker rushed from the room, followed closely by several students. The rest scooped up their books and papers, everyone speaking at once. Peter stopped a young woman who'd given careful attention to his lesson and asked what had just happened. She told him the students were planning a strike in solidarity with the Palestinian people.

Peter thanked her, walked to the doorway, looked back at the empty classroom. Several crushed cigarette butts along with a few sheets of loose-leaf paper lay scattered on the floor. He turned off the overhead lights, shut the door.

So much here baffled him that he was pleased whenever he was sure of something. He thought that at least he could recognize poverty. He thought that the deformed and destitute were what they appeared to be. Each day they were the same, in the same place. The poor were one of the few consistent things he experienced. Now as he stood on the street looking back on the boy who'd pretended to be lame he felt as aggravated as if he'd caught a beggar slipping behind the wheel of a fancy car and, radio blaring, driving off to a mansion in the suburbs. "Where are your crippled legs now?" he asked the boy.

"Hey you, he don't speak."

A voice from the curb. Peter turned. A boy in a navy-blue stocking cap and dark inside-out sweatshirt pointed at Peter and then at the beggar boy. "In his mouth there is a tongue, but it is broke since he was a baby."

"Broken," Peter said. "How do you know this?"

The boy in the stocking cap grabbed the other by the shirt and drew him close, then pulled down on his jaw. "See, there is his tongue." He grasped it with his fingers, gave it a hard squeeze. Then he punched the boy's arm and kneed him sharply in the groin. The boy dropped the postcards and doily and fell to the ground. "See, he don't make no sound."

"You don't have to be so rough."

"He don't mind. We beat him up all the time."

"You shouldn't."

The boy stared at Peter, as if considering his words. Peter crouched over the mute boy. His eyes were glassy with tears and stared, unmoving, at the tires of a parked car. Peter lifted the boy to his feet. The other picked up the doily and postcards.

"Do you know where he lives?"

"Sure. In the mellah."

"Will you take me there?"

"Twenty dirhams, sure."

Peter laughed. The mute boy seemed to have caught his breath and was no longer crying. "Tell me your name."

"Abdu. You got a name?"

Peter told him. The three started down the boulevard. "Abdu, I'd be a fool to give you twenty dirhams to take me to the mellah, which is a place I know well."

"Any way you like, but you don't know which zanka. Give me eighteen."

"Once I'm there all I'll have to do is ask."

"There won't be nobody to understand you. Sixteen dirhams. Hey, I know every place and can show you everything."

"But all I want is to take this boy home." The boy was touching the tips of Peter's fingers. Abdu walked backward a few paces ahead of them, eyes fixed on the man's face. "I'll tell you what, Abdu, for helping me I'll give you two dirhams."

"Find the fucking place yourself," Abdu said. He turned his back on the pair.

"Sure," Peter said after a few moments. "If that's what you'd like."

Abdu turned. "I like fifteen dirhams."

"Five," Peter said, "and I want you to promise never to hit him again."

"No problem," Abdu said with a smile. "I don't hit him no more for five dirhams. And I take you to his house for another ten."

Peter paused to give a coin to a blind beggar. The mute boy still held Peter's hand. Abdu watched, arms folded across his sweatshirt. "All right," Peter said, "six dirhams for not hitting the boy again and telling me everything you know about him."

Abdu laughed. "You ask for this and this and this and this and you don't give me nothing."

"There are more important things in the world than money."

"Sure. That's what everybody say when they got a whole lot in their pocket." He was sniffing the air. "You smell that?" They had walked the length of the boulevard, and now the avenue narrowed into a commercial lane lined with starkly lit shops and sidewalk peddlers offering everything from food to jewelry. At the end of the street were the ancient walls that opened into Rabat's medina. Abdu had stopped walking and stared into the window of a grill. Several

young Moroccans were inside, sipping bottles of Coca-Cola and
smoking cigarettes as they stood around a pinball machine. Peter
pushed the door open, led the boys to a table, then ordered from
a low glass case displaying roasted chickens and a variety of meats.
He returned to the table with half a chicken, a plateful of grilled
kefta, salad, bread, a liter bottle of Sidi Ali mineral water, and many
napkins.

Abdu dug into the food at once. Peter raised a piece of bread
to the mute boy's lips and tempted him with a ball of kefta. Once
the boy began, he ate as energetically as Abdu. Peter drank a cup of
water and encouraged the boys to eat the salad after they'd finished
the meats and bread. Abdu sucked his fingers loudly when he
was through, then drew the two postcards out from beneath his
sweatshirt.

"My cards," Peter said.

Since both were bent Abdu smoothed them with his hands. He
studied their pictures, then asked Peter to read what he'd written.

"The one with the three snakes is to my wife." He stared at the
words he'd put there. Instead he said, "So I wrote, 'Dear Ellen, I love
you and miss you more than I'll ever be able to say.'"

"You love her very much," Abdu said, nodding. "It is in your
eyes."

"Sure." Peter tried to laugh, then told the boy the joke about
where sheep get their hair cut.

Abdu shook his head. "It is not a good joke. I don't think men
take sheeps to a barber." He rubbed his nose vigorously with the back
of his hand. "Listen, I tell you a good joke. One about Djoha, the old
man from the South."

Peter nodded.

"Once Djoha had a rooster that he needed every morning to
wake up, but the rooster begins to crow at all the wrong times. On
the first day one hour late, on the next two hours, then three, until

Djoha goes later and later to his job. His boss tells him to be on time or else. So Djoha takes his rooster to the city to the man who fixes broken clocks. Djoha asks if he can fix his broken rooster. The man says he will do what he can. Djoha leaves and the man kills the rooster and makes of him a very nice tajine. After he eats he puts all the bones into a bowl. The next day Djoha comes back to see if his rooster is fixed. The man shows Djoha the bowl of bones"—Abdu pointed to the pile of chicken bones on the table—"and says, 'Well, as you can see he is not fixed yet, but be patient I am still working on it.'"

Peter and Abdu laughed. The other boy was eating crumbs from the table. Abdu pulled off his stocking cap and fiercely scratched his head for several moments. Peter asked, "Can he hear?" He pointed to the mute boy. Abdu settled on a spot that seemed to require vigorous scratching. Peter saw that his eyelashes were thick and long and, for a boy, rather lovely. He picked the postcards up from the table and put them in the inside pocket of his jacket. Beneath the dirt on Abdu's face his sallow complexion was smooth and fair.

"Maybe he don't want to," Abdu said.

Peter frowned. "Hearing's not something you want or don't want."

"If all the time they yell at you." Abdu shrugged. He sucked one of his fingers. "He's a Jew, I think."

"What's that got to do with whether he can hear?"

Abdu raised his eyebrows, as if considering the question. He lowered his head, put on his stocking cap, and spoke sharply to the boy in Arabic. The boy watched Abdu's face, then averted his eyes and licked a fingertip and reached for another crumb.

"We'd better go," Peter said. He reached for the mute boy's hand.

Outside the crowds were heavy, walking to and from the medina's walls. Peter held the mute beggar's hand tightly. He knew Abdu would stay close because he expected to be paid. The dark sky above sparkled with stars and held a narrow crescent of moon. A pair of

ghaitas, the horns shrill and piercing, accompanied by the furious
beating of barrel drums played from a loudspeaker outside a shop.
Peter listened to the dizzy, hypnotic music. If he had been alone he
would have lingered beneath the speaker, entered the shop, tried
to strike up a conversation, but the boy's hand pulled him past the
sound. He was certain now the child was deaf. Peter knew the way to
the mellah and turned and started heading toward the river outside
the medina's walls until Abdu grabbed his free hand and said he knew
a shorter way, through the medina.

Lights strung on wires hung across the narrow street. The naked
bulbs swayed in the wind. Beneath them a throng filled the medina's
narrow pathways. A motorbike rushed past in a whirl of sputter and
exhaust. On the side of the street lay a man whose bare brown thighs
were as thin as Peter's wrists. Peter wondered if the man was dead.
An old man crouching beneath a pair of crutches called out to Peter,
and Peter's hand dove into his pocketful of coins. He knew the beggar
and gave him a dirham each time he saw him. Tonight the old man
accepted Peter's coin with a smile and a muttered prayer. A veiled
woman with a sleepy infant in her lap raised her hands in a gesture
that by now was so familiar to Peter he saw it in his sleep. "*Oui,
madame,*" he said, pressing a coin into the center of her palm. Her
doleful eyes stared up at him. He held her gaze until she looked away.
Then he saw a legless man, walking on his knuckles, swing himself
near. The man's midsection was wrapped in cloth that matched his
turban. Peter gave him a coin. Abdu yanked the sleeve of Peter's
jacket. "Come. There are too many. You cannot give to them all."

"I know," Peter said sadly.

Now Abdu was holding the deaf boy's hand. From both sides of
the street men called out from their piles of wares, which lay on the
ground on plastic sheets the men would scoop up whenever an auto
tried to thread its way through the medina or a policeman waved
a hand at them to move away. Each open stall was brightly lit, and

unlike more traditional medinas Rabat's wasn't arranged strictly by trade. A spice merchant's colorful baskets and bottles were next to a butcher's display of sheep heads. A souq selling radios and kung fu posters stood next to the fluttering folds of a tailor's array of scarves, kaftans, djellabas. Beneath them a bearded man bent over a sewing machine that he pumped with one foot. The deaf boy pointed at the stacks of Orange Fanta in a stall that smelled of grease and ketchup. Abdu pulled him away, leading them past a souq selling colorful leather poufs and down an empty street whose bare walls were broken only by an occasional gangway or closed wooden door.

As soon as they were off the central streets Abdu recited the names of the families who lived behind each door. "Here is the place Lalla Fatima fell the day she broken her hip," he said, stopping along a stretch of wall that was not unlike any other stretch they'd passed.

"Broke," said Peter. "The day she broke her hip."

Abdu shrugged. "Two days after, she died. The same day Rashida, the tailor's daughter, births a baby girl."

Peter nodded, took a breath. "I have a little girl."

"No sons?"

Peter shook his head.

"As they say," Abdu said, "it is a long life." He shook his head too. "Your wife, did you beat her?"

"No. Of course not."

"Perhaps that is the mistake."

"No," Peter said. "Truly. No one ever deserves to be beaten."

"My father beats my mother many times, every night, until she makes no screams."

"I'm very sorry to hear that."

The boy laughed. "Don't be sorry for her no more. She is dead."

"Then I'm sorry for you. That you had to live with that."

"It was more worse for her than for me. My legs are very fast, the most fast perhaps in all of Rabat. When he came to beat me I ran away."

"He's no longer living with you?"

"No. He leaves the day she was dead."

"So who takes care of you?"

Abdu smiled. "Ar-Razzaq."

"Ar-Razzaq?"

"Allah the Provider."

The man and the two boys walked from the shadows into the lights of a busy street, which they crossed as Abdu explained that *mellah* was Arabic for *salt*. In the ancient days, Abdu began in a practiced voice, it was custom for the mighty sultans and pashas to give the heads of those killed in battle to the Jews to be salted, then impaled on poles placed outside the city's walls as a warning to all who passed. Though Peter knew it was largely myth, he let the boy tell him the story. Now he walked with a hand on Abdu's shoulder, the other in the deaf boy's gentle grasp. He felt foolish for his earlier anger, for the frustration he'd felt fill him, like a bitter liquid filling up a flask. The deaf boy had every right to pretend he was crippled. Things didn't exist to be consistent or understandable to others. Peter felt foolish and painfully arrogant for having made a judgment about another person's life.

They entered the mellah and walked down its curved, narrow streets until Abdu paused before a dark doorway, then wordlessly entered and led the man and the deaf boy into a small courtyard. Peter could make out a three-wheeled cart with a metal bar for pushing or pulling it. He stepped across the courtyard's cracked paving stones to what had once been an elegant tiled fountain set in the stone wall. A trickle of rust bled from the spigot. Few of the tiles were intact. The house once must have been magnificent, he thought. A rat half as long as his arm ambled across the courtyard's stone wall. Abdu stood before a cracked wooden door, gesturing for Peter to follow.

He followed the boy into a dark hallway that opened into rooms on either side. The high, biting odor of urine was overwhelming.

Peter had to step back and take shallow breaths to keep from gagging. A heavy drape hung over the doorway to his right. Abdu disappeared behind it. Then the deaf boy appeared, carrying a heavy pail. Peter held the cracked door open for him. In the dim light filtering from the courtyard he could see the bucket was filled with waste.

Peter didn't want to go beyond the drape. Whatever was there wasn't meant for his eyes. He should turn around, leave. The deaf boy was safely home. And downtown, right about now, the promenade would be in full swing. He could leave five or ten dirhams on the narrow table that stood before him in the shadows.

His eyes were growing used to the absence of light. In the shadows on the table was a squat metal tank of what was probably butane, the jet and valve enclosed by a metal ring. He could leave twenty dirhams beneath it, he thought. It would be more than enough. He turned, swung the door open, propped it with a stone lying in the courtyard, to allow the rooms to air.

By the time he arrived downtown the promenade would be ending. Peter tried to imagine it, as if he were a muezzin standing in the high tower of a minaret or a bird flying over the city. He pictured first the women, walking arm in arm, heads bowed to one another in rapt conversation, and then the men, who often held hands, though sometimes they linked their arms too. In his imagination all of the people in Rabat were strolling down the wide boulevard, arms linked, connected, a chain of djellabas and blue jeans, burnouses and suits, skirts, haiks, turbans, skullcaps, beggar's rags. Berber and Arab, Muslim and Christian and Jew. Among them he felt like Djoha, the foolish old man from the South. I've come here to learn, he thought, to be humbled, to be taught how little I know.

Moonlight washed over the courtyard, bleaching the cracked stones so that they looked like silver. In the distance he heard a rooster crow. Once, the sound a rusty scratch. Then again. He waited for the bird to call a third time. He wanted to fall to his knees. He held no idea, only desire. For several moments he fought the desire but then he surrendered to it, raising his hands to the sides of his face, then dropping at first to one knee, then both, as he leaned forward and pressed his cheek and then his forehead against the gritty, moon-washed stones.

He stood and walked past Abdu leaning in the doorway and pushed aside the heavy drape to see an old man lying on a pallet. The man wore a tan cloak and lay beneath a woolen blanket. Peter bent over him and smoothed the hood of his cloak, which had bunched at the man's neck. Lifting the head was like picking up a big egg. Breath rasped from the gaping mouth. The eyes stared ahead, unmoving. Then the deaf boy returned and squatted next to the pallet, and something from the other room rustled in the hall behind the drape.

There was a thud and the sound of something heavy being dragged across the wooden floor. A hand peeled the bottom of the drape up from the doorway. A head thrust through the opening into the room. In the dim light it might have been a giant crab or scorpion pulling itself forward with its claws, dragging its dark, immobile shell behind its head and pincers. The beast waved a bent claw in salute. Then it fell forward clumsily and righted itself, pulling its useless legs forward as the head again twisted in the air and an arm reached out in the darkness and fell onto Peter's leg. Without thinking Peter leaned down and lifted the crippled boy into his arms.

Now the wheeled cart in the courtyard made sense. It was how the one with the good legs brought the other to the center of the city to beg. Peter felt a warm flush of shame.

The crippled boy smiled as the other turned to touch him. For a moment their faces were perfect reflections of each other. The deaf twin stood and raised his arm in a graceful arc, reaching for his brother, for himself, Peter thought, who didn't know if he could ever let go now that he held them in his arms.

THE HAND OF FATIMA

"It's a talisman to ward off the evil eye," Rosemary said and sipped her cup of espresso.

At Sarah's suggestion they were taking their morning coffee on the rooftop terrace of the Café de France, overlooking Marrakesh's famous open square, the Jemaa el Fna. On this clear summer morning a jumble of tricksters and snake charmers, acrobats and monkey trainers was already performing on the square for everyone who passed. Their elongated shadows played on the ground as the two women, now traveling together, crossed the square on their way to the café, and then suddenly a boy ran up to Sarah and without a word or even a moment's hesitation pressed something small into her palm. Sarah stared at the object—it was a hand, made of brass, and in the center of its palm was an eye—and then her eyes tried to follow the boy. He disappeared behind a man clutching a trio of leashed squirrels, then materialized near an old woman who sat on the ground before a plastic sheet on which she displayed a bowl of green paste, several stylos, and a mounded pile of ground henna, then vanished again by a long row of stands offering tall glasses of freshly squeezed orange juice. A man in a turban held out a pair of pigeons that turned one-legged somersaults in his hands. Next to him an old man crouching behind several curious instruments and a spread of human teeth drew out his sebsi to smoke his morning bowl of kif. A muzzled monkey on a leash did a quick series of backflips. Her hair the color of flame, Sarah stood still, breathless.

"The evil eye," Sarah said. She was drinking café au lait and trying to ignore the waiter who, each time she happened to meet his gaze, lifted his eyebrows and gave her an indecipherable series of winks. "I thought that was Italian."

"It is," Rosemary said. "*Il malocchio*. Sometimes *occhio morto*, the eye of death. Most Mediterranean countries have some version of it, though I believe it originated in ancient Greece. Bill knew all about things like that."

In the distance around them, beyond the many minarets lancing the sky and the flocks of dark swallows that soared and swooped just above the level of the roofs, loomed the High Atlas mountains. They stood at sufficient distance from the city to be seen in their full height, ringing the city majestically, their jagged peaks brushed by an occasional passing cloud. Sarah knew they insulated the oasis of Marrakesh from the desert. She watched the clear morning light play against the higher ridges, some of which were still capped with ice and snow, bringing each into focus as a gauzy shadow of clouds passed overhead. Later in the day the peaks would appear to recede, fading behind a hazy curtain of rippling heat. But for now the mountains seemed so immediate Sarah imagined she could touch them if she reached out her hand.

Her hand held the brass amulet. She uncurled her fingers, stared at her palm. "It has a small eye."

"In the middle of the palm," Rosemary said knowingly. She pushed aside her demitasse of espresso and lit a cigarette. Her face, particularly her eyes, looked exhausted, as if she'd once possessed boundless energy but had since used it up. It was a face people would say had character, and it attracted Sarah strongly from the moment she saw it. Sarah could tell from Rosemary's high cheekbones and the delicate turn of her mouth that when she was younger she had been beautiful. She dropped the match into the ashtray. "It's the eye of evil."

"You mean bad luck." Sarah wore a short-sleeved cotton blouse and a modest, full skirt. With her fingertips she brushed back her long hair.

"I mean evil. It exists in many forms here. You know that djinn, ifrits, and demons can snatch away your soul if you're not careful." Rosemary gave a slight shake of her head. A hint of color played in her cheeks. "In the countryside they believe pools of water are the eyes of subterranean monsters. Mothers caution their children against staring at their reflection in a body of water lest the demons within gobble them up. Devils use these openings as passageways between hell and earth. They travel between both worlds freely. They look for any crack in your body—your eyes, your ears, nose, mouth, sex—as a way to invade you."

Sarah laughed lightly and stared at the talisman in her hand.

"You can draw evil to someone," Rosemary continued, "through gossip or praise. We may praise a thing but some part of us might also relish seeing it undone. So the rich man hides his wealth as the lovely woman hides her beauty. If people see, they may talk, and their words may lead to envy, their envy to a curse." She drew on her cigarette. "No magic here. The evil exists in people, in their perception. It's best never to comment, say, on a stranger's child. A compliment invites misfortune."

"So they block the evil with the hand. The eye is the evil, the hand the protector." Sarah held the amulet up first toward the Jemaa el Fna beyond the terrace railing and then toward their waiter, who leaned against a wall leering at her with arched eyebrows.

Rosemary nodded. "You might see a newborn baby and say, 'My, how strong he is!' Immediately the mother will extend her hand to block your words and say, 'Five on him!' or 'Five on your eyes!' The best present you can give a newborn is a small hand that the parents will tie in the child's hair. The charm provides protection. It's like the Sicilian cornicello. The hand or abstract forms of it—five dots or lines for the five fingers—are sometimes tattooed on the face, particularly among Berbers here in the South. Muslims associate the five fingers with the five pillars of Islam. You'll see women wearing a silver hand—or hamsa, the Arab word for *five*—on a chain around their neck. You'll see door knockers in the shape of Fatima's hand, to ward off any evil that might try to pass over the threshold."

Sarah thought of the mezuzah nailed to her grandmother's doorpost and remembered how, when she was a small child, her father would lift her up so she could touch the tiny scroll before they entered the house. "Who was Fatima?"

"The Prophet's daughter, whose descendants conquered most of the Middle East and North Africa"—Rosemary gestured with her cigarette—"and who built Cairo and founded Al Azhar, the world's oldest university. The Fatimids made Egypt great and attempted to unite the Muslim world, but failed. They're the sect that gave birth to the Twelve Imams, whose most famous descendent no doubt is Khomeini of Iran."

"They're the Shiites," Sarah said, unsure.

Rosemary nodded. "It's really quite intriguing, how all these things are connected. You know the Sunni sect of Islam doesn't hold any individual higher than another. In a Sunni mosque anyone, even the least of men, may preach. Shia bases itself more on charisma, believing that power, even infallibility, lies concentrated in individual descendants of the Prophet, the bloodline that passes through Fatima."

"So Fatima stands above other women in the Muslim world."

"Certainly. She comes closest to anything Muslims have resembling the Virgin Mary. Remember that the angel Gabriel visited them both. Fatima is also know as Maryam al-kubra, or Mary the Greater."

Sarah sipped her coffee. "I'm not Catholic."

"I know, dear." Rosemary reached across the table, patted Sarah's arm. "Forgive me if I sound as if I'm lecturing, but since you're here you might as well understand . . ." She let her thought trail off and took a long suck off her cigarette, then stubbed it out.

"I agree." Sarah glanced at the waiter, who was strutting over to a foursome of American college girls in T-shirts, jeans, sunglasses, who'd just sat down at a nearby table. "You seem to be feeling very well this morning, if you don't mind my saying so."

"I had some quiet time earlier this morning, before you awoke."

From the square below, Sarah could hear the sudden, rhythmic beating of a drum. She stared across the Jemaa el Fna at the stately Koutoubia minaret stretching in the distance. She wanted to remind Rosemary that she wasn't like the college students, down from Europe for a week, maybe two, hoping to see some sights that would make her cool in her peers' eyes when she returned to the States. Neither was she here for fancy meals, a souvenir kaftan, as many photographs as she could snap. She didn't know precisely why she'd traveled to Morocco except that everyone had told her not to. Because she was Jewish. Because she was a woman. Because she would be by herself. The quickest way to get Sarah to do something was to tell her she shouldn't do it. She wanted to be what Anaïs Nin called "a woman of the future," free of guilt about her own self-development. She watched the creepy waiter as he pandered to the college girls, who grinned up at him with their pink, dimpled cheeks as he passed out their cups of cappuccino.

Rosemary sat, eyes down as if meditating. "I'm surprised you're not more curious about why you were given the amulet."

"Oh," Sarah said. For several moments she considered why. "I know the reason. I'm a lightning rod."

The older woman nodded. "I imagine you're right."

"People see this red hair—" She broke off her thought to finger her hair, then reached for her purse and drew out a scarf, self-conscious.

"It's quite beautiful, particularly when you brush it out."

Sarah shrugged. "It's hair." She snapped the scarf open, folded it into a large triangle, tied a loose knot beside her neck. She knew that if she were truly a woman of the future she'd have her hair cut or shave her head entirely. Her hair was her central vanity. It drew attention to her, and she both liked and disliked that.

In college she took a Shakespeare class and learned the Elizabethans believed hair was an external manifestation of the soul, an outgrowth of spirit, an abundance of internal energy. Though she was too young for the 1960s, her older brother wasn't and had hair that hung down to his shoulders. He wore soft cotton work shirts that would fade to azure, blue jeans, sturdy work boots that laced down to the toe. In college he did political work and read Kropotkin and Beat poetry and smoked pot. Sarah envied him for being born first, in a time when possibility was untainted by cynicism. By the time she got to junior high, kids argued that the students killed at Kent and Jackson State got what they deserved. In college they were busy making a verb out of the noun *party*. The prevalent feeling then was to make money while you could, as fast as you were able, while the earth was still in one piece and there was still money to be made. So she hung out with the socialists and the geeky outcasts from the fine arts, who at parties threw themselves on the floor and writhed on their backs when they danced, and she took classes in literature and feminist studies. She wrote her undergraduate thesis on Nin's journals and diaries. She dreamed of Morocco and for several weeks dated a student from Jordan until one evening he insisted they have sex and tried to rape her. She gouged his eye and slapped the side of his head so hard she ruptured his eardrum. Her women's group encouraged her to report the attack, but she knew that if she did he'd be sent back and the scandal would ruin his life, and who was she, Sarah argued, to destroy someone else's life, particularly someone from the Third World?

Her friends told her she was too full of liberal guilt. You owe it to the next woman he dates, they said. Send the sexist pig to jail or back to the desert. Sarah called her brother, who was completing

his law degree. He explained her options, said there was no right
or wrong decision, whatever she decided would be best. She didn't
report the Jordanian, but to do something she cut her hair with a
dull pair of kitchen scissors the night her group denounced her as
spineless and weak. The cut was so severe it made her look punk, as
if the mutilation were intentional, a consciously chosen style. Her
brother, who'd moved to D.C. where he did mostly pro bono work,
blanched visibly when he saw her. "God," he said, "what did you do
to yourself?" She vowed she wouldn't cut her hair short again.

"I can see them coming a block off," Rosemary said.

"Who?" Sarah said, caught not listening.

"Usually middle-aged men in Western dress, suit and tie, or
sometimes a sports shirt open at the neck. Seldom in anything
traditional."

Sarah understood now. Rosemary was talking about gropers,
men who sidled next to you, trying to feel you up when you were out
alone or with another woman on the street.

"I used to be able to spot them a mile away. In a minute I'd be all
elbows."

"They're worse in crowds." Sarah tied her head scarf more tightly,
then shuddered. "Suddenly you feel a hand running over your
breasts."

"With me it's usually my ass. They get me from behind."
Rosemary laughed, then shook her head "I guess they grab what they
can."

"It seemed worse in Fez." Sarah looked out over the tangle of
people on the square, and then her eye climbed the graceful lines of
the Koutoubia.

"No, it's just as bad here. You're just getting used to it."

It was time to surrender the table. The waiter pounced at once
on the back of Sarah's chair, pulling it out for her, standing too close
over her, smiling. Sarah turned and nudged the chair back sharply

with her leg as she stood, pushing him back. She gave his dark eyes
a monotone *merci*. Rosemary snapped the clasp on her purse and
dropped two dirhams beside the ashtray.

The college girls looked like students in class, blonde heads
down, arms crooked, busily writing postcards. Sarah wanted to say
something as she walked past them, send out some warning, tell them
about the handsome student from Jordan, but she knew anything
she'd say would sound banal and, even if phrased eloquently, would at
best be only advice. She turned to Rosemary to see if she'd noticed the
studious girls.

Their eyes met. Both women laughed.

There are things you learn directly or you don't learn them at
all, Sarah thought as she and Rosemary made their way down the
staircase of the busy café. You can't be told these things. There are
things you just have to experience.

For the rest of the morning they lost themselves in the Marrakesh
medina. The ground was flat. The winding streets and alleyways
were open and surprisingly wide. Many sections were covered with
latticework that protected those below from the hot summer sun
and cast slanting shadows on the ground, making everything appear
zebra-striped. Water sellers in tasseled hats, wearing necklaces of
brass cups over their traditional red robes, softly rang their bells to
those who passed. Within moments Sarah forgot herself. The medina
gave her the feeling of being swallowed up. As she and Rosemary
walked past the souqs offering olives, mint, spices, past the barber
shops and tiny five-table cafés, the entranceways to mosques where
there was always a heap of babouches and shoes, the tiled fountains
where beggars mumbled their pleas, hunching hopefully with an
outstretched hand or bowl, the potters whose wheels spun with clay
red as the rosy red earth of Marrakesh, the copper- and silversmiths
whose busy hammers tinkled like hundreds of wind chimes, the

woodworkers whose quarter had the crisp, biting smell of cedar, where several donkeys stood tethered beneath a date palm that stretched its curved fronds toward the sky, Sarah forgot that anything else existed. In the dyers' quarter, lush skeins of wools drooped from poles set high above the street. As Sarah walked with Rosemary beneath rows of turquoise, scarlet, saffron, emerald, she noticed how the sunlight filtering through the drying loops of wool and silk bled the same hues onto their faces and hands. It was as if they'd stepped into another world. Sarah leaned against a rack holding the long bamboo poles the wool dyers used to lift and remove the skeins and gave the air a sigh and crossed her arms and held herself. She held the moment, and time's passing matched her breath. Then it took flight, like a small brown bird.

"*Balak!*" she heard. Watch out! And a pair of donkeys loaded down with skins ambled down the street's center. An old man in a filthy djellaba beat the lead donkey's rump with a stick. A shopkeeper stood at the edge of his stall, beckoning eagerly to Rosemary, who told him in Arabic that she lived in Fez, or so Sarah guessed. Sarah understood only a few words of Arabic. Then the shopkeeper shrugged and said something that made Rosemary laugh, and Rosemary followed with something that made him laugh, and Sarah stood outside on the street, not understanding, watching Rosemary saunter into the shop.

Sarah followed the donkeys, which she was certain would lead her to the tanners' quarter. She called into the shop to Rosemary. "I'm going to have a look at the tanners."

"But he's offered us tea," Rosemary said. She was resting on what appeared to be a sofa, feet up on a leather pouf. Sarah found it difficult to see into the shaded shop. She didn't want to stop, sit for twenty minutes beside Rosemary while she and the merchant went on endlessly in Arabic.

"Stay. Have a glass of tea. I'll be just ahead."

"I'll be five minutes," Rosemary said. "I promise."

By now the donkeys had moved out of sight, but Sarah trusted her own sense of direction. She walked down the wide street. She very much liked Marrakesh, its easy feel, the quality of its light, its pinkish earth and rose-colored walls. In Fez life seemed concentrated and intense, contained beneath and within the jagged mountains enclosing the city. The mountains seemed to turn Fez in on itself, reflecting what emanated from the city like a mirror, isolating the city, making its people look inward, inside. She was no expert, but that was her impression. Fez was mysterious and closed. If Fez were a woman she'd be wrapped in a black djellaba, and her face would be veiled. You'd see only her dark eyes over the edge of her veil. The eyes would make you gasp in appreciation of their beauty but would tell you nothing.

Here it seemed there was room to breathe. It was open and light. The city itself sat on a high desert plain. Marrakesh was a woman you could walk up to and say hello, though she'd be wearing traditional dress, a stylish djellaba—something modest but colorful—and high heels. Her face would not be covered. Her eyes would be outlined seductively with kohl, and she'd be wearing a hint of lipstick.

As Sarah walked on she considered perhaps the difference lay not so much in the cities as in her. Perhaps she was beginning to relax. Perhaps traveling with Rosemary made all the difference. Sarah took her thought no further because it was then that she caught a whiff of the tanners' quarter. She quickened her step.

In the medina there was no activity as medieval and interesting to observe as the leather tanners. Their round pits lay full of dye, like shiny pockets of color in a gigantic paint box. Men in loincloths moved between the vats carrying raw skins, which they dipped into the dye, then worked with their feet, standing in the dye up to their knees, stomping the color into the leather. Between the pits rivulets of blue, yellow, and purple ran in the mud. Though the stench was quite high, particularly in the heat, Sarah lingered by the side of the vats and realized that a tanner's legs would be forever discolored by his work, and she thought of the famous blue people of Goulimine, so named because their deep blue indigo robes, after years of wear, stained their skin, giving them a bluish tint. She hoped to see one now that she was in the South.

Her thought was interrupted by a man standing suddenly at her side, saying, "Pardon me," with downcast eyes, in his fist a bunch of mint. He offered the mint to Sarah like a bouquet. He was slight, not much taller than she, and wore a blue suit and white shirt open at the neck. When he raised his eyes, Sarah found him attractive. She took a step back.

"Pardon me," he said again. "I thought you might like some mint, to smell"—he raised the bouquet to his nose—"as you stand here."

"No, thank you," Sarah said and turned away.

"Here. I brought it for you. As a gift. The aroma is—" He looked up and to his right, as if searching for the next word.

"Thank you, but I'm perfectly fine." She appreciated his gesture and that he spoke in English. She felt less threatened speaking to him in English than if their conversation were in French. She turned to look back at the way she'd come, hoping to see her friend.

"The aroma here is not very nice," the man said, continuing to offer her the mint. "Please take it, for me. I mean you no harm."

She liked the way he looked. The hand holding the bouquet had the soft color of chestnuts, and the fingernails were clean, neatly clipped. His teeth were exceptionally white. His shoulders appeared broad beneath his jacket though he wasn't muscular or bulky. He seemed wiry, like a dancer. His eyes implored her. They were round and full, the color of bittersweet chocolate. Sarah imagined they were the envy of every girl he knew.

"All right," she said at last. "Thank you." She took the mint from him and held the bouquet to her face.

He reached forward and crushed a leaf between his thumb and first finger, then sniffed his fingertips and smiled. She smelled the leaf he had crushed. It had a clean, pleasant scent. She nodded.

"Forgive me. I should make an introduction of myself. I am Ramzi Talib."

"Thank you, Mr. Talib, for the mint."

"You are most welcome." He smiled again and sniffed his fingers. His hands appeared to be soft, unused to work. "You do not have a name? When you were born, your parents did not think of something for your family and friends to call you?"

"No," Sarah said. "They didn't give me a name to share with you."

Ramzi's face grew sad. "I am very sorry to hear it." His strong chin was clean shaven. A thin, nearly imperceptible scar creased his upper lip. Sarah noticed a second scar, crescent-shaped, over his cheekbone. "I will leave you alone at once. No problem. But I am happy to have given you the Hand since a lovely woman with no name must be in certain need of it."

He'd turned, was leaving. "Wait," Sarah said.

"We should not speak together since we are not introduced. To speak more, I fear, would give you insult."

"You gave me this?" Sarah reached into her purse and took out the brass amulet.

Ramzi nodded.

"May I ask why?" When he didn't answer, Sarah asked, "Was it to give you a reason to come up and talk to me?"

"No," Ramzi said, "but the thought entered my mind, and things like that are sometimes done." He was walking from the tanners, in the direction from which Sarah had come. "In truth I gave it to you because I thought you had need of it."

"But why?" She followed him. It was the way back to Rosemary.

"Because I watched how others look on you."

She was afraid he knew of some new danger of which she was not yet aware. "And how do they look at me?"

Ramzi stared at her as if she'd asked an unanswerable question.

"Like men sometimes look at women?" Sarah asked, frowning.

"Men whose eyes look on women," Ramzi said, waving a hand at the men around them, "most of them mean a woman no harm. They look mainly just to see what is there. You'll admit women present several faces to the world. Some enjoy being looked on. Many are fond of bright colors, shiny things they hang from their heads to attract the eye."

"You're not answering my question."

He turned down his mouth, then smiled. "Because I don't understand why you ask it, since you know the answer better than me."

They walked on for a while in silence. She thought of the Jordanian student, how he'd blamed her—the same old story—said it was the way she acted, dressed. She knew better than Ramzi, no doubt. She noted that she was still holding the bunch of mint. She dropped it to the ground.

"But really," he was saying, "there's not too much here to fear. Tourists are protected here. There are police all around, particularly in touristic cities like Marrakesh, watching out so that no harm comes to them. It is very Moroccan to be kind to our guests, and tourists are the bread for many, you understand? If harm falls to one, he will tell five others who in turn will tell twenty more, and soon the hotels will be empty and all here will suffer."

"But I seldom see police around."

"You think they all wear a uniform?" Ramzi laughed. "Then everyone would know who they are. Even the pickers of pockets. No, many are dressed just like me."

She was walking beside him now, an eye out for the familiar.

"Perhaps even now police observe us." He swept a hand in the air. "Seeing a Moroccan walking with you, they might think I am leading you to a place where you would be hurt. They might step up to us, ask you if you are OK, ask who I am, if I have passed myself as a guide. Guides, as you know, must have official registration. They might take me over there"—he pointed to a nearby alleyway—"and demand to see my ID. If my answers are not satisfactory they might take me to where I can be questioned."

"You seem to know an awful lot about the police." It occurred to her that he was a policeman. She glanced at the crescent scooped out of his cheekbone, as if from a knife. Or was he a criminal who knew their ways? She noted his air of confidence as they strolled back from the dyers' quarter. They were retracing her steps exactly. It was as if he'd followed her from the time she'd left Rosemary in the shop.

"There is much I don't know, much I must still learn." He paused. "You will let me give you advice? Dress as you like outside the walls, but here in the old city it's best for a woman's arms to be covered, even though it is hot, and wear a scarf over your hair. Or else people will look on you too much. Otherwise, you have little to fear."

Sarah laughed. "The way you describe things, it hardly seems I'm safe." She stroked her bare arms. It seemed she had a great deal to fear.

He shook his head. "But I thought I made it clear. There is a hand of protection always around you."

She looked at the charm in her hand, then at his dark eyes. "You mean this?"

He smiled. "In part."

She held the Hand up to him, then clutched it in her fist. They walked past a boy twining silk on a stick. She wasn't sure of the man. Barefoot children ran past them, disappearing into an alleyway. The silk stretched to a second boy, who held a skein in his hands.

"Two women here alone, not part of a tour group, with no husbands or brothers." He shrugged. "I first saw you last week, the moment you stepped onto the Jemaa el Fna. Like a child in a store of sweets, your eyes, they were very wide. Many noticed you."

"And that's why you gave me this charm?"

"I thought it would please you."

She said nothing.

"I had the boy give it to you so you wouldn't be—" He stopped, turning toward her. Again his eyes searched the sky for the right word.

"Afraid?" Sarah said. "You must admit, in a foreign country, a woman traveling alone, there's a certain wisdom in fear."

"Of course, you are correct. But I was thinking more of something like in the dark." His stare was open, direct. He raised his eyebrows. "You know it, what I mean? When someone is, how shall I say, unaware."

She nodded. Of course she knew what he meant. It was how she'd felt since she'd arrived. She decided to trust him. He wasn't a criminal. "When the boy ran up to me so suddenly and placed it in my hand"—she laid the amulet in her palm, trying to recapture the feeling—"it was so surprising. I felt I couldn't breathe."

"Though now you are fine, in good health, again breathing." He gave out a laugh, apparently pleased.

"I should thank you." Sarah didn't know what else to say.

Then because the shop where Rosemary remained came suddenly into view and the light, now at a slight angle to the medina's walls, filtered down through the loops of cherry-colored wool and golden silk so delicately that the street was more lovely than anything in Morocco Sarah had seen, and the sun overhead resembled a shining brass plate, and now that they were no longer downwind of the tanners she noticed that Ramzi smelled of some rich oil or perfume that drew her unthinkingly closer to him—because the smell was everything Sarah had once dreamed Morocco would smell like, like cedarwood smoke

and oiled leather, like a tale from *The Thousand and One Nights*—and
because at precisely that moment, as she recognized the desire within
her, Ramzi suddenly grabbed her arm so that she wouldn't step into
a dark, rushing river of steaming dye and ruin her shoes, and the
aproned dyer who'd tumbled the boiling cauldron onto the street
waved and shouted something and grinned, and Ramzi responded
sharply in Arabic and laughed, and they stepped out from beneath the
hot brass bowl of the sky into the cooler shadows beneath the skeins,
and the scene—the sudden breeze, the dye soaking into the crevices
between the cobblestones, the shifting quality of light, the pleasant
smell of his hair oil—made Sarah think of Anaïs Nin, something in
one of the diaries or erotic stories or in the book about the women of
the future, and because at that moment Rosemary ventured out from
the shop and raised a hand and hailed them, like a New Yorker calling
for a taxi, standing on her tiptoes, her hand leaping up and down in
the air, Sarah turned to Ramzi and asked if he would care to see her
again, if he'd consent to show her more of Marrakesh.

That evening, an hour or so before the sun set, Ramzi chose a
carriage from the long line of them waiting in the shadow of the
Koutoubia, beside the busy splendor of the Jemaa el Fna. Already
paraffin lamps shone from the food stalls on the square. Water sellers
rang their bells. There was the clang of tambourines. Ramzi bargained
with the drivers as they walked beside the line of carriages until a
driver in a brown burnous agreed with him on a price. It would be all
right, Sarah told herself. Though she was apprehensive, she stepped
up into the carriage.

As the pair of horses trotted away from the curb she turned to
gaze up at the Koutoubia minaret. In the light its rough walls had
the texture and color of gingerbread. Her eye traced its lines past its
domed tower to the golden balls and pear-shaped drop that topped
it. She looked beyond the minaret at the snow-capped mountains
in the distance, then back at the crowds filling the square, the

people moving up and down the busy sidewalk. It seemed everyone
who lived in Marrakesh was outside, going somewhere. Women
in djellabas and head scarves hurried home with rounds of bread
alongside others in jackets, skirts, and pointed heels, clutching
briefcases to their chests or in the crooks of their arms. They rode
with the top of the carriage down. The horses' hooves tocked on the
cobblestone street as the carriage weaved its way through the traffic.

Then the street opened up and they were outside the ramparts,
and Ramzi pointed at the walls that glowed a deep golden red in
the sunlight. Swallows swung out from pits in the red walls, looping
in the air and then returning in dark flurries to where they began.
Ramzi recited the names of towers and gates, but Sarah listened
only to the sound of his voice, which was as dark as the swallows
and, like the birds, made little forays into the air and then returned
to silence. He sat well apart from her, on the other end of the seat.
The earth was pink, barren, covered with crumbled rock between
stands of date palms. A few camels rested in the shade of the trees,
legs folded beneath their bodies as if they weren't there. An old man
in white walked among them with a stick. The city fell away entirely.
Just behind them the carriage's long shadow bumped along the road,
racing to keep up. The earth stretched around them toward the
distant mountains, which were veiled in shadow and haze. Sarah gave
Ramzi a smile and with the flat of her hand shielded her eyes against
the sun.

After a while they reached the Gardens of Menara. As if they
knew the place, the horses came to a halt beside a grove of olive trees.
The driver gave Sarah a gap-toothed grin and helped her to step
down.

As the sun set, Sarah and Ramzi walked around an enormous
reflecting pool fronting a pavilion with a green tiled roof. The
entranceway jutted toward the water and opened into three graceful
arches. The western face of the building had a soft, golden glow.

Ramzi told her the place had been built long ago by a sultan as a gift for his concubines.

"It's very peaceful," Sarah said. She gazed at the entranceway, then at the golden reflection of the building in the pool.

"Now the students have made it their favorite place." He swept his hand in the air, and Sarah noticed students walking singly about, a book or sheaf of papers up to their faces, their lips moving as if in prayer. Along the walkway's walls sat pairs of students—couples— heads together, bent in whispers, some holding hands, others sharing a cigarette.

"They prepare for their examinations."

Sarah smiled, though she knew he hadn't intended to be humorous. By the way he stood at some distance away from her she could tell he was uncomfortable, unsure of his place, what to do. They strolled around the water's edge, and he took her up a staircase and showed her a grotto in the concrete and stone where the local women came to pray. The narrow mouth of the cave was russet with henna from the women's hands. Inside they leave offerings, Ramzi told her. He walked back to the staircase. Sarah ran her hands over the stone, which was caked with dried henna. The grotto seemed too dangerous a place to enter without a light. Standing just inside the grotto's lip, Sarah could hear the rushing spring that fed the pool.

What did the women pray for? she wondered. She took a step forward. For the health and safety of their children, she guessed. For protection against abuse from their husbands. Certainly that. And she hoped they had time to pray for themselves, for their own concerns. Sarah stepped fully into the cave and whispered a prayer for herself. The rushing water swallowed her words, and she wondered how often English was spoken in this place. She took the brass talisman from her purse and prayed for the women who'd come before and those who were yet to stand where she now stood.

In the shadows she could make out on the ground beside the water several bowls and clay pots of what was most likely henna. She crouched and stuck the amulet in the ground alongside the bowls and pots, fingers raised, so that the palm faced the water.

No harm would come to her. She was sure of it. The power of the thought beat within her like a pulse. If you decide evil isn't going to happen to you, it won't. She stood and considered that negative thoughts were themselves cracks through which demons could enter. She raised the flat of her palm to the darkness. She understood that her power was covered, like the henna in the bowls or the eggs within her body, like the palm is contained by the hand. She closed her hand, then opened it and pressed her palm with the thumb of her other hand until she could feel her pulse.

The light was failing. Ramzi leaned against the steps. The students who sat on the wall appeared cloaked in fuzzy gray.

"I was afraid you'd fallen, that I'd have to go in after you."

Sarah shook her head and smiled to show him she was all right.

"Look at you. There's dirt all over you."

She looked down at her smudged blouse, which her fingers had marked with henna. "No matter."

"Are you tired? We can go back."

"No. It's nice here. Let's walk."

"You seem sad."

"No. Just quiet."

They began walking. She allowed the back of her hand to brush against his. By the time they walked the pool's length back to the pavilion she'd let her fingers entwine in his.

"See," Ramzi said, "there are no eyes here."

In the olive groves just beyond the walls Sarah could see blankets spread out on the ground, the shapes of bodies reclining on the blankets. She stared back at the dark water in the pool.

"But what about the water?" She meant her question to be playful. She knew the water was supposed to be an eye that opened into the underworld.

"What about it?" Ramzi said. He clutched her hand tightly. They stopped and faced each other.

"The pool. The pool is itself an eye."

"You don't believe that," he said, drawing her close to him. She felt his hand on her back. The touch was light but firm. His lips brushed her ear, and she breathed in his scent of oil and smoke. A warmth radiated from him that was reassuring.

"We can't believe that," he whispered.

Though she understood then that he didn't really believe and that he'd lied when he told her the talisman wasn't just a trick he'd used to meet her, she kissed him anyway. And when his tongue edged against her lips and she felt a dizzy surge of pleasure, she kept the flat of her palm pressed against his chest, blocking any evil she hadn't foreseen, able to push him away if he tried anything against her wishes.

POSTCARD FROM OUARZAZATE

The mountains broke the country in two, dividing the fertile plains of the Maghreb from the Sahara. Henry steered the rented car up the road—a ledge of more or less level concrete skirting the mountainside—giving it as much accelerator as it would take. Lush terraced fields lined the valley floor on his left. To the right was a sheer wall of jagged rock. Henry hummed "In the Mood," buzzing his lips in imitation of a saxophone. Wherever space between the roadway and mountain afforded squatted a stand covered with glittering chunks of green or purple rock, geodes big as heads split in two, shining slabs featuring fossils of ancient underwater creatures. The larger stones lay beside the stands, set carefully in rows against the mountain. Henry hummed "A String of Pearls," beating time with his palm on the steering wheel. He slowed the car to gaze out Ahmed's open window at the polished stones dotting the roadside. It was as if the way to the desert was lined with marvelous jewels. The windshield was a greasy blur of smashed insects. Henry gave the Peugeot gas. On the seat beside him Ahmed Ousaid slept as if dead, head lolling back, mouth slack against the afternoon's thick heat.

They stopped outside Taddart Oufella, a drowsy Berber village edging the road that would take them over the back of the High Atlas mountains through the Tizi n'Tichka pass and then down to Ouarzazate, the Drâa valley, and the Sahara. Henry urinated against a wall, then began cleaning the car's windshield. Ahmed stretched beside the open door of the car, rubbing his eyes with the knuckles of his first fingers. "Usually in the afternoon I do not sleep." He scratched his curly hair and smiled. "But my eyes fell closed by themselves."

"It's the mountain air," Henry said. Since they'd left Fez he'd lost a considerable amount of weight. His khaki shirt and pants hung loosely on his frame, at least a size or two too large. He wore his old brown sweat-stained fedora and scraped the crushed insects off the windshield with a stick, then splashed mineral water over the glass and wiped the mess with an old sock. The petrol station had a single pump that was out of petrol. A lone café—smoke and the enticing smell of grilled meat wafting from the brazier outside its doorway—stood beside a few open stalls offering wool carpets and polished stones. An untended flock of sheep nibbled the weeds growing next to the empty pump.

Their long shadows stretched ahead of them as they walked. Inside one stall was a cage of chickens, the smell of blood.

"You are feeling OK?" Ahmed said.

"Fit as a fiddle," Henry lied. He patted the swell of his stomach. Whenever he felt himself start to slide into self-pity, Henry reminded himself that everyone was dying of something. The main difference was that he knew. Many who suspected nothing would be dead long before he was dead. The thought comforted him. At least he had warning. So you danced for as long as you heard the music. A bellyful of cancer wasn't so much cause to complain. "Thanks for asking," Henry added. He pushed the fedora back on his head, then wiped his brow with the back of his hand.

"I do not want you to die here."

"I'll do my best to cooperate."

"But if you are very sick and have much pain—"

"Then you'll give me permission."

"My permission," said Ahmed with a grin. "Sure."

A man grilled kefta and kebabs on the brazier outside the café's door. Henry sampled some of the rare, spicy kefta, eating the ground meat with a sliver of bread, then entered the café with Ahmed and sat near the bar, where he watched a squadron of flies land on a nearby table. For several moments, while a waiter prepared their coffee, the flies were still—some feasting on the bread crumbs dusting the tabletop, others walking peaceably about—and then one jumped into the air and buzzed in small circles around the others, and then the others leapt up and buzzed in a larger oval and the entire squadron flew high into the air, and then one settled again on the table and the others followed, one by one lighting on the table of plentiful crumbs.

Ahmed dipped sugar cubes into his coffee, then sucked them nearly white. Henry stared at the flies. Now that he knew about his cancer he sometimes indulged himself with grand thoughts, imagining there was truth or relevance in everything that happened to him, in all he could see. These flies, certainly they said something about being alive. He wanted to discuss the flies with Ahmed but he was busy sucking sugar cubes, then happily crunching the crumbling pieces with his back teeth.

The sun glittered in the thorny treetops—argan trees, famous for the herds of goats that climbed their low, twisted branches and ate their fruit and leaves—as they walked back to the car. It was all these fossils, Henry thought, all this calcified, petrified death that was making him feel so morose. He took a deep breath and told himself to cheer up. He tried to think of cheerful things. Cinnamon houses, the color of the earth, rose suddenly from the ground between the trees on the far mountainside. He stared at the dried earth houses, stunning in their utter simplicity.

Then Ahmed called him from one of the fossil stands. Ahmed and a dark man in a striped maroon djellaba were shaking hands, and Ahmed said, "This man, he knows my village and is a friend of one of my uncles."

"Small world," Henry said. He introduced himself, shook the man's outstretched hand, smiled. Before Henry knew it they were buying several rocks, small enough to keep in a deep pocket, and then Ahmed was pointing at a fossil nearly as long as Henry's hand.

The stone was black, rounded at one end, pointed at the other, like a teardrop, polished so finely it shone even in the shade. A slender gray dart creased the stone's face—an orthoceras, a four hundred-million-year-old cephalopod—its straight shell tapering toward the rock's sharpened end. Henry held it in his palm. It was a stone made for the hand, to hold, to stab with. Henry drew his arm back, like a quarterback about to throw a football, fingers wrapped lightly around the stone's smooth surface.

The fossil seller grinned apprehensively. "You want to hit something with it, yes?"

"Me?" Henry said. "I'm a peaceful guy. I wouldn't think of it."

"Peace," the fossil seller said, smiling now with his bad teeth. He made a *V* of his fingers. "You like the hippies?" He slapped his open palm with his knuckles and fingertips, then lowered his voice to a near whisper. "I know where you buy some kif. I give you a very good price."

"Thanks but no thanks," Henry said.

"As you like, but is the best outside of Marrakesh, believe me." He slapped the palm of his hand again. "Very good price."

"These stones are enough for me."

Ahmed covered Henry's hand with his own when Henry took out his money. "No, I wish to pay. These are a gift."

"A gift," said Henry. "Oh, happy day."

"Sure," Ahmed said. "All our days are happy days."

The sun fell between the trees. Before they started back to the car Henry stared at his long shadow. The stone in his hand felt as good as anything he'd ever held.

Night slipped across the sky before them like a rising veil. Henry sped from the dying light into the darkness. He had the sense he'd never return this way again, so he felt nostalgia for everything he saw—a flock of black-faced sheep blocking the roadway, a house made of round off-white stones, roofed with sheets of corrugated tin, a shadowy stand of juniper, clematis, and nearby a tumble of acacia mixed with lavender and oleander. The road twisted along the mountains, winding through the Tizi n'Tichka pass, which rose above the height at which vegetation grew, then snaked down the southern slope of the High Atlas, curling down to the vast desert plateau on which stood Ouarzazate, a sudden swell of gray buildings and streetlights. By then darkness had overrun them. Henry's sweat-soaked shirt stuck to the back of the seat as Ahmed's uncles and cousins spilled from the metal doorway of a house next door to a mosque. The men kissed and embraced Ahmed, who smiled so broadly his face looked made of rubber. Henry took his time setting the hand brake, wiping sweat from his forehead, adjusting his fedora, making sure the incomprehensible rental papers were in order, the glove compartment secure.

"*Labas!*" they called to him, thronging around him as he unfolded himself from the car. They grinned, pumped his arm. They were darker, rounder versions of Ahmed. All had his almond eyes, his curly hair.

"*Labas, hamdullah,*" Henry answered carefully. He'd memorized the phrase for the occasion. I'm fine, thanks to God. He smiled into each face, shook each outstretched hand, repeating the phrase like a trained mynah.

The dark eyes of the children peeked out from behind a draped doorway inside the house. The men led Henry past the drape up a stairway, proudly showing him a vacant bedroom and adjoining bathroom, which held a sink and a tub. "A thousand thanks," Henry said with a bow.

"They say all they have is yours," Ahmed told him.

"*Eyah,*" the men said, nodding.

"You wash now," one of the uncles said. Another uncle offered him a towel. A third handed him a white tasseled robe. Then, as

quickly as they'd swept into the room, everyone disappeared, softly
shutting the door behind them.

He threw his fedora onto the bed, then dropped the rocks from
his pockets into it. After he undressed, he washed. The robe was cut
like a wool djellaba but made of a lighter fabric, most likely cotton.
Putting it on over his boxer shorts, Henry felt like a kid in his old
man's nightshirt. His black socks ruined the effect, so he took them
off. He wished he had a pair of yellow slippers, curled slightly at
the toe. His feet were cold on the bare tile floor. Then he saw that
someone had left a worn pair of babouches just outside the bathroom.
Slipping them on Henry felt like a sultan out of *The Thousand and
One Nights*. He closed his eyes, clapped his hands, made another
wish. No dancing seven-veiled girl appeared.

He could hear the others gathering in a nearby room. He closed
his eyes again and wished not that he could be cured—he was beyond
the point where he expected miracles—but that the darkness destined
to swallow him up would come easily, quickly. He pressed his hand
against his abdomen. He felt nauseous waves of pain. He guessed
the beast sleeping inside him had awakened. He thought of the story
of the Spartan boy who concealed a stolen wolf beneath his cloak,
denying its presence even after the wolf began to claw and eat him.
The story had so impressed him when he was a boy that it became his
model for manliness. Walking to school, he tried to practice the silent
endurance of great pain. In truth he was a mama's boy, a fraidy-cat,
what the others called a pansy. When the older boys knocked him
down on the playground, he wailed like the world's biggest crybaby.

Their nut-brown eyes rose to behold him as he shuffled into the
room, deep and formal, lined with a long red sofa and more pillows
than he could count. At once they stopped speaking. There was a
palpable silence. They gazed at him with a collective "Ahhh!"

"*Labas?*" Henry offered.

"*Labas!*" they laughed. "*Labas, hamdullah!*" They led Henry to a place on the sofa surrounded by many pillows, and everyone at once offered him something to eat. On two large brass platters before him were brochettes, bread, several kinds of salad, large speckled hard-boiled turkey eggs.

"Eat," Ahmed said, his cheeks already fat with food. "Please. Do not be shy."

Henry tried some of the salad, chewed a piece of the bread. After a while the uncle who had handed him the robe—a slight man badly in need of a shave who had a single tooth in the center of his lower jaw—rushed at Henry with a pointed silver bulb and doused him with scented water. At first Henry didn't know what to do. He put up one arm to ward off the crazy man. The uncle cackled as he splashed the rose water on Henry's head, shoulders, chest. The scented water burned Henry's eyes. He had to ask for a towel.

"Now you have been welcomed," Ahmed said with a smile.

"Don't come near me with a match," Henry answered, drying his eyes. "I'm flammable."

"My uncles say all they have is yours."

"Tell them I wish Allah will return to them all they've given me."

"*Barak'Allahu feek,*" Ahmed told the uncles, who turned happily to Henry and nodded. Henry nodded, waved an arm, smiled.

After supper they drank mint tea and ate almonds and small cookies flavored with anise. Henry's eyes drooped. He hoped he hadn't given offense when the madman came after him with the after-shave. He hoped he wouldn't have to wear the white robe all the time. Then all at once he no longer cared what was or wasn't expected of him. He sipped some of the very sweet mint tea, then leaned back.

Being here was like watching a foreign movie without any subtitles, he thought as he lay back on the cushions. For a moment the room seemed to be moving ahead of him, like the mountain road. He shut his eyes. Well, here he was. He'd journeyed to Morocco because it was absolutely unexpected, and because he believed life needed a dash of adventure and romance. Ahmed suggested they travel together, first north to the imperial cities of Meknès and Fez, then back to Rabat so he could sit for his exams. Ahmed then offered to show Henry his home, so they drove south, their friendship growing like the beauty of the passing landscape. They traveled to bustling Casablanca and the lovely walled town of Essaouira on the Atlantic coast, then on to the dreamy pink spectacle of Marrakesh, where they shared a carriage ride at twilight and ate from the open-air stands of the Jemaa el Fna. Now they were venturing beyond, to the land the guidebooks called the Valley of the Kasbahs, which would lead to the Sahara. After reaching the Sahara, Henry had no plans. He imagined himself walking from one sand dune to the next, searching the horizon for the next oasis.

A sudden clenching seized his abdomen—the squeezing fingers of an unforgiving hand. Henry winced from the pain. His heart fell. So it was true, he thought. The beast inside him was waking. He took shallow breaths though the pain was so sharp his forehead broke into a sweat and he had to pant for air like a dog. "Forgive me," he said to the others in the room. He gripped his sides, writhing beneath hot spasms of pain.

One very old uncle with wet, clouded eyes and a sharp jaw rough with whiskers patted Henry's shoulder and said something to the air near Henry's ear.

"Lord God, the pain's bad," Henry told him. He was puffing now, arms wrapped around his gut, as if he were about to give birth.

Then he sat up and bolted for the toilet, next to the room where he'd washed, where he squatted over a tiled hole in the floor and let loose such misery he moaned audibly. His bowels released a searing flame from hell. A sadist with a blowtorch could hardly have made him feel worse. All at once he remembered the raw, spicy kefta he'd eaten in Taddart Oufella.

It wasn't until early the next morning, after the muezzin from the mosque next door wakened him with an uncompromising call to prayer, that Henry wondered what Ahmed's relatives had thought as they'd heard his moans followed by his laughter.

Ouarzazate was a more or less sleepy town strung along a single main street. It had none of the mystery or romance of Marrakesh. Villagers in hooded djellabas walked up and down the cracked sidewalks, pausing for conversations that sometimes lasted longer than an hour. In this region of extended families it was considered impolite not to inquire about the health of every brother, nephew, and cousin of everyone you encountered on the street. Henry grew used to sitting on curbstones, watching tinny cars and fly-infested donkeys amble past him. He'd gaze west at the great stretch of mountains they had crossed. His eyes traced the paths of soaring birds. He watched women enter shops, transact business. He watched boys play soccer on empty lots beside the street. Curiously, few of the women wore veils. When he asked Ahmed he learned that veils were more typical in the city, where you would be seen by many people who do not know you, than here where you live, at home. Soon Henry referred to Ahmed's uncles' house as *home*. Each day after a breakfast of bread and hard-boiled eggs and coffee they left home, walking up the long avenue named for Mohammed V, the great king who'd led Morocco to independence, past the cafés where sunburned French tourists sipped *limonade* beneath umbrellas, writing postcards and adjusting the settings on their Japanese cameras, and where Moroccan men, their faces dour, impassive, drank café noir and read newspapers and smoked an endless row of cigarettes. They walked to the Taourirt Kasbah, where an old man with a pair of tethered camels waited with a Polaroid for tourists eager for an out-of-focus souvenir. Henry and Ahmed scaled the kasbah's ocher walls, gazing down at the river beyond that trickled between groves of luxurious date palms. Each

night they walked back, silently, as the sun set in an orange blaze
behind the high ridge of mountains before them, and then Henry
would bathe and put on the clean, pressed shirt and pants he'd
discover in a pile in his room, and as night fell he'd go to the sala and
sit and write postcards to his landlady, his oncologist, the manager of
the corner bar, between sentences playing with the pointed black rock
he now kept in his pocket.

I'm in the south of Morocco. Weather's pretty darn hot. In the desert beyond
it's so hot snakes are said to stand on their tails. We drove through the Tizi
n'Tichka pass, nearly 7,500 feet high. The big C is still in remission though
at times I can feel it rolling over in its sleep. Best wishes, Henry

Then Ahmed would return from evening prayers at the mosque
next door, and they'd sit together as the room grew dark, then gather
a few of the carpets and take them up to the roof where they'd roll
them out and sit with the uncles, nephews, and cousins beneath
the stars. They'd eat couscous, sometimes a saffron chicken tajine,
sometimes rice with sugar and sour milk. The women had their own
roof, Henry learned. He never saw them, and when he asked about
them conversation grew short. Surely someone was responsible for
preparing his meals, changing his sheets, making his bed, washing
and ironing his clothes, putting a fresh towel in the bathroom. He
would have liked to meet them, to tell them *Barak'Allahu feek!* May
the blessings of God be upon you! But to him they existed only as
shadows that pulled their daughters' curious eyes away from the
draped doorway. Only if he woke early and sat waiting for breakfast
in a corner of the sala could he catch a glimpse of the girls, who were
thin and dark and beautiful, and who ran like deer from his sight.
He'd sit silently, like a hunter in a blind, as soon as he heard their
shoes tapping softly on the stairs. They wore plain cotton dresses that
fell to the knee. Their dark hair tumbled freely to their shoulders.
They'd set the trays of food on the low tables with care, then peek

out the front windows, chatting like birds, until their big brown eyes caught him spying in the corner. "Hello," Henry would say in a soft voice, trying his best to be disinterested, nonchalant. They'd freeze, look at him and giggle, hide their mouths with their hands. Then the one closest to the doorway would break for the stairs, and the others would follow, the hems of their dresses whirling as they ran. Henry would listen to their shoes scamper up the stairway.

On the roof at night he'd teach their brothers English phrases.

There's no place like home.

Have a nice day.

Beam me up, Scotty.

When the boys grew inattentive, the uncles gathered in a tight circle around Henry and instructed him.

Mnin gi ti? Where are you from?

Fin rha di? Where are you going?

Ash brhi ti? What do you want?

Each night the uncles asked him the same questions. Henry repeated whatever he heard, polishing his pronunciation like the fossil seller did his stones. It didn't occur to Henry that these questions were ancient, central to the uncles' lives, or that they expected him to offer them his answers.

The next day they drove to Tiffoultoute and then Aït Benhaddou to see their magnificent kasbahs. They were the stuff of children's dreams, these mud-brown castles that loomed suddenly on the horizon like something out of a fairy tale. Henry preferred the kasbah at Aït Benhaddou, perhaps because it lay on the side of a picturesque hill across a wide but shallow river dotted with large stones. Tourists on donkeyback crossed the river on their way to the kasbah. Ahmed and Henry rolled up the cuffs of their pants and walked in the trails left by the donkeys. The kasbah seemed to rise from the earth by itself, its crenellated walls and towers stretching against the bare mountainside. In the dry air Henry thought the fortress looked perfect, untouched, as if it had always been here and always looked this way. He tried to ignore the tradesmen gathered around its base. The boys selling trinkets, postcards, three-stringed guitars made from sticks and the shells of box turtles. The men offering jewelry—each piece guaranteed to be an antique—or kaftans stitched aimlessly by machine, or camel rides. "Picture, I take your picture," a mustachioed man with a Polaroid called. Behind the mountain hung a pale blue sky. Now that Henry no longer carried a camera, he wanted his picture taken. "For posterity," he told Ahmed as they posed, Mutt and Jeff, squinting into the sun, grins splitting their faces, one arm around the other's shoulder.

Later, in Ouarzazate, Henry wanted a newspaper, so they headed for the row of hotels overlooking the Taourirt Kasbah. They parked the Peugeot near the mosque and walked through the town's old section, down its dusty streets and alleyways, past houses and shops made of dried mud, their soft walls crumbling into mounds of dust that lined the base of the walls. "It's late," Henry told Ahmed as they walked. "No time to chew the fat with your friends."

"I do not chew fat," Ahmed said, as if he'd been insulted. "When I find fat with some meat I swallow it."

"I mean chitchat. Gab. Palaver. Baloney. You know, flapping your gums, shooting the breeze. '*Labas, labas,* got half a day? Here, let me run down the medical history of my ancestors.' I mean the way you filibuster, Berber style."

"You do not wish me to be polite."

"I'm not saying that, amigo. I just think you could say howdy-do in under twenty minutes."

"But these people, they have known me all my life. This is my home, and I have been away a long time."

"I just want to get a newspaper before sunset, that's all. I'd kind of like to catch up on what's happening in the world."

"It is the same when I stop to talk."

They walked in silence past a man squatting in the shade beside several watermelons, then headed up a steep hill, beyond a courtyard wall overgrown with flowering red hibiscus. In an empty lot pocked with rubble and garbage grazed a spotted goat. Cicadas made a high, winding screech in the weeds. Henry could see the green stretch of several tennis courts ahead, below the crest of the hill that faced the Taourirt Kasbah. On the choicest hilltop, commanding the best view, sprawled Club Méditerranée. Beyond the tennis courts and the kasbah lay the airport, a jet circling overhead.

Henry hummed "Chattanooga Choo Choo" as they walked past a couple on the way to the tennis courts. Their matching sweaters lay flat on their backs, the sweaters' arms crossed idly over their chests. Henry nodded to the man, most likely French, and tipped his fedora to the woman. A doorman in a blousy red shirt, cream-colored pants, canary-yellow babouches curling up at the toe held the double glass doors of the hotel open for them. The man's face was deep black and expressionless. On his head he wore a small red fez. The lobby was filled with overstuffed sofas and chairs positioned around spotless glass coffee tables. Henry headed for the newsstand left of the long front desk and looked among the magazine racks for something he could read—the Paris edition of *The International Herald Tribune* or a copy of *USA Today*. The stand was sold out, though the Moroccan behind the cigarette and candy case told Henry he'd have a copy of either paper sent to Henry's room the moment they arrived. "Whatever is your pleasure," the man said.

"Thank you, no," Henry said. "That will not be necessary."

"As you like," the man behind the case said.

Ahmed was waiting uncomfortably in the center of the lobby.

"No luck," Henry called out. "What do you say we wet our whistles?"

"Wet our what?"

"Follow me," said Henry, marching up a red carpet through
the lobby and several stairs that curled beneath a brass handrail and
enclosed a lush display of immense potted plants. Henry turned back
to Ahmed and smiled broadly. They entered a sunroom, walls lined
with chaise lounges. The humid air held the faint smell of chlorine.

He led Ahmed around the pool—its emerald water glistening
in the fading sunlight—and then back through the sunroom to a
courtyard where a set of drums stood beside a piano on a small stage.
Kelly green napkins towered like pyramids at each place at the tables,
made of opaque glass. Henry pushed his fedora back on his head. He
grabbed the center table, motioning generously for Ahmed to sit.

Immediately a waiter hovered at Henry's elbow. Henry ordered
their drinks—mint syrup and Oulmès water for himself, lemonade
for Ahmed—and then leaned back and gave out a long sigh.

"I can't for the life of me tell you why," Henry said, raising his
glass, "but I have an incredible desire to drink something green." He
mixed the sparkling water with the syrup.

Ahmed sipped his drink, reached for a packet of sugar.

"Not too shabby a place," Henry said, looking about. Ahmed said
nothing. Nearby on the ground a brown sparrow nervously seized a
fallen crumb of bread. Then it flew away as the shiny black shoes of
the waiter returned to their table.

Outside they paused on the sidewalk. Henry looked out at the
kasbah and the magnificent valley beyond. Ahmed said, "Someday I
wish to see this hotel destroyed."

Henry laughed. "The lemonade was that sour?" He had put his
hat back on and fingered the black fossil he kept in his pocket.

Ahmed waved his words away. "I hope to see it fall, stone by
stone."

"You're against these hotels?"

"I do not want Ouarzazate to become another Marrakesh."

Around the corner another deluxe hotel was going up. Already the workmen were setting its elaborate façade with green tiles. "Well," Henry said, "you can understand why tourists want to come here."

"For now," Ahmed said sadly, "I think yes. But I pray it will not always be this way."

"You can't stop progress."

"What you say is progress others would say is a death."

"Whoa," Henry said.

"You do not understand," Ahmed said, mouth twisting with sudden vehemence, "what it means when your home is not your own. I remember when I was a small boy, listening to the radio at my uncles' house. It was when the Israelis crushed the armies of Egypt, Syria, Jordan, all in six days. Do you not understand what that meant to us? The humiliation. The shame. All Muslims feel it."

"But Morocco and Israel aren't at war."

"In this all Arab countries stand together. I say it even though I am Berber. It is like waking up and seeing that a stranger who you hate and who hates you lives in your house. He sleeps in your bed and eats your food. You want to throw him out, be your own master."

"But no one hates you."

"No one in the world hates Arabs or wants their land or wishes to destroy Islam?" Ahmed looked as if he were going to laugh. "For someone who has been given much you know very little. The early settlers of your country threw out the English, did they not? We should be friends on this, Henry. Morocco was the first country to recognize America's independence. Ask anyone here how they were treated by the French when Ouarzazate was a military outpost."

"But the French don't occupy—"

"Who are these palaces for? Me? My uncles?" Ahmed snorted. "Moroccans? Certainly not Palestinians." His face grew long, sad. "During the whole time we were there, the Palestinians were all that took up my thoughts. Though Moroccans built these places I know they are not for us. Without you I could not even walk in the door."

Henry shook his head.

"If a mob came to destroy these hotels, I would join them. With the fallen bricks I would help them build houses for those who sleep on dirt while here they sleep on the soft feathers of gooses. You understand so little I am surprised. You are free to travel the entire world, and what do you see when you go? Do you see the things people see who live day to day or just the pretty things on postcards?"

"I came here for both," Henry said.

"Yet when I try to show you both you argue. I explain how some feel and you say I am wrong. No one hates you, Henry, because of who you are as a person. But many hate your country because it and Israel lie together like two whores."

"My country is not a whore."

"Then the evil it does is even worse! I thought it was the love of riches that makes it so blind to the situation of others."

"You're pretty insulting."

"Forgive me, truly." The young Berber bowed, as if to his master. When he looked up again his eyes appeared wet with tears. "I thought you might be different because you are so close to death."

A dark butterfly sailed past Ahmed's shoulder. "That's why you became my friend." The awareness of the truth caught in Henry's heart and hung there, heavy as stone.

"I do not want you to die here alone. It would not be—what is the word?—hospitable. Is that it? The politeness you show to a guest? After coming here, without your family or even a friend, all alone."

"Your uncles, cousins, all the others," Henry said, "they know about my cancer? That's why they welcomed me into their home?"

"Of course. But there is one aunt who is very afraid. After you have touched a glass or plate or slept beneath a sheet she boils it right away to kill the germs. We have tried to tell her you are not catching but she is old and does not believe."

"Go away," Henry said.

Ahmed stood his ground.

"Leave me alone."

"As you like," said Ahmed, turning at once and walking away.

Henry knew he'd given insult. For several moments he stared at the back of Ahmed's checked shirt as it receded into the waning light. A jet roared suddenly overhead. Henry stared past the hotels at the sun setting over the ridge of mountains and clouds in the west. Then, because Ahmed walked one way, Henry walked the other.

He hurried toward the Taourirt Kasbah, though he hardly noticed where he was. All he knew was that something had ended, like waking up suddenly from a dream. One moment you're inside it, and its physics are the laws by which you and all else exists, the rhythm that fills your head, the rhyme you accept without question. The next moment you're lying in a puddle of sweat, and the dream is a crumbling shadow on a wall inside your mind. How stupid to think he and Ahmed could be friends! He crossed the road and nearly stepped in front of a truck rattling by with great urgency. The driver didn't brake or even swerve to miss him, only shouted something at him in Arabic as he sped past. The polished stone Henry kept in his shirt pocket banged against his heart.

An old man in a tattered djellaba drove his pitiful donkey down the street with a stick. Henry stared at the man's downcast eyes, at the flies crawling on the flat of the donkey's back. Pity, that's all it was. He'd mistaken it for friendship. Henry knew that one of Islam's five pillars was paying a tithe to the poor and destitute. His mind pictured the great bowls of couscous sitting outside the doorways of mosques on feast days, food left by the fortunate for the poor. Perhaps their hospitality fell into the same category, he thought. Allah would give them extra blessings if they were so lucky that he died while under their care.

He stood on a ridge near a mound of high weeds, gazing down at the crumbling tan walls of the kasbah. A pair of tourists was snapping photos from the walkway that ran inside its high walls. The old man with his two miserable camels stood in his usual spot in the shade, unrolling his prayer rug.

The ground around Henry's feet was laced with orange peels, curved downward, dotting the ground like little frowns. He took the fossil out from his pocket and squatted in the dirt and drew a circle, then arranged the orange peelings to make a sad face. From town he heard the muezzin give the call to evening prayer. The prayer was called the Maghrib—the word meant *sunset*—just as this part of North Africa was known as the Maghreb, the land of the setting sun. He stood, gazed at the sunset. Over the next minute, for as long as he could hear the muezzin's plaintive cry, he thought about the fertile valleys that were behind him, the desert that lay ahead, and in between the steep and treacherous mountains he had successfully crossed with Ahmed, only to see their friendship shattered once they'd reached the desert plains.

He pushed the round end of the rock into his abdomen to feel his cancer, but it was sleeping. Then he heard the sound of something rustling toward him in the weeds. He parted the high weeds with his hands. It was a turtle, crawling toward the silly face he'd made of orange peels. He squatted. The box turtle poked its head through the grass, eyes red and wild, looking about. Then it scraped its way slowly forward until Henry could see the whole of it. He stepped back. The turtle nosed the peeling that was the sad face's left eye, then gaped its mouth open and snapped it up. The peak of the turtle's carapace had been broken—likely struck by a passing car or truck—and the raw, exposed flesh beneath the cracked, open shell now teemed with maggots. The turtle held the peel patiently aloft in its mouth. The swarm inside the turtle's shell shimmered obscenely in the light.

Henry's first impulse was to walk away, leave it there in the dry grass. For several moments he didn't look at it as he decided. The tourists who'd been climbing the kasbah's walls were gesturing to the old man with the camels, and now the woman was petting the smaller camel's side. There wasn't really any choice, he thought. He stepped on the maggots swarming inside the shell, pressing the turtle tightly down to the earth. He gripped the pointed rock, raised it high over his head. His shadow leapt along the ground, then collapsed. He had to strike the animal twice before he was sure he'd pierced its head. Then he edged the dead thing into the weeds with the tip of his shoe.

The sun fell back behind the ridge of mountains. Henry tossed the bloody fossil into the weeds. The tourists scrambled onto the backs of the two camels, posing gaily as the light completely gave out.

THE FIRE-EATER

"The people here have an expression," Rosemary said, lighting and then taking a long drag from a cigarette. "When you've been to jail or the hammam, everyone knows you've been doing something."

A smear of lipstick, red and sudden as a bruise, appeared on the cigarette's white filter. The hammam was the public bath. Sarah blushed, red as the lipstick on the cigarette.

"So you think I've been doing something?" She tried to laugh as she reached across the table for a cigarette from Rosemary's open pack.

"I thought you'd stopped."

"I have. It's just one."

"It's the first one," the older woman lectured, "the one with coffee, unless you're as bad as me and have your first in the shower."

The women were finishing their morning coffee at a sidewalk café in Gueliz, the modern French quarter lying outside the walls of old Marrakesh. Here Sarah could forget for the moment that she was in Morocco, a place she found magical and exotic beyond her expectations as well as harsh, even cruel and unrelenting. Though the books she'd read before her trip informed her that Morocco was a happy land of contrasts, she found its blend of Arabic, Berber, and European influences at times overwhelming. In the words of its king, Morocco was a country rooted in Africa, watered in Islam, and rustled by the winds of Europe. Even now, as Sarah sipped her café au lait and nibbled the delicate flakes of a croissant served to her by a uniformed waiter whose expression was as flat as the starched white cotton cloth spread across their table, she noticed the grizzled beard of a toothless man in a brown burnous driving a miserable donkey laden with green-stemmed oranges down the street alongside the opposite curb, and on the curbstone sat a woman in black nursing a baby and begging. How horrible it must be to sit at the side of a filthy street with a baby at your breast! With each step the man hit the donkey's side with a stick. Traffic sped past, spewing exhaust. Men in nondescript suits streamed past the beggar, likely on their way to work. Some men were without jackets and carried folded newspapers beneath their arms. Sarah guessed they were the men who spent their days talking and smoking cigarettes at the uncovered tables in any one of Marrakesh's thousand mid-block cafés.

Sarah's café fronted a spacious hotel spanning a wedge of sidewalk thrust between the intersection of three busy streets. The sky was pink and bright with the promise of heat. The fronds of the date palms lining the roads stirred in the early morning breeze, though Sarah couldn't feel a breeze. She fingered the crumbs of her croissant. The air around her stood still, heavy. She lit her cigarette and sucked in its smoke, then held the hot smoke deep in her lungs, allowing a dizzy wave of nicotine to wash over her. Her eyes fell on the watch on Rosemary's wrist. It was barely seven. Already it was hot.

Rosemary spoke suddenly. "You'd be a fool if you weren't." She leaned forward, as if revealing a confidence. Her face was slack and puffy from her years of hard drinking, and her hair had gone gray, but Sarah knew men still ran their eyes over Rosemary in the streets.

"I'm sorry," Sarah said. "I must not have been listening." Men stared openly at Sarah, who was lean, lithe, with her head of marvelously full, long, dark red hair. This morning she'd tied it in a loose ponytail and wore a patterned scarf she'd purchased in the medina.

Rosemary's face collapsed into a laugh. "Honey, I'm trying to talk about your man." Smoke spilled through her nose and teeth.

Sarah gave her eyes a roll, then looked down at her nails. They were short, unpainted, sensibly clipped. With her thumbnail she pushed back a cuticle. Her fingers were slender, uncluttered by rings. Hands announced to the world the kind of person you were. Her mother taught her that. The familiar strength of Sarah's hands lent her comfort, reassured her in this foreign place. She remembered she was a no-nonsense girl from the North Side of Chicago, Rogers Park, a neighborhood of shops and yeshivas, modest brick homes, everything clean but nothing too fancy, where the streets were parallel or perpendicular, where the women wore babushkas and house dresses and traded with the same kosher butcher their entire lives, and the men carried metal lunch pails to and from their factory jobs and every few months squirreled away a little something in the neighborhood savings and loan or a rusted coffee can hidden inside an old tire in the garage, for the rainy days that loomed with certainty on the horizon, the pogrom everyone was never quite sure wasn't massing just beyond the edge of their sight.

"He was hardly my man," Sarah said. The buzz from the cigarette made her dizzy. Now she was a Jew three times a year, on Yom Kippur, Rosh Hashanah, and Passover. She stubbed the cigarette out in the ashtray, then reached for her coffee cup.

"Did I miss something?" Rosemary's face broke into a smile. "Was? As in the past tense?"

Sarah shrugged. "I don't know. I suppose." She thought of Ramzi's eyes, which were full and round, the color of bittersweet chocolate. That he was an Arab, forbidden, made seeing him all the more sweet. She recalled the clean, silver taste of his tongue, the crescent-shaped scar that scooped his cheekbone, like a sideways moon, his chestnut skin beneath the curls of fine dark hair on his chest. She remembered the way they fit when he held her, smelling of a perfume made of oil and smoke. She was just taller than he was, and when they embraced his bones locked with hers like the wooden blocks of a puzzle she'd owned when she was a child. Each piece fit like a grooved mouth atop the other piece. When you pushed them together just right they connected with a satisfying click. "He wants to see me again, but, I don't know, I can't see it leading anywhere."

"Men that handsome," Rosemary said, "hold a special appeal for foreign women, as well as for some men. I've seen it happen dozens of times." She lit a cigarette off the one she'd just smoked. She chain-smoked since she'd quit drinking. "A woman travels here from France, Spain, Italy, the States, and before you can blink she's shopping for that just right something to wear to the wedding. The groom gets her citizenship, his name on all her bank accounts, a permit to travel, a chance at a real job."

Sarah laughed. "You make it sound very romantic."

"Oh," Rosemary said, "but it is. Before the inevitable divorce she gets a year or two of marriage to a Moroccan prince."

Sarah shook her head. "It's too early in the day for sarcasm."

Rosemary sat back and smiled like a medina merchant who'd just made a good sale.

"I'm not like the others," Sarah pointed out.

"Of course you're not."

"But it's true. This thing, it's run its course."

"I never said it hadn't."

"I'm sorry. I thought you had."

Rosemary drew on her cigarette. "That's precisely the problem with love. If you're not friends, after bed it just goes bad on you. And if you are friends you take the risk that some afternoon when you least expect it he'll drop dead."

"Did Bill die suddenly?" Sarah asked.

The older woman nodded, exhaling a cloud of smoke. "I thought I'd told you. His heart. It just gave out. One afternoon in his office at the consulate." Her face sagged into a frown. "I remember rushing to be with him after they called, not knowing if he were dead or alive, just as the sky was splitting open with the first big autumn rain. Everyone in the hospital was very happy. Even outside the surgery you could hear the thunder. Of course there was nothing they could do. They were doing their best, they kept telling me. In the streets outside the rain ran ankle-deep. Very good news for the crops. Everywhere you looked people were happy."

Sarah reached across the table and touched Rosemary's hand. The skin was wrinkled, dry.

"I was drinking a little then—not any yet that day—but in general, evenings, after Bill would get home. He had one of those big open American faces. He'd loosen his tie, slip off his shoes, and we'd have a drink, very civilized, as we waited for Halima to serve dinner. Or we'd have a drink waiting to go out that evening to some consulate function where someone else's maid would serve us dinner and drinks. It's what people in our position did. We entertained, or were entertained. I seldom drank anything before Bill got home. But afterward there seemed no reason not to."

Sarah squeezed the hand in hers. It felt limp, like a dead bird.

"I'm sorry."

"Don't be. Just be careful."

"I try."

Rosemary laughed. "No you don't. You're like a kid taken with a dog behind a fence. You can't resist banging the fence with a stick. You know how that story ends."

"The big bad wolf." Sarah dropped the hand and laughed.

Rosemary wagged her head. "I'm not talking about something that's benign. I mean there are things beyond the scope of everyday life that are capable of consuming us, devastating us, entirely, in a flash." The fingers of her hand flew apart. "Suddenly, without a moment's warning. I know."

From the street came a honk and the sharp squeal of brakes. A truck and a petit taxi slid at angles to each other across the intersection. Several green melons tumbled from the truck's open bed and burst in brilliant red splashes on the pavement. All traffic stopped. The drivers argued, leaning out their open side windows, angrily waving their hands. The howl and scrape of their Arabic leapt hotly through the air. Both drivers threw their hands up over their heads, as if blame for the near collision were a ball they could hurl back and forth.

A boy in a white T-shirt ran out into the street, grabbing up pieces of the broken watermelons. Smaller boys followed. Traffic bunched around the stalled pair like a tightening fist. If either driver backed up, the other could get by and the knot would be unsnarled. But neither moved. Only men on foot and their donkeys and those on bicycles and motorcycles could pass. Sarah looked past the honking cars for the beggar woman and her child but couldn't see them.

"This afternoon," Rosemary shouted above the noise from the street, "let's do what real Marrakeshi women do after love's paid them a visit. Let's go to the medina and find a nice hammam."

"Fine," Sarah shouted back, though she feared the hammam would be dank, sordid, an ideal environment for the spread of disease. "If you're sure there is such a thing."

The older woman laughed. "Just wait. A good sweat, a scrubbing, you'll feel like a new woman."

Sarah smiled, imagining herself in a dark djellaba and veil, her body concealed except for her eyes. "Like a real Marrakeshia."

Rosemary laughed again and pushed her chair back from the table to leave. "Sure, but for that we'll have to scrub a little harder, pay a little extra."

The traffic remained snarled, bumper to bumper. Horns honked long and impatiently. Everyone argued with someone else. Only the street boys eating watermelon weren't waving their hands. They thrust their chins out at the street to spit out seeds. Sarah saw that one of them had brought the beggar woman a jagged wedge of the fruit, the red flesh of which the woman ate, gazing abjectly at the sidewalk as her child nursed.

Rosemary pulled Sarah's arm. "Let's go. It'll stay this way until the police come and order them both to back up."

Sarah understood. "And they'll have saved face."

"But of course," Rosemary said, "and life will go on, *insha'Allah.*"

Instead of going with Rosemary to window-shop the boutiques that dotted the avenues of the Gueliz, Sarah decided she wanted to be by herself. She agreed to meet Rosemary later, at the Jemaa el Fna.

By week's end she'd be leaving. She hadn't told Rosemary yet. They were doing as many new things—touristy things, Rosemary called them—as their time together allowed. They toured the obligatory palace ruins and visited the gilded honeycombed tombs of the Saadian sultans—direct descendants of the Prophet's daughter, Fatima—where several storks nested high atop worn, crumbling walls. They had tea and croissants at La Mamounia, the posh hotel made famous by Sir Winston Churchill. That Churchill had loved Morocco, particularly Marrakesh, was a fact Rosemary repeated until Sarah had to tell her to stop. One evening after strolling all afternoon about the courtyard of an ancient medersa the women took a taxi to La Mamounia's grand casino, where Rosemary played roulette and baccarat, sipping a glass of Oulmès water that cost more than a meal outside the hotel's walls. Sarah felt out of sync there, as if she'd stepped out of a page in the Old Testament into a scene in a film with James Bond, though none of the men in the casino were even a quarter as attractive as any of the actors who'd portrayed the British secret agent.

Sarah was weary of the tourist routine. She made her way across the intersection and dropped a dirham into the woman's palm. It was hennaed gold. The curled green rind of the melon lay beside the

woman's foot. She whispered a blessing. The infant in her arms was
fast asleep.

Sarah made her way easily through the streets. She learned that
if she didn't carry a camera or gape like a lost lamb no one bothered
her. It was mainly a matter of where you placed your eyes and how
quickly you walked. She used the Koutoubia as a point of reference.
As long as she could see the graceful minaret jutting above the palm
trees against the mountains that formed the horizon, she could orient
herself. Everything in Marrakesh stood in relation to the Koutoubia.
Inevitably she found herself walking toward it, as if the stone tower
were a magnet.

She paused across the street from the noisy Jemaa el Fna, near a
group of tourists—German, she guessed by their accents—who were
snapping photographs of themselves in a carriage with their Berber
driver. She remembered her first evening date with Ramzi. After their
carriage ride to the Menara Gardens, they returned to the Jemaa el
Fna, where shadows shivered on the ground to the sound of ghaitas,
drums, tambourines, and flutes. Sarah had watched the dizzy shadows
and let herself be carried away. In Ramzi's room in the medina, they
lit a candle melted atop a cracked plate. Their shadows washed across
the walls as they kissed before they made love.

She remained on the sidewalk, forming a swirl of people forced to
walk around her, as if she were a stone in a stream, until a boy asked
if she would like a tour of the medina, very good shopping, I know a
special place, good jewelry, silver, filigree, at a good price, come with
me now, follow me, I show you, very good price. Sarah walked away
from him, and as he began to follow her she turned and told him
sharply in Arabic to leave her alone, she was no tourist, she lived in
Fez, exactly as Rosemary had taught her. The boy stared at her for a
few moments, then shrugged and said something in response. Sarah
pretended to understand and nodded. The boy bent his head and

spoke softly, as if praying or apologizing. Then he smiled and ran off into the crowd.

She felt no need to see Ramzi and hadn't since the night they'd been together, yet she found herself following the same path they'd taken before and worked her way through the Jemaa el Fna, past the scribes and fortune tellers, the toothless conjurers selling herbs and potions, the barbers and dentists, storytellers and snake charmers, Gnawa dancers, oud players, drummers, Chleuh dancing boys. Sarah walked past the jugglers, the acrobats, the monkey trainers, the pigeon man, the man who pretended to swallow a snake, the man standing on broken glass. She was able to move through the crowds unbothered since she'd crossed the square so often with Rosemary that many knew them as a pair of outsiders here for the summer, two *berrani* women from Fez.

She entered the medina and immediately slowed her pace. Here she was not known. Shopkeepers beckoned to her as she passed. She kept her head lowered, her eyes down, trying to blend in with the waves of women walking past in djellabas, the men in burnouses and skull caps, trying not to resemble the graceless groups of tourists herded like goats by their officious tour guides. Like tourists anywhere these expressed the poorest manners, talking too loudly, pointing, displaying expensive photographic equipment around their necks, as if declaring that the sights around them were less to be experienced in the present moment than to be captured and reduced to something two-dimensional, something one could hold in one's hand in a miniature, flattened version. Now that she'd lived in Morocco for several months, Sarah hated the tour groups. They embarrassed her. They were like relatives who did senseless things in front of people you were hoping to befriend. Though you couldn't really be blamed for their actions, you were still somehow responsible for them. How they behaved reflected on you.

She found herself at the doorway of the courtyard that led to Ramzi's room. He lived alone, in a room with a gray door, on the second floor. The yard door scraped against the paving stones as she pushed it open. A pair of cats—one black and white, the other long-haired calico—tumbled in the courtyard's center. Someone's wash hung limply on a rope stretched across the far corner, near a broken fountain bordered by cracked tiles. A green snake lay curled, asleep, amidst some dry leaves in the bowl of the fountain. Sarah walked up to Ramzi's room and knocked on the door. It gave way as she knocked, creaking open. The long-haired calico mewed and rubbed suddenly against her ankle. Ramzi wasn't there. She thought he'd be inside, sleeping. Curious to see his room in daylight, she stepped inside.

Against the wall on the right was the narrow bed in which they'd made love. The sheets were rumpled but appeared clean. Beside the bed was a table strewn with empty cigarette packs, a chair beside the table, another chair against the wall, which supported a bookcase filled with paperbacks in French, Arabic, and English. Sarah recognized titles by Alain Robbe-Grillet, Joseph Wambaugh, and Albert Camus as well as *Children of Dune, Serpico, Crime and Punishment*. Atop the bookcase was a ceramic mug featuring a red basketball. Taped to the wall were photos scissored from magazines— Yves Montand with both arms around Simone Signoret, Michael Jackson performing the moonwalk, Samira Said singing into a microphone, a shirtless David Bowie holding a cigarette, Catherine Deneuve looking unruffled and suave. The other walls were bare except for a corkboard near the door covered with postcards. Neatly pinned in the center was the one of Marilyn Monroe on the subway grate, gleefully pushing down her upblown skirt.

"They told me someone was here. I didn't expect it was you."

He stood in the doorway, one arm raised against the jamb. The light glared behind his head. Sarah couldn't make out his face.

"I didn't know you'd lived in the States."

"Sure. I studied there. For one year." He walked up to her and took her face in his hands and kissed her. He ran his hands lightly along her back, then down the length of her arms. His tongue tasted sweet, like mint, as if he'd been drinking tea. Though Sarah was aroused by the kiss she nudged him away.

"I didn't come here for that."

"Oh," he said and closed the door. "Then you must be a thief, here to steal my things."

His arms were cinnamon against the pale yellow of his shirt. His teeth were too white as he smiled. Sarah tried not to look into his eyes, the color of café noir, or at the way the soft curls of his hair fell back from his forehead. He was wiry, with a gymnast's body. She remembered how light and muscled he felt atop her as they had made love.

"I came to tell you I'm leaving."

He sighed "Would you like tea? I can make some."

"Rosemary's going back to Fez now that her nephew has returned to the States, and I'll be going with her. A few days of shopping, a last look at the medina in Fez el Bali, at least this time around."

"It is *baa-li.*" He was plugging in a hot plate. "The first syllable takes the accent. It is very easy to say. *Baa-li.*"

"Ramzi, please, don't make this difficult."

"Roll the *r*, just a little bit. Watch my mouth. *Rramzi.* Say the rest of the word fast, almost as if there is no vowel. Clip the end."

"Ramzi, don't."

"Still too slow, too much *ah*. *Rrmzi*. Like an engine you are starting. Don't be afraid to jam your foot down on the pedal. Give it some gas."

"You didn't think I'd be staying permanently, did you?"

"Put it in gear. Burn some rubber. Floor it."

"So now you give me language lessons."

He crossed the room and stared at her. His eyes melted, then fell. "Of course I knew you'd be leaving. But not this fast."

Sarah kissed him then, not knowing anything better to do, realizing it was indeed the reason why she'd come here. She became aware of the heat outside, the glare of light spilling into the room from the window. She pushed Ramzi to the bed, crossed the room, pulled the curtain on the window. The room fell into a soft darkness. Beyond the courtyard she could hear the muffled voices of passersby.

She unbuttoned Ramzi's shirt and ran her hands across the smooth, fine muscles of his chest. When he began to speak she put a finger to his lips. "No, don't," she whispered, slipping the shirt from his shoulders. There was no noise from outside now. She had him stand as she unbuckled his belt and unsnapped his pants button, then pulled the pants and the tongue of his belt out from his waist as she eased down his zipper. He was breathing heavily, his eyes closed. She imagined he could be heard in the courtyard. She kissed his lips, which were slightly parted, and whispered for him to be silent.

She had him sit on the edge of the bed as she undressed herself, taking off one piece of clothing at a time as slowly and deliberately as she could, performing in the near darkness an act that was less tease than dance, less for him than it was for herself. For her it was a new way she could be, a possibility, in a place she could leave behind forever if she wished, an act of sex with a man whom she would never have to see again if that was her desire. She drew each item of clothing across her skin so gradually the fabrics made her tingle and flush. When he reached for her she told him if he moved again she'd leave.

By the time she eased off her brassiere the touch of cloth on her skin was like a breath. A drop of sweat worked its way down between her breasts. She caught it with a fingertip, licked the droplet into her mouth. She peeled her underpants to her knees and lifted a leg free, then the other. Then she untied her scarf and ran it up the inside of her legs, over her stomach and breasts, then down the inside of each arm. She stepped to the edge of the bed and kissed him, then had him kiss the trail of her scarf, beginning with the insides of her arms. She pressed her fingertips to the nape of his neck and with the pressure of her touch led his mouth to her sex. She felt in harmony with her strength, confident in what she was doing.

"There," she said. He knelt before her on the floor. After a few minutes she lay on the bed. "Yes, that's it, that's it. Yes, yes, right *there.*"

Swirling light. The white, softly beating wings of a dove, hovering before her at the bed's edge. Light from the window pooled on the ceiling. Then the bird flew out from under her and became a thousand doves, all of them furiously beating their wings. The birds flew higher until they disappeared into the puddle on the ceiling, like sparks or jagged bolts of lightning, until she had to push his head away. She knotted her fingers in his hair, unaware that she'd cried out. He said something deep, dark, and her hands in his hair eased their grip, and then the dove again began beating its wings, transforming into one of the storks that flew high above the ruins, the courtyards and palaces, minarets, the stately Koutoubia, the crumbling rosy-red walls of their Marrakesh.

Later, in the hammam in the medina, Sarah was bathed in a white tiled room by a tall bare-breasted woman who made soft clucking sounds with her tongue. Sarah guessed the clucks were the audible part of some private song the woman sang to herself, a song she sang all day, that no one else could hear. The woman wore a mitten of cloth and used soap that was black and oily and soft as butter.

It seemed a great indulgence to Sarah to allow someone else to wash her. In the steamy room the woman poured buckets of hot water over her, then began to rub Sarah's skin with the cloth mitten until little rolls of dead cells and surface dirt fell from her hand and

Sarah's skin glowed red as sunburn. The woman scrubbed Sarah with
the dark soap as if she were a doll whose limbs were stuffed with rags.
She pushed Sarah's head to the tiles so she could wash Sarah's arms
and the mound of her back, then had Sarah stand so she could get at
the legs, then had her sit while she washed the red hair that tumbled
past Sarah's shoulders. Sarah closed her eyes and let the muscles
of her neck go limp. Her body tingled. The strong fingers worked
rhythmically in her hair, massaging her scalp, and then the hands
began on Sarah's face, thumbs smoothing the forehead, the heel of
palms gently pressing against her temples, thumbs stroking her eye
sockets and then moving down across her cheeks and jaw and the
layers of muscles in her neck.

Sarah could hear the woman's bare feet slap the tiles, the drip
of water, the steady clucking, Rosemary's occasional moan. Another
woman was washing Rosemary. Sarah lay now on her back and again
closed her eyes. Soft circles of color popped behind her eyelids. The
tall woman was massaging Sarah's hands now. Sarah gave herself up
completely to the woman's touch.

Lying on the hammam's floor on the edge of a dream, Sarah felt
something within her drain out her fingertips and merge with the
water swirling around her. It was more than tension or a tightness.
She felt she'd reached some point where her life could be more her
own. Whether it was the bath and massage or the raw boldness with
which she'd pulled Ramzi's mouth between her legs she didn't care.
All she knew was that she realized some difference. Now there was no
going back.

The Jemaa el Fna pulsed with music and Arabic's rasp and swing,
illuminated by the bright gas torches over the food stalls, offering
an unimaginable variety of grilled meat, vegetables, fish. The sky
overhead popped with stars. Rosemary bought a round loaf of
khubz and ate from it as they strolled about. Sarah closed her eyes

and listened to the shrill cries of the ghaitas, the soft jangle of tambourines, the drip of a strummed guembri, the velvet beat of drums, the tumble of human voices that filled the crowded square like the darkness now filled the sky. The sounds were so thick Sarah felt she could swim in them. She opened her eyes and followed her friend, who turned around to smile, one cheek bulging with bread.

They walked past a group of men and boys who circled a storyteller, hands chopping the air as he weaved a sentence that had no ending. Sarah wished she understood him. She knew that some storytellers retold the adventures of *The Thousand and One Nights*, taught to them by their fathers who'd learned it from their fathers who'd learned it from theirs in a near endless chain. And while the men of Marrakesh listened to ancient stories, the women gathered in loose clusters of five or six around fortune tellers who placed cards down on a worn rug and whispered to the bent covered heads all that was certain to come.

The juxtaposition made Sarah wonder if there was something in men that turned their gaze to the past, something in women that compelled them to wonder about the future. Was it that women gave birth and as a result were more directly responsible for new life? She pictured the streetside beggar woman in Gueliz. Before Sarah could complete her thought a grinning Gnawa dancer leapt into her path, castanets clacking between his fingers, the tassel atop his checked cap spinning as he danced. The boy's face was as dark as the night. Sarah gave him a coin. Immediately the monkey trainer's muzzled monkey performed a backflip beside her, then took off his miniature fez and raised it toward her with one hand, while the other hand tugged viciously at his penis. The pigeon man thrust out his hands, on which two pigeons performed a sequence of clumsy hops. The young Gnawa dancer was now joined by his older brothers, one of whom beat a drum. Sarah pushed past them to keep up with Rosemary, and it was then that she noticed the fire-eater.

He was standing off by himself to one side of the square, juggling several flaming batons, first high over his head and then behind his back and beneath his legs. Then he gathered the torches in one hand and with a flick of the wrist extinguished all but one, which he slowly raised to his mouth. The other sticks dropped on the ground behind him. Sarah pushed her way forward to see him. He was arching his head and back as he began easing the flaming baton down his throat. Then the fire-eater drew the black stick from his mouth, and all was darkness, and then his coiled form sprang forward and he spat a long flame into the dark sky. He dropped to one knee and like a dragon breathed fire back onto the torch, which blazed again suddenly with fury, and then a boy behind him rushed forward and gave him the other batons, which the fire-eater again juggled, allowing each to catch the fire that for a magnificent moment had completely disappeared.

Sarah clapped her hands, hard, sure she had seen the fire disappear completely. The fire-eater juggled the flaming sticks. The boy gave him a cup to drink. Between gulps the fire-eater shouted something to the crowd that made them laugh, and then the boy lifted the hem of his djellaba, making a basket of his lap, and worked the crowd for coins as the fire-eater juggled the flaming batons high over his head, and the Gnawa dancers once against banged their tambourines, and ghaitas wailed in the silky night.

Rosemary drew on her cigarette. They were back in Gueliz, again at the hotel where they'd taken their morning coffee, though now they sat at a table on the hotel's rooftop terrace, which overlooked both old and new Marrakesh. "That's precisely the problem with love," the older woman was saying. "It always comes to an end."

"I hope he understood. I tried to explain."

"Oh, don't worry yourself about him. He was using you. He expected it, I'm sure."

Sarah reached for a cigarette. "No. It hurt him. I caught him by surprise." She remembered how sad his eyes looked. She lit the cigarette, pulling the smoke deep into her lungs. Though they'd stopped at their hotel room for sweaters, Sarah felt cold up on the dark rooftop. "And if one of us was using the other, it was me using him."

"The way it should be," Rosemary said with a laugh.

Sarah smiled, not wanting to be disagreeable. "We both went into it with our eyes open."

"You can be sure he's had plenty of affairs with foreign women."

"No." She pictured him, how for a moment he'd watched her as she dressed to leave. Then he cleared his face and smiled gently. "Not plenty." She sighed. "No matter." She drew hard on the cigarette. It did matter, though she felt she couldn't admit it. "If we'd met back in the States—"

"He wouldn't be the same person there."

"I know." She let out a long stream of smoke. "I'm not the same person here."

Rosemary nodded. "Travel does that."

Sarah stared at her hands. "Some things, you can't outrun them, though in a different light, in a foreign place"—she looked about, at the others at their rooftop tables and then up at the suddenly clear stars in the dark sky overhead—"you can try new possibilities." She nodded for emphasis. "Do you ever think of going back?"

"To the States?" Rosemary shook her head. "What for? To live in some condo off the Beltway? In my clean, narrow widow's rooms, with some potted plants, a caged canary?" She opened her hands and laughed. "For one thing, I simply don't have the money. I could rent a palace here for half of what an apartment costs in the States. You know how inexpensive it is here. As long as you have sugar and bread. Very poor people in the countryside, they live on that."

Sarah nodded.

"But even if I were rich I doubt I'd go back because here I know people, I have friends, I have place, I'm someone, Rosemary Fisher, of Rue de l'Atlas in Fez." She drew out from her purse the red roulette chip she'd kept the night they'd visited the Mamounia casino. She fingered the chip as she spoke. "Some come here because they've failed, like my nephew, who thinks every bad break he's been given is someone else's fault. I knew he couldn't stay because he was never really able to see this country for what it is. He never searched for his place here, if you understand what I mean. On the other hand you, someone like you could find a life here."

"I'll return," Sarah said and then added quickly, "*insha'Allah*."

"*Insha'Allah*," Rosemary replied. She sipped a glass of water. "It's more than that Bill's buried here. Our life together was here too. Why do you think out of all the hotels in Marrakesh I picked this place?" Her face eased into a smile. "The first time Bill and I drove down here we stayed in a suite on the fifth floor." Her eyes grew dreamy. "That night, after we had some time together in our room, he brought me up here to see the view."

Sarah stared up at the stars and then down at the twinkling lights of the city below. "And the next morning you looked for a hammam."

Rosemary laughed devilishly. "But of course."

Sarah excused herself from the table. She stepped across the terrace to the railing, one hand drawing the folds of her sweater together.

And did she have place? she wondered. She stood in a suddenly stiff wind, gazing down at the yellow headlights of the traffic on the wide avenue below. She was Sarah Rosen, of Rogers Park in Chicago, an American woman, a Jew, who'd traveled to this edge of Africa and the Arab world in part because she wanted to and in part because people told her she couldn't, and there was nothing she wanted to be unable to do. Whether it was travel or break off an affair with a man or ease a fiery torch down her throat and live to spit out the flame.

At once she understood how the fire-eater did it. Fire required not only fuel but oxygen. By breathing out and trusting what he knew, he wasn't burned.

Sarah smiled, pleased. She hadn't been burned either. She scanned the horizon, looking for the graceful, elegant lines of the Koutoubia. When she could locate it she'd know for sure where she was. She gripped the terrace railing firmly and stared across the lights of Marrakesh into the night. The tower stood in the distance to her right.

VALLEY OF THE DRÂA

They reached the point near Agdz where the land leveled off.

"All these trees," Ahmed Ousaid said, gesturing toward the groves of date palms beyond the windshield, "come from the seeds spit out by the traders who brought dates from Zagora to Ouarzazate and Marrakesh. They grow near the river, where the traders stopped to take water and rest."

"You mean pits," said Henry, who was driving. He reached up and pushed back his fedora.

His hat was the kind Humphrey Bogart wore in the film Henry had rented from one of the hotels in Ouarzazate to show Ahmed and his uncles. The film made Casablanca look like a remote outpost on the Algerian border. Expecting to see a movie about the modern city that Casa in fact was, Ahmed was sorely disappointed with the story of the unhappy seller of alcohol who lusted for another man's wife. Where was Morocco? Ahmed wanted to know. At the end after Bogart accepted his fate without complaint, Henry turned to no one in particular and announced, "Hey, he's got my hat." Just as well, Ahmed thought, for no Muslim would want it. Muslims had no time to be taking off hats with brims each time they prayed. Ahmed decided that in the movie Morocco was portrayed as primitive because in America's eyes it was. Still, Ahmed wanted to see the world the way Americans saw it, with American eyes.

"Yes, pits," he said and let out a sigh. They'd been arguing. It was late summer, too hot for Henry's word games. Ahmed grew annoyed whenever Henry listened not to what he said but how he said it. With Henry, words had to be one way or else they were wrong. You would think he was a professor or the first man to be ill. "That is what I told you. Pits."

"Not to pick bones with you, pardner, but clear as a bell I heard you say *seeds*." Beneath the hat's shadow Henry had pale, pink skin that broke into red splotches whenever he stayed out too long in the sun. In his guts sprawled the crab of cancer. His little eyes, that at times reminded Ahmed of a hedgehog he once kept as a pet, squinted at the road ahead.

Seeds, pits—did Professor Hedgehog really think it mattered? Ahmed took a breath and said, "Henry, here they are the same."

That silenced him. He sucked in his cheeks, then let his jaw go slack. In the glare of the sunlight his face resembled a skull.

They sat on the sticky plastic seats of the rented Peugeot, windows down, speeding through the swirling dust from Ouarzazate. The narrow slash of roadway spilled out ahead of them, running parallel with the Drâa, which at this time of year was less river than trickle of mud. Thick groves of date palm swayed lazily alongside the Drâa's banks. On the slopes beyond, houses made of mud and straw squatted in the shadow of the barren mountains. Here animals and men shared the same house, scratching out a miserable life from the useless sand peppered with rocks and weeds that resembled dark sticks. The high sun above bleached the sky so white it hurt to look.

Ahmed stared instead at his feet. They were bare now that he'd slipped off his shoes. He wore a cotton djellaba, tan with mahogany stripes. It was soft to the touch and cool, easy to wear in the heat, which shimmered in dizzy waves on the concrete ribbon of highway. He ate from an open bag of almonds resting between his legs. His uncles had given him the almonds, along with a sack of dates, before they left Ouarzazate. Food for the desert, they told him. Positioning the next nut with his tongue, he crunched it with his back teeth.

"And where did the dates in Zagora come from?"

Where did he think? From the djinn? "Other traders."

"From across the desert?"

"Of course."

"Ever been out this way before?" Henry shouted over the noise of the car's engine.

"Once." He didn't feel like elaborating. Before he'd left Ouarzazate to study at the university in Rabat, he'd ventured into the Sahara with one of his uncles, the youngest son of Hajji Izem, visiting villages so desolate they barely deserved names. The houses huddled there made Ahmed think of clutches of graves. The desert held no appeal. Beyond Zagora there was nothing else. Beyond Zagora there was only the hot, rolling waste of the Sahara broken by an occasional oasis. Ahmed considered Zagora the end of the world.

"So why'd you go there?" Henry said.

Rushing in through the open windows was the wind's hot, stale breath. Here they gave names to the wind. *Chergui* was the hot, dry wind that blew in from the desert's heart. The air vent above Henry's knee spat out a fine spray of sand, dusting his pants.

"Because my great uncle Izem crossed it twice, on his way to and from Mecca."

"What'd he have"—Henry wiped a drop of sweat working its way down his nose—"something with four-wheel drive?"

Ahmed laughed. "He did not go by automobile." One day long ago, decades before Ahmed was born, the uncle made preparations to leave their village, saying he was going to make a pilgrimage to Mecca. So began the story the uncles routinely told. But how will you go there? the others asked. By the blessing of Allah, the uncle replied, on foot. So the uncle set out and crossed the desert, walking to Algeria, the south of Tunisia, then Libya and Egypt, reciting the Shahada with every step, until he crossed the Red Sea. The journey took three years. "He walked the whole way, on foot."

"Better by foot than by hand," Henry said with a grin.

Ahmed shook his head sadly. He didn't recognize the joke, only that once again Henry had found something he'd said amusing.

"So tell me, why would a guy do something like that?"

"I already told you." Ahmed didn't mind that his voice revealed his impatience. "To make a hajj to Mecca."

"Ahh, a hajj to Mecca, that explains it." He reached across the gearshift for an almond. "Don't tell me the poor guy hoofed it the entire way. Didn't he even have a donkey?" He put the almond in his mouth and sucked on it.

"In the desert a donkey would soon die."

"Oh yeah?" Henry said. "Quicker than a horse?"

Ahmed nodded. Henry was playing another one of his games. "Perhaps. But why would anyone take a horse into the desert?"

"I give up. To get to the other side?"

"That would not be wise. A horse would die very quickly."

"Quicker than a man?"

Ahmed considered the riddle. "No. I think the man would die first. Then the horse would die after some days, then the donkey. Only the camel would live."

"Where'd this camel come from?"

Where did he think? Ahmed grinned before he answered. "From its mother's womb."

"Well, why didn't your uncle take a camel?"

"He was too poor."

"Camels are expensive, huh?"

Ahmed was smiling. "Sure." He felt the strong rush of air outside his open window. He was relieved he had been able to keep up. "When we get to Zagora you can buy one, if you like."

"What would I do with a camel?" Henry spat the unchewed almond out his window as they sped past the dusty little village of Agdz.

"What you do with everything else," Ahmed said. "Take a picture of it."

Henry laughed. His head no longer looked like a skull. "So what did your great uncle do in Mecca?" he said in a soft voice. "I mean, really. I'm curious. I'd like to know. Did he go there to pray?"

Of course he prayed in Mecca, Ahmed thought. He performed the tawaf, seven counterclockwise circles of the Kaaba, then made seven trips between the hills of Safa and Marwa in imitation of Hagar, who was left by Abraham in the desert valley with their son Ishmael, who was dying of thirst. Because Hagar did not lose hope that she would find water for her child, Allah sent the angel Gabriel to her, and the angel led her to the Zamzam well. Pilgrims making a hajj were allowed to drink from the Zamzam well. Ahmed always imagined its water as cool and sweet. Then the pilgrims traveled to Mina and rested before the day of standing at the Mount of Arafat, where the Prophet delivered his final sermon, sealing Islam and its teachings. As dusk descends, the pilgrims rush through the narrow pass at Muzdalifa—the place where one makes oneself agreeable— purging themselves of all ill feelings for others. They gather forty-nine stones which later they throw in groups of seven at the three pillars in Mina. Mounded around the base of the ancient pillars are more stones than anyone can count. The stoning cleanses the faithful of evil. Then all celebrate the Feast of Sacrifice by slaughtering a sheep. So many offered sheep to Allah, the great uncle said after he returned, the ground ran ankle-deep with blood.

Before Ahmed could answer, Henry bleated like a startled goat and swerved the Peugeot onto the road's shoulder, which was strewn with rocks.

Ahmed cried out. He grabbed the door to steady himself.

Henry eased the car back onto the road. "Jeez! Did you see that? He could've killed us!"

Ahmed shook his head. "I had thoughts only of Hajji Izem."

"I don't believe it! He was heading right toward us!"

"Yes, as he should," Ahmed said, trying to be agreeable. Though he did not drive, he knew that steering down the road's center was the way it was done.

Henry pushed up the brim of his hat. "I hate to clue you in on the rules of highway safety, but the son of a beehive is supposed to stay in his own damn lane."

Ahmed pointed out the windshield at the road, thumb and first finger curled into an oval. He didn't know the rules of highway safety but he knew that here there were no laws, only the narrow road ahead, which they were indeed fortunate to have. "Do you understand where we are now, how there is nothing ahead of us?"

"I know where we are." Henry glared at the road. "I'm not lost."

Now people go to Mecca by airplane, Ahmed thought. He took another almond between his teeth. They arrange their hajj as they would a trip to Italy or France, with the aid of a travel agent and the efficient click of a computer's keyboard. Though he respected his great uncle, Ahmed was quite sure that if he ever made a hajj, Allah willing, he'd take a jumbo jet.

"Look!" Henry cried.

The car slowed. Henry pointed. There, to the north on the horizon, was a caravan of about a hundred camels. They walked nose to tail into the sun along a high ridge, driven by one of the Blue Men from Goulimine.

"Isn't that something!" Henry cried.

"Sure," Ahmed said, though to him the sight was not much. From a distance camels are beautiful and move with a graceful sideways sway along the sand, but when you get up close they are mean creatures that spit and try to tear your clothing with their sharp teeth, and the men reek of the sour stench of seldom washing.

"Let me try another one," Henry said, extending his hand. "Lord knows, I should eat something."

Ahmed placed a date and an almond in the man's open palm. "You are not hungry?"

"Not at all. Haven't been for days. Just hot." He banged the dashboard with his fist, then slid the date between his lips and mouthed it.

Ahmed stared out the window at the sand. He would never walk across a desert. He was a modern young man, the first in his family to attend the university. If he were going anywhere, it would be to America, where he would view the Statue of Liberty, Disneyland, Epcot Center, the monuments of the District of Columbia. Ahmed wanted to see the cowboys of Texas, eat a hot dog with mustard at Coney Island, float on a raft down the Mississippi like Huckleberry Finn. In Ahmed's vision of America all the young men looked like James Dean or Michael Jackson, the women like Whitney Houston, Madonna, Elizabeth Taylor. Though it was said that the homeless beggars of New York were worse than the beggars of Fez or Tangier, and everyone in America owned a gun, and the alleyways were full of drug addicts who would slit your throat for the few dirhams in your pocket, in Ahmed's eyes America was a wonderful place filled with neon light. Next to Morocco, America was the greatest place. Ahmed wondered if he would attempt to walk there if an impossible ocean did not lie between them.

Then Henry cursed and said, "If you don't like it, go around me."

Ahmed turned. In the dust behind them a car flashed its yellow headlights, the signal for Henry to give room so it could pass.

Henry held the car to the road's center.

"No," Ahmed said.

The car came up fast alongside them, forced out onto the shoulder of the road. As it sped past them there was the sound of cracking ice.

The windshield turned white as wool. The car spun in lazy spirals, looping through the dizzy swirls of dust raised by the car that had passed them. Ahmed drew up his knees and cradled his head in his arms. Henry shouted *whoa!* over and over, unable to control their motion, his pale arms clinging to the wheel as the car skidded crazily through the sand whirling thickly around them.

*

He wore the wide-brimmed hat to conceal his head, made bald
by the invisible rays of a machine designed to kill cancer. Beneath
a streetlight outside Rabat's American Center, Henry had shown
Ahmed photographs of how he'd looked before. Did the hair burn up
in a puff of smoke? Ahmed had wanted to know. No, Henry replied,
it just fell out when I combed it. Then this—he took off his hat—
grew in its place. On his head were wisps of straw. See, Henry said
after Ahmed made a face, you'd cover it up too.

As long as it was someone else's, death held out a fascination as
enticing as a woman's veil, as mesmerizing as a flute waving before
a hooded snake. Ahmed was quite taken with the progression of
Henry's disease. Ahmed wondered about the pain, imagining himself
in the dying man's place. Every few hours Henry covered his palm
with pills from a bag packed with brown plastic vials, whispering
like a madman remembering his prayers. Two of these, one of these,
four of these directly after meals three times a day. Some pills were
intended to ease the crab's pinching, others to lull it to sleep or at least
make it lie quietly. Several more were for problems—complications—
brought on by the first pills. In turn they raised more complications,
solved by even more pills that required still others hiding deeper
down in the bag in still more brown bottles. It seemed the American
was always swallowing something, always checking his watch, always
muttering like a beggar with one hand extended for the red pills, the
green pills, the pills with the blue stripe, the big white ones that were
so bitter they sometimes made him gag and choke.

The crab slept so soundly when Henry first arrived in Morocco
that Ahmed was tempted to believe it did not exist. But then, when
Ahmed least expected it, Henry would wince and turn the color of
bone, then puff his cheeks and breathe in great spurts, like some
immense fish pulled out of the water into the air, until Ahmed
believed again.

It was easy for Ahmed to believe in what he could not actually see. The world was a place where the invisible had surprising power. Ahmed knew about spells and spirits, both good and bad. He believed in *maktub*, that what is written is certain to pass. He surrendered his petty personal will to Allah, whose supreme wisdom placed the dying American in his path. Ahmed did not consider he had any choice in the matter.

So the pair traveled about doing whatever Henry wanted to do, which was to see all there was to be seen. It seemed to Ahmed that, if Henry was typical, Westerners believed mainly in what their senses could perceive. They valued the visible so highly they liked to take photos of all the physical things standing before them. Rather than travel to Morocco and try to know it, to feel the rhythms and repetitions of its ordinary life, to hear the silence of its art and architecture, understand their search for forms, patterns, variations, most Westerners seemed to prefer only to photograph their presence there, as if posing before a ruin with a grin on one's face was sufficient reason to make the long journey across the ocean.

Though he was as poor as a rag in comparison to them, and he felt their inferior whenever he considered their mastery of machines and their ability to wage war, he knew in his heart he was at least their equal. In moments of pride he felt their superior because he believed he was closer to God. He believed his religion, Islam, was in truth superior to Judaism and Christianity since his prophet, Muhammed, had been sent after theirs. He held no desire to convert Christians or Jews since as a Muslim he believed faith comes from within and cannot be imposed from without. He thought it telling that while they did not acknowledge his prophet his religion accepted theirs. In the matter of religion Ahmed felt he, the one in the djellaba, was the more advanced.

He liked the opportunity travelers gave him to practice speaking English, and he liked the dirhams the days of guiding them around left in his pockets. Henry paid for everything with the endless wad of money that fattened his pockets or sprang, as if by miracle, from his wallet's plastic cards. Ahmed knew his efforts spared travelers the disappointments of encountering hustlers or pickpockets, who plagued all cities and who saw tourists not as people made by the same God who had fashioned them but as potential sources for riches beyond imagination. It pleased Ahmed to think that the travelers he guided returned home with the knowledge that Morocco was a good place, which in nearly all ways it was.

Of course he is more than welcome, Ahmed's family said when Ahmed brought Henry inland over the mountains to Ouarzazate, but why have you brought this one home and not others? Because he has no one, Ahmed replied, and because he is dying. And would you have us fall ill with his disease? they asked. It is a thing inside him only, Ahmed answered, not a germ we might breathe in. It eats him from the inside, like a worm hidden in fruit. Worms crawl out, they told Ahmed. Not this worm, he replied. It is too busy killing him. And what are we to do when it succeeds? Ahmed's family asked. What we do for all deaths, he answered. Wash his body, dig a grave, cover his body with dirt and stones. There is no one else to do it. Though he is rich, he has no family. His faith in God seems to play no part in his life. No one in his country cares about him. Ahmed described how Henry would die if they did not help him—alone, surrounded by machines. No hands would touch him. One machine would make a long sound, *beeeeep*, when his heart stopped. Poor man, they said, but he is not an Arab, not Berber, not Muslim. Yes, Ahmed said, he is very poor. Allah be thanked we are not so unfortunate. He told me he did not know what he would do until one day his finger found Morocco on a globe. The finger of God! Ahmed's family said knowingly. They accepted him then, believing Allah had led him to them.

Everyone got along well enough until Henry and Ahmed argued about politics—the Palestinian situation, America's support

of Israel—and Henry decided to move to a hotel. He sent a boy to
Ahmed's house to get his bag. Perhaps the bed was not soft enough,
Ahmed's family wondered after the boy carried away Henry's suitcase.
They sat up on the roof around a bowl of couscous. Or perhaps he
left because he preferred a toilet like a chair, or he did not enjoy
their company. Whatever, the insult was clear enough. The men ate
the couscous, rolling it first with their fingers and palms into balls.
Henry's name was dropped like gristle or a piece of fat sucked clean of
meat. In all hearts but Ahmed's he was forgotten.

In Ahmed's heart there was a jagged rip.

The next week they were told Henry had been taken to the
hospital, rushed there from the lobby of his hotel after he'd passed
out. The crisis restored their honor, allowed them to speak of him.
Like a dog that goes off by itself into the countryside when it is
sick, so Henry must have felt the turn in his condition, so he had
no choice but to abandon their house. They hurried down the main
boulevard to the hospital to see him.

In the crowded men's ward he lay on a cot, hairless as a newborn
rat, flies sipping the sweat that pooled in the yellow hollows beneath
his eyes. A sturdy plastic tube connected his arm to a bag of fluid
suspended in the air. After a while he groaned, then opened his little
eyes and spoke, saying their names and that he was sorry for being so
much trouble. You are not much trouble to us, they told him. They
spoke in Berber, forgetting he did not understand.

Henry gave them a rusty laugh and told them to ixnay the Pig
Latin. Then he gazed at Ahmed and announced that now he was one
of them—Arab, Berber, maybe even both—now that their blood ran
in his veins.

They had to punch out the shattered windshield before they could
continue. The car squatted motionless in the sand not too far off the
road. Henry wrapped his hand and forearm in a shirt he took from

the trunk, and the glass shattered into tiny blue-green cubes. Ahmed
scooped them from the floor and car seats by the handful. Henry
tossed the rock the passing car's rear wheels had spit back at them
back onto the other rocks lining the road.

"Lucky it held together." He seemed like his old self, full of
sudden energy. "Or else we'd be looking at a couple of blind guys."

"Yes," Ahmed agreed. He was surprised at how beautiful the
cubes of glass were, how they did not cut his hands or otherwise harm
him. He made a neat mound of the glass in the sand. "But Henry, if
we were blind we could not look at anything."

"That's good. No slipping the obvious past you." Henry poked
his fist through the rest of the windshield, then paused and picked the
remaining pieces out of the shirt. "Yeah, we'd have to beg together in
the medina. You'd have to teach me some of those chants."

The thought of the rich *Nasrani* begging made Ahmed smile.

"The way I look nowadays, we could make ourselves some real
money."

"Sure," Ahmed said. He felt giddy, ecstatic they had not been
killed.

"Or maybe we could just roam around the desert. We'd have to
get canes, white ones with little red stripes. Maybe a couple of good
German shepherds. That way people would know we were blind."

"Here people know you are blind when you stumble into them."

"Oh, we could stumble all right. We could get ourselves a pair of
those camels from that guy in the blue bathrobe, then go from oasis
to oasis to Algeria like your great uncle."

"Algeria is very far. Beyond Zagora it is many kilometers."

"Not a problem." Henry tossed the shirt in the trunk, slammed it
shut. "You know, I always thought the desert was an especially weird
place. That's true, isn't it? Hermits living in caves, eating grasshoppers
and honey. Prophets going there for visions. In the States some native
tribes still go into the desert for peyote buttons, claim it's a religious

experience. Of course, the Jews wandered around the desert for forty years."

"Peyote buttons?" Ahmed pictured the buttons on a shirt.

"Mushrooms. Psychedelics. Turn on, drop out. Dig it?" He gave Ahmed a big grin. "Or were you nowhere during the Sixties?"

He'd read about the 1960s, the American hippie movement, when many traveled to Morocco for kif. "Henry, I was not yet born."

"Well, it's about time you were." Henry slid behind the car's wheel, then clutched his abdomen and winced. "The rooster's crowing." He rested his forehead against the wheel and let out a long breath through his puffed cheeks. "Wake up, smell the coffee."

Ahmed knew better than to ask about the pain. Instead he smiled. "I wish there was some coffee here to smell."

Henry cranked the engine. "I wish we had some peyote buttons. I'd try 'em. Let's go, Berber King, hop in the car. I'd eat a whole handful of hallucinogens and check out of this motel in a blaze of glory."

"Sure." Ahmed gave Henry's shoulder a pat.

They sped toward Zagora along the empty strip of road. "Don't need air-conditioning after you knock out the windshield. Whooee! Makes you grit your teeth." He shifted gears and relaxed, color seeping back into his face. "You know, during the Sixties I was nothing. I was a black hole, a worker bee, doing whatever I was told. Now I wish I'd loosened my collar for a minute, taken off my tie, enjoyed more things, know what I mean?" Ahmed could hardly hear him through the rushing wind. "Kicked back, stepped off the hamster wheel, did whatever I wanted for a damn change."

Ahmed nodded, confused. He did not understand *black hole, worker bee, hamster wheel.*

"Like your great uncle, the guy who walked to Mecca. Now that sounds like a life worth living. You get through with a life like that and you can think back and say you actually did something with the time you had. Me? Up until the time I came here, I wasted my whole life." He nodded at the road ahead. "I worked for other people, always put myself last. Nose to the old grindstone, shoulder to the wheel. Oh Ahmed"—Henry paused—"I was a good donkey. I never complained, was always on time, where I was supposed to be. I was the kind of guy who carried two pens in his shirt pocket in case one ran dry. Instead I ran dry. I ended up selling my life to the highest bidder. It hurts now even to say it. You know, the only true-to-myself thing I ever did was to come here to Morocco."

"I am sorry to hear it," Ahmed said. His eyes teared from the wind. He wished he knew the right words to say.

"Don't look so glum, chum. Just a final epiphany. Can you drive a stick shift?"

"Me?" He felt a warm flood of worry. "I have never tried. Why, do you need me to drive?"

"Not just this moment, no. But remember, this is a rented car. Eventually you're going to have to take this baby back. Open the glove compartment, let me show you the papers. There's probably a drop-off at the airport in Ouarzazate. Don't worry, it won't cost you, it's all on plastic. I better give that to you too, and sign over my traveler's checks. Now tell me about the great uncle who walked to Mecca. What'd he do after he got there?"

Ahmed was not sure he understood. "Please do not speak foolishly." He put his hand on Henry's shoulder. "You have plenty of time."

"Sure I do." Henry patted Ahmed's hand, then pushed back his hat. "I got a first-hand look at the level of health care around here. Believe you me, now I know why they call this the Third World."

"We do our best," said Ahmed. There was Henry again, making him feel defensive.

"No one said you didn't."

"The big cities have very excellent hospitals."

"Amigo, at this point I wouldn't walk into the Mayo Clinic. The fat lady's standing off in the palm trees clearing her throat. So tell me about this great uncle and Mecca. I want to hear all about Mecca. C'mon."

Ahmed began with the tawaf. Then he hitched up his djellaba and sat in the driver's seat after Henry pulled over and insisted he learn to drive. Once the car was past first gear and rolling it was easy, even pleasurable. Ahmed drove slowly—thirty kilometers an hour— to keep the wind down and so he could hear Henry when he talked. After Henry fell asleep Ahmed imagined he was in Hollywood driving down the road like Paul Newman or Robert Redford. He smiled and waved out the windshield at beautiful imaginary American women.

In Zagora it was very hot. They drove past the town's gate and down its main street, deserted except for a pair of tethered donkeys, tails flicking away flies, necks bent by the heat. Henry was awake and wanted to walk around, so Ahmed pulled the car over. When he took his foot off the clutch, the car bucked forward and died. Henry showed him how to turn the key off, then had him start the car up again, put it into reverse and back out, then pull over again. The second time Ahmed did it right. Turn the key off first, then take your foot off the clutch. Henry locked the glove compartment and told Ahmed to keep the keys. The sun dipped lower in the sky, edging back toward Agdz, Ouarzazate, the High Atlas mountains, Marrakesh. Ahmed's mind traced the geography, the path he and Henry had traveled together. He pictured Rabat's coast, the pounding blue sea.

There was no breeze. The town itself was not much more than a main street tacked onto the end of the highway. It seemed smaller to Ahmed than the last time he was here. The muddy river bed nearby was fringed with date palms. Here the Drâa came to its end. They found a café at the far edge of the street and sat down in the shade. Henry drew circles and lines in the fine layer of sand on the table. A scrawny brown dog slinked down the center of the street.

Henry was ghost white. "Be right back," he said, walking into the café. "Gotta see if I can whiz."

When he returned he shook his head at Ahmed and said, "No cigar." Ahmed shouted in Arabic to the boy inside. "Wake up, can't you see?" The boy got up from his stool and came to their table, staring at the street. Henry asked the boy for something cold, with lots of ice. Ahmed knew the café was too poor to have ice. They would be lucky if the sodas were even slightly cool.

"We should go to the hotel for ice," he told Henry. He was covering his palm with pills. "You should have a rest."

"We don't need a hotel. Unless you want a room."

The boy brought them their sodas and two glasses. Both bottles were warm, as if they had been kept in the sun.

Henry spilled the pills onto the dusty tabletop. "Captain, the engines have shut down." He spoke with a strange accent.

"What engines?" Ahmed thought he must mean the car. He was sure he had turned it off properly.

"I need all the power you can give me, Scotty," Henry said in a different voice. He raised his bottle of soda, pushed back his hat and gave Ahmed a wink. "Let's see if this gets the old engines up to warp speed."

Ahmed didn't like this game. "I do not understand a thing you say."

Henry set down the bottle and grimaced. "Tastes bad to me, like drinking sweat."

Ahmed did not know how to answer. He knew the taste of sweat. The soda was warm but nothing like it. He was about to exchange bottles with Henry when Henry stood and dropped a coin in the dust alongside his pills on the table, then started up the street. Ahmed finished his drink—he was very thirsty from the heat—and hurried after him.

At the end of the street there was something for tourists, a large painted sign.

TOMBOUCTOU 52 JOURS

Below the words was a painting of the desert. A Blue Man posed with his camel on the left. In the clear sky was a large red arrow. "Tombouctou!" Henry shouted. "We can make that, easy."

"No," Ahmed said, as if to a child.

"I love this," Henry said. "A sign to Tombouctou!"

"Henry, we should go back to the car."

"Just remember to give it a little clutch. The Peugeot likes a little clutch. Or else she'll die out on you."

Henry walked past the sign into the desert. Ahmed followed. Only later would Ahmed learn that the crab in Henry's guts had grown beyond imagination, that it had spread out its arms, strangling everything it could touch and embrace. The doctors in the hospital in Ouarzazate would have to cut Henry open so the authorities could issue an official cause of death. Ahmed did not want them to cut Henry's body open, but the doctors would not accept his explanation that Henry had died from the heat, nearly three-and-a-half kilometers from Zagora, after turning as red as the arrow in the sign to Tombouctou.

He had stopped sweating. His face was covered with the ugly splotches he got whenever it was too hot. After they trudged beyond the first few sand dunes he had to sit, breathing like the bellows of a silversmith.

"Let's go back," Ahmed said. He wanted to pour water over Henry's face, cool him down, before he burned up.

Henry waved at the words as if they were flies. Go away, his hand said. After a while he stood and told Ahmed he had to urinate.

Ahmed turned away, to give him privacy. Henry said, "No good. No damn good. I'm tapped out."

What could Ahmed do? "We must go back," he pleaded, as Henry walked on.

It was growing late. Their long shadows stretched ahead of them in the sand. The dunes rolled on, as if without end. On the sides of some of the dunes were pebbles and the dark tufts of weeds.

"Just look at this place!" Henry said. He grabbed Ahmed's shoulder, grinning so wide his red skin looked about to pop. "God, it's so beautiful! So still, like a frozen sea." He pointed at the dunes ahead of them, glowing orange in the fading light. They climbed the next dune, then stopped on its crest. "Ever since I was a kid I wanted to come here, to be in this place." Kneeling, Henry sifted a handful of sand through his fingers. "The Sahara!" He threw a handful of sand into the air. "The Sahara! Can you believe it? Come on, let's see how far we can go."

When it was clear that his words could not make him return, Ahmed followed his friend deeper into the desert. They walked into their shadows, which raced playfully ahead of them, clinging fast to the sides of the steep dunes they climbed, bounding down each hollow they descended. Ahmed prayed to Allah for wisdom to be opened up to him, saying aloud the name Ya-Fattah until his tongue felt thick.

Finally Henry slumped to the ground, the sand mounding around him as he fell. Ahmed took his friend's hand, later cradled his head in his lap. "If I knew what to do for you," he told Henry, "I would do it." He felt shame for his earlier pettiness. A hint of breath hovered over Henry's nose and lips. Henry's eyes wandered back into his head, fluttering between his lashes. Ahmed held Henry's hand and prayed as dusk fell and the air began to cool, until the hand no longer held warmth.

The next day night the authorities took Henry's body back to Ouarzazate. Ahmed waited until the following morning, until after the Fajr, to return. Even though the sun was behind him he wore Henry's hat, though now he was much less sure that he wanted to see the world with American eyes. He feared that his preference for American things might lead him to Henry's same desperate situation. Beneath the hat's generous brim Ahmed's eyes searched for the spot where the windshield had exploded. He drove slowly, scanning the roadside for the mounded sparkle of shattered glass.

Afterward Ahmed could not think of the desert without picturing Henry kneeling on top of a dune, tossing sand into his shadow. At night on the roof of their house in Ouarzazate when Ahmed's uncles gathered to talk and eat, and the stars above were so full and shiny that Ahmed would dream they were holes he could climb through to reach somewhere he had never been, the story of Hajji Izem's journey across the desert would be retold, and Ahmed would imagine Henry walking beside the old great uncle to Mecca.

THE BARAKA OF BEGGARS AND KINGS

"You don't know prices and can't bargain," Khadija protested from the kitchen doorway. "Pardon me for saying it, but it is so."

"But you already do so much for me." Peter put his passport and wallet in his back pocket, preparing to leave. In his passport he kept the letter he'd received from the embassy, explaining his role in the exchange. They were standing in his modest, nearly bare apartment near the Assounna, Rabat's Grand Mosque.

"Allah knows, someone must."

"How am I going to live here if you do everything for me?"

Khadija was the gray-haired widow of a Moroccan soldier who died fighting for the French. She licked her gold front tooth, as was her habit, then drew the folds of her blue head scarf in and around her neck. In appearance she was slight—excessively thin—and often reminded Peter of a bird by the way she held her bony head at odd angles to her body. "If the little I do is everything, you have been without a wife too long."

"Thank you, really," Peter said, reaching for his jacket, "but it's time I started to do some things by myself."

"Then may Allah be your guide. But if you ask me you'll be fleeced like a lost lamb."

They were talking about bargaining for carpets, which Peter's new apartment lacked. Once he decided to remain in Morocco, he checked out of the hotel where he'd been staying and found a small apartment on Avenue Moulay Abdelazziz near Place Jemaa Assounna. Every day after teaching at the university he went to the mellah, where he spent time with the two boys, Omar and Najib, the twins— one grotesquely crippled, the other deaf and unwilling to speak—who lived with their sick grandfather and begged each day in the streets. Peter found that he could not turn away from them.

Omar told him their lives had twined because of Allah's will, but Peter suspected it was more the result of loneliness. He enrolled the boys in the Lalla Asmaa School in Rabat's Hassan Quarter so that by the time he left the country they would be educated and more able to provide for themselves. He saw in his action a paradox, that by surrendering to the boys and their needs he'd actually found more freedom. Because of them he felt able to remain. During his daily walk from the university to the mellah he was content, even happy. It was there in the mellah that he met Khadija.

He noticed her sitting at her window just below the mellah's highest rooftop, obviously watching every aspect of the district's goings-on. He nodded to her each time he neared the boys' house and again upon leaving. One afternoon, after he brought the brothers several sacks of food, she descended and stood in their courtyard. In slow, exact French she told Peter the boys' history, that their father might as well have been the wind for all the time he passed with them, that their mother died the previous winter from a congestion of the lungs.

"Can you help me find a doctor to treat the grandfather?" Peter asked. He explained that the grandfather refused to take the pills prescribed him by the doctor Peter had brought the week before.

The gray-haired woman turned away without a word, but the next afternoon as Peter entered the courtyard there stood Khadija with a local healer. After examining the old man, the fqih took out a bottle of dark syrup and in Arabic painted suras from the Quran on first a spoon and then the inside of a bowl. The grandfather licked the spoon clean. The fqih fed the old man the writing in the bowl, then had him lick that clean too. Outside in the courtyard, Peter paid the healer what he asked.

Soon Khadija appeared each afternoon in the courtyard. She
told Peter she wanted some of the rain she saw falling there to fall
on her too. She gave him a dry laugh and called him *Rumi*, which
Peter knew meant outsider, someone from Rome. Khadija told him
she understood that what he was after was baraka. You are clever
just like me, she told Peter, waving a pointed finger. You understand
giving alms to the cursed twins and their sick grandfather will cleanse
you—she used the French verb for *purify* and made a scrubbing
motion with her hands—and in the last days when the earth rocks
in her final convulsion and the oceans roll together Allah will couple
you with your deeds. Her gold front tooth glistened as she spoke. Her
deep brown eyes sparkled confidently. She licked her shining tooth
and smacked her lips several times, then turned and walked back
to her house, smoothing the worn folds of her djellaba, whispering
enigmatically beneath her breath.

After a while their conversations became less philosophical, more
practical. She knew all the shopkeepers, she told Peter. She assured
him she was an excellent bargainer, held in respect and fear by every
merchant in Rabat. She could obtain everything he wanted, all he
desired, at the best price. Peter was persuaded to agree with her.
Soon Khadija arranged the purchase of food for the boys and their
grandfather, though at a price considerably less than what she charged
Peter. After all, she told him when he discovered the difference, some
butter must stick to the dish. She arranged for a local girl to come
in each day and prepare the food—Khadija didn't cook for beggars,
though she was willing to accept a portion of the girl's pay for her
part in setting up the situation—but after learning that he took his
meals from street vendors or occasionally from restaurants she offered
to cook for him herself.

Peter was quite thankful for Khadija's cooking, though she put
cinnamon in nearly everything. Otherwise she was a palatable cook
and able housekeeper, but soon she complained that his apartment

was so bare it depressed her to enter it. She offered to buy furnishings
for him and purchased with his money a stack of hammered silver
trays Peter saw little use for and a table so squat he had to sit on
the floor to use it. When she suggested he purchase a carpet—or
better yet, several—and added quickly that she knew of an extremely
reliable dealer who handled only rugs of the highest quality, carpets fit
for a professor, for a king, Peter shook his head and said, "Thank you,
no, really, I prefer to do this myself. Truly," Peter added, "I don't want
to live here like a foreigner, removed, waited on hand and foot. Even
if I end up paying twice what a rug is worth, I have to learn to get by
on my own wits."

"If you pay twice as much I'll have the merchant's head on a
stick," Khadija said.

"No you won't," said Peter, "because I'll be too smart to be
taken."

"A month ago you couldn't even buy a bunch of carrots. You'd
point like a child, then give twice the amount they asked."

Peter smiled, then laughed.

She measured him, smacking her tongue against her gold tooth.
"Like every *Rumi* you know less than you think."

He put on his jacket. "Then I must be capable of learning more."

"There's no stopping the lamb who thinks briar is clover," Khadija
said in a tone that Peter knew ended the conversation. "So we'll see
how far your wits can take you."

On the outer edge of Rabat's medina, the side nearest the cemetery
and ocean, blessed by the warm tangerine glow of the setting sun, a
Berber carpet the color of poppies marked the entrance to Hamid
Benjelloun's shop. The rug hung crookedly by two dangling threads
of its red border knotted around a pair of nails driven into the
plaster wall. Beside it was a soft, subtle carpet the color of crushed
saffron. Peter admired them at once. He ran his fingertips over the

multitude of knots in their designs. There were triangles, circles, delicate hexagons in beautifully repeated patterned mazes so dizzy and delightful that Peter could barely pull his eyes away. Then he noticed a thicker gray wool rug that in the slanting light nearly appeared silver. The motifs in its central medallion were mirrored in four sets of squares marking its borders. Peter touched this rug as well—its nap was so thick and soft he was tempted to rub his cheek against it—and then he admired the rug beside it, and then the exquisite royal-blue carpet it overlapped, and before he realized what he was doing he had stepped over the threshold into the shop, and there stood the shopkeeper, tall, imposing, hands behind his back, smiling, generous belly protruding beneath a djellaba whose broad white-and-apricot stripes made Peter think at once of an awning.

"Greetings," the man said with a husky voice. He rocked momentarily on his heels, then brought his hands forward in a flourish of welcome. The shopkeeper had a hooked nose, fair skin, the thinnest mustache. Set atop his graying hair was a red fez. "I am Hamid Benjelloun. You come in, please, yes? Don't be shy."

Peter nodded and smiled. He'd already visited two shops, trying to get a sense of what was what, a grasp on prices. Hamid flicked his fingers toward the wall and in a moment a row of fluorescent bulbs twinkled from the ceiling and the shop filled with light. Peter reviewed in his mind what he'd learned. The thick wool Rabati rugs were ordinarily sold by their size and their rating—very good, superior, extra superior—listed on a seal glued to the rug's underside. Extra-superior rugs had the tightest weave, the most knots per square inch. The embroidered Berber carpets were generally sold by the piece according to the degree of their handiwork. All prices had to be negotiated. To bargain, you had to know what you were doing. The system was based on mutual respect and was as much a social occasion, replete with its own etiquette, as a financial transaction. A ludicrously low offer could give insult and put an end to the

conversation. You had to understand what an object cost the dealer
as well as what it was worth to you. Then you settled on a price
somewhere in between.

Peter considered how to begin. "You have a beautiful shop," he
said, looking about the vast first room, which was full of carpets.
Some hung on the walls or from the sides of high piles that reached
nearly to the ceiling. Others lay in imposing rolled stacks, waiting to
be unfurled.

"It is nothing," Hamid said, gesturing broadly with his arms, "if
it does not hold what you desire."

Hanging from a wire on the far wall was a framed photograph of
Hassan II, as was the practice in nearly every shop in the medina. In
this photo the King wore a white djellaba, hood raised, as if he were
on a journey. In fact Hassan was out of the country, at a summit of
Arab nations. The dark smells of incense and damp wool hovered in
the air. Peter smiled. By far this shop appeared the most promising of
those he'd visited. "Oh," said Peter, "I'm sure what I desire is here."

Hamid smiled. "You are very kind. Welcome. Here, sit." He
pointed toward a cushioned bench in the far corner, then turned into
the shop and called out in Arabic.

"You like tea?" Hamid asked, turning again to Peter, who
nodded. A boy with dark hair ran breathlessly into the room, glanced
at Peter, then began nodding furiously as Hamid spoke in a low,
rapid voice. In a moment the boy had disappeared. Hamid ran the
flat of his hand down his djellaba, pausing at the wide expanse of his
stomach, then met Peter's eyes and smiled.

"He will be only a few minutes. Sit. Relax. Allow me to show you
some nice things."

He turned and unrolled a thick pale-yellow carpet that Peter
guessed was sheepskin. "Here," Hamid said, "you feel this. Very
soft. All wool. And as you can see it is all natural, undyed, Berber,
from the Atlas mountains." He turned and unrolled a second, which

was streaked with black. "Here is another. See? Again, like the first, all natural." He unrolled a third, slightly mottled. "See? Each one different. No two are alike."

They weren't at all what he wanted. "They're very lovely," Peter said. "Very plain."

Hamid frowned. "Yes, they are very plain. Exactly so. Not for everyone, yes?" He left the three on the floor and pulled out something orange from a tall stack of folded carpets. "You want something with more color?" He snapped the carpet open in the air, then let it fall at Peter's feet. The rug was raw, unbordered, blindingly orange, slashed with large white and black *V*'s. Peter thought of Halloween. As the dark-haired boy returned with a tray holding a teapot and three glasses, Hamid brought out carpets that were lemon, crimson, turquoise, plum. Each was marked with a different geometric design that repeated itself exactly and without variation, as if the rugs were made by machine.

"You are from Spain?" Hamid said. He raised the teapot to eye level and poured some of the steaming liquid into the first glass, then set the teapot on the tray and raised the glass to the light, as if to gauge its color, then poured the tea back into the pot.

"America."

"Sure. OK. U.S. So we talk dollars."

"These are very colorful." Peter didn't know what else to say. He pointed at the rugs on the floor.

If Hamid heard him, he gave no sign. Hamid stared at the small silver teapot on the tray, then took in a robust breath and as he raised the pot again to eye level splashed tea into the remaining two glasses.

"But they do not make you love them." Hamid exhaled sharply. "I agree. They are good but cheap. Some who come in, this is all they want. Or else they buy the first thing they see." He handed Peter a glass of mint tea. "But you, you are a man who knows quality."

"*Shukran*," Peter said. Thank you. He blew on the tea, then took a tentative sip, savoring the sharp bite of mint and sugar.

"You speak some Arabic?" Hamid said with a sideways glance.

"So far, only a few words. My students teach me."

"You are a teacher?"

Peter nodded.

"You teach speaking English, yes?"

Peter shook his head. "American history."

"Ahh, history!" Hamid said, as if the fact impressed him deeply. After a few moments he sighed. "And do you know Moroccan history?"

"A little. I'm learning, bit by bit. I read and study every day."

"Good." Hamid's mouth moved as if he were chewing. "Do you know the Quran?"

"I've read through it once, but I don't know it as you would."

"You read the book in English, a translation, yes?"

"Yes, a translation."

Hamid shrugged. "You must read the Quran in Arabic, as it was meant to be read, as it was written by Allah through the Prophet."

"Someday I will," Peter said, "*insha'Allah*."

"*Insha'Allah* you will read it as it has been written." Hamid sipped his tea, then set the glass on the tray. The tassel on his fez swung as he turned. "Here we sit, a pair of dogs barking, while the caravan passes by. I show you the best. The highest quality."

The merchant walked to a far corner of the room and pulled out a pair of embroidered Berber carpets. He unfolded them with a slight bow. The rugs were similar to the beautiful hangings that first attracted Peter's attention outside in the street in the medina, but their colors were deeper, more vibrant, their handiwork even more precise.

"See?" Hamid said. "Look at these stitchings. Zemmour. Sheared wool. Pure. Entirely hand crafted. The finest quality. One of a kind. Everything handmade."

He wasn't exaggerating, Peter thought. He stared at the carpets—the smaller one featured a myriad of striped zigzags and triangles over a regal purple background while the larger offered similar designs across a background the color of flame—and imagined them hanging in his house in the States. At once he realized he was picturing his house as it had been before he and Ellen had broken up. The thought made him frown.

"But these aren't to be walked on," Peter said, looking for some other reason to reject them.

"Sure, you walk on these." To prove the point Hamid stepped across both carpets, then stomped his feet.

"What would one of these cost?" Peter said, hearing his heart begin to pound.

Hamid's face grew sad, as if he didn't wish to part with either. "A carpet of this quality is very hard to come by. But for you, I make you a very good price. In dollars, each one, fourteen hundred."

Peter guessed he could bargain the price down to less than half that, but the image of these carpets, so beautifully lush and ornate, hanging on the walls of his empty house back in the States made him sad. In his apartment here in Rabat he had no use for them. He guessed Khadija would think them an indulgence. "It is a good price," he told Hamid, "and perhaps I'll buy one at some other time, but for now I think I'd prefer another style."

"But of course," Hamid said. He reached behind another stack of rugs and brought out several large rolled carpets looped with rope. On their backs Peter could see their tan seals, EXTRA SUPERIEURE, that indicated their quality. Hamid's fingers were fat and blunt but impressively nimble as he loosened the ropes that bound the thick rugs and allowed them to unroll over the others lying on the shop's floor, and at once Peter knew these rugs were right and that he'd buy one.

The one he liked most was just over four square meters in area,
deep red, double bordered in shades of blue and white and gray that
made him think of sea and sky. Within the borders the colors mixed
to make a repeating pattern of symmetrical round blossoms on the
outside and slanting ellipses on the inside that twisted at opposite
ends in a knot. Beyond the borders the deep colors curled and jutted
into the central sea of red, thrusting toward the rug's medallion,
which twirled eight curlicues of color back at the borders and
repeated its ornate design. The medallion's center was ringed by a thin
field of white. The white lay like snow on a mountain peak on a blue
island in a red sea. The medallion held a jagged circle of light blue
that enclosed a splash of the red that made up the sea, and then Peter
noticed tiny traces of red tumbling from the center toward the rug's
four corners.

"These are of the classic Rabati style," Hamid was saying proudly,
"though these were made in Fez, extra superior quality. Here, feel.
Run your fingers over, like this. You have been to Fez, yes? The Fassis
are famous the world over for their craft." He bent and pulled a bit of
thread from one rug's border, tried to light the thread with a match
he'd taken from inside his djellaba. "See, it does not catch. Pure wool.
With synthetics there would be burning. Here, smell. Wool, one
hundred percent. Genuine. I guarantee. The best you can find. If you
like, I can give you a very good price."

"I like," Peter heard himself say. "The price is by the square meter,
isn't it?"

"Or by the piece," Hamid said. He was smiling now. "I am a
modern man and can do business either way."

Indeed, thought Peter, as he watched Hamid withdraw a
calculator from inside his djellaba, then a small pad of paper, the
stub of a pencil. They were going to do business. Peter took in a deep
breath. He knew from those with whom he'd spoken at the university
that extra superior Rabati rugs could easily run over one hundred fifty

dollars per square meter, though he guessed that for a Moroccan the price would be less than half the amount. Hamid began him high, at two ten.

Peter smiled and said he wished he could pay such an amount since Hamid's shop was so handsome, so full of treasures, without doubt the best in all of Rabat. But I'm a poor university professor, Peter said, not a rich tourist from New York or Paris. He offered seventy-five.

Hamid's face fell as if he'd been stabbed. His hands clutched the great expanse of his abdomen. A badly tuned motorbike sputtered by in the street outside the shop. There was a shout, the clank of metal. Peter could hear a beggar calling out, "Alms! Alms for the love of Allah!" Hamid puffed through his mouth like a steam engine. Peter wished he could reach back into the air and retrieve his low price, offer eighty, ninety, an even hundred. He stared at the magnificent rug on the floor before him. In the States he'd never be able to afford such a luxury.

"Because you are not a rich tourist," Hamid said at last, "one ninety."

Peter pulled at his chin. His mouth had gone dry. "Eighty," he said carefully.

"One seventy-five."

"A little over four square meters. I'm still thinking eighty."

"Just for you, last price, one sixty," Hamid said with such sudden authority that Peter nearly said thank you, yes, I'll take it.

But now it was Peter's turn to pause. He set down his empty glass and stood, then inspected the rug, searching it for defects. He wanted to make Hamid think he was mulling the price over. There were no imperfections he could see—in fact, the rug was even more beautiful now that he ran his hands over it. He decided to pretend. He pulled at a stray piece of wool, made a soft *tsk* sound with his tongue, then wagged his head. The more he looked at the carpet the more he wanted it. He turned over one corner to study the government seal of quality and made a show of removing and polishing his eyeglasses on his shirt.

"It's a good price," said Hamid with strained patience. "Of that you can be sure."

Peter nodded, then forced his eyes to read the writing on the seal again. Finally, as if he'd come to a final decision, he said, "Eighty-five."

"My friend," Hamid said with a dismissive wave of his hand, "I am trying to help. I make you a good price, best in all of Rabat. You will not find better anywhere else, believe me. For you, one hundred forty. A good price, believe me, you will find nowhere else."

Peter swallowed. "Ninety. It's all I can afford."

"Final price," said Hamid, "only because you are a poor professor and will send all of the other poor professors and their wives here to my shop to buy my rugs. You understand? For you, I make a special price. One time only. Take it or leave it. One twenty. Last price. Final price."

Peter crouched and looked at the rug again. "If you don't let me buy it," he told Hamid, "I can't send my friends here." He stood, walked toward the doorway. "Ninety-five."

Hamid turned away and began folding the carpets on the floor. Peter stood in the doorway watching. He knew Hamid was aware that he remained. Had Hamid begun rolling up the rug they were bargaining over, Peter would have concluded that the deal had fallen through and he would be forced either to leave or to ask Hamid to sell it at his price, but Hamid ignored Peter's splendid carpet and put away everything else, and Peter stood silently in the doorway, watching, waiting. Hamid paused in the room, hands resting on his stomach, and then one hand leapt into the air like a lizard's tongue and grabbed a fly in flight. Hamid turned, clutching the fly in his fist like a trophy. "You can pay in dollars?" Peter nodded. "So in dollars, we agree, one hundred ten."

"Ninety-five is all I can afford." Peter wanted to smile. His heart was beating happily. "It's a fair price."

Hamid gazed at his fist, then made a sour face. "OK, just for you, in dollars, for each square meter, an even one hundred." He opened his hand, releasing the fly in the air. "Will you carry it or should I have the boy deliver it to your hotel?"

"Ninety-five is my price." The words were out before Peter realized what he was saying. What did he want more, he wondered, the rug or the upper hand in the deal?

Hamid shook his head. "You argue over only a few rials."

"*You* argue over only a few rials," countered Peter.

Hamid looked pained. He ran one hand over his mouth. "So we split, OK?" He moved one flattened hand over his palm, as if he were slicing his palm in half.

It was his, Peter realized. They'd reached the point where each could agree. "Ninety-seven fifty," he said. "Yes?"

"Yes, ninety-seven fifty," Hamid said with a smile.

Hamid computed the final price and wrote out a receipt as Peter paid. The boy who'd brought the tea rolled the rug and tied it securely with string. "I'll send all my friends here," Peter said happily. "And I'll be back before long, to buy more."

Hamid nodded as his fingers deftly counted Peter's money. "Sure, I have a whole shop full. You buy more of my rugs before too long, *insha'Allah*."

"*Insha'Allah*," said Peter.

The men shook hands, then touched their hearts.

Peter carried the rolled rug on his back through the crowded medina, resisting the many boys who ran up to him with offers to help. He

wanted to carry it by himself even though his apartment was across
town. He walked up Avenue Mohammed V past the beggars and
the banks, past men in dark suits, women in high heels and red
lipstick, past the traders who spread their wares on plastic sheets
on the sidewalk and who called out to all who passed, past a stand
where a man with clear-framed eyeglasses sold ice cream, the taste of
which once made Peter so homesick that he no longer ate it, past the
newsstand outside the post office where, during his first few weeks
in the country, his eyes hungrily scanned the racks for anything
American—*Newsweek*, *Time*, *USA Today*. Now Peter read *Lamalif*,
like a true Moroccan intellectual, and *L'Opinion*, with the desire to
learn more about the Arab world and at the same time strengthen his
weak French.

He sprinkled coins in the open hands of beggars as he passed
them, as was his habit. They knew him and called his name as he
approached, then repeated his name in blessing after he moved
on down the boulevard, tiring from his load but pleased with his
purchase and quite proud of his bargaining. If he was going to live
in this country, he'd have to learn to bargain. He noticed a pair of
wooden sawhorses blocking the sidewalk up ahead and thought of
how he'd recount the experience in Hamid's shop to Khadija. Of
course she would say she could have purchased the rug for less than
what he'd paid, but inside she'd have no choice but to be pleased.
He was sure he'd gotten it at a good price. On the stone steps of the
railroad station stood several uniformed guards, rifles at the ready.
Across the station's white façade hung a large Moroccan flag—a field
of brilliant red in which stood a green, five-sided star. Across the
sidewalk just ahead were the two sawhorses. Too tired to cross the
busy avenue, his mind preoccupied with the aftertaste of his success,
Peter stepped around the wooden barriers.

He walked past a truck from which men were unloading rolled
carpets. Already, he could see, the top steps of the station were

covered with rugs. Peter had no idea what was going on. One of the guards shouted at him in Arabic, pointing his rifle first at him and then at his carpet, then at the ground. Confused, Peter stopped. He asked the guard in French what was going on. The guard pointed his rifle at him again.

"You'd better do what he says," a worker called to Peter in French. The worker was spreading rugs across the steps and sidewalk.

"Do what?" Peter said.

"Lay your rug on the ground."

"But this is my rug."

"So what? He thinks you're stealing it."

"But I have a bill of sale."

"It's your head," said the worker.

The guard was shouting now, walking closer, thrusting his rifle at Peter's chest. "But I have a bill of sale!" Peter shouted again. The guard said something, low and mean, in Arabic. The rifle remained pointed at Peter's chest.

What other choice was there but to drop the rug to the ground, crouch, untie the careful loops of twine the boy in the shop had so deftly knotted? Even as Peter unrolled his carpet across the dirty sidewalk near the bottom of the station's steps, he expected someone to recognize the situation for what it was, then intercede. He positioned his rug precisely in the center of the station's steps and high, arched doorways. It should be obvious to anyone that his rug was different, he thought. The others, though perhaps just as beautiful, were much more worn.

"But can't you see that this is mine?" Peter said one last time.

The guard with the rifle waved him away. Peter stood, resigned. As he walked toward the onlookers milling curiously on the oval area fronting the station, a hot anger flared and then rippled inside him. No sooner had he succeeded at doing something than he failed! How stupid of him to have crossed the barrier! He considered that staying

on in Morocco was idiotic. He should go back to where he belonged,
back to where he could understand what was going on around
him, where life could be read, comprehended. Then in a moment a
gnawing sadness filled him. He gazed back at his rug, at the armed
guards, at the growing field of carpets. How dumb of him not to have
understood something so painfully obvious.

He walked past the other side of the station and then, as he saw
several groups of Moroccans sitting on the squat wall that overlooked
the station's tracks, he understood what was taking place. The King
must be returning from the Arab summit. Peter pushed his way
through the people gathered beside the wall. Yes, just as he thought,
the platform below was covered with a patchwork of rugs. Peter
could see more rugs lining the steps leading to the station, and he
imagined that the inside of the station was carpeted as well, so that a
near-endless Moroccan rug made of many, many rugs would greet the
King's feet as he stepped from the train and walked to the limousine
that would speed him to his palace.

His own fine rug was now part of that mosaic. He put his hands
in his pockets, let out a long sigh. He considered that now the rug
was no longer his. Now it belonged to the King.

He had coffee at his favorite café, La Chaine, a busy, sometimes
raucous place where students from the university gathered. Tonight
no one he knew was there. The usual lot of young men in denim
jackets, gesturing grandly as they talked, and young women in bright
lipstick, jangling earrings, and short skirts filled the tables. A cloud of
cigarette smoke hung perpetually in the air. Peter sat alone with a café
noir, facing the front door, and watched the evening light fade into a
hard darkness.

Night was his most difficult time. He stared at the trace of
grounds on the bottom of his cup, then gazed back out the doorway.
Night had to be waited out, endured. Or used, somehow, in a manner

which he hadn't yet discovered. He was embarrassed to admit that
what he sometimes wanted most at night was to be able to curl before
the flickering images of the latest show on TV and allow his mind
to be numbed, his senses glazed by television's impersonal electronic
embrace. He hadn't watched much TV back in the States but
surprisingly he now suffered from withdrawal. There was television
here—national news and soccer matches, Egyptian soap operas and
old black-and-white American movies with all the kisses censored
out—but for him it held little interest. What he craved was a familiar
half-hour of news following by an evening of glitzy American
commercial television.

He gazed at a young woman at the next table, at her deep dark
eyes, black hair, long painted fingernails that held a cigarette. For
several moments he stared at her full lips.

Of course, he thought, if he had a lover he'd hardly crave
television. He looked away, not wanting to make the young woman
feel uncomfortable or draw attention to himself. To have a lover here
would be complicated, if not dangerous, for both himself and the
woman. The plain truth was that he was lonely. He leaned back in his
chair, gave a sigh. So what was a little loneliness compared to others'
hunger and pain? He thought about Omar and Najib. Compared
to them he'd been blessed with all the advantages, all the riches, of
royalty.

He should go to his apartment, eat what Khadija had left for
him, write a few letters, read a book. When he didn't return to his
apartment by sunset, she left him food on top of the stove in a
covered tajine. He pictured the tajine's blunt conical top, its thick
ceramic plate. In a global sense, he reminded himself, his problems
had the magnitude of a flea bite. He told himself he was a rich prince
who complained of a grain of sand in his shoe in a world in which
many went shoeless, in a world in which many did not even have
feet. But when he pictured his bare apartment and remembered his

magnificent rug, the rug he'd so wonderfully bargained for but then so stupidly lost, his heart ached.

He pushed his empty cup aside, standing from his table, and walked past the beautiful young Moroccan with long raven hair and smooth olive skin, fetching dark eyes, who laughed behind her painted fingernails with her friends. A silver hamsa hung from her neck. Their eyes met and locked, before hers fell discreetly to her hands.

The square outside the railroad station was flooded with so much light that Peter had to squint as he squeezed his way though the crowds. He wanted to have one last look at his rug. The people were held back by metal barricades behind which stood expressionless armed soldiers. Already several limousines had pulled up to the Hotel Terminus side of the station's steps, and around the steps stood guards in ceremonial dress—red jackets, baggy cream-colored pantaloons, white turbans, long antique swords at their sides. A group of men in white djellabas, hoods over their heads, strolled past the guards and stood off to the one side near several men in suits, no doubt dignitaries and government officials. Then a woman—short, hunchbacked—at Peter's side elbowed him sharply. Peter said, "*Pardon*," as the woman resumed standing in her place. The hump on her back shifted and squirmed, and when a curled fist emerged from beneath a fold of cloth Peter realized the hump was her baby. A man with rotted teeth turned and spoke to Peter in Arabic so rapid Peter couldn't understand a word, though he guessed by the tone the man was trying to tell him something important. Peter said he was sorry, he didn't understand, and then a man behind him said, "He told you tonight you are a most lucky one to look on our king." Peter nodded. "Yes," he said, "tonight I'm a lucky one." He nodded vigorously until the man with bad teeth smiled. Finally Peter saw his rug—new, untouched—there on the sidewalk in the center beneath the station's steps.

Then the crowd surged forward and Peter was nearly lifted from
his feet, and a host of young women in Berber costumes and silver
spangles the size of half dollars dangling from around their heads
emerged from the yawning doorway of the station tossing out rose
petals from straw baskets they held in their hands. Peter thought
he could hear music—the clean, sudden shrill of horns—but every
sound was drowned out by the women who began their ululations.
"Luuluuluuluuluuluuluu," the women trilled. The sound was endless
and joyous and so thrilling that Peter's spine tingled and the hair
stood out on his arms and the back of his neck. Then the King strode
grandly from the station, smiling, waving his hand, and the air
throbbed suddenly with song that seemed to come from everywhere
at once.

"Hassan the Second, Noble Alaouite!" the crowd sang. Others
cheered, ululated. "Hassan the Second, Noble Alaouite!"

The King was dressed handsomely in a light-colored suit. He
put his fingers to his lips and threw the crowd kisses. Several steps
behind him walked his two sons, in dark suits, hands crossed at the
waist. The dignitaries greeted the King, kneeling before him, kissing
his hand, and one of the limousines backed up behind the line of
armed soldiers, and then Hassan walked to the edge of the barricades,
smiling, waving, touching the outstretched hands of his people.

"Hassan the Second, Noble Alaouite!" the chant repeated, faster,
faster, like a whirling Sufi, until the words tumbled and spilled,
spinning in the air like the dancers' skirts, and the pulsing rhythm
made the crowd sway in response. Hassan and his two sons stepped
into the limousine. Then Hassan appeared through its open sunroof,
standing, waving, again throwing kisses to the crowds as the limo
inched up the boulevard and the people screamed and raised their
palms at their king. Peter noticed people cheering from windows,
from rooftops. The limousine rolled from sight, and the crowd surged
past Peter, swallowing up the King's path. Then Peter saw that the

people on the rooftops were armed soldiers with binoculars scanning the windows and the crowds.

Peter admired Hassan, and for a moment his lips whispered a prayer for Hassan's safety, and for Morocco, which he was beginning to love. He looked back at the station, at his rug.

The costumed girls had gathered in a circle on the steps. Car doors slammed as the dignitaries disappeared behind the tinted windows of their limos. One of the guards behind the metal barricade relaxed, slung his rifle downward, took out a cigarette. The match flared against the darkness of his chest. Peter walked over and in French asked him who was in charge, and the guard called over an officer who stepped arrogantly forward, and Peter put on his best face and began his explanations.

Though Peter tried to tell him precisely all that had taken place, through the tumble of translation and cultural difference the facts dangled unconnected in the cool night air. The officer grew frustrated, absolutely refusing to consider the idea that his soldiers would force a foreigner at gunpoint to give up a carpet he'd purchased as a souvenir. There must be some other explanation, he told Peter. They were joined by another officer, then a third and a fourth. Peter showed them his bill of sale. He pointed at his rug, then at the receipt, then at his rug again. When they asked him for his passport, he surrendered it to them along with the letter from the embassy about the exchange. Already workers were busily rolling up the King's carpets and loading them onto the backs of several trucks. The Moroccan officers discussed their different interpretations of Peter's story, arguing heatedly, with blunt gestures of the hand, with feeling and passion, like men in the medina discussing a price or a difficult sura in the Quran. One by one they inspected his passport, the bill of sale. They had the workers drag the rug over, which they then inspected.

Then another officer walked over and the others stood at attention. For several minutes they spoke quietly among themselves.

Then one called Peter over. In careful French he explained to all present that Peter was an American with the U.S. Embassy here to see the King, may he be blessed by Allah, and in Peter's admiration for the King purchased a rug for him to walk upon. That much is true, yes?

Peter hesitated, then said yes.

"Then is it not a gift to the King?" the officer inquired.

Peter thought quickly. He didn't want to make a mistake here. He feared that if he said the wrong thing he'd give offense and all would be lost. "Forgive me if I am wrong," he said in his best French, "but I did not think the King, may Allah bless him and his children, who already owns several trucks full of rugs"—he gestured toward the trucks, which the workers were in the process of loading—"would want another rug from me." He looked into their eyes to see if he had given the right answer.

They remained unconvinced. "But then why did you bring your carpet here?"

Peter thought quickly. "For the baraka."

"Ahh, baraka," they all said at once.

"Yes," Peter said. Now he knew he'd won. "Baraka."

"For the King's baraka. But of course."

Late the next morning, as the sun began wedging its way in through the wooden shutters on the bedroom window of his apartment on Avenue Moulay Abdelazziz, Peter dreamed of a barbeque in his backyard in the States. It was a sad dream, one of the homesick dreams he had now and then since he'd been given approval to stay on. The fire in his backyard was burning wildly, out of control, and he was running in slow motion for water to douse it, fearing that if he didn't run quickly enough everyone he loved would be doomed. Ellen was there, though in the dream she and Peter were still married. Rachel was there too, sitting at a picnic table beside Omar and Najib.

The three children were hungry, waiting to be fed. Peter was doing his best to hurry. He whimpered as he ran across the green lawn in his backyard, as his legs thrashed beneath his sheet and he reached toward the King, who stood in an open limousine, for the water.

He heard a key scrape open a lock, then footsteps. The limo was beginning to pull away. Behind him the fire was burning. Peter's legs and arms felt heavy, as if they were asleep or buried in sand. He lunged a final time toward the King for the water. Then he heard Khadija's call, and as he opened his eyes the dream fled the room, slipping between the blazing cracks of the shutters toward the unreachable light of the morning sun.

Khadija was in the next room, unrolling his new rug with the toe of her shoe. The carpet looked majestic beneath the shafts of morning light. Khadija stooped in the light, gathering in the bowl of her apron pieces of something that lay scattered on the rug's surface. Watching from his bedroom, still wrapped in the fuzz of sleep, Peter thought at first the scraps were bits of bread, some strange manna that had fallen on his rug in the night. He couldn't recognize what Khadija held up to him in her cupped hands. He cinched the belt of his robe and stepped forward to take a closer look.

The gray-haired woman stretched out her hands to him, smiling. A pair of rose petals drifted down from her apron. She opened her hands and the other petals fell back to his new carpet like rain.

"From the King," he explained. "The sign of his baraka."

"The King's baraka?" Khadija said, wide-eyed.

"Yes," Peter said. He was sure of it now, and after the dream felt doubly blessed. "Baraka for us all, *insha'Allah*."

Acknowledgments

I want to thank Anthony Tamburri, Fred Gardaphé, and Paolo Giordano for their interest in and support of my writing, and Diane Prokop, Nick Grosso, and Siân Gibby for their generous help with this edition. I remain extremely grateful to Abdelkrim Abdellahi, Said Abdessamad, Mohammed Dahbi, Lahcen Haddad, and Brahim Moussabbir for their encouragement and advice, and once again I thank Diane Kondrat, my work's first reader.

I also want to express my gratitude for support received from the Office of Research at Indiana University Bloomington and the National Endowment for the Arts.

I'd also like to acknowledge and thank the literary magazines, and their editors, in which the stories in this book first appeared:

AGNI: "Sons of Adam"
Beloit Fiction Journal: "The Fire-Eater"
Black Warrior Review: "Expatriates"
The Georgia Review: "The Whore of Fez el Bali"
The Gettysburg Review: "The Unfinished Minaret" and "Postcard from Ouarzazate"
High Plains Literary Review: "Exchange"
Ploughshares: "In the Garden of the Djinn"
Prairie Schooner: "The Arab's Ox" (under the title "Larabi's Ox") and "The Surrender"
Shenandoah: "The Beggars" and "The Baraka of Beggars and Kings"
Sonora Review: "Valley of the Drâa"
Witness: "The Hand of Fatima"

About the Author

Tony Ardizzone is the author of the novels *The Whale Chaser, In the Garden of Papa Santuzzu, Heart of the Order,* and *In the Name of the Father,* and the short story collections *Taking It Home: Stories from the Neighborhood, Larabi's Ox: Stories of Morocco,* and *The Evening News.* He also edited the anthology *The Habit of Art: Best Stories from the Indiana University Fiction Workshop.* His writing has received several awards and honors including the Flannery O'Connor Award for Short Fiction, the Virginia Prize for Fiction, the Milkweed National Fiction Prize, the Chicago Foundation for Literature Award for Fiction sponsored by the Friends of Literature, the Bruno Arcudi Short Fiction Prize, the Lawrence Foundation Award, the Pushcart Prize, and two individual artist fellowships from the National Endowment for the Arts. He has taught at Saint Mary's Center for Learning (Chicago), Bowling Green State University, Old Dominion University, Vermont College, and Indiana University, where he was named Chancellor's Professor.

In 1985 Ardizzone taught at Mohammed V University in Rabat, Morocco, as part of a University Affiliation Program funded by the United States Information Agency. He returned to Morocco in 1988 for further travel and research for this book.

Born and raised on the North Side of Chicago, he currently lives in Portland, Oregon.

VIA Folios

A refereed book series dedicated to the culture of Italians and Italian Americans.

PHYLLIS CAPELLO. *Packs Small Plays Big*. Vol. 124. Literature.
FRED GARDAPHÉ. *Read 'em and Reap*. Vol. 123. Criticism. $22
JOSEPH A. AMATO. *Diagnostics*. Vol 122. Literature. $12.
DENNIS BARONE. *Second Thoughts*. Vol 121. Poetry. $10
OLIVIA K. CERRONE. *The Hunger Saint*. Vol 120. Novella. $12
GARIBLADI M. LAPOLLA. *Miss Rollins in Love*. Vol 119. Novel. $24
JOSEPH TUSIANI. *A Clarion Call*. Vol 118. Poetry. $16
JOSEPH A. AMATO. *My Three Sicilies*. Vol 117. Poetry & Prose. $17
MARGHERITA COSTA. *Voice of a Virtuosa and Coutesan*. Vol 116. Poetry. $24
NICOLE SANTALUCIA. *Because I Did Not Die*. Vol 115. Poetry. $12
MARK CIABATTARI. *Preludes to History*. Vol 114. Poetry. $12
HELEN BAROLINI. *Visits*. Vol 113. Novel. $22
ERNESTO LIVORNI. *The Fathers' America*. Vol 112. Poetry. $14
MARIO B. MIGNONE. *The Story of My People*. Vol 111. Non-fiction. $17
GEORGE GUIDA. *The Sleeping Gulf*. Vol 110. Poetry. $14
JOEY NICOLETTI. *Reverse Graffiti*. Vol 109. Poetry. $14
GIOSE RIMANELLI. *Il mestiere del furbo*. Vol 108. Criticism. $20
LEWIS TURCO. *The Hero Enkido*. Vol 107. Poetry. $14
AL TACCONELLI. *Perhaps Fly*. Vol 106. Poetry. $14
RACHEL GUIDO DEVRIES. *A Woman Unknown in Her Bones*. Vol 105. Poetry. $11
BERNARD BRUNO. *A Tear and a Tear in My Heart*. Vol 104. Non-fiction. $20
FELIX STEFANILE. *Songs of the Sparrow*. Vol 103. Poetry. $30
FRANK POLIZZI. *A New Life with Bianca*. Vol 102. Poetry. $10
GIL FAGIANI. *Stone Walls*. Vol 101. Poetry. $14
LOUISE DESALVO. *Casting Off*. Vol 100. Fiction. $22
MARY JO BONA. *I Stop Waiting for You*. Vol 99. Poetry. $12
RACHEL GUIDO DEVRIES. *Stati zitt, Josie*. Vol 98. Children's Literature. $8
GRACE CAVALIERI. *The Mandate of Heaven*. Vol 97. Poetry. $14
MARISA FRASCA. *Via incanto*. Vol 96. Poetry. $12
DOUGLAS GLADSTONE. *Carving a Niche for Himself*. Vol 95. History. $12
MARIA TERRONE. *Eye to Eye*. Vol 94. Poetry. $14
CONSTANCE SANCETTA. *Here in Cerchio*. Vol 93. Local History. $15
MARIA MAZZIOTTI GILLAN. *Ancestors' Song*. Vol 92. Poetry. $14
MICHAEL PARENTI. *Waiting for Yesterday: Pages from a Street Kid's Life*. Vol 90. Memoir. $15
ANNIE LANZILOTTO. *Schistsong*. Vol 89. Poetry. $15
EMANUEL DI PASQUALE. *Love Lines*. Vol 88. Poetry. $10

ANTHONY VALERIO. *The Little Sailor*. Vol 49. Memoir. $9

ROSS TALARICO. *The Reptilian Interludes*. Vol 48. Poetry. $15

RACHEL GUIDO DE VRIES. *Teeny Tiny Tino's Fishing Story*. Vol 47. Children's Literature. $6

EMANUEL DI PASQUALE. *Writing Anew*. Vol 46. Poetry. $15

MARIA FAMÀ. *Looking For Cover*. Vol 45. Poetry. $12

ANTHONY VALERIO. *Toni Cade Bambara's One Sicilian Night*. Vol 44. Poetry. $10

EMANUEL CARNEVALI. *Furnished Rooms*. Vol 43. Poetry. $14

BRENT ADKINS. et al., Ed. *Shifting Borders. Negotiating Places*. Vol 42. Conference. $18

GEORGE GUIDA. *Low Italian*. Vol 41. Poetry. $11

GARDAPHÈ, GIORDANO, TAMBURRI. *Introducing Italian Americana*. Vol 40. Italian/American Studies. $10

DANIELA GIOSEFFI. *Blood Autumn/Autunno di sangue*. Vol 39. Poetry. $15/$25

FRED MISURELLA. *Lies to Live By*. Vol 38. Stories. $15

STEVEN BELLUSCIO, *Constructing a Bibliography*. Vol 37. Italian Americana. $15

ANTHONY JULIAN TAMBURRI, Ed. *Italian Cultural Studies 2002*. Vol 36. Essays. $18

BEA TUSIANI. *con amore*. Vol 35. Memoir. $19

FLAVIA BRIZIO-SKOV, Ed. *Reconstructing Societies in the Aftermath of War*. Vol 34. History. $30

TAMBURRI et al., Eds. *Italian Cultural Studies 2001*. Vol 33. Essays. $18

ELIZABETH G. MESSINA, Ed. *In Our Own Voices*. Vol 32. Italian/American Studies. $25

STANISLAO G. PUGLIESE. *Desperate Inscriptions*. Vol 31. History. $12

HOSTERT & TAMBURRI, Eds. *Screening Ethnicity*. Vol 30. Italian/American Culture. $25

G. PARATI & B. LAWTON, Eds. *Italian Cultural Studies*. Vol 29. Essays. $18

HELEN BAROLINI. *More Italian Hours*. Vol 28. Fiction. $16

FRANCO NASI, Ed. *Intorno alla Via Emilia*. Vol 27. Culture. $16

ARTHUR L. CLEMENTS. *The Book of Madness & Love*. Vol 26. Poetry. $10

JOHN CASEY, et al. *Imagining Humanity*. Vol 25. Interdisciplinary Studies. $18

ROBERT LIMA. *Sardinia/Sardegna*. Vol 24. Poetry. $10

DANIELA GIOSEFFI. *Going On*. Vol 23. Poetry. $10

ROSS TALARICO. *The Journey Home*. Vol 22. Poetry. $12

EMANUEL DI PASQUALE. *The Silver Lake Love Poems*. Vol 21. Poetry. $7

JOSEPH TUSIANI. *Ethnicity*. Vol 20. Poetry. $12

JENNIFER LAGIER. *Second Class Citizen*. Vol 19. Poetry. $8

FELIX STEFANILE. *The Country of Absence*. Vol 18. Poetry. $9

PHILIP CANNISTRARO. *Blackshirts*. Vol 17. History. $12

LUIGI RUSTICHELLI, Ed. *Seminario sul racconto*. Vol 16. Narrative. $10

CPSIA information can be obtained
at www.ICGtesting.com
Printed in the USA
FFOW03n2044161017
41182FF